A Hard, Cruel Shore

A Hard, Cruel Shore

An Alan Lewrie Naval Adventure

Dewey Lambdin

THOMAS DUNNE BOOKS
ST. MARTIN'S PRESS
NEW YORK

THOMAS DUNNE BOOKS.
An imprint of St. Martin's Press.

A HARD, CRUEL SHORE. Copyright © 2016 by Dewey Lambdin. All rights reserved. Printed in the United States of America. For information, address St. Martin's Press, 175 Fifth Avenue, New York, N.Y. 10010.

www.thomasdunnebooks.com
www.stmartins.com

Maps by Cameron MacLeod Jones

Library of Congress Cataloging-in-Publication Data

Names: Lambdin, Dewey, author.
Title: A hard, cruel shore : an Alan Lewrie naval adventure / Dewey Lambdin.
Description: First edition. | New York : Thomas Dunne Books/St. Martin's Press, 2016. |
    Series: Alan Lewrie naval adventures ; 22
Identifiers: LCCN 2015039020 | ISBN 978-1-250-03009-2 (hardcover) |
    ISBN 978-1-250-03008-5 (e-book)
Subjects: LCSH: Lewrie, Alan (Fictitious character)—Fiction. | Ship captains—Great Britain—
    Fiction. | Great Britain—History, Naval—19th century—Fiction. | BISAC: FICTION /
    Action & Adventure. | FICTION / Historical. | FICTION / Sea Stories. | GSAFD: Sea
    stories. | Historical fiction. | Adventure fiction.
Classification: LCC PS3562.A435 H37 2016 | DDC 813/.54—dc23
LC record available at http://lccn.loc.gov/2015039020

Our books may be purchased in bulk for promotional, educational, or business use. Please contact your local bookseller or the Macmillan Corporate and Premium Sales Department at (800) 221-7945, extension 5442, or by e-mail at MacmillanSpecialMarkets@macmillan.com.

First Edition: February 2016

10   9   8   7   6   5   4   3   2   1

To my agent, Jake Elwell, a long-suffering man

Full-Rigged Ship: Starboard (right) side view

1. Mizen Topgallant
2. Mizen Topsail
3. Spanker
4. Main Royal
5. Main Topgallant
6. Mizen T'gallant Staysail
7. Main Topsail
8. Main Course
9. Main T'gallant Staysail
10. Middle Staysail
11. Main Topmast Staysail
12. Fore Royal
13. Fore Topgallant
14. Fore Topsail
15. Fore Course
16. Fore Topmast Staysail
17. Inner Jib
18. Outer Flying Jib
19. Spritsail

A. Taffrail & Lanterns
B. Stern & Quarter-galleries
C. Poop Deck/Great Cabins Under
D. Rudder & Transom Post
E. Quarterdeck
F. Mizen Chains & Stays
G. Main Chains & Stays
H. Boarding Battens/Entry Port
I. Cargo Loading Skids
J. Shrouds & Ratlines
K. Fore Chains & Stays
L. Waist
M. Gripe & Cutwater
N. Figurehead & Beakhead Rails
O. Bow Sprit
P. Jib Boom
Q. Foc's'le & Anchor Cat-heads
R. Cro'jack Yard (no sail fitted)
S. Top Platforms
T. Cross-Trees
U. Spanker Gaff

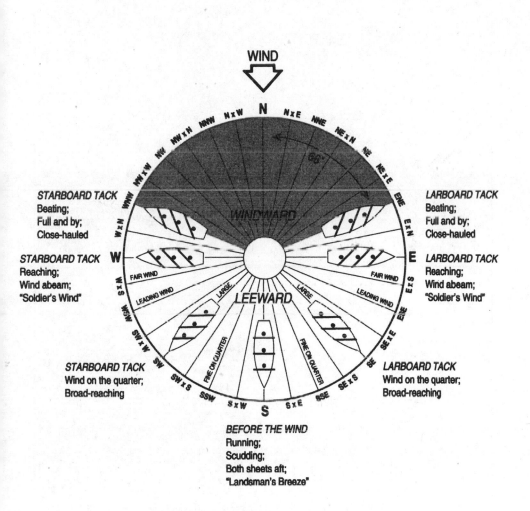

POINTS OF SAIL AND 32-POINT WIND-ROSE

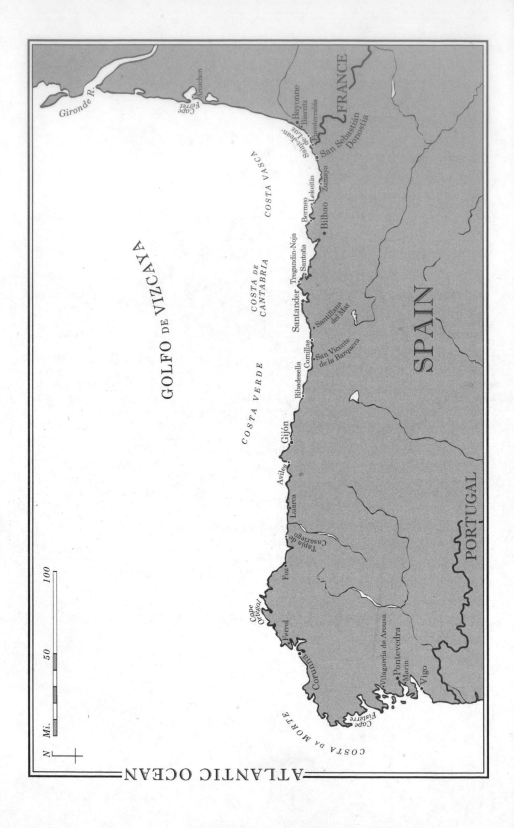

Praeda vago iussit geminare pericula ponto,
bellica cum dubiis rostra dedit ratibus.

Booty made men double the perils of the surging deep, when it fitted the beaks of war to the rocking ships.

–ALBIUS TIBULLUS, *THE COUNTRY FESTIVAL*, BOOK II, LINES 89-40

BOOK ONE

He that commands the sea is at great liberty and
may take as much and less of war as he will.
—FRANCIS BACON (1561-1626),
OF THE GREATNESS OF KINGDOMS

CHAPTER ONE

*A*h, it looks bad, right enough, sir," Mr. Posey, the Surveyor of the Portsmouth Dockyards, gloomily said as he gave the main topmast a thump with his fist. He would have said more, but had to go for his calico handkerchief once more to contain a massive sneeze, then a huge, phlegmy, gargling cough.

Thought he'd sneeze himself right off the shrouds on the way up here, Captain Sir Alan Lewrie, Baronet, thought. He would have taken a step away from the man to avoid catching whatever he had, but for the fact that they were standing in the mainmast fighting top, having come up through the lubber's hole, most un-seamanly. It had been ages since Lewrie had ascended any higher than the cat harpings of the mainmast, and if either one of them had taken the proper route, hanging upside down from the futtock shrouds and clawing up and over the rim of the top, they would now both be smashed to jelly on the deck, far below.

Now, there's *a cure for his sniffles,* Lewrie told himself.

"Your pardons, sir," Mr. Posey continued. "Lightning, was it?"

"Aye, one Hell of a crack, and I haven't trusted it with even a handkerchief, since," Lewrie told him, taking a half-step back as Posey whipped his handkerchief from the turnback of his coat's cuff and captured yet another massive sneeze.

⚓

The weather on their way back from the evacuation of the army at Co-runna had been brisk, and the seas rough, requiring reefed top-sails, and the striking below of the royal and t'gallant masts. That had brought the lightning conductor head down to the lower mast cap. Rain was pouring down, cold and hard as ice pellets, and lightning could be seen all round them, miles away, fork-flashing at the seas.

Suddenly, there had come a flash brighter than day, sizzling the air, rais-ing mens' hair on end, a searing explosion of light and heat, so bright that everyone's eyes were nigh-blinded for long seconds. The clap of thunder that accompanied the flash was so sudden, and so loud that, for a second or two, Lewrie imagined that the ship had blown up! Lost in the titanic roar had been the splintering of the topmast, and the splitting of the lower main mast just above the fighting top. The cap had been set afire, to boot, quickly extinguished by the rain, leaving a plume of thin grey smoke spurting to leeward. Three men in the top had been killed outright, and another two had been rendered senseless, deaf, and half-blind for days after.

Oh yes, it had been lightning!

"We fished it, as you can see," Lewrie said, pointing out the spare anchor stocks that had been nailed to the main mast, woolded with wraps of haw-sers, and shimmed. "The iron bands all the way down to the upper deck partners had t'be re-enforced, too. So . . . I expect she'll need an entire new lower mast?"

"Oh, indeed, sir, indeed," Mr. Posey heartily agreed, done with his sur-vey, and returning to the lubber's hole in the top for a climb back down to the weather deck. "Ah-achoo! Ah, pardons. If you would be so good as to strip her down to a gantline, and un-ship all shrouds and backstays, I can have the sheer hulk alongside by Monday. Though . . . fashioning a lower mast to the proper dimensions may take awhile, sir . . . ah-achoo! At least we can have the bad'un out 'til then. I will need the length of the main course and tops'l yards for my calculations, if you please, sir."

God, I'm stuck in port 'til next *Epiphany,* Lewrie thought, despairing. There weren't many Fourth Rate 50-gunners left in the Navy inventory; most had been turned into troop transports minus guns, or were used as harbour stores hulks. Warships of roughly the same class and design had their specifications drawn up to strict mathematical calculations of mast thickness, lower taper, length, upper diameter to fit through the partners of the lower and upper gun decks, and how they must be stepped to the keelson deep below, with the length of their yards laid out to yet another set of calculations. It might take weeks for the dockyards to fashion one, if none was laying about ready for use, which was extremely "iffy"!

Posey seemed free enough of sneezes to assay the climb down the narrowing main stays and ratlines, and swing out and around to the outer face of the larboard main shrouds. Lewrie followed him, gingerly. But, damned if the bastard didn't pause to sneeze, again, with both hands busy, and expel a cloud of snot and droplets without his handkerchief. The air was so cold in harbour that Posey's breath—along with snot—resembled a sudden burst from a 6-pounder gun!

Lewrie waited 'til that cloud dissipated, then clambered down, slowly and carefully, to the larboard bulwarks and dropped to the safety of the sail-tending gangway. He hoped that he wasn't infected!

Lewrie saw Mr. Posey to the starboard entry-port, made some polite departure small talk, then doffed his hat as the side-party rendered debarking honours.

"A whole new lower mast, is it, sir?" Lt. Geoffrey Westcott, HMS *Sapphire*'s First Officer, glumly asked once Mr. Posey was in his boat, and its crew stroking for the distant shore.

"Aye, if they can find one," Lewrie told him, "or make a new one."

"Oh, good!" Westcott replied with a glint in his eyes, and a quick, fierce grin. "*Bags* of shore liberty, then. Mirth, glee . . . wine and women."

"Most especially women," Lewrie said with a roll of his eyes.

Geoffrey Westcott and Lewrie had been paired for nigh six years, come May, in the same ships, first the *Reliant* frigate, and now *Sapphire*, and Lewrie had stood in awe of how aggressively his First Lieutenant pursued "quim". Lewrie, no slacker when it came to discovering a willing lady, felt like a monk in comparison!

"Well, at least we can still use the main course yard for hoisting stores aboard," Westcott commented, looking aloft, "even if we had to jury-rig."

"Aye, continue loading fresh stores, but when the sheer hulk comes alongside on Monday, everything will have t'be stripped away," Lewrie told him. "And, we'll have to stretch some canvas over the gaps when it's extracted, from the weather deck right down to the orlop, else all the rain and snow get in."

"I'll see to it, sir," Westcott promised, touched fingers to the brim of his cocked hat, and walked away.

Probably t'stay warm, Lewrie told himself as he lingered by the starboard bulwarks to gaze at the shore, and the town. Portdown Hill was almost obscured by the low, grey, and swift-scudding clouds, and the spires of the churches were almost brushed with them. Under that unbroken gloom, the coal smoke from thousands of chimneys spewed an even darker pall. It had snowed before HMS *Sapphire*, the other escorting warships, and the clutch of troopships had entered port and had come to anchor, then warmed and melted what snow had fallen, turning Portsmouth and its environs into a dingy grey and black sketch with the red brick of manufactures, warehouses, and government buildings the only discernible colour. What accumulations of snow that remained had gone to dark mud and coal-soot grey.

It was trying to snow again, in a lacklustre fashion, in swirls and gusts that played out before any new accumulation could sugarcoat the winter's ugliness. As Lewrie paced along the quarterdeck's rails, his boots found icy patches of snow just half-melted then re-frozen to sound crunchy, then another patch of fresher snow just deep enough to muffle his steps. When he turned to look forward towards the bows, he could see some of the ship's boys trying to make the best of what had fallen on the decks to make snowballs. They had formed two sides in roughly equal numbers, but there wasn't much to work with, and after a few volleys back and forth, the game was played out for lack of "ammunition".

"Mister Fywell," he said to one of the Midshipmen standing Harbour Watch, "break out the brooms at the end of the Second Dog, and have the ship swept down. No sense in someone breakin' their necks on an icy patch, not after survivin' the voyage here."

"Aye aye, sir, I will see to it," Fywell replied, coming out of his shivery in-attention. He was swaddled in a heavy grogram watch-coat, a colourful civilian wool muffler, and mittens, but still had to stamp his buckled shoes to keep life in his feet, and his cotton duck slop-trousers were no help in repelling the chill wind that stirred the harbour waters to confused chops.

"Carry on, then," Lewrie said, knowing that the older Mids had put the "younkers" in their place on such a day, and made a note to himself to check on the watchstanders of the First and Second Dog Watches to see if Hillhouse, Leverett, and Britton, the eldest, were taking their proper turns.

As was his wont when seeking a wider view, he went on up to the poop deck and looked over the anchorage for the *Undaunted* frigate, in which his youngest son, Hugh, served, then for the two brig-sloops, *Blaze* and

Peregrine, which had been with him since they had left Gibraltar weeks before. All appeared to be in good order. They *should* be, after all; *they* hadn't been struck by lightning! Capt. Chalmers had fetched *Undaunted* close aboard soon after the strike to offer aid, but could not help from teasing, asking Lewrie "What sins has the Good Lord punished you *for,* sir?" and she was close enough for Lewrie to see Hugh at her rails, laughing his young arse off!

Once in port, Lewrie had summoned his crew to tell them that they'd done a grand thing in fetching off every last survivor of the late General Sir John Moore's army, all the wounded and sick, from the clutches of the pursuing French armies, along with all the army's supplies, leaving the starving enemies with not a morsel of loot, and only the brief warmth of the great pyres of burning supplies that they could not load aboard the hundred-odd rescue ships before they had sailed away. And, despite the brutal weather on-passage from Corunna, not a single troopship had been lost, which he'd told his men that they should be proud of doing.

Privately, though, Lewrie had had a hard time believing that, himself. He had been a Midshipman at Yorktown during the American Revolution, escaping by the skin of his teeth the night before when the hasty evacuation of Cornwallis's army had been scotched by a storm that had howled down from inland, turning the York River into a maelstrom that had flushed his shoddily and hastily built greenwood barge, along with a few others, as far as Guinea Neck, leaving them to make a skulking further escape past the French fleet to the sea beyond the Chesapeake Bay capes, and rescue by a passing British warship.

He'd been a Lieutenant at the evacuation of Toulon, seconded off the *Cockerel* frigate to command a captured French Third Rate, cut down to a *razee* and turned into a large mortar ship, which, by the by, had been hit in the wrong place whilst shelling Fort LeGarde to ruin, and blown up underneath him. He'd had temporary command of a French frigate to get as many of the captured enemy fleet away before the French took the city, at last, and butchered or guillotined the French Royalists that the ships of the First Coalition could not find room for.

And now he had been at Corunna, and had plucked yet another British army to safety before its destruction.

Christ, but it gets old, don't it, he sadly thought; *And I'm cold,* he noticed as the winds picked up and a few icy pellets of snow began to flurry about him.

Despite wearing itchy woolen underdrawers beneath his dark blue wool trousers, woolen stockings inside his Hessian boots, and his coat buttoned double over his chest, he still shivered, and wished that he had not sold off his furs that he had not had a real use for since he had sailed into the Baltic in winter, just before the Battle of Copenhagen, to scout the ice and the naval ports of Sweden and Russia which were allies of the Danes. It was time to stop dawdling in depressing thoughts, and go below to his great-cabins, where, with any luck, it might be a *touch* warmer, out of the wind.

"And where's old Captain Speaks' Franklin stoves when I really need one?" he muttered to himself as he went down the starboard ladderway to the quarterdeck.

He heard a tentative *woof!* from the improvised dog house under the ladderway. Lewrie ducked down to peer in, and sure enough, the ship's dog, Bisquit, was in there, getting to his feet and shaking off one of the cast-off old blankets which he'd half-pulled over himself.

"Hallo, Bisquit," Lewrie said, "what the Devil are ye doin' in there? You should be below on the gun decks, where it's warmer."

Bisquit perked up his stand-and-fall ears and whisked his bushy tail, taking that for an invitation, and wriggled out to stand on his hind legs with his front paws on Lewrie's coat, eager for some "wubbies", which Lewrie was happy to supply, making the dog break out one of his glad grins.

"I'm goin' in, out o' the wind. Care t'join me, just this once?" Lewrie said, cupping Bisquit's head and rubbing his ears. "Can't promise it'll be that much warmer, but there's a carpet for you t'curl up on."

He turned to the door to his great-cabins, just under the poop deck's overhang, and Bisquit frisked at his heels. Hardly had Lewrie nodded to the Marine private who guarded his sanctuary and laid hold of the knob than Bisquit dashed through the narrow gap, galloping into the cabins.

The Marine sentry lowered his musket from Present Arms and turned up the wide collar of his little-used greatcoat after saluting the Captain, muttering under his breath "Wisht I could roll up on a warm carpet, too!"

CHAPTER TWO

"Have we anything hot, Pettus?" Lewrie asked his cabin-steward as he blew on his hands to warm them. His cabins were a bit warmer, only due to being out of that wind, and closed up snugly, but five warm bodies—Lewrie, Pettus and young Jessop, Bisquit and the cat, Chalky—did little to heat it, not like the upper and lower gun decks where the body heat of hundreds of off-watch sailors and Marines was trapped beneath closed hatches and behind sealed gun ports. They had small lanthorns or glim candles by the dozens, too.

"Aye, sir!" Pettus piped up. "There's a pot of tea just brewed on the sideboard, with a warming candle under it. Would you care for a dollop of rum or brandy with it, sir?"

"That I would," Lewrie eagerly agreed, "a mug that I can wrap my fingers round, not a dainty cup. Hallo, Chalky, and how are you?" he asked his cat, which had been napping on the starboard side settee. One of his servants had tucked a tea towel over the cat, a white one, making it hard to distinguish where the tea towel ended and the whiteish furred Chalky began. He was so comfortable that even the dog's exuberant entry and quick scout of the great-cabins hadn't stirred him.

Lewrie gave Chalky some head strokes, and ran a finger along his jowls that brought him to all fours, and an arching of his back. Which bliss lasted but a moment, for Bisquit decided to come to the settee to see what the animated towel was all about, and Chalky was off in a dash for the bed space and shelter atop the hanging bed-cot where the dog might not be able to leap.

"Oh, well," Lewrie sighed, transferring his attention to the dog for a moment before crossing the day cabin to his desk to seat himself, open a drawer, and pull out writing paper. "Damme, I've the last quire o' good paper left, maybe less."

"Mister Faulkes, he said he wuz almost out, too, sir," Jessop spoke up from the wine cabinet, where he was fetching out the rum, "an' thought he might haveta borry from you, afore we got new from a chandler."

"Well, that's one of many shortages soon t'be solved," Lewrie said, jerking his head shoreward. "Be aboard by morning."

Pettus brought him a large ceramic mug of steaming-hot tea, redolent of a *large* dollop of rum, and Lewrie held it under his nose for a good long time, letting out an "aahh", holding it with both hands. A second satisfied "aahh" followed his first, deep sip. Pettus had laced the tea with lots of sugar, and some goat's milk from the nanny in the forecastle manger, and it was heavenly going down, warming him even down to his toes.

Lewrie transferred some of that warmth with one hand on the dog's furry head, bestowing some more "wubbies" as Bisquit sat at his side.

"Gotten spoiled, ye have," Lewrie gently teased, "all that one winter at my father's house in the country, after I got shot. All of the fireplaces, and the kitchens, when Mistress Furlough wasn't lookin', hey?"

Oh, Bisquit had had a fine time of it, that winter, even to the point of leaping to the foot of Pettus's, Jessop's, Liam Desmond's, or Patrick Furfy's beds for the night . . . or curling up in front of the fireplace in Lewrie's bed-chamber some nights, truth to tell.

Lewrie turned his attention to his letter writing. As soon as *Sapphire* had dropped anchor at Portsmouth, pre-written reports to the Admiralty of his doings, and his ship's damage, had gone off in the post, along with personal correspondence. Now, he would have to write a fresh report concerning his damaged lower main mast, and what the yards would do to pull it like a rotten tooth and replace it with . . . what?

This'll take some careful *doin'*, he thought, steeling himself.

If he was brutally honest about the severity of the damage to the mast, and the slim odds of there being a spare in the mast ponds to replace it, Admiralty might deem *Sapphire* redundant to the needs of the Royal Navy if she was forced to sit idle long enough for a new mast to be fashioned for her, and relegate her to an un-armed troop ship or harbour hulk, jerking his quarterdeck right out from under his feet, and casting him ashore on half-pay in the middle of an active commission!

Can't have that! Lewrie fretted to himself; *She's still a good fightin' ship, we've* proved *that, over and over, and her crew's been honed t'the peak of perfection, with the best gunners ever I did see!*

In point of fact, Lewrie had gotten her six months into her re-commissioning, when her former Captain and First Officer had shot each other in a duel—piss-poor shooting on their parts—and she was now about one year from the necessity of being de-commissioned and turned over to some dockyard graving dock for a complete rebuild before some other Captain got her, in one form or the other. Lewrie *knew* he only had a year of commanding her left before being forced to give her up, anyway, but he *wanted* that one last year, dearly!

To The First Secretary of The Admiralty,
The Honourable Mr. H. H. W. Pole,

   Sir, it is my Duty to Inform you and The Lords of Admiralty further anent the damage which my Ship suffered on passage from Corunna to Portsmouth. The lower mast, sadly, is so damaged that it must be drawn out and replaced. I am assured by the Surveyor of the Dockyard that it can, and shall be, speedily replaced and that HMS Sapphire can return to full Service as soon as that is done.

Well, he sorta *promised, didn't he?* Lewrie qualified, tongue firmly planted in one cheek; *It ain't an* outright *lie!*

He mulled over how much more he could add, but there was an interruption. His Marine sentry stamped boots, musket butt, and shouted "Cap'um's Cook t'see th' Cap'um, SAII!"

"Enter," Lewrie called back, and James Yeovill came into the great-cabins, shaking flakes of snow from his watchcoat and swiping a shapeless wool cap from his long and frizzy hair which was bound back with a hank of ribbon into what looked like a fox's brush.

"Thought you might not mind a cup of hot broth, sir," Yeovill offered.

"I would, indeed, Yeovill," Lewrie perked up, for his mug of tea was empty, at last, and the cabins were still chilly. "Bring it on! What's planned for supper?"

"That would depend on whether you're of a mind to dine some of your officers in, tonight, sir," Yeovill said, coming to the desk with his offering.

"No, just me and the beasts, tonight," Lewrie told him.

"Nothing in the way of a salad, sir, the last greens have gone over."
Yeovill ticked off on his fingers. "But I thought that a soup of salt beef
could start it, then a quail or a rabbit, your choice, would go down well,
and there are some decent potatoes left, along with *garbanzos,* that lot of
Spanish chick peas we took aboard at Gibraltar are still in quantity *and*
quality. There's shore bread come aboard, and I can do a bread pudding
with caramel sauce."

"Rabbit, if it's a fat one," Lewrie decided. Long ago he had been advised by a senior officer to stock his share of the manger with both rabbits
and quail, for they bred and matured rapidly. "The cat, and Bisquit will
find rabbit toothsome, too. Along with their sausages or jerky, o' course.
Sounds grand. I leave it to you to produce another of your miracles."

"Aye, sir," Yeovill said, turning to go.

"Has it started to snow, again?" Lewrie asked, taking note of the back
and shoulders of Yeovill's watchcoat.

"Off and on, sir," Yeovill said with a grin. "And thank God for a warm
galley, even one with Mister Tanner in charge of it."

Bisquit whined and whuffled at Yeovill's side before he left the cabins;
he was smart enough to be friends with the source of all good treats, and
all those delicious smells! Once he was gone, the dog padded round about a
couple of times and settled down in front of Lewrie's desk, on the deep and
soft Turkey carpet.

Lewrie read over what he'd written, wondering if there was anything
more to add, wondering if going further would be "gilding the lily", or
sounding a tad too desperately smarmy to keep his ship.

"Shore messenger t'see the Cap'um, SAH!" the Marine sentry bellowed,
slamming boots and musket butt on the deck.

"Christ, what now? Enter!" Lewrie shouted back.

A shivering, teeth-chattering Midshipman came in, hat under his arm,
and advanced to the desk as Lewrie rose to his feet.

"A message from the flagship presently in port, sir," the Mid told him
as he handed over a wax-sealed letter. "There are at least twelve senior
Post-Captains that have come in with the Admiral and his squadron, and
in two days they will sit aboard the flag to hold examinations for all qual-
ifying Midshipmen."

"In two days," Lewrie queried, opening the sealed letter and discovering
pretty-much what the Mid had just stated. "I've several who will eagerly
attend, and thankee for bringing news of it, young sir. Mister . . . ?"

"Tominy, sir, George Tominy," the Mid replied.

"Thinkin' of tryin' your luck, yourself, are you, Mister Tominy?" Lewrie jested.

"I lack a year on ship's books before I could, sir," Tominy said with a moue of disappointment, and a shrug.

"Well, you'll have your turn, in time," Lewrie assured him. "Thanks again, Mister Tominy."

"Thank you, sir," the Mid said, and headed for the door, and the foul weather. He was snow-flaked, too, Lewrie noted.

A Midshipman's Board, well well, Lewrie thought; *And is there a chance that I can get rid of Midshipman Hillhouse, at long last? Oh, just please Jesus!*

It wasn't that Hillhouse was not competent, no; he was one of the oldest and most experienced of *Sapphire*'s ten Mids, well into his mid-twenties. Hillhouse's problem was that he seemed to have a bad case of the "sulks" over his few chances to shine and be mentioned in reports, to command a prize into harbour, be given grander duties.

"Jessop?" Lewrie called out to his cabin servant. "I'd admire did ye run this letter down to the Mid's cockpit, and inform them that if letters of recommendation are desired, they should let me know at once."

"Me, sir?" Jessop replied, sounding put-upon. "Oh, aye, sir."

He took the letter, found his wool watch coat for his brief exposure to the foul weather, and dashed away.

Lewrie looked over his damage report to Admiralty some more, wondering if he could hint that his proficient, and well-drilled, crew and their impeccable gunnery skills would prove valuable, and deadly to the French, and should be kept together and gotten back to sea, instanter. *Is that beggin', or boastin'?* Lewrie pondered.

He dipped his precious steel-nibbed pen in the inkwell and began to add to his report, but Chalky got over his fear of the sleeping dog, left the comfort of the bed-cot, and leapt into Lewrie's lap without even a warning mew or trill. Lewrie's hand was jounced, and a large glop of ink spoiled the report.

"Damme, but you're a hazard," Lewrie said with a weary sigh as he balled up that sheet of paper and tossed it aside. He gave Chalky some long strokes along his back and tickled his jowls and cheeks, anyway, getting him settled into a white-furred pot-roast atop the desk before pulling out a fresh sheet to begin again.

The door opened, admitting an icy blast as Jessop returned, shaking snow from his coat like a dog shedding rain, and emitting an audible *Brr!*

"They's three wantin' letters, sir," he said, handing over the letter, with the aspirants' names now pencilled in at the bottom.

"Oh, good," Lewrie said, groaning faintly. "More scribblin' to do."

"Niver saw such a pig-sty me whole life, sir," Jessop went on, sounding offended. "Ever'thing hangin' on pegs'r spillin' outa their sea chests, filth in ev'ry corner, an' it stinks worse'n a corpse's armpit. Don't think they *ever* sponge off. You oughta do somethin' about it, sir. Why, even the table-cloth ain't white, *anywhere* you look, nothin' but stains an' spills, an' their steward . . . he were cleanin' the meat fork by stabbin' it *through* the table-cloth t'get some crusty black stuff off'n it!"

"Don't be bothering the Captain with all that," Pettus said, making a shushing motion over his mouth.

"Mister Kibworth, sir," the outraged Jessop went further, ignoring the warning, "he wuz drinkin' cider outa a glass so filthy it'd gone brown, an' when Mister Leverett wanted some, he had nought but an old *shoe* t'drink from, an' they laughed an' said they *all* used shoes when they got soup, 'coz Mister Kibworth had the only glass left!"

"And someday, God willing, Jessop," Lewrie told him with glee, and remembrance of his own Midshipman days, "they will all become exalted Post-Captains . . . if they don't poison themselves, first. That is very much like what I saw back in my day. You've been spoiled."

"Spoiled, sir?" Jessop said, cocking his head to one side.

"The way Pettus keeps these cabins, how neatly, and cleanly," Lewrie told him, "My father's country house, the way the Coneys keep the Old Ploughman back in Anglesgreen. You're used to it, by now."

"Oh, Well, s'pose I am, then," Jessop agreed after a long ponder. He had wandered into a "rondy", a tavern hired out for recruiting volunteers, when Lewrie was fitting out his last frigate, HMS *Reliant*, in early 1803, before the Peace of Amiens was broken, and Britain went back to war with Napoleonic France. He'd been a street waif, living hand-to-mouth and sleeping rough wherever he could lay his head, nigh-illiterate, and completely alone in life, filthy in clothes and body, and lice-ridden. A thorough wash under a hose from the wash-deck pump had made him screech in horror after he had come aboard and had scrawled a shaky attempt at his name in the ship's muster book.

Now, though, Jessop was almost sleek with good living, and a guaranteed three meals a day, with meat four days a week, dressed in clean "pusser's slops", shod and stockinged, with a short blue coat with brass buttons, a flat, tarred hat on his head, and, as a ship's servant, he had "all night in" to sleep soundly in a corner of the upper gun deck near the Marine complement.

Jessop even had something to aspire to, learning his knots, learning to box the points of the compass, to hand and reef, if not yet steer, to go aloft as agile as a monkey, and serve as a member of one of the starboard carronades' gun crew.

He'd also learned to chew tobacco, drink to excess, curse as grandly as a Bosun's Mate, and had gotten himself two very nautical tattoos, and on shore liberty at Gibraltar, had taken runs at the whores.

"Lay the table, Jessop," Pettus ordered, "and mind that the settings are clean."

Lewrie re-wrote his letter to the First Secretary, carefully fudging the wording on the second try, and signing his name and "the etcs" at the bottom, pleased with the result. He reached into a side drawer for sealing wax and a seal, weighing whether he would use the plain one with only his initials, or the one that bore his crest of knighthood.

Knighthood, and a baronet to boot! Most gentlemen of his ilk would leap over the moon to hold such an honour, would fight and claw to attain such a gift from King George, but it had always left a bad taste in Lewrie's mouth, suspecting the reason for his elevation to be a cynical, backhanded sop from the government. And, there was too much lost.

He and *Reliant* had been part of a four-ship squadron ordered to seek and bring to battle a French squadron rumoured to be sailing for Spanish Louisiana to reclaim that vast territory, and the strategically sited city of New Orleans, in exchange for some duchy where a relative of Spanish King Carlos could hang his new crown. They'd found them after weeks of fruitless cruising, just off the Chandeleur Islands near the Eastern pass into the Mississippi River, and beaten them quite handily. Since it had been the first, and nigh the only, significant sea action that year, all the national papers were full of it for days, and the victors were lauded to the skies . . .

Captain Blanding, their Commodore, had been certain to be knighted. Lewrie, though, even in command of the most powerful of the three frigates present, putative second-in-command, usually could not expect to be included, but, oddly, he was. He knew why.

Lewrie and his wife, Caroline, had reconciled after years of bitter recriminations over his extra-marital dalliances, and had gone to Paris for a "honeymoon". He still didn't know quite what he had done to anger Napoleon Bonaparte when presented at the Tuileries Palace to exchange dead French officers' swords for a hanger that Lewrie had had to surrender into Bonaparte's hands at Toulon years before, but they'd been warned to flee at once, and with the aid of a fraudulent Sir Pulteney Plumb, who styled himself as "The Yellow Tansy", and his wife they had made it to

Calais in one disguise after another, and almost into a waiting rowboat, where the French caught up with them with orders to kill them, and Caroline had been shot in the back and died minutes later as the boat neared a waiting schooner.

The papers had been full of *that*, too, for days; NAVAL HERO AND WIFE PURSUED UNDER DEATH SENTENCE, WIFE SLAIN BY PERFIDIOUS FRENCH ON ORDERS OF THE CORSICAN OGRE. And it went on being beaten like a drum as England had prepared to go back to war, on and on, mentioned in the same breath with which nation would keep Malta, demands for France to end their occupation of Switzerland, and an host of depredations and atrocities the French had been capable of.

Much like Lewrie forever being a somewhat useful "gun dog" to the agents from the Foreign Office's Secret Branch over the years, he had been *useful* to stir the nation's patriotic fervour, and his wife's death had been . . . productive! Even fortuitous!

So, Lewrie had found himself a year later at Saint James's Palace in unaccustomed silk finery, with an irritating powdered wig, kneeling before King George the Third and a bored Prince of Wales who had seemed more concerned with the dirt under his fingernails, and it had turned into a shambolic farce, for the King was having one of his bad days, and after dubbing several before Lewrie with baronies, knighthoods, and baronetcies, it must have stuck in his head, so when the dangerously swinging Sword of State had touched Lewrie's shoulders (very near his ears!) out had come "Knight and Baronet", which was repeated several times in search of the proper word to emphasize, then a question from his Sovereign as to why he was on his knees in front of him. He was told in an anteroom moments later that the Crown did not "err", which had been pronounced much like "grr" and there it was, what what?

Well, it cost me enough, Lewrie sadly thought as the stick of wax was melting over a candle; the fees for such honours at the College of Heralds for his crest, ring, and seal had been horrendously steep. He dripped a large blob of hot blue wax over the fold of the letter, then chose the crest seal to press into it. *One down, three to go,* he told himself with a sigh as he began to scribble praise for Midshipman Leverett.

"More tea, sir?" Pettus asked in a soft voice, sidling up to the desk with the shiny pewter pot.

"Aye, fill me back up," Lewrie said with his head down over his writing, wondering just what he could say for Hillhouse that would improve his chances of promotion.

CHAPTER THREE

And, that's why they pay me the glorious sum of ten shillin's a day, Lewrie told himself over the next few days, as one problem after another cropped up.

First came the men addled by the lightning strike. The Ship's Surgeon, Mr. Snelling, a tall, and skeletally gaunt fellow, came to him with the bad news that it was not two hands affected, but five, all prime topmen.

"They were so close to the strike, sir, that they came within a breath of perishing, themselves," Snelling reported. "Since then, they have all lost their sense of balance, their co-ordination, their sight has been impaired, and they show difficulties with forming words and thoughts. In addition, they seem as if their strength has vanished. Lassitude, general weakness of their limbs . . ."

"Ain't playin' a 'fiddle', are they? Shirkin'?" Lewrie had to ask.

"No sir, it's quite real, and most mystifying to me," Snelling said with a shake of his head. "Do recall, sir, that we were both on the quarterdeck when the lightning struck, and we both felt a strong *frisson* of the electrical aura, as if the very atoms of our beings were being stirred, or somehow re-ordered. Who is to say what force it really was that re-ordered the wits, and the strength of those poor fellows. I fear they must be medically discharged, sir. Even light duties out at sea would be the death of them."

"Damme, Mister Snelling, that's eight experienced topmen of the main-mast crew, and hellish-hard t'replace!" Lewrie barked with a wince. "Christ on a crutch, three dead and five sent ashore? Well, I s'pose there's no helpin' it. Send my clerk your findings and I'll handle the discharge papers."

Next, it was the First Officer, with more bad news.

"The lightning strike, sir," Lt. Westcott said with a scowl on his face, "it transferred itself down the lower stays to the channels and dead-eye blocks, and the metal sheaves are damaged. And the iron bolts that tension the blocks beneath the channel platforms, well . . . they look to be partly *melted*, and may have to be replaced, as well."

"Mine arse on a band-box," Lewrie growled. "I thought Mister Posey passed 'em."

"Best we send for him, again, sir, for a second look, before we step a new mast and re-rig the stays," Westcott suggested.

"Right, then, I'll see to it," Lewrie replied with a much put-upon sigh. "God, I wonder what it did to the bolts that hold the iron knees of the lower decks!"

"Oh," Westcott said, wincing himself. "I'd best check with the Bosun and his Mates on that head, sir."

"The iron water tanks . . ." Lewrie grimly mused.

"I'll look for leaks, sir," Westcott promised.

"Now, as if ye didn't have enough on your plate, Geoffrey," Lewrie went on, "Mister Snelling says it's five cripples, not three, who need discharges. Where d'ye think we're going to find replacements for 'em?"

"Five?" Westcott gawped, then let out a thin whistle. "All of them Able or Ordinary, and all topmen? Damn my eyes. Hmm, we have some teen boys who've gone aloft, mostly for fun so far. And, there may be some younger Landsmen who might be trained. The slight increase in pay 'twixt a Landsman and an Ordinary Seaman ain't much, but I could use it as a lure. I'll see to it, sir," Westcott said with a morose expression.

The next day, and Mr. Posey was back aboard with some of his artificers to have a look-see at the dead-eye block sheaves and the channel platform bolts, and, after a long inspection from outside, a tight tramp through the carpenter's walks 'twixt the inner and the outer hull scantlings, he surfaced with a dour look on his phyz.

"You're right, Captain Lewrie," Posey said, whipping out that sodden handkerchief for a blow of his nose, a gargle of phlegm, and a spit alee over the side. "We'll have to replace them all, before we fetch the sheer hulk alongside."

"You found a mast?" Lewrie hopefully asked, perking up.

"Ah, in point of fact, no, sir," Posey had to impart. "There is nothing of the proper dimensions in stores, at present. Though I may have hopes of employing a Third Rate's foremast, it may take a few more days to see if it can be re-fashioned."

"Very well, then, Mister Posey," Lewrie had to allow, feeling that his ship and his active commission could be doomed. "I leave it to you and your artificers."

Three pounds, ten shillings a week, he gloomily thought; *ain't nowhere near enough!*

A day later, and his senior Mids made their way to the towering Second Rate 98-gun flagship for their examinations, looking cleaner and neater than he'd seen them in a year entire. He saw them off from the entry-port and wished them well.

Hours later, he heard the cutter coming alongside, and went on deck to welcome them back. And oh, but they were a merry crew! Well, two of them were.

"Welcome back aboard, gentlemen," he said. "And how did you fare?"

"I am passed, sir!" Midshipman Britton crowed. "There were a few real posers, but all in all, it wasn't *too* terrifying."

"Speak for yourself," Midshipman Leverett said with a laugh as he pulled the precious certificate from an inside pocket of his coat. "I am passed as well, sir, and that with not one relation on the board, or the slightest smidgeon of 'interest', hah hah!"

Lewrie turned to Midshipman Hillhouse, whose stony expression gave him a quick answer as to how he had fared. "And?" he asked the man.

"I . . . I was told to try again at a later date, sir," Hillhouse slowly and carefully replied, too disappointed and crushed in his hopes to give his tongue freedom.

"Ah, I see," Lewrie said, hiding his own disappointment that he might at last be shot of the fellow. "My condolences, young sir. A real cobbing, was it?"

"No, sir, not all that bad, not like a time before, when the questions came so quick that I barely had time to get through one before they posed a second," Hillhouse replied, rasping as if his voice would break. "I *knew* the answers, but I couldn't get them out, I stammered and lost track, and . . . they must have thought me daft, or feeble-witted, or a complete, lubberly *fool*!"

"Again, you have my condolences, Mister Hillhouse," Lewrie said, feeling sorry for the fellow for real. "Well, I shall let you all go below and 'splice your mainbrace'."

They all doffed hats and departed for the cockpit far below, and Lewrie suspected that the younger Mids would have a rough time of it, what with Britton and Leverett celebrating, and everyone walking on tip-toe round Hillhouse, who would most-like be deep in his cups, and ready to rage at the younger ones.

Lewrie doubted the sense of accomplishment would last long, though. While surviving the ordeal of the Examining Board and being rated Passed Midshipman was a significant milestone in a young gentleman's naval career, it did not guarantee future advancement. The Navy teemed with Passed Midshipmen in their thirties and fourties, men with no patronage or "interest" to speed them upwards to the coveted promotion to Lieutenant, Passed Mids who served lacklustre roles in ships on the blockades or foreign stations which offered no opportunities to win fame, or notice sufficient to make Admiralty deem them worthy of promotion. And, it was a cruel fact that Midshipmen didn't get half-pay after their current ship paid off.

Lewrie reckoned that Britton and Leverett would wake up with groggy heads in the morning and feel as frustrated as Hillhouse that there was yet another steep hill to climb!

Lewrie headed back to his warm cabins, wondering if he should enquire of the Port Admiral about the availabilty of a spare Midshipman, in addition to spare topmen. If Lord Gardner still ruled Portsmouth, he could help on both matters. Why, with any luck at all, and an abundance of warmth in his flinty heart, Lord Gardner might even whistle him up a new mast!

Two older Ordinary Seamen *were* available ashore, fresh from the Naval Hospital, men who had been topmen before falling sick and being left behind when their ship sailed for the Brest blockade. A pair of Landsmen weary of un-ending "pully-hauley" on the gangways volunteered to go aloft and begin to learn topmens' duties, and among the many ship's boys aboard, Lt. Westcott found some in their "tweens" who were eager, as well, so that was one of Lewrie's worries put to rest.

A day later, though, and there came an announcement from the Marine sentry at the cabin door. "Midshipman Britton t'see th' Cap'um, SAH!"

"Enter!" Lewrie called back, and in breezed Britton, wearing a smile as wide as his ears.

"Sir, I am appointed Third Lieutenant into a frigate!" Britton burst out. "She's being re-commissioned, at Deptford. I received my promotion, and posting, in this morning's mail!"

"A Commission Sea Officer, well, well!" Lewrie congratulated, rising from his desk to shake Britton's hand. "That was quick I must say. I am sorry to lose your services, Mister Britton. I s'pose you wish to leave us, instanter . . . coach up to London, see a good tailor, and get aboard her before Admiralty changes its mind?"

"Something like that, sir, aye," Britton said with a hearty laugh, full of good cheer at his marvellous stroke of luck.

"Clear your accounts with the Purser, and my clerk will have your records ready for you by . . . when, Mister Faulkes?" Lewrie asked his clerk, who was scribbling away at a side table.

"By one P.M., sir," Faulkes replied, looking only the slightest pained at the additional task, "ehm . . . Two Bells of the Day Watch, mean t'say."

Faulkes secretly didn't care for doing his work in the great-cabins, nice though they were, and under constant scrutiny by Lewrie and the rest. He had a wee drinking problem, kept in check most of the time. When Lewrie and his retinue had first come aboard *Sapphire* there was a snug cabin right off the quarterdeck on the larboard side which would have been his private hidey-hole, the clerk's office, but Lewrie had decided that it would make a grand chart space convenient for the officers of the watch and the Sailing Master, who had a small sea cabin on the opposite side.

"When you come for your final papers and pay chits, we will send you off in my cutter, Mister Britton," Lewrie promised.

"Thank you for the honour, sir, and may I say . . . my time in *Sapphire* under your command has been the grandest experience of all my time in the Navy, and I can only hope that my new ship gets into but *half* the adventures that we have."

"Well, thankee for that, sir," Lewrie replied, taken aback a bit, "that was well, and kindly, said. A glass of something before you go crow to your messmates?"

"I would admire one, sir!" Britton said, beaming and fit to bust with pride of his advancement.

Now I'll have *t'go see Lord Gardner,* Lewrie told himself as Pettus fetched out claret and a pair of glasses.

"Ah, Captain Niles, good t'see you again," Lewrie said as he was allowed to enter the anteroom of the Port Admiral's offices where Niles stood as guardian to the gate, and kept his own office, and the Admiral's affairs, running smoothly. Captain Niles was one of those grand fellows, seemingly all affable and charming, who could make a refusal, or an admonition, almost sound pleasant.

"Ehm . . . aha! Captain Lewrie, aye," Niles said, rising to greet him, "I got your note requesting a moment of Lord Gardner's time. I fear, though, that he's so much on his plate at the moment that he cannot see you today, and indeed, for some time. So sorry."

And here I thought he'd remember me, Lewrie thought, sensing that Niles could not place a name with a face for a moment.

"Well, it's not a pressing matter," Lewrie allowed, "perhaps you could give me a leading wind."

"It does not involve finding you a new mast, does it, sir?" Niles asked with a brow up in jest; he *did* remember Lewrie at last.

"No, it's more a matter of personnel, Captain Niles . . . a lack of a Midshipman," Lewrie told him, explaining how two of his Mids had passed the recent Examining Board, and one had been ordered away. "Were I in London, I'd be ankle-deep in parents lookin' for a post for their boys, but, here in Portsmouth, I don't know a soul, and I wondered if you, or the Admiral, might have some likely lad in mind."

"Oh, I say!" Capt. Niles said, suddenly getting a crafty look. "Will you take tea, sir? Sit you down, sit you down."

He rang for a steward to fetch a fresh pot, rubbing his hands together as if to warm them. Or, to take advantage.

Over his long career, Lewrie had been the recipient of very little "Interest", patronage, or "petti-coat influence", and what he had gotten had come from much older officers who'd soon retired and dropped out of the Royal Navy's behind-the-scenes sponsorship of favourites, cater-cousins, sons, and the "give-and-take" manoeuvring.

The one good thing about the informal system was that a poor recommendation reflected badly upon the patron, so that senior men usually were very careful anent whom they chose to foster. Capt. Niles, and Lord Gardner, would not stick him with a "pig in a poke".

"No relations who might have a second or third son waiting in the wings, sir?" Niles teasingly asked as the steward returned with a laden tray.

"None, sorry t'say, sir," Lewrie told him, "and, I've been so much at sea since Ninety-Three that I fear my circle of friends and acquaintances ashore is quite limited."

"Hmm, I do believe that the Admiral has just placed a young fellow aboard a Third Rate, one of his distant relations' boys, and sounded relieved that he'd done so, and was now free of finding posts for a time," Capt. Niles related as he spooned sugar into his tea, poured fresh cream with a heavy hand, and slowly stirred, as if in deep thought. "On the other hand, though . . ."

"Aye, sir?" Lewrie asked, wishing that he would come to the point. "Ah, good tea, pipin' hot, too. Perfect for such a day."

"I was thinking that my wife's family, the Holbrookes, have a likely prospect," Niles said off-handedly, "her eldest brother's boy, George, has just turned thirteen, their youngest of three sons, I've met him a few times, and he seems as smart as paint, and has done well at his studies. Rides and shoots well, a wickedly fine cricketer, and has a happy, outgoing demeanour. I suppose I could send for him to coach down so you could take your measure of him."

"Just so long as he's not a swaggerin' brute with servants and fellow students," Lewrie said after a long sip of his tea.

"He struck me as sunny and delightful," Niles said quickly.

"No need for me to vet him, Captain Niles," Lewrie said with a shrug and a chuckle. "I will take your word on him. Aye, send for him, and tell him to kit himself out and be ready to report aboard *Sapphire* at his earliest convenience. It ain't as if we'll be sailin' on the next tide, so long as Mister Posey is still lookin' for a new lower mast."

"Quite decent of you to oblige me, Captain Lewrie, quite decent indeed!" Niles said, suddenly beaming with joy, "and I'm certain he'll not disappoint. You do me an honour, sir!"

And if you're still here in future, you will owe me a favour next time, Lewrie thought, quite satisfied with the morning's work.

"Ah, welcome back aboard, sir," Lt. Westcott said, doffing his hat as Lewrie gained the deck in-board of the entry-port. "We have just gotten good news from Mister Posey. He's determined that there is a foremast from a

Third Rate that will suit us admirably, and he vows to have the sheer hulk alongside two days from now, sir."

"Why, that's capital!" Lewrie cheered. "And thank God for it! By the by, we've a new Mid to come aboard to replace Britton . . . some kin of Captain Niles, a Mister George Holbrooke."

"Better and better, sir, and I've shifted a man from both the foremast and mizen mast crews to fill out the mainmast crew, so we'll have as many as needed to man it."

"You *do* work wonders, Mister Westcott," Lewrie praised him. "All fresh provisions have come aboard, everything stowed away?"

"Aye, sir," Westcott told him.

"We'll put the ship Out of Discipline *after* we've stood up the new mast, then," Lewrie decided, "but we will allow tomorrow to be a 'Make and Mend' day. Finally give the people a bit of ease."

"Very good, sir,"

"Sir, sir! Captain, sir!" Midshipman Leverett called up from the waist in great agitation. He was waving a parchment document over his head. "Permission to speak, sir?"

"Aye, come up, Mister Leverett," Lewrie bade, sure that one more problem had just cropped up.

"I have just received my promotion, sir," Leverett said after he had clomped to the quarterdeck, and doffed his hat. "There is an opening as Fifth Lieutenant aboard a Third Rate that just came up . . . she's lying here in Portsmouth this instant, and I am to report to her at once!"

As he had with Midshipman Britton, Lewrie put a cheerful face on it, congratulating him and telling him how much his services would be missed, and have a glass with me aft, before you finish your packing, get your papers from Faulkes, etc. and etc.

"Mail's come, sir," Pettus informed him before he poured them both a claret to celebrate, in Leverett's case his "stirrup cup" to see him off to his new ship and his new career.

Lewrie picked through the slim pile of his personal mail on his desk, noting the weight and distance travelled, and toting up the cost in his head, wondering if the government would ever collect the postage due from the sendee, and not the recipient.

"What the Devil?" Lewrie muttered as he found the official one atop the pile. As Leverett expressed much the same sentiments as had Midshipman Britton a day or two before, about how grand an experience and how high the adventures he'd had aboard *Sapphire*, Lewrie tore it open and read the first few lines. "Mine arse on a band-box!"

"Ehm . . . sir?" Leverett stopped in mid-spiel.

"Sorry, Mister Leverett, thankee for the kind sentiments," he finessed, setting the letter aside for a moment. "I expect that you'll make a good show of it aboard your new ship. You're more than ready to advance, and, again, my heartiest congratulations. Just keep fond memories of your time here."

"The fondest, sir," Leverett said, raising his glass.

"Well, remember the old Navy adage, 'growl you may but go you must', and I'm certain you've packing to do."

"Aye, sir. I'll be on my way." Leverett told him, draining his wine and bowing from the waist as he made his departure.

"Damn, damn, damn!" Lewrie fumed once Leverett was on deck and out of earshot.

"Trouble, sir?" Pettus asked as he reclaimed the glasses.

"The Goddamned Admiralty's summoned me t'hear what I have t'say before they decide to de-commission the ship and turn her over to the bloody Transport Board!" Lewrie raged, looking for a piece of furniture to kick. Chalky, who had been footballing one of Lewrie's personal letters cross the waxed desktop, froze in fear, then dashed off for refuge under the settee. "I have t'go up to London, before dawn tomorrow. Christ, arrange a coach, pack . . . you'll accompany me, of course."

"Happy to, sir," Pettus said.

"Mine arse on a band-box! Just when we finally get a new mast, too!" Lewrie growled.

Fourteen pounds a month, and a bloody lunar *month at that,* he furiously thought; *it ain't* anywhere *near enough!*

CHAPTER FOUR

*O*n such short notice, a private equipage was impossible to hire, so Lewrie and Pettus booked passage on the early morning post coaches, plumping for inside seats, given the weather. To put his steward on top with a precarious grip on a madly swaying, rocking coach would have been the death of him, either being frozen solid, or tossed off to smash his brains out.

It had been some time since Lewrie had travelled in one of the so-called "flying coaches" or "diligences", and the trip was as bad as he remembered. Only a few of the nine people crammed inside were Navy, and none were in a mood to be talkative at "first sparrow fart". A quick request of "Shall we caulk or yarn?" favoured that they caulk, try to nap in uncomfortable, cold silence. The rest of the coach's passengers were civilians, a very fetching young daughter and matron warily guarding the girl's virtue; several contractors or jobbers associated with HM Dockyards, some who snored loudly or snorted, gargled and snuffled with winter woes, after attempts at flirtation with said virtuous young daughter. The last pair were older women whose accents and choice of canting slang words made Lewrie think that they were either pickpockets, whores, or fishmongers from the Billingsgate market.

Lastly, to make things even worse, winter was a bad time to bathe, or wash what little clothing one possessed, so the aromas of most of Lewrie's fellow passengers were "high", and grew worse after body heat in the closely sealed coach shared the smells about, and any attempt to lower a sash window was greeted with cries of alarm.

They all had to get out and help push near the crest of Portdown Hill, as per usual for overloaded coaches, where a fresh snow only masked the semi-frozen mud of the roadway.

From there on, the roads were actually better than Lewrie remembered, better drained and gravelled, not so badly rutted as he had experienced the last time he'd gone up to London, and a fresh snow of several inches softened what bumps there were; along with better suspension straps to lessen the swaying and rocking of the coach body, Lewrie almost could drift off with his chin on his chest.

The glass windows were glazed over with frost outside, and fog inside, so there wasn't much to see for the most part, not 'till they rolled into a posting house every fifteen or twenty miles on for a change of horse teams, and a chance to get out, stretch their legs, take a quick trip to the "jakes", and rush inside the inn for a hot beverage or a bite of something, always too short a time, for one of the coachmen would wind his long horn, "tara-tara-tara!" and it was back inside the coach, crammed arsehole-to-elbow for another couple of hours before doing it all over again.

With a great sense of relief, Lewrie and Pettus finally alit at the Elephant and Castle posting house in London, retrieved their belongings from the coach top (hoping that the semi-frozen passengers up there hadn't pilfered them looking for spirits or more clothing to warm them) and hired a hackney to bear them to the Madeira Club, at the corner of Duke and Wigmore Streets, where Lewrie was a member and could always count on a set of rooms when in town. After all, his father, Sir Hugo St. George Willoughby, Sir Malcolm Shockley and several other gentlemen had founded the club years before, and Alan Lewrie was almost a "legacy"; he even got a decent discount!

They trooped up the steps of the stoop into the grand foyer, where the clerk's high desk, the mail slots, and cloak room were located. It was nigh six of the evening, and the Common Rooms beyond teemed with members, full of good cheer, and the heat from the large fireplaces.

"Yes, sir?" a new desk clerk asked as Lewrie shed his cloak, cocked hat, and wool mittens.

"Captain Sir Alan Lewrie," Lewrie replied, leaving off the "Baronet" for now. "I'm a member? My man and I need rooms."

"Oh, dear Lord, sir," the clerk quailed, looking through his ledger for a moment, then stuck a finger in the air. "Might you excuse me a moment, sir? I must summon Mister Hoyle."

Lewrie waited as patiently as he could, but sensed that something was amiss, this time. He hadn't been back to the Madeira Club for over two years, but surely . . . ! In its own quiet way, the club set an excellent table, and had one of the most extensive wine cellars in London, even stocking a crock or two of his favourite Kentucky corn whisky. Deliciously tempting aromas were wafting in from the kitchens, and . . .

"Sir Alan, so good to see you back, again," Hoyle the longtime manager of the club said, coming forward with both hands outstretched. "We had no word of your coming, I'm so sorry. It seems that, ehm . . . over the last year and a half, the club has gained an host of new members, and a fair number of those long-term lodgers. I am afraid that we are quite booked up. You would be staying how long?"

"Only a night or two," Lewrie told him, feeling quite let down, and a tad miffed, in point of fact; along with starving, of course.

"I fear that we are so full that several of our bachelor members have consented to share a set of rooms," Hoyle went on, wringing those hands, "with two bed-steads per room, quite . . . crowded. Also, I must advert to you that we have to turn away many would-be lodgers, who are unaware that it is members-only. They think that we are a common hotel! It may be . . . ehm, difficult to find rooms this time of night, anywhere in London. The times, d'ye see?"

Lewrie went through a short list of former lodgings in his head, letting out a long, disappointed sigh as he wondered if he and Pettus would have to return to the Elephant and Castle and hope for the best.

"If it is possible, Sir Alan, you are more than welcome to partake in the supper," Hoyle offered as a sop. "Turbot, turkey for the fowl course, and of course our usual beef roast," he tempted.

"Much as I desire it . . . no," Lewrie had to decline. "I must find lodging, first, and can brook no delay, temptin' though it is. If someone would be so kind as to whistle up a hackney for me, I'll be on my way. Perhaps I'll drop in tomorrow afternoon, sir."

"But of course, sir!" Hoyle replied, sounding relieved, and turned to one of the footmen to go out into the cold and flag down a conveyance.

⚓

"Where are we going to go, sir?" Pettus asked as they bundled into the small one-horse coach.

"We're goin' to the one place we *can't* be turned down, Pettus," Lewrie said, wondering if he should cross the fingers of his right hand for luck, anyway. "Coachman, Duke to Oxford Street, down Audley, and thence to Upper Grosvenor."

"Roighty-ho, sir!" the coachman said as he whipped up.

"A den of iniquity, Pettus," Lewrie told him with a derisive laugh. "Where we can't be refused . . . my father's place!"

"Your father, sir?" Pettus asked, perplexed. "Don't know that anyone's ever met him. I know I haven't."

"Then they're more fortunate than I am," Lewrie said, rolling his eyes.

Lewrie's father, Sir Hugo St. George Willoughby, had suffered more than a few financial ups and downs in his life. His family had once been well-off Kentish gentry, rich enough to purchase him a commission in the 4th Regiment of Foot, the "King's Own". But, through a series of bad investments, mis-adventures, and to be perfectly honest, his family's penchant for spending too freely and gambling too deep, they had gone smash, had sold off their estates in Kent, and had reduced young Hugo (not yet knighted for bravery) to hunting potential wives with rich dowries so he could even pay his regimental mess bills.

Alan Lewrie was the result of such a calculated marriage which was not, in the cruel light of day, strictly legal. There were still in those days "false justices" who wed people without the posting of the banns, which made the sole issue from Elisabeth Lewrie and Hugo Willoughby, Alan, therefore, a bastard. And, when it was determined that there would be no dowry coming from the Lewries in Wheddon Cross, Devonshire, the "happy couple", *both* dis-illusioned and ready to tear each others' throats out, Hugo Willoughby took the low road, abandoning the pregnant Elisabeth in Holland, absconding with her jewelry, and dancing a jig back to England.

With creditors cleared, mess bills paid, the young Hugo sported himself rather grandly; he had much better fortune at gambling than his father and elder brother, got involved with the Hell-Fire Club for a time (bailing out just before it was exposed, but not evading *all* the opprobrium), and went abroad briefly to win his spurs and receive his knighthood. At Bath, Sir Hugo now, wooed and wed an incredibly wealthy widow, Agnes

Cockspur, who, unfortunately, came with two children of her own, Belinda and Gerald whom he would not have wished for if they'd come with the crown of Prussia attached. Some *grand* spending followed, a poor turn or two of the cards in the Long Rooms at Almack's and the Cocoa-Tree, and the Lewries in far-off Devonshire, seeking the grandson reputed to have been born in St. Martin-in-the-Fields parish before Elisabeth had succumbed to child-bed fever, put Sir Hugo in a frantic search for another source of income. He'd struck gold when he found the orphan, pounding oakum with his little hands in a parish poorhouse, and had taken him in to his St. James's Square house as his own, clothing, tutoring, and sending young Alan to a series of public schools.

When Alan was seventeen, an idle, foppish Buck of the First Head back in London after being expelled from Harrow for the destruction of the governor's coach house in youthful emulation of the Gunpowder Plot (all the horses managed to escape), it appeared that Granny Lewrie was about to expire and join the Great Majority. Sir Hugo was by then a very relieved widower, but just about "skint" and in debt. If Alan, the only male Lewrie heir, was to inherit, he would be saved.

Sir Hugo had drawn Belinda into a plot (for a share) to entrap Alan in incest, replete with pre-arranged witnesses, so he could be press-ganged into the Navy as a Midshipman and be an ocean, and a year apart when the money came in.

Perhaps one now understands why Alan Lewrie was never a *glad* sailor!

Granny Lewrie, however, refused to perish, proving harder to kill than breadroom rats, the creditors came calling, and Sir Hugo, ever the responsible sort, sold everything he owned or could lay his hands on, including his commission in the King's Own, right out from under Gerald and Belinda, and lit out for Oporto in Portugal where many an English gentleman hid out when in arrears, and creditors in England could not collect, abandoning everyone and all responsibilities, as usual. Belinda had become a much-in-demand courtesan round Covent Garden and Drury Lane, eventually opening her own house of prostitution, and Gerald, a sodomite, worked his way down to whoring himself round Wapping. Undesirable children, indeed!

Sir Hugo did never reveal how he'd prospered in Oporto, but it was rumoured to involve rich Portuguese widows and "gifts" of their jewelry. Cleared of debts at last, and with the help of old friends (some members of the old, dis-banded Hell-Fire Club who had never been exposed) and some old military contacts, he had finagled an appointment with the

Honourable East India Company army, command of the 19th Native Infantry, where he performed wonders. Cad he might be, but he was always a damned good soldier! He returned from India and his campaigns a full *nabob*, worth over an hundred thousand pounds in *loot*, which is a wonderful Hindoo word for . . . loot.

More circumspect in his middle age, Sir Hugo had run up a fine house in London, had bought an estate from Phineas Chiswick uncomfortably close to Alan and his wife's rented farm in Anglesgreen, and had invested to establish the aforementioned Madeira Club, wealthy, comfortable, in the centre of the West End, and still able to indulge his lusts whenever he felt an itch.

Is it any wonder, then, that Alan Lewrie might still harbour a smidgeon of suspicion, resentment, and outright loathing for the old fart?

Here he was, though, going up the stone steps of the stoop to the door to raise the brass lion door knocker, taking only an instant to admire the grandness of his father's house. Unsure of what sort of reception he might get, Lewrie had bade the coachman to wait 'til he and Pettus had actually been allowed in!

Locks turned, bolts were drawn, and the door was opened by a butler in fashionable new black livery, a man who could have been a retired Sergeant-Major or a servant worthy of St. James's Palace.

"Yes, sir? And who is calling, please?" that worthy asked.

"Captain Sir Alan Lewrie, Baronet, to see Sir Hugo," Lewrie told him, striving for a top-lofty and confident air.

Before replying, the butler gave Lewrie one of those irritating look-overs from hat to boots, with one brow up as if asking whether the creature who stood before him was even human.

"Sir Hugo is not receiving callers, sir," the butler drawled in a clench-jawed Etonian accent. "Have you a card, you may leave it for his consideration."

"Tell the old fart that his son is here, and is in need of a night's lodging," Lewrie shot back.

"His son, you say, sir?" the butler replied, showing no sign of surprise.

"Why, his other bastards show up once a week?" Lewrie asked with a cock-headed grin. "He's home, is he? Well, go tell him that Alan's home from the sea."

The butler grumped and harumphed, but stepped back and swung the door a tad wider. "If you will be so good as to wait in the parlour, Sir Alan. Your man may bide here, in the foyer."

"Pay the coachman, Pettus, and he can go on," Lewrie called over his shoulder, and went inside, removing his cocked hat and shrugging his boat cloak, holding them out for the butler, who *had* to take them and hang them up before he could go re-lock the door, on the way giving Pettus another of these dis-believing head-to-toe inspections.

It had been years since Lewrie had been at his father's house, understandably, and he looked the public rooms over with a new eye.

The entry hall was the usual black and white chequered marble, with an expensive Turkey carpet, and some rather nice pieces of furniture, a large sideboard dominating. The old wood panelling had been painted over with white, the ornate millwork picked out with gilt to lighten the old gloominess that had once welcomed visitors. Several scenic paintings lined the walls, in gilt frames, as well.

The front parlour had been turned into a library/office where his father could have in people he *had* to deal with, done in a pale mint green with more white millwork, more anonymous scenics suggestive of a Grand Tour of the Continent that Sir Hugo had *never* taken, and a wall or two of books that Lewrie suspected had never had their pages cut, or their bindings opened. There was a large marble fireplace, though, and a roaring fire to which he was drawn like a half-frozen moth to warm his hands and lift the back of his uniform coat to bring some life back into his buttocks. He tapped at the mantel to determine if it was really marble, or the old contractors' fraud, painted slate.

"You are to come up, Sir Alan," the butler said as he returned from the upper storey, where the proper parlours, dining rooms, and such would be. Lewrie trotted up the marble staircase and was shown to yet another, larger parlour where the gleaming wood floors were almost lost under several Turkey or Axminster carpets, yet one more roaring fireplace, some rather surprisingly tasteful settees, chairs, and side tables, and . . . his father, standing before the fire, warming his own hands. He looked over, scowling.

"So, you've turned up, again, like the bad penny," Sir Hugo scoffed.

"Said the counterfeiter," Lewrie rejoined as he crossed the room to join him. "What is it, regimental mess night?"

Sir Hugo was wearing a new-style army uniform, a long-tailed cutaway coat doubled over his chest with bright gilt epaulets on his shoulders, wide black lapels that featured the blue and white button holes of the 4th Regiment of Foot, a gilt waist-belt and a large silver buckle plate very snug white breeches, and top boots. Damn his eyes, he still kept a fine, lean soldierly figure, and looked quite impressive, to the un-familiar, at least. The only odd thing about him was his wig, which fit so close to his head that it looked more like a head of real hair, right down to the sideburns.

What, he's gone completely bald, at last? Lewrie wondered, recalling a rapidly-thinning head, and liver spots, under the powdered peruke that Sir Hugo had worn to witness Lewrie's presentation at court when he'd been knighted. It looked damned expensive an expedient.

"In point of fact, it's a supper with old comrades," Sir Hugo told him, nigh sneering, "among which I very much doubt anyone from the Fourth will attend. And, if I do not leave this instant, I will be late. Harwell said something about you needing lodging? What's the matter with the damned club?"

"Full up with long-term lodgers," Lewrie said with a shrug. "Admiralty summoned me on short notice, too little to write and ask if there were rooms available."

"In trouble with 'em again, are ye?" Sir Hugo posed.

"Got struck by lightning on the way back from the evacuation of Corunna, and there's a question whether my ship will be repaired, or turned into a trooper," Lewrie told him. "I intend t'save her."

"Corunna?" Sir Hugo blurted. "You were there?" At least he could take professional interest. The news of the evacuation, and the death of General Sir John Moore, had come with the first ships to make port, only days before, and the papers were full of it, though with little deep details, yet.

"Aye, I was," Lewrie told him, "and a right mess it was. We beat the French to a stand-still, then got the army off that night and the next day, leavin' 'em nothing. Whoever dreamt up marchin' into Spain in Mid-winter deserves shootin' . . . but, Sir John Moore paid for it."

"I never met him but the once, and that was briefly, back in Oh-Four, when the French looked ready to sail cross the Channel and invade," Sir Hugo said. "Knew Baird. Did he survive?"

"Sir David?" Lewrie said. "Met him when we re-took the Cape Colony from the Dutch, three years ago. He lost an arm, but I hear he's still with us. Good fellow."

"Aye, he is," Sir Hugo said, looking deep into the flames with a pensive expression. "What a bloody waste. I suppose that'll be the end of any more nonsensical adventures in Spain and Portugal. Let the Dons tend to their own affairs. The damned French are just too powerful."

"They can be beat," Lewrie objected. "I saw it, at Vimeiro. I went ashore and had a hand in the fighting. We put Arthur Wellesley back in Lisbon, with fresh re-enforcements, and you'll see."

"You actually *were* at Vimeiro? Just damn my eyes!" Sir Hugo exclaimed with real excitement. "Pop up here, there, everywhere, hah!"

"About a room for a night," Lewrie reminded him. "I've my man with me, and he needs a bed, too. And some supper'd be welcome."

"Harwell?" Sir Hugo bellowed in a raspy parade ground voice. "Ah, there ye are. Prepare a room for my son . . . lay a good fire, mind, and his man will need a place to doss down. Is there anything edible in the larder for them?"

"I will see to it, Sir Hugo," the haughty butler replied with a bow.

"Sorry t'dash off so quickly," Sir Hugo apologised, gruffly and quickly, as were most of his apologies. "I'll most-like be back long after you've re-tired. Perhaps we'll have a moment in the morning over breakfast before you head off to the Admiralty."

Short, semi-sweet, and quickly done with, Lewrie thought of his usual in-teractions with his father.

"Hang it!" Sir Hugo barked, stepping abruptly after he had taken only a few steps towards the landing and the staircase. "You were at Vimeiro, *and* Corunna! My old army friends would be eager to hear your accounts. Fresh-washed?"

"Reasonably," Lewrie told him.

"Come sup with me and the others, then," his father said with a laugh. "Bring your star and sash? No? No matter. We'll feed and shelter your man. Let's go. I'm already late enough as it is."

Lewrie hardly had time to inform Pettus where he was going at such short notice, how the house would look after him, that he would be very late returning and not to worry about him 'til morning, and don his hat and boat cloak on his way to the door.

Lewrie was sure that Pettus would be in good hands, and enjoy his stay, for, as he prepared to go out to another hackney that someone had whis-tled up, he saw two very comely housemaids headed up the stairs to the bedchambers with sheets, blankets, and pillows to make up a room for him. *Very* comely, young and promising!

If the randy old goat can't top 'em, by now, Lewrie drolly thought; *at least my father can still* look *at 'em and whinny!*

CHAPTER FIVE

*U*p, are you?" Sir Hugo asked as Lewrie entered the smaller breakfast room the next morning. "Bathed, shaved, and wearing full kit, well well." He said that with a sarcastic tone, as if taking glee. "Risen, and ready to shine, hah!"

"Up, aye . . . bleary, too," Lewrie had to admit as he sat himself down, whipped a napkin under his chin, and peered round for a coffee pot. "I wasn't countin' on such a *long* night of it."

"It ain't just 'younkers' like you who stay up late," his sire told him with a knowing, worldly-wise leer. To add insult to injury, he threw in a "tee hee" of amusement, delayed enough to irk. "But, you had so much to impart, you held their interest that long, so the late hour was *your* fault. Did quite well, though . . . went down well," he added with faint praise.

Retired Generals and Colonels, officers still on Army List who had no field commands, and might as well be on the equivalent of Navy half-pay, *had* been interested in Lewrie's views and observations of what had transpired in Portugal and Spain, and there had been many questions put to him about Sir Arthur Wellesley, the battles of Roliça and Vimeiro, that worthy's arrangements for supplying his troops in the field, the disastrous Convention of Cintra which had doomed the careers of General Sir Hew Dalrymple and General Sir Harry Burrard, the mis-calculations and poor intelligence that had ruined the Mid-winter thrust into Spain by General Sir John Moore and General Sir David Baird, then the disastrous retreats to Vigo and Corunna which had saved what was left of their soldiers.

Well, that was all to be expected from older gentlemen who might never see battle, again, and who'd most-like game it all over on tabletops, then write scathing letters to *The Times*. What Lewrie had *not* expected was how boisterous, drunken, loud, and at times so bawdy Sir Hugo and his old friends could be, and sit up so late into the wee hours, when most men their age would long have been abed.

He was paying the price this morning; a thick head, a tinge of wine and brandy still fuzzing his senses, and suffering the lack of a good night's rest. Lewrie had had no more than four hours of sleep, and had been roused from a deep stupor, feeling as if he had been drug up by the scruff of his neck from a vat of treacle.

"Coffee, sir?" a servant enquired at last, and Lewrie almost leapt for the silver pot to pour a cup for himself. He stirred in the offered white sugar and thick, fresh cream, took a sip, and thought himself in Heaven, letting out a long, blissful "Aahh!"

"Defending your ship at Admiralty today, are you?" Sir Hugo asked.

"Just lettin' 'em know I'm in town and ready to do so," Lewrie told him between restorative sips of his coffee.

"Good, 'cause ye look like Death's Head on a Mop-stick," Sir Hugo cackled, "no matter your sash and star." To which compassionate comment, Lewrie could only cast him a slit-eyed glower.

"With any luck, I can retire early tonight and be bright-eyed and bushy-tailed for 'em tomorrow," Lewrie told him, rubbing his hands together in anticipation as another servant presented him with the serving dish of cheesy scrambled eggs. A dish of bacon strips followed that, then another of piping-hot potato hash. Finger-thick slabs of toast were set before him, there was the jam bowl, the fresh butter, and once his plate was laden, Lewrie dug in, famished beyond all measure.

"Bushy-tailed?" Sir Hugo sneered. "Another Colonial colloquialism, is it? Well, that's what happens to good English when one spends so much time overseas, I suppose."

"You still sling Hindi about," Lewrie rejoined, a fork-load poised halfway to his mouth. "By the way, where's your man from your old 'John Company' regiment, Trilochan Singh? I haven't seen him about the house."

"Ah well, Singh," Sir Hugo said, looking rueful. "After old Zachariah Twigg passed over, his man, Ajit Roy, was left enough for a goodly pension, and passage back to India, if he wished it. Twigg's whole native staff, his cook and major-domo, too. They met at the funeral, Singh spoke with them, and wished to see his kinfolk before he died, so I pensioned him and bought his passage, too. Hated to lose the old one-eyed *badmash*, but, he was gettin' on in years, and English weather didn't agree with him . . . never did, really."

That must've been a wrench, Lewrie thought, feeling a touch of sympathy for his sire despite their edgy relationship; *the end of a link to excitin', younger times.*

Well, his father still had arrays of Hindoo *tulwars*, *jeʒail* muskets, and other diverse exotic weapons scattered round his house, along with tiger pelts and mounted heads of hunting kills from the Far East, even a poised-to-strike cobra that had threatened Sir Hugo one morning in his *gusulkhana*, seated on his "thunder box" with his breeches round his ankles, but . . . gathered *things* were not the same as old compatriots.

"Sorry 'bout that," Lewrie felt need to say. "So, what are you doin' today?" He noted that his father was not fully dressed in either last night's dress uniform, or civilian suitings, and wore a richly embroidered and lined dressing robe.

"First, I intend to take a good, long nap, after you're gone," Sir Hugo told him with what could only be called an evil grin, "then I may coach over to Lackington's new bookstore in Finsbury Square."

"Finsbury?" Lewrie scoffed. "Isn't it a dirt field full of trash and dead animals?"

"Was when ye left," Sir Hugo said with a purr. "Now, it's almost as fashionable as the West End, totally re-done, and the store is the largest bookstore in London, perhaps in England, which means in the world, haw haw! Oh, London's just explodin' in all directions lately. Ye go away for a spell, they change things all round!"

"Well, if I have some time on my hands, I might have a look at the place, then," Lewrie said. "I could use some new reading material."

"Ye'll find all the caricatures along Piccadilly," Sir Hugo said, "the ones with the simple words?"

And that's why I love you so much, you old bastard! Lewrie told himself; *At least he sets a damned good table.*

Admiralty in Whitehall was much the same as he had left it two years before; the courtyard inside the curtain wall was a bustle of arriving and departing officers and officials. The tea and sticky-bun carts still did a thriving business, and the arms of the semaphore tower still whirled with orders down the chains of towers to Falmouth and Tor Bay, Plymouth, Portsmouth, the Nore, and Great Yarmouth. And the Greenwich Pensioners hired as the tilers to tend the doors were just as surly, short, and disparaging.

Inside, the infamous Waiting Room was just as arsehole-to-elbow crowded with hopefuls, and the hopeless, sprinkled here and there with people who had a reason to be there, fresh from paying off their latest active commission, or there to receive a new one, like raisins strewn through a cheap duff.

Lewrie checked his hat and boat cloak with a clerk, found someone who could dash abovestairs to announce his presence and deliver his letter to the First Secretary, Mr. Pole, then readied himself for a long, possibly pointless wait 'til getting word as to when he could present his ship's status to anyone who'd listen. He looked about the large room for a seat, or a newspaper or magazine with which to while away his time, but that turned out to be fruitless. Turned out in his best, with the sash and star of his knighthood prominently displayed, one would think that some quick-witted soul in search of a new ship *might* spring to his feet and toady to him, but . . . no.

And here I thought I was famous, *or something,* he thought with a wry grin, slowly pacing the room to appear as if he didn't care and had no need for a sit-down. The better part of an hour of that soon palled; his feet told him he needed to get off them, soon!

At last, another Post-Captain, grown weary and impatient with his own delayed appointment with those abovestairs, rose, groaning, and growled that he would "up-anchor, and take a leading wind out to a mid-day mess," and Lewrie dashed, with as much dignity as he could to seize the hard, wooden chair, much like the parlour game, beating out a Commander and a Lieutenant, who shied off in deference to his senior rank. Wonder of wonders, there was a copy of *The Gazette,* too!

It was getting on for one P.M. by the time Lewrie finished the paper, even reading all the advertisments for hernia trusses and undergarments for ladies with as much deep concentration as he would give to reports of the impending Apocalypse. Despite his ample breakfast, he was getting peckish, shoving aside a fantasy of a chop-house quite nearby where he'd dined well in past, relishing their meat pies, pork chops, ales, and sweet duffs . . . even their mushy pease pudding!

"Captain Sir Alan Lewrie, if you please?" a clerk announced at the bottom of the staircase. "Is Captain Lewrie still present?"

"Here," Lewrie replied, making a nonchalant show of getting to his feet, as if it was no matter to him if he got a ship or not, or kept the one he had.

"The First Secretary wishes you to return tomorrow, sir," the clerk, the one Lewrie had long-ago deemed the "happy-making clerk" told him, handing him a folded-over sheet of paper. "Would ten of the morning be suitable, sir? Good. He and the Chief Surveyor of the Navy, Sir Henry Peake, wish you to bring along all pertinent papers pertaining to your ship's condition, sir."

"Most happy to oblige them both, and ten tomorrow it'll be," Lewrie replied, plastering a gladsome and confident grin on his phyz. "And, good day to you, sir."

The note was only written confirmation of what the clerk had just told him, so he shoved it into a coat pocket, and retrieved his hat and cloak from the coat room, then went out into the courtyard and took a deep sniff. He could smell neither snow nor rain in the offing, though the day was still very cold and grey, with low-flying clouds, mingled with the pall of ever-present coal smoke. Lewrie felt himself in need of some warm liquid refreshment, and went to the tea cart to queue up to buy a cup.

Looking about whilst waiting in line, he shook his head in awe that, in all the times he'd called at Admiralty, it was the rare day when anyone he knew even slightly was there at the same time, just as it was today. He had scanned the faces in the Waiting Room, perking up at every arrival in the faint hope that he'd spot an old shipmate, to no good result. The courtyard was much the same; not a single familiar face.

He did take note of a civilian hesitantly entering the courtyard, a man in his fifties dressed in the black garb of a churchman, in "dominee ditto"; black-coat and waist-coat, black breeches, stockings, and buckled shoes, a flat-brimmed black hat on his head, broken only by his white shirt and neck-stock,

Lookin' for a Chaplain's post, is he? Lewrie took note, though he wondered why the fellow ushered a younger lad along at his side; *Well, he's a faint hope!* On paper at least, ships of the Royal Navy were supposed to carry Chaplains, but it was a poor, "mar-text" sort who would give up the hope of a shore living, even as a poor Curate in a rural parish, to go to sea and its misery. Lewrie knew of senior officers far more religiously observant than he who carried one with them, mostly aboard warships of the Third Rate and above. Admiral "Dismal Jemmy" Gambier sprang to mind, the old croaker, who would demand every officer he met with the question "Are you saved, sir?"

The churchman looked round as if lost, or uncertain that he was in the right place. Lewrie made the mistake of holding his gaze too long, and the fellow approached him as if invited, making Lewrie put his stern "quarterdeck" face on.

"I say, sir, you are a Captain?" the churchman began.

"Aye," Lewrie gruffly replied. "Captain Sir Alan Lewrie, Baronet. And you are, sir?" he added with an arch tone to his voice, hoping that his rare use of his title might scare the man off.

"Your pardons, sir, allow me to name myself . . . Reverend James Chenery, Rector of Saint Anselm's, in Piccadilly," the man said with a sweep and doff of his hat. "My son, here, Charles, is eager to go to sea as a Midshipman, but, knowing no one nautical, we have no clue as to how such might be accomplished. My parish has only a sprinkling of army officers, you see."

"Hmm, well, the normal practise would be to have kin in the Navy who might have an open Midshipman's berth," Lewrie informed him, still wary and stand-offish, "or know someone who commands a ship."

He glanced at the son, who appeared to be around fifteen or so, a well-formed lad with straight limbs, hair so dark it appeared almost black, and surprisingly dark blue eyes. He *looked* likely.

"Barring that, sir," Rev. Chenery continued with several nods, "I heard a rumour that perhaps some small *fee* might be entailed?"

"Absolutely not, sir!" Lewrie rejoined with a bark. "Whoever told you that knows nothing. That'd be criminal."

Though I still *wonder what my father paid my first Captain to take me on,* Lewrie recalled.

"I see, sir," Rev. Chenery replied, looking relieved.

Lewrie also wondered why Rev. Chenery looked so "out at the heels", for as he recalled, the man's West End parish was a rich one, and should come with a substantial living, and a grand manse. There was something—thready—about the fellow, as if he was one of those who took a vow of sobre poverty seriously, and it was the rare Church of England man who really did. Yet, when he was told that a fee was not necessary, he looked as if he quit fingering his coin-purse. As dowdily as he was garbed, Lewrie could almost mistake him for a Methodist, or a Dissenter!

"So, one applies in person, inside Admiralty, or does one send them a letter, then, sir?" Chenery further enquired.

"That would be fruitless, I'm afraid," Lewrie told him. "Such applications would be quite ignored. Young sir," he said, turning his attention to the son. "You are determined to make a career of the Navy? How old are you, and what do you know of navigation, and ships in general?"

"I am fifteen, sir, and I have earned high marks at my school in mathematics, trigonometry, and we did some practise at celestial navigation," young Charles Chenery answered, very matter-of-factly, with none of the shyness or reticence expected of a young lad. "As for ships and the sea, I only know what I have read, or found in my books, sir, though some of us at school have done some boating on the Thames, the upper reaches, really . . . rowing, sailing. And, father has tutored me well."

"Swim, do you?" Lewrie demanded.

"Quite well, sir, yes," the lad replied.

"I would not have allowed him to go boating, else, sir," Rev. Chenery stuck in. "Alas, Charlie doesn't seem eager to follow the family tradition."

"My uncle and my older brother are in Holy Orders, as are my sisters' husbands, do you see, Captain Lewrie, sir," Charles Chenery said with the faintest *moue* of distaste for such a life for himself. "I, though, would prefer to take a more . . . active part in life, sir," he announced with a shrug and a tentative smile.

There's an imp in him, Lewrie determined; *just* achin' *t'kick over the traces.*

"Well, young Master Chenery, Nelson's father was a churchman, and he turned out well," Lewrie said, which raised grins on both of them. "As a matter of fact, two of my own Mids passed their Examining Boards recently, and have been posted away into other ships as Lieutenants, and I am still one short . . ."

"Hallelujah, sir!" Rev. Chenery crowed, looking skyward for a moment. "The Lord works in mysterious ways, and answers the prayers of the faithful! How serendipitous, all of us being here at the very right time. Ehm . . . may I understand that you are offering Charlie a place, Captain Lewrie, sir?"

Hell's Bells, why not? Lewrie thought.

"I do believe that I am, Mister Chenery," Lewrie told them, smiling for the first time since their meeting. "My ship, *Sapphire,* is currently anchored at Portsmouth, undergoing some repairs. Mind now, Mister Chenery," he said to the lad, "she ain't a frigate, with all the dash, and the promise of prize-money, but she does well," explaining that she was a two-decker 50-gun Fourth Rate.

"If you would be so good as to inform us all what he will need at sea,

Captain Lewrie," the Reverend asked, almost wheedling for the list of necessities.

"Hmm, have you eat yet?" Lewrie asked them. "No? Good. There is
a rather good chop-house near here, and I'm famished. Let us go there and
I can fill you in whilst we dine. You have pen and paper?"

The Reverend did; pencil and a few sheets of foolscap.

The chop-house was a slight cut above the usual two-penny ordinary,
closer to a reasonable six pence for everything per diner, and that included
a hard-boiled egg, lashings of bread and butter, roast beef, pease pudding,
an albeit small roast potato that day, beef broth, a currant duff, and ale.

"Now, t'start with, you'll need uniforms," Lewrie began, "and any decent London tailor worth his salt'll know the current patterns. Round
jacket, brass buttons . . . don't go for gilt, it's a gyp . . . and white waist-
coats, white breeches, white cotton stockings, and good buckled shoes,
brass'll do, no need for silver or 'pinchbeck', for there's no need for a grand
show."

He ticked off the need for a stout sea-chest with strong hasps and locks,
and spare keys; borrowing back and forth among Mids was one thing, but
it's better to be asked. He mentioned the need for thicker dark blue wool
trousers for cold weather and undress, along with the necessity of a grogram
watch-coat, mittens, and a couple of mufflers. Hats, well . . . Charlie might
need but one cocked hat for inspection and Sunday Divisions, but a short,
curl-brim top-hat would come in handy, as would a wide-brimmed straw
hat for hot weather in the tropics, but he could get one of those in a foreign port.

"Several linen shirts, black neck-stocks, perhaps just the one silk shirt,"
Lewrie told them as the Reverend Chenery scribbled away, "again, that's
for Sunday Divisions, or formal occasions when away from the ship t'make
a good impression. Silk stockings, too, though cotton ones are more useful. And, once aboard, the Ship's Purser will have slop-trousers, which
you'll wear more often than breeches."

"Will I need weapons, sir?" Charlie asked, looking hopeful.

"If it comes to action, the Navy sees to that, young sir. Cutlasses, boarding axes, Sea Pattern pistols," Lewrie said to the lad's disappointment.
"You'll need a dirk, only as a mark of distinction. Any sword shop, or a
chandler's, will have them, and you can usually find a good, used one at a

fair price. Again, there's no call for anything too showy, just . . . sharp and serviceable."

Books? Lewrie recommended the latest edition of Falconer's *Marine Dictionary*, his old steward, Aspinall's, book of knots, which he would have to learn to tie by heart, and quickly, along with something on rigging, both standing and running, and more on the use of a sextant, and the stars.

"You might provide yourself with your own tableware, knife and fork, a teaspoon and soup spoon," Lewrie said, recalling the pig-sty that Jessop had described of the Midshipmens' cockpit aboard *Sapphire*. "And, it wouldn't hurt to take a spare plate, soup bowl, and a pewter tankard, just in case what you're issued gets broken or lost. It happens after a few months at sea. Something that'd serve for wine, small beer, even soup if it comes to it."

"As I am given to understand, Captain Lewrie, Charlie will be paid?" the Reverend hesitantly asked. "A trifling sum, I suppose."

"Six pounds a year, since Seventeen Ninety-Four," Lewrie said. "Before that, Midshipmen weren't paid at all. What they earn, now, usually is six months in arrears, so . . . it might do well did you send him aboard with about, oh . . . at least five pounds of spending money, all in small coins'd be best, for me and my clerk to hold for him. Like clean shirts, money has a way of vanishing in the Mids' quarters."

"Ah, I see," Rev. Chenery said, nodding sagely. "Five pounds in change, aha."

Why do I get the feelin' I'm squeezin' his last farthing from him? Lewrie asked himself.

"Mids are fed the same rations as the ship's people most of the time," Lewrie cheerfully explained as he picked at his dinner, "salt beef, salt pork, duffs, bisquit, cheese, oatmeal, but . . . Lord, it do get old, so . . . before a voyage begins, all the Mids in the cockpit mess do a whip-round to purchase sacks of potatoes, a crate of apples, mustard, Worcestershire sauce, better cheeses, and such. I and my clerk, Mister Faulkes, hold all their coins, and dole it out for the purchases, *and* keep a weather eye on *what* they buy, so it doesn't go for trifles, or pamperin' luxuries."

"What of Charlie's further instruction, sir, and his religious observance?" Rev. Chenery enquired. "Languages, the classics?"

"Well, we don't carry a Schoolmaster, or a Chaplain aboard," Lewrie had to tell him, which made the Reverend drop his jaw. "Our Sailing Master and his Mates see to instructing the Mids on navigation, the use of charts, weather signs, and such. Anything beyond what pertains to the ship and the sea must be done on your son's own time, so you might pack a few books in his sea-chest.

"As for religious observance, well," Lewrie further admitted, "we hold lay services after Sunday Divisions . . . hymns, prayers from the Book of Common Prayer, and perhaps I will read a short homily from a book I picked up, if the weather allows, of course."

"Perhaps I could supply you with some of my old sermons," Rev. Chenery quickly offered, "with the pertinent verses noted so that your sailors could look them up and be edified."

Lewrie didn't have the heart to tell him that he doubted if the ship had more than half a dozen Bibles aboard, about the same number of prayer books, and maybe only two song books; what hymns were sung were old favourites known by heart from childhood, the lustier they could be belted out the better.

"Your offer of sermons would be most welcome, sir," Lewrie told the man, wondering what-all he'd gotten himself into by taking the lad aboard as a replacement Midshipman. Still, young Charles Chenery *appeared* to be a likely sort. Time would tell.

As to when the lad must report aboard seemed to put Rev. Chenery in another wee dither. Lewrie laid out the facts that it was up to Admiralty, and his meeting with the Chief Surveyor of the Navy on the morrow, how long that worthy would ponder *Sapphire*'s fate, how long the repairs would take, whether fresh orders came determining where she would go, and how soon, and whether the "dead muzzler" weather allowed her to sail. It could be a week from now, or it might be a fortnight.

"I may be required to bide in London 'til the decision is made, which shouldn't take all that long," Lewrie concluded with a lift of both hands, and a puzzled shrug, "but were I you, sir, I'd make haste to kit your son out, perhaps by the end of this week? Then, when I coach back to Portsmouth, he could ride with me . . . sparing him the discomfort of the 'flying coach', and the fare."

I thought *he'd perk up t'save the coach fare!* Lewrie thought as he saw the Reverend take and release a brief breath of relief.

They exchanged addresses and promised to inform each other at once should circumstances change. They paid their bills, Lewrie with no thought of the six-pence coin and one pence for the waiter, though the Reverend drew out his coin purse, gave a long look in, and only then laid out twelve pence with nothing for their waiter.

⚓

Well, that's one problem solved, Lewrie thought as he strolled back to Admiralty, where he stood a better chance of hailing a hackney to bear him to his father's house. Now that his official business was over, the idea of a good, long nap was very appealing.

He had half an idea to detour up to Piccadilly and take a squint at St. Anselm's, and the Chenery's manse, just to see how grand it may be, for Rev. Chenery's seeming miserliness seemed rather odd.

Ensconced in a hackney and out of the wind, he pondered the circumstances. Hadn't the lad said that his sisters were married to other church men? How many of those were there, then? If the Reverend had dowried them proper, that might mean at least an hundred pounds per annum, perhaps sixty at the very least. That might be one reason for his abstemiousness, but . . . the man's church in Piccadilly, and near the up-and-coming neighbourhood of Mayfair, quite near Whitehall, St. James's Park, Green Park, and Hyde Park bespoke wealthy and influential parishoners who paid their tithes in specie or bank notes, not in kind, chickens, or rabbits.

Rev. Chenery's brother was also a churchman, which meant that the family, and the daughters' husbands, might represent an entire set of parishes, perhaps country churches where lowly Curates did all the work, and the Chenerys collected a further share of all the tithes. So, why was he such a purse-strangler, then?

And, didn't his clothes look a tad . . . rusty? Lewrie recalled.

Black suitings worn too long went brownish-black at the knees, elbows, and cuffs, sometimes upon the coat lapels, and Chenery's had given that impression in the weak light of the chop-house candles.

I'll 'smoak' it out, sooner or later, Lewrie told himself as he stifled a groaner of a yawn, more concerned at the moment with an image of a settee near a warm fireplace, a glass or two of brandy, and an hour or more of restorative sleep!

CHAPTER SIX

*E*hm . . . might I ask how it went at Admiralty, sir?" his man, Pettus, asked after Lewrie returned the next afternoon.

"Main-well, I think, Pettus, main-well indeed," Lewrie told him as he shed hat and cloak on his way to the nearest fireplace for a warm-up. "Oh, they were sceptical at first, but I b'lieve I brought 'em round, at the end. Had to boast most immodestly about all we'd done the last two years." He pulled a wry face and shrugged as he rubbed his hands together near the fire, and not because of the cold. No, he rubbed them together as if gloating over a good performance.

"Her bottom might need a de-fouling, but she ain't all that bad off, yet," he went on in a slightly louder voice as Pettus stowed his things away in the entry hall, "and, Surveyor or not, Sir Henry Peake sounded appreciative of our battle record, and seemed as if he agreed that it'd be a cryin' shame if the crew was broken up just at the acme of their gunnery skills. They said I should stay in town for a few days, and they'd send me word, by next Monday at the latest."

"Why, that sounds just grand, sir!" Pettus exclaimed as he came into the first storey parlour. "Rough as it is to be going back to sea in Midwinter, it sounds as if you will still have a ship, and a going concern."

"Fingers crossed, mind," Lewrie joshed, holding up his right hand to demonstrate that it was still up to luck. "A few more days of shore liberty in London, well! They'll be *more* than welcome. Do some shopping . . . replenish my stores? I may actually break down and buy one of those infernal bicorne hats!"

He had come up in the Navy when large cocked hats were the norm, and it was only lately that the "Frenchified" fore-and-aft bicornes had become "all the go"; it seemed that almost every officer he'd seen in Portsmouth, and at Admiralty, now wore them.

"Should I ring for tea, sir?" Pettus asked. "The cook says they've some fresh-baked scones and jam, and some lovely fresh cheese from Martini and Company in New Bond Street . . . where your father shops."

"Aye, ring . . . if they bother to answer," Lewrie decided aloud.

Their welcome in Sir Hugo's house was rather thin, as if his father had passed the word to his household staff that his interloping son should not be made *too* comfortable. Lewrie reckoned that Pettus might have to go fetch the tea service, himself, if the haughty butler, Harwell, was of a mind to be un-cooperative.

"Come t'think on it, Pettus," Lewrie said, turning his back to the fire to warm his other side, "when you're in the kitchens and the pantry, ye might make a list of all the places my father favours. It may be that they're all closer, and better than my old haunts, so that I don't have t'tramp from one end of the Strand to the other, or roam all over t'see if my old'uns are still doin' business."

"That I already have, sir," Pettus replied, looking pleased as punch to have anticipated his master's wants and needs, "and the cook and the others have assured me that your father's tastes are finely discriminating . . . and that their prices are more than reasonable."

"Topping!" Lewrie declared. "We'll spend tomorrow at shoppin', then! Make a whole day of it! Lock's Hatters . . ."

"I'll go see about the tea and all, then, sir," Pettus said, departing.

Lewrie flung himself into a wing-back chair near the fire and discovered a stack of new books on a side-table, his father's latest purchases at Lackington's Bookstore. One title took his fancy and he almost began reading it, but rose and went to the row upon row of book cases in the office-library parlour, plucking a few off the shelves at random, and was amazed to discover that the old lecher really *had* cut the pages and had read them!

There was a pounding on the entry door, and Harwell rushed from wherever he'd been hiding to answer it, admitting Sir Hugo and taking his hat, gloves, walking stick, and greatcoat for him.

"Spitting damned sleet, again," Sir Hugo grumbled, entering the parlour. "How'd ye do at Admiralty?"

"I think I won the day, and will keep my ship," Lewrie told him.

"Fine, fine, off and gone again," Sir Hugo dismissively said, going to the fireplace for his own warm-up. "I had tickets for the theatre tonight . . ."

"Want company?" Lewrie asked, just to see how quickly his father would say "No".

"Know what the bloody prudes've done?" Sir Hugo fumed. "That damned Society for the Suppression of Vice declared that the play was too damned *lewd,* and forced the theatre to re-schedule something else. The bloody *nerve* of those people! William bloody Wilberforce, Hannah bloody More, and their whole simperin', tea-lappin' lot. D'ye know that the Bishop of London shut a play down in mid-performance a month ago? Right at the stroke of midnight, 'cause it was then Sunday morning, and the Sabbath must be observed proper! Just when everyone in the theatre were really enjoyin' themselves, and the show! Bah!"

"Well, Sunday's always been dull as ditchwater in London," Lewrie said, puzzled. "Everything shuts down."

"Oh, but now it's a deal worse!" Sir Hugo went on in a raving pet. "At the bookstore the other day . . . a new edition of the entire works of Shakespeare, sonnets and all, but annotated by some joyless bastard, a Doctor Bowlder . . . all the good parts've been taken out! No cursin', drinkin', wenchin', all the bawdy *entendres* are just gone!"

"Why the Devil would anybody do that?" Lewrie asked, puzzled.

" 'Cause Wilberforce and More, and that Bowlder, think that the children must be exposed to the great works of English literature, the histories," Sir Hugo gravelled, "be read aloud to in the parlour so their mushy little minds are uplifted . . . but never exposed to anything . . . *disturbing*! Same with fairy tales, classic poets, about everything . . . gutted beyond all sense! If I wasn't too old, I would apply for a foreign posting where a man can still have a little fun!

"*You* started it!" Sir Hugo accused, jabbing a stiff finger at Lewrie. "If it hadn't been for you stealin' those dozen slaves in Jamaica, bein' Wilberforce's fair-haired hero t'get his Society for the Abolition of Slavery goin' . . ."

"Me?" Lewrie gawped.

"Wasn't for that, he'd *still* be a back-bencher scold!" Sir Hugo accused. "Nobody'd give the little bastard the time o' day!"

Sir Hugo went on, stomping round his parlour raging against all the changes over the last twenty years; church ales were now thought scandalous, bear baiting, cockfighting, dog fights, goose pulls, and even Maypole dancing, Morris dancing, had been slowly suppressed by an host of reformist societies . . . why, it'd be steeplechasing and fox-hunting, next!

"Well, you have little t'worry about," Lewrie pointed out once his father began to run down like a cheap pocket watch. "I see that you have just about ev'ry scandalous book here, arranged alphabetically and by author. Pornographic prints here . . ."

"Preservin' 'em for future generations, once this ridiculous shit's run its course," Sir Hugo declared, striving for "nobility of purpose".

Lewrie had to fling himself into his chair and have himself a good, long cackle over that. Sir Hugo fumed some more, gnashed what passed for a full set of teeth, stamped his foot, and announced that he'd see Lewrie at supper, once he'd come to his bloody senses.

"Yours, or mine?" Lewrie shot at his departing back but got no response beyond what he might have deemed a growl. "You old scandal," he added, under his breath.

At least the "old scandal" had hurled aside the day's copy of *The Times* in his pet, leaving Lewrie something to read whilst savouring his tea and scones, with a pot of strawberry jam. There were a few advertisements for the theatres that he found tempting, a notice for a symphony by some Italian something-or-other, a subscription ball which he considered for a moment, then rejected after recalling just how insufferably crowded they usually were, and how "odiferous" were the attendees.

After exhausting the newspaper, Lewrie rose and went to the front windows to check the weather, and, at the sight of the accumulation of fresh snow and sleet, decided that he would stay in and wait for the morrow to do his rounds. He yawned in boredom . . . until he discovered an untidy pile of caricatures and satiric prints, hand-coloured at a shilling apiece, by Gillray, Isaac Cruikshank, Rowlandson, and others.

"Oh, what fun!" he muttered as he sifted through them. "They're as good as a newspaper *any* day!"

Everything and everyone was mocked and skewered, and the politics of the nation, and the peccadilloes of the rich and titled, were laid bare, along with the scandals, a great many of the prints sexual in nature, contrived to be risible.

The old fart must've spent a bundle on 'em all, Lewrie thought, even discovering some older Hogarths near the bottom of the pile. On the backs or at the bottoms, he noted that they mostly had come from S. W. Fores in

Piccadilly, Hannah Humphrey's in New Bond Street, William Holland's in Oxford Street, James Brotherton's in New Bond Street, and Thomas Cornell's Picture Gallery in Bruton Street, which was just off New Bond, all conveniently close by.

Hmm, now there's *a distraction for tomorrow,* he told himself, expanding his day of shopping with a few hours of gawking. With any luck, there'd be coffee or tea available, too!

Assuming he got through supper with his father, of course.

CHAPTER SEVEN

*H*uzzah!" Lewrie shouted at the top of his lungs once he'd read the letter from Admiralty, thrusting it aloft in triumph. "Whoo, and about damned time!" He sprang to his feet from the breakfast table, upsetting his chair.

"One'd suppose you've a reason to be boorish," Sir Hugo laconically said in the midst of buttering his toast. "And too bloody loud, to boot."

"*Sapphire*'s to stay in commission!" Lewrie hooted, "and I still have a ship! They say . . ." Lewrie quickly re-read the letter to find the pertinent sentence, "they say that orders for her continued service will be forthcoming. I must get back to Portsmouth with the good news, at once."

"*After* breakfast, or right this instant?" his father said with a scowl. He bit off a large mouthful of toast and chewed, with a wee glint in his eyes. After swallowing, he further said, "Sorry to see you go, parting is such sweet sorrow, . . . all that. Though it will be grand to have my house, and its peace, back."

"God, but you're the soul of hospitality," Lewrie scoffed as he came back down from his sudden elation, righting his chair, and sitting back down to resume his breakfast. "If you hold me to be your Prodigal Son, you could at least *send* me off with the fatted calf!"

"Then we shall have roast beef for dinner . . . or will you be staying on for supper tonight?" Sir Hugo enquired with pointed sarcasm.

"A carriage to arrange, packing to do," Lewrie ticked off, "and a Midshipman to collect. Thank God my shopping's done already. It'll take a full day t'get back to Portsmouth, if the weather and the roads are passable. Start before first light tomorrow? Ehm . . . do you still maintain a coach and four?"

"What?" Sir Hugo barked, leaning back in amazement. "Bang up my coach, leave my picked team at some shoddy wayside inn to be stolen? You'll have to hire your own, boy, and the best of luck to you."

"The soul of Christian charity you are, too," Lewrie snapped. "I should have known better, by now, to even ask."

"I'll lend you the use of my footmen to hunt up a hired coach, and pass what letters you must," Sir Hugo grudgingly allowed, as if he felt he'd gone too far towards selfishness. "You *are* my Prodigal Son, after all, the only one I'd care to claim, anyway."

"Well, thank you for that," Lewrie replied, then returned to his breakfast, His father paid closer attention to his own plate, and several minutes passed in uncomfortable silence.

"Mean t'say . . . ," his father said after stirring cream and sugar into a fresh cup of coffee, "I will allow that I've never been what most would call a proper, dutiful father. It ain't in my nature, d'ye see, never has been. Children, my God, what bothers they are! Get in the way of a man's life, they do! I've *tried*, in my own way . . . ," he trailed off, shaking his head.

"Believe me, I've noticed," Lewrie said with an ironic smile.

"They're best dealt with when they're grown and on their own," Sir Hugo said, sighing. "And, what with the Navy, and the wars, I've got used to you being . . . somewhere else, with the odd letter now and then to keep me up with your doings."

"Well, the acorn don't fall far from the tree," Lewrie allowed, confessing his own lacks as a parent. "I was never home with mine, not after Ninety-Three. I've seen Hugh of late, haven't clapped eyes on Sewallis in years, and Charlotte, well . . . I don't *care* t'see *her* and that's mutual. I *did* enjoy 'em when they were little, in the few years I was home, but . . . you may be right."

"And, I must confess that I've become . . . set in my ways," his father said, making a wry face. "At my age, I prefer things to be . . . sensible, with no upsets. It really has been grand to have you, even for a few days, but I *will* enjoy the quiet once you've gone."

"I love you, too, you old rogue," Lewrie said, chuckling.

"Ahem!" Sir Hugo replied, grimacing in acknowledgement, as if to put an end to a maudlin moment, as close to saying "I love you, too" as he would come, and that was the end of the matter.

Sir Hugo had offered his leave-taking blessings an hour or so after the night's supper, preferring to sleep through Lewrie's departure before sunup. He had, however, directed his kitchen staff to lay on a small basket of food for the journey. Lewrie had perhaps his last hot, shore bath for some time, and a close shave, before retiring for a few hours of rest. All his preparations were a strain on the house staff, to heat and fetch up the water to fill the copper tub, then remove it when Lewrie was done, to prepare that basket of food, and for one unfortunate footman to sit up and watch a mantel clock so he could wake some of the staff, and Lewrie and Pettus. The butler, Harwell, turned up in a quilted dressing gown to unlock the door when the coachman arrived, and knocked. Sleepy, bleary-eyed footmen bore Lewrie's traps to the coach's boot and interior, a last-minute mug of tea for the coachman had to be fetched, and when the empty mug was reclaimed, and the coach rattled off, Lewrie was sure that everyone was perfectly sick of his presence, and glad to be shot of him!

"There are lights in the windows, sir," Pettus said as their coach drew to a halt in front of the rectory of St. Anselm's, "so they must be up."

"Aye," Lewrie agreed as he kicked the folding metal steps down and dismounted from the coach. He took a deep sniff of the night air, before climbing the stone steps to the front door. At that hour the smell of coal smoke was less, and he could imagine that the cold was not as biting as the day before, and the fog that haloed the lanthorns either side of the door was not as thick, or wet-smelling.

He rapped with the heavy iron door knocker, and a sleepy maid in a mob-cap over dishevelled hair turned the locks and opened it and waved him in. She could not stifle her wide yawn.

"Good morning," Lewrie said, right-perkily for that early hour, "Captain Alan Lewrie, come to collect Midshipman Chenery."

"The family's in the parlour, sir . . . this way," the maid said, leading him deeper into the house.

"Good morning, Reverend Chenery," Lewrie said, sweeping off his new bicorne hat and bowing from the waist as he took in the new faces. There was young Charles Chenery, now in uniform, and standing by his sea-chest, looking quite eager to go.

"Sir Alan," the Reverend replied in like manner, fully dressed himself but not yet shaven, "allow me to name to you my long-time house guest, Madame Bernice Pellatan. She and her late husband were Royalist refugees who have resided as the parish's guests for some time, now."

"*M'sieur chevalier Capitaine, enchanté,*" a blowsy, over-done older woman cooed as she performed a deep curtsy, with a graceful incline of her head.

"Madame Pellatan, *enchanté, aussi,*" Lewrie replied, bowing and making a "leg" to her.

Must sleep *in all that bloody make-up*! he thought.

"And, may I name to you my youngest daughter, Jessica," the Reverend Chenery continued. "Jessica, this is Captain Sir Alan Lewrie, Baronet, and Captain of Charlie's new ship."

"Mistress Jessica, so happy to make your acquaintance," Lewrie said, repeating his "leg" as she dipped him a curtsy less grand than the older woman's.

"Sir Alan," the young lady replied, looking him right in the eye as she rose, "you will excuse me if I am of two minds regarding making your acquaintance . . . you are taking my little brother to sea, and war."

I think I'm in love! Lewrie thought; *Well, maybe lust. Hands t'yerself, idiot. Am I droolin'? Good Lord, what a beauty!*

Jessica Chenery had not made the same effort as her father or Madame Pellatan to make a proper show. She wore a high-necked winter wool drab-brown gown, with a pale grey shawl over her shoulders, but then, that was more than enough.

She had her younger brother's dark hair, so dark brown that it was almost black, and, like her brother, her eyes were dark blue. Her brows were dark, thick, and nicely arched. At that early hour, she'd not braided, plaited, or pinned her hair up, either, but had bound it back in a loose fall, though loose locks draped part of her face.

Jessica Chenery's face was a very English long oval, with good cheek bones, tapering to a square-ish wee chin; her nose was long and straight; her mouth in rest was not too wide, and even when closed had hints of amusement that lifted the outer corners.

"My pardons, Miss Chenery," Lewrie replied to her, after a moment of surprise at the boldness of her statement. "At this moment I am sure you look at me like a Turk in a turban, and I know your concern. Both my sons are in the Navy, d'ye see, and I worry about 'em the same way. Trust me that your brother is joining a good ship, and that I will do my best t'see him through his early days."

Lord, what a flawlessly creamy complexion! he marvelled further as he tried not to ogle too noticeably; *slim, too!*

"I wonder, Sir Alan," Rev. Chenery broke in, as if she had given offence to a guest, "if you have time for a cup of tea, or . . ."

"I'd *relish* one, sir," Lewrie quickly and eagerly assured him. "It's not as cold as it was yesterday morning, but it *is* very early. I wonder . . . our coachman is in need of hot tea, as is my cabin steward, Pettus, here."

"Yes, let us all have tea," Rev. Chenery enthused. "Betty? Tea for all, if you please. Let us sit. Thoughtful of you, sir."

"Yes, sir," the sleepy maid replied, curtsied, and departed for the kitchens, with Pettus in her wake.

"What a strong countenance you have, *M'sieur*," Madame Pellatan drawled after studying Lewrie closely. "A face to be painted, *n'est-ce pas,* Jessica? Though, without the scars, perhaps."

"Never," Lewrie said, laughing, "I earned 'em fair and square. Nobody'd recognise me without 'em."

"Madame Pellatan and her late husband were renowned portraitists before they were forced to flee France during the Terror," the Reverend supplied, "and Madame still takes commissions from some of the finest clients."

"And so does Jessica," Madame Pellatan imparted with a coo and a lean in the young lady's direction. "From her earliest days, she has shown a remarkable talent, which we were happy to develop . . . though she prefers a starker realism that is not to most people's taste. My husband and I follow the style of the famous Élisabeth Vigée-Lebrun . . . so much softer, *romantic,* and *flattering* to customers, *n'est-ce pas, M'sieur Capitaine?*" She said with a coy titter.

Damme, is the old baggage tryin' to flirt with me? Lewrie had to wonder.

"Ah, you paint, Miss Chenery?" Lewrie asked, thankful for an entry to conversing with her.

"Yes, Sir Alan, I do," Jessica told him, darting a quick look at her father. "As Madame Bernice says, I can't remember when I did not have a brush or a pencil in my hands . . . sketches, watercolours, or oils, pen and inks?" She became more animated as she told him that, impatiently brushing the stray locks back from her forehead, and her smile made her even more fetching. "I have done several portraits in the last year or so, though

I've had better luck with fanciful illustrations, amusing scenes suitable for engraving which I have to colour myself, unfortunately, not trusting to the inkers that most printers hire. Madame is right . . . you would make a fine subject for a portrait."

"I haven't sat for one since . . ." Lewrie replied, furrowing his brow to remember just when he had, "since I was back from the American Revolution, when I was a Lieutenant. Lord, I was a *child*. And the painter kept chidding me to look stern so often, that I told him it was off if I couldn't smile. If I was leavin' my phyz for the ages, I preferred that people knew I had a sense of humour!

"If I wasn't awaiting sailing orders, I'd be tempted to sit for a new'un," Lewrie offered. "Perhaps when I return?"

"I am quite reasonable, Sir Alan," Jessica told him, smiling at him. "Fifteen pounds is my usual fee."

"Ahem!" Rev. Chenery said, squirming and coughing.

"And da . . . quite reasonable, too," Lewrie told her, grinning from ear to ear.

"I'll show you one of my works," Jessica said, springing to her feet, and going to a painting near the fireplace. "This is my sister Portia and her first baby," she proudly said.

"I'm sure that Sir Alan has little time to admire your . . ." the Reverend Chenery interrupted.

"I see what you mean!" Lewrie exclaimed, going to join her as Jessica shifted a candelabra to better illuminate the painting. "It's so true to the life that one could imagine they're sitting behind the wall, holdin' their breath!"

So taken with the young lady as he was, if the sister and her newborn looked like a cross-eyed sow and a piglet, he would have found a way to praise the work, but . . . he really was impressed.

The tea service was brought in, and they returned to their seats. Madame Pellatan took the opportunity to produce some more of Jessica's work, stating that her prints could be found in many of the galleries that sold satiric caricatures.

There was one of a group of children running cross a grassy lea flying a kite, another of a kid goat in the lane of a stable, nose to nose with a horse that leaned down over its stall door to sniff at it. Sleeping kittens, jumbled atop each other; hares springing through some truck garden . . . all amusing and innocent, suitable for children for the most part.

"Oh, here's my latest," Jessica said, "though I must confess that I know little of hunting, or steeplechasing."

"Hah hah, I love it!" Lewrie said with real delight.

She'd painted a pack of hounds in a country lane, riders in the rear just clearing a gate, most of the hounds looking serious on the scent, but the one in the foreground looking the viewer right in the eyes, tongue lolling comically, and its long ears winged out.

"I toured the galleries yesterday," Lewrie said, "barely managing t'get close to the windows, or the doors, for all the crowd, but I didn't see any of these. If I had, I would've bought this'un."

"When it's printed, I would send you one, Sir Alan," Jessica offered, her earlier sadness quite flown, and quite outgoing.

"Don't know where I'd hang it, though," Lewrie told her. "And, my old cat, Chalky, would hate it. He can barely tolerate the ship's dog, already. But, thankee kindly for the offer, Miss Chenery."

"Well, I would suppose if you wish to reach Portsmouth by dark, we must say our *adieus*," Rev. Chenery declared as a mantel clock struck five A.M., and, their tea finished, all rose and paid heed to young Charles at last. Madame Pellatan smothered him in a great, voluminous hug, servants curtsied or bowed and said their goodbyes, his father shook his hand and bade him make them proud, and Jessica took him in her arms for one last sisterly embrace.

"Oh Lord, poor Charlie," she muttered, stroking his hair back into place, "it is so hard you have to go into the world so young. I will miss you horribly, and pray for your safekeeping every day."

"Oh, I'll be alright, Jess," Charlie assured her, "but prayer will still be welcome."

"Yes, well," Lewrie said, donning his boat cloak and taking his hat from a footman. "I fear it is time to depart. Ready, Mister Chenery?" he asked his newest Midshipman.

"Yes sir, I am," the lad said with a firm note in his voice.

"Let's get your dunnage aboard the coach, then," Lewrie ordered. "Reverend Chenery, Madame Pellatan, Miss Chenery, I dearly wish I had the time to make more of your acquaintances, but . . . time and tide, all that. I bid you all *adieu*," he said, with a last bow with his hat on his heart.

"And do you return, Sir Alan," Jessica dared say, looking impish, "I will be honoured to do your portrait."

"I look forward to that, Miss Chenery," Lewrie agreed.

They saw Lewrie, young Chenery, and Pettus to the door, house staff hefted the sea-chest into the boot, and waved them away as the coachman cracked his whip and set off into a gathering fog.

"Well, there it is, then," Rev. Chenery said with a sad, but relieved, sigh once all were back inside, warming themselves at the fireplace. "I thought Sir Alan a most . . . distinguished gentleman, who knows what he's about."

"So handsome, *aussi*," Madame Pellatan commented, "and a gentleman possessed of a fine physique . . . though rather young to be so distinguished, *oui* Reverend? I expected the hard-bitten, stern sea-dog, all salt and tar, but . . . he is so merry and charming, so polite and, I think, reassuring. Did he not strike you so, Jessica?"

"After meeting him, my qualms over Charlie's future are *somewhat* eased," Jessica said as she dabbed her nose and her eyes with a handkerchief. She sat down in a wing-back chair by the fireplace and drew her shawl closer round her shoulders. "Yes, Sir Alan is all that you say, Madame. Did you note his eyes? Such a striking blue-grey colour they are, which make him seem even more merry. Do I ever get to paint him, he *must* be rendered with a smile, as he insisted his first portraitist do."

"Oh, painting, painting!" her father said with a groan.

"How old do you think he is?" Madame Pellatan wondered aloud. "In his fourties, perhaps?"

"His young fourties, I should imagine," Jessica agreed, reaching beside her chair for a tablet of sketching paper and a pencil, trying to recall as much as she could of their visitor while her memory was still fresh. Lost in that endeavour, Jessica Chenery began to smile, and hum a tune to herself.

CHAPTER EIGHT

*O*h, father said to give you this, sir," Midshipman Chenery said as the coach reached the open country round London's outskirts. "Five pounds in pence, six pence, and shillings."

"Hold onto it 'til we're aboard ship, Mister Chenery," Lewrie told him with a wave of his hand. "You might have need of your money at one of our stops for fresh horses."

"Though your father saw to it that we've more than enough food in the basket, sir," Pettus told him after digging through it. "Cold ham, sliced beef, bread, mustard, jam, a jar of pickles . . . and aha! There are even some berry tarts! Did us proud, he did."

"Wish there was a way t'carry hot coffee," Lewrie replied, "a crock of some kind that'd keep it warm."

"Hmm, a crock jar filled with boiling water, sir," Pettus fancied, "with a metal bottle inside that, and a screw-down top?"

"I'd hug the bloody thing, first off," Lewrie grumbled, yawning, "and worry 'bout the coffee, later. Less cold than yesterday is a damned thin comparison. Brr!"

"Thank you for the lap-robe, sir," Midshipman Chenery said, for all three of them were so supplied, and the coachman out in the wind was swaddled in one, along with his greatcoat.

"Don't want you t'freeze to death before you've signed ship's books, Mister Chenery," Lewrie told him, grinning.

"Ehm . . . should I be armed as well, sir?" the lad asked, casting a glance at the brace of double-barrelled pistols in an open case by Lewrie's side, and the pair of single-barrelled pistols in Pettus's lap.

"No, I think not, Mister Chenery," Lewrie told him with a reassuring smile, "Pettus and I can deal with any highwayman we might encounter, though anyone up to mischief this early'd be a truly desperate thief."

"Who'd be out in the cold, this early, aye," Pettus agreed.

"Damn my eyes, you said 'aye' 'stead of 'yes', at last," Lewrie joshed him.

"Well, sir," Pettus replied, "after hearing it said all this time, I've become accustomed. The Navy insists on 'aye, sir' or 'aye aye, sir'," Pettus said, leaning toward Chenery and tipping him a wink. "Oh, the strange words and terms you'll hear, and have to learn, the customs you must follow! Why, you'll be all 'at sea', hah hah!"

"I didn't know you were such a wag, Pettus," Lewrie pretended to grump. "It must be the early hour. So sleepy that you're giddy."

"Oh, it must be, sir!" Pettus agreed, most happily.

So passed the first two hours before reaching a posting inn for a change of horses, a quick warm-up before a roaring fire, hot drinks, and a trip to the "necessary"; filling Mr. Chenery in on the most basic things that he should know about boarding ship, and what to do and how to carry himself once there, all of which at times made the newly gape.

"So, tell me about your family, Mister Chenery," Lewrie asked of him once they were back on the road. "I believe you said that all of them were churchmen?"

"Yes . . . aye, sir, sorry," Chenery was happy to relate. "My uncle is in Holy Orders, and a Fellow at Oxford, though his interest is mostly in classical history. Greeks, Romans, Phoenicians, Carthagenians, and such. Ehm, there's my older brother, Henry, who has the living of Saint Crispin's at Windsor . . . visiting with him and his family is where I learned to swim and boat . . . then there's my oldest sister, Portia, and her husband, who's Rector of a parish in Hampstead, my sister, Miranda, and her husband, who's the Rector of Saint James's in Woolwich, and Jessica, of course. Father adores Shakespeare, d'ye see . . . which explains our names. The plays about King Henry the Fifth, *The Tempest, The Merchant of Venice*. . . ." He shrugged.

"Your sister Jessica really is quite the talented artist, and I was taken with what little I saw of her work," Lewrie idly prompted. "So very realistic, even the fanciful illustrations she does. Even a hare leapin' about was so realistic one could conjure that it could be touched, and it would take fright, or the sleepin' kittens would wake up and stretch, haw!"

"Aye, she's very good," Mr. Chenery agreed, though tilting his head and looking less than gladsome, "and, the last few years, she's even managed to make a decent living from her art, though my father thinks it scandalous. Not the proper thing for a young lady to be doing, engaging in what amounts to . . . Trade."

"Oh, it's good enough for Madame Pellatan to scratch out a living, but not your sister?" Lewrie posed.

"Madame Bernice, well, sir," young Chenery imparted with a *moue,* "she and her husband *were* well-renowned before they came away from France, and they catered to the aristocratic and wealthy, so it's fine for *her* to continue working, but . . . it's not what father would prefer for Jessica. He fears that the life, and the circles in which artists associate, are too . . . Bohemian and . . . barely a cut above actors and idle *poseurs* . . . jaded sinners and . . . seducers," he concluded with a deep red blush. "He'd much rather see her married, but for our . . ." He clamped his mouth shut, fearing he'd revealed too much, and wakening Lewrie's suspicions about the Chenery family's finances.

He's too "skint" for a dowry, is he? Lewrie thought.

"Ehm . . . is anyone feeling peckish?" Pettus asked, obviously famished himself, despite a rather hearty cold breakfast at Lewrie's father's house. "I forgot to mention that there are hard-boiled eggs, as well."

"Aye, I'd take one," Lewrie told him, perking up and shifting his rump on the thinly padded seat, "by way of a beginning, at least. Care for something, Mister Chenery?"

"Most kind of you, sir, and . . . aye, I will," the lad replied with a boyish grin.

"Your uncle's at Oxford, is he?" Lewrie re-started his questioning as he cracked the shell of his egg and began to peel it. "I never have been there. Senior Fellow, is he?"

"Aye, sir," Chenery related, busy trying to find a place to discard his bits of egg shell, "Been there for years. We coached up a few times to visit

Uncle Richard and his family, and Oxford is . . . nice, if a bit confusing. All the winding streets? He's the eldest, of course, so he began his teaching post even before father took Holy Orders. I've a grand batch of cousins, though they are a touch . . . wild, so going there is quite fun, and . . . eye-opening."

Lewrie fell silent while he munched on his egg, pondering that fact. The Oxford uncle was eldest, so he would have inherited what wealth the Chenerys had, and Rev. Chenery in London would have had to find some career to sustain him.

What's the goin' rate for a minister's daughter? he wondered; *It can't be more than one hundred pounds per annum, even for a man with a* good *living! Maybe closer to fifty or sixty.*

Years ago, Lewrie had given his French ward, Sophie de Maubeuge, away to one of his former First Lieutenants, Anthony Langlie, and had supported her with an hundred guineas, or 105 pounds, thankfully matched by the Langlie family, but if he hadn't been extremely fortunate when it came to prize-money, with several thousand pounds earning interest in the Three Percents, the girl might have had to get by on much less. Thinking of his un-married daughter, Charlotte, and his brother-in-law, Governour Chiswick, and his hints that she should be exposed to the marriage market of a London Season, and a dowry of at least an hundred pounds as well made his head ache. Which further made him think of his former lover, Lydia Stangbourne, Viscount Percy's sister, and *her* dowry, of two thousand pounds a year. *Damned* if he would! Charlotte might get sixty pounds for her "dot", only when she quit being a spiteful little bitch!

Lewrie gave Midshipman Chenery a closer look as he joshed with Pettus; his dirk was definitely a used one, as his sea-chest had been, and the lad's uniform coat and watch-coat could have been made from finer material. Two married daughters to support, a third unable to marry for a lack of a dowry, and earning her own small living with her artwork? It was a wonder that Rev. Chenery could afford meat on the table three days a week! It made Lewrie wonder if that Madame Bernice was a paying lodger, and not a guest, or even worse . . . that Jessica's earnings went toward the family's up-keep!

"Romans and Phen . . . what-you-call-'ems?" Pettus asked, sounding astonished.

"The ancient Phoenicians," Midshipman Chenery was relating to Pettus, "the boldest seafarers in the ancient world. They sailed open-sea voyages beyond the Pillars of Hercules, called at the Canary Islands, maybe the Azores, too, and might even have discovered America long before Co-lumbus! If anyone tried to follow them out into the Atlantic, they'd turn and fight to the death to keep their secrets, Uncle Richard says. He's ex-amples of their copper wafers, like two triangles joined at the points, so they could stack them up and bind them with rope so they could carry them about, and that's the same way that the Red Indians traded *their* cop-per! He and father think that the Phoenicians sailed to America, found copper deposits . . . copper was as important as iron or steel then . . . and brought it back home. Then, there are the Roman coins . . ."

"Roman coins?" Lewrie blurted out, intrigued by the theory.

"People in New England, in Massachusetts, now and then find old Roman coins washing up on the beaches, sir," Chenery excitedly said, "and Uncle Richard got hold of a couple of them, all dated round 380 A.D. or so, a silver *sestercius,* and a gold *denarius.*"

"How the Devil did the Romans get there?" Lewrie objected.

"Oh, they had big ships, sir," Chenery said with a laugh. "Do recall Saint Peter who sailed to Rome on a ship with five hundred passengers. Now the *intriguing* thing is that both coins bear the head of Emperor Val-entinus, a very young fellow, who was murdered by his mother and a Gothic general, round 383 A.D. Father, Uncle Richard, and their fellow antiquarians believe that Valentinus sent out ships to find him a refuge, knowing they were going to do him in, using the lore of those ancient Phoenicians, but he was killed before they found it and came and told him about it, maybe wrecked and *never* returned! I don't know if they'll ever really get round to looking into it properly, but they do try to raise funds for several lengthy expeditions, sir."

"Sounds like a very iffy proposal, to me," Lewrie concluded, "and an *expensive* one, with no guarantees that it would *ever* result in anything."

A hellish expensive hobby, the Reverend Chenery has, Lewrie told himself; *He'd do better bettin' on horses, or Shove-Ha'penny! Even findin' old books and such'd cost him dear. No wonder he's so "skint"!*

"The Pillars of Hercules," Pettus mused. "We've seen *those.* Gibraltar's been our home port the last two years, and we've prowled round Ceuta, on the other side of the Straits almost as long."

"Oh, if we're going back there, I can't wait to write father and tell him all about it!" Chenery exclaimed.

"No guarantees on that, either, Mister Chenery," Lewrie told him. "It'll be up to the Admiralty where we'll go next. Perhaps they would find us useful in the Great South Seas."

He shrugged himself deeper into his boat cloak and drew his lap-robe higher on his chest, crossed his arms, and closed his eyes to take a little nap. The coach's suspension straps rocked the coach body as restfully as a swinging hammock, and they were on a good stretch of decent road.

Where are *we goin'?* he had to ask himself. He hoped that they'd send him back to Spain and Portugal where he had a nagging feeling that there was still some un-finished business with the French . . . back to Gibraltar and the Andalusian coast, or Lisbon, if the rumours about a fresh British Army presence in Portugal were true. He could see Maddalena, again, or move her to Lisbon.

The coach's motion, and his lack of sleep, lulled him to dream in fits and starts, but not about Maddalena Covilhā. No, the images that arose were of a slim and lovely Jessica Chenery, the way that she swiped her loose locks back from her forehead, and the long, slim, and talented fingers with which she did it; a bright smile . . .

He jerked awake.

Here, that'll *never do!* he chid himself.

BOOK TWO

The dusky night rides down the sky,
And ushers in the morn;
The hounds all join in glorious cry,
The huntsman winds his horn,
And a-hunting we will go.
  –HENRY FIELDING (1707-54),
   "A-HUNTING WE WILL GO" (1784), STANZA 1

CHAPTER NINE

*T*heir coach reached Portsmouth round seven that evening, long before the dockyard gates were closed for the night, and Lewrie, Pettus, and Midshipman Chenery took time to dine at the Fountains Inn before hiring a boat out to *Sapphire*, and their respective beds.

After a hearty breakfast, Lewrie could take great satisfaction in strolling his quarterdeck, then forward along a sail-tending gangway as far as the forecastle so he could admire his new main mast and all its standing and running rigging, now set up as good as new, and all that mile of rope taut and geometrically perfect. There was even a new commissioning pendant aloft at the royal mast truck, streaming to the wind in lazy snake-tongue flickers.

"Mister Posey's done us proud, Mister Westcott," Lewrie said, quite pleased after returning to the quarterdeck.

"Indeed he has, sir," the First Officer agreed, looking up in admiration, too. "As has Admiralty, to keep us in full commission. I wonder, though . . . have you given any thought to putting the ship Out of Discipline, now all the heavy work's done, sir?"

"All stores aboard?" Lewrie enquired.

"Aye, sir, and the Bosun's lockers, the Carpenter's stores, and the holds are bung-full," Lt. Westcott reported, then slyly added, "and our Augean

Stable has been mucked out, too," referring to the Midshipmens' cockpit berthing space. Whilst Lewrie was in London, the quarters had been sluiced with sea water, scrubbed and holystoned, then scoured with vinegar, smoked with burning faggots of tobacco leaf, and re-painted to make it even a bit more liveable. Both men took glee in the relation of how the ship's Mids had groused over being forced to purchase mugs, plates, bowls, new tablecloths, and glasses. Their mess boy, typically the filthiest "git" aboard, even dirtier than the "duck fucker" who tended the forecastle manger, had howled like a banshee when he was scrubbed clean for the first time in months!

"Aye, then, Mister Westcott," Lewrie said, after making up his mind, "hoist the Easy pendant and let the bum-boats come alongside at Noon. Warn the Surgeon and his mates t'do what they can t'spot any of the Polls who might be poxed. Bosun Terrell and his mates, and the Master at Arms and Ship's Corporals are to keep their eyes peeled for smuggled spirits, too . . . and, I'd admire did you pass word for Midshipmen Holbrooke and Chenery to report to me in my cabins."

"I'll see to it directly, sir," Lt. Westcott said, touching the brim of his hat in salute. "Oh, by the way, sir . . . nice new hat you have," he slyly teased. "Bicornes . . . all 'the go' these days. Maybe I should get one, too."

Lewrie's answer to that was a scowl and a snort.

"Midshipmen Holbrooke an' Chenery t'see th' Cap'um, SAH!" the Marine sentry announced from without the cabin doors.

"Enter!" Lewrie shouted back. The two lads came to stand in front of his desk in the day cabin, hats under their arms. "Gentlemen, did you enjoy your first night below?"

Both of the lads seemed to shiver in dread of that experience, looked at each other, and swore that it had been fine, though Lewrie imagined that their introduction to the rough-and-tumble of the cockpit was more like shoving a stray dog into a pen full of hounds to be savaged.

"Very well," Lewrie went on with a faint smile of remembrance, "I wish you both to enter your names in the muster book, making your presence aboard, and your membership in the Navy, official. From now on, Admiralty will know to pay you the handsome sum of six pounds per annum, less the deductions for the Chatham Chest and Greenwich Hospital, and our Surgeon, Mister Snelling. That comes to one shilling a lunar month, twelve shillings a year. I suppose your relatives told you that there is no half-pay for Midshipmen should your current ship pay off and you're unable t'gain another berth? Oops, too late, and as the old saying goes, 'ye shouldn't've joined if ye can't take a joke'. So . . . it will be vital to your future careers to learn quick and take every opportunity to learn even more, everything that matters to the safe performance of your duties, as well as the proper handling of a ship, and . . . the management and safety of the ship's people you will supervise.

"I will not tolerate a brute or a bully who treats the hands as objects of derision," Lewrie went on, turning stern. "I've seen it, and I detest it, and any sign of it will get you bent over the breech of a gun and thrashed by the Bosun or one of his Mates 'til you learn to treat our people decently. You must walk a fine line 'twixt keeping good order and being lax, playin' 'Popularity Dick'. That'll get you despised, no matter if they laugh at your jokes. On the other hand, you'll not let them take advantage of you, or show you even the least respect. You are considered 'gentlemen in training' by the Navy, and rank among the petty officers. *Sapphire* has ten of you, roughly in charge of about fifty hands each, though that will vary depending on the tasks at hand.

"Are you both sure you still want to stay on?" Lewrie asked as that sank in, cocking his head to one side with a wry expression. "Good. It ain't all 'claret and cruisin' for you, it's a damned dangerous profession you've entered, and a demanding one. I sincerely hope that you're both up to it. Mister Faulkes?" Lewrie called to his clerk, "I'd admire did you tend to the paperwork regarding Midshipmen Chenery and Holbrooke, here. I believe that you young gentlemen also have some funds to be banked with Mister Faulkes?"

"Aye, sir," Chenery said, laying a slim wash-leather purse on the desk with his five pounds in coin.

"Ehm, my uncle, Captain Niles, advised my father to bring only coins, sir?" Midshipman George Holbrooke tentatively said, producing a fatter purse. "I have twelve pounds, in all, sir . . . Mister Faulkes, and ehm . . ." Holbrooke dug into a breast pocket of his coat and drew out a sheet of paper which he laid beside his purse, turning shy.

"What's this?" Lewrie asked, picking it up and reading it.

Midshipman Holbrooke was tall for thirteen years old, lean and spare, with light brown hair, green eyes, and freckles. He blushed as Lewrie read the letter and looked up at him.

"Hmm, it appears that Mister Holbrooke has two years on ship's books already, Mister Faulkes," Lewrie said.

"A friend of the family, of Captain Niles, sir," Holbrooke stammered, "I was to join his ship next year, but he caught Yellow Fever in the West Indies last summer, and . . . I was told it counted, sir."

"Oh, it does," Lewrie said with a sage nod.

It was official, noted at Admiralty, a thing done for aspiring young lads, even if it was a humbug. Samuel Pepys long ago had laid down that no one could qualify for a Lieutenant's commission if he was not "upwards of twenty" and had been on ship's books for at least seven years, now in time of war reduced to six years. But, there were hundreds of hopefuls carried on ship's books who never set foot on an oak deck 'til most of their useful schooling ashore was done, even more listed as Captain's Servants pretending to be "Gentleman Volunteers" as young as eight, so they could have the requisite years at sea to speed their jump from Midshipman to Commission Sea Officer.

Thank God for Examining Boards, Lewrie thought; *At least they weed out the stupid and ignorant.*

"In a way, Mister Holbrooke, your uncle and his friend did you no favours," Lewrie told the lad. "You only have four official years t'learn all you should know to meet *one* of the qualifications, then must wait another two before you're old enough to stand before an Examining Board, at the earliest. I count Captain Niles as a good acquaintance, but I give no guarantees. Both of you are now 'on your own bottoms', and must make the best of it that you can.

"I will speak with Midshipman Hillhouse and enlist him to be your senior instructor," Lewrie promised, which made both of them look as if they'd been made a present to a demon, "and I'll speak with the First Officer, Mister Westcott, to find you each a 'sea daddy' to show you the basics, knots, rigging, and such. You'll be standing Harbour Watch today . . . try not to be too shocked when the Easy pendant is hoisted, and the ship is put Out of Discipline at noon. I'm certain someone'll explain what that means to you, hey? That's all for the present. You're both dismissed."

Just moments after Eight Bells were struck to mark the end of the Forenoon Watch, up went the Easy pendant on a signal halliard, and the bumboats which had been swanning about the harbour in search of trade began to make their way toward HMS *Sapphire*. Lewrie made his appearance on the quarterdeck to assure himself that the Surgeon and his Mates, the Bosun and his Mates, and the Master at Arms, Baggett, and his Ship's

Corporals, Wray and Packer, were on deck and alert, then retreated to the aloof perch on the poop deck above it all, to play with Bisquit.

> *Don't you see the ships a-coming,*
> *don't you see them in full sail,*
> *don't you see the ships a-coming,*
> *with the prizes at their tail?*

The eager whores and bum-boat traders belted out their ditty, lustily and loud, if nowhere near on-key, some sounding more like the squawks of riled parrots.

> *Oh, my little rolling sailor,*
> *oh, my little rolling he,*
> *I do love a jolly sailor,*
> *Blithe and merry might be be!*

There was a time long before in his own Midshipman days when he had goggled and gawped over the arrival of the "wives" when one of his past ships had been put Out of Discipline, and had invented excuses to pass down a mess desk when the crew and their doxies were in full carouse, when breasts and bare bums could be seen two-a-penny, and Jacks and Polls had had sex between the guns on the deck, sometimes screened by a hung blanket, sometimes not once the rum began to flow.

> *Sailors, they get all the money,*
> *Soldiers, they get none but brass,*
> *I do love a jolly sailor,*
> *Soldiers they may kiss my arse,*
> *Oh, my little rolling sailor,*
> *Oh, my little rolling he,*
> *I do love a jolly sailor,*
> *Soldiers may be damned for me!*

There had been times when Lewrie had been sorely tempted to get in on the carousing, though it would have meant "kissing the gunner's daughter" bent over a gun, and a round two-dozen strokes for behaviour not worthy of a gentleman volunteer. There had been one or two young and comely waifs aboard each bum-boat not yet ruined by the life, so tempting that he, long-deprived of release, had stiffened as hard as a marling spike, and had to walk crouched over, hoping to be allowed ashore where Captains, Lieutenants, and Mids could rantipole a sweet young whore in "gentlemanly" privacy. Most of the time, though, he'd been reduced to "boxing the Jesuit" in his hammock, hoping that his mess-mates didn't notice and tease him un-mercifully.

"Lord, what an ugly lot, sir," the Sailing Master, Mr. Yelland, spoke up from the bottom of the starboard ladderway from the quarterdeck, as the first of the whores made their way up the side and faced quick inspections at the entry-port. "There must be *honest* work somewhere, in spinning mills and such, that recruited the young and good-looking. Your typical 'Portsmouth Poll', the most of them."

A fair number of the whores were as brawny and round as female versions of "John Bull", tawdrily over-dressed in cast-off finery. The Surgeon, Mr. Snelling, a very tall and skeletally lean fellow, turned some away at once, sure that they were poxed to their eyebrows. Once, Ship's Surgeons had been able to deduct fifteen shillings from a man's pay to treat venereal diseases, which explained why so few sailors admitted they'd caught it. Even now, when treatment was free at Navy expense, it was a rare sailor who would come forward, either, for the so-called "cure" was brutal, with doses of mercury shot down the urethra with a metal clyster, oral doses of mercury that turned one's teeth to grey, brittle powder.

"Oh, now there's a stunner," Mr. Yelland said appreciatively as a slim, young blond angel came aboard to be inspected.

"Aye, she is," Lewrie agreed, though she was no angel, if she ever truly was; she was openly flirting with Mr. Snelling and his Mates, obviously used to the routine. Bosun's Mate Plunkett grabbed at her bottom, heard clinking noises, and reached up her gown to rip away a canvas appliance filled with pint bottles of gin or rum.

"Off ye go, lass," Plunkett growled, "ye'll have no trade on *this* ship."

The girl tried to wheedle, then began cursing as she was sent back to her boat, raging at a loss of income in a Midlands accent.

"Shiver me timbers, you're grown so out of compass I can hardly embrace ye!" Plunkett hooted at the next to arrive, a monstrously fat older whore.

"Damn yer eyes, I've come t'see me 'usband, sure!" she shouted back, "Ord'nary. Seaman McQuade, an' 'ere's me papers t'prove it!"

"Poor Seaman McQuade, then," Mr. Yelland sniggered. "She'll crush him to death, does he allow her on top, hee hee!"

"Too tawdry for me, Mister Yelland," Lewrie said, trotting down to the quarterdeck, on the way to the sanctity of his cabins. "Come on, Bisquit. They won't appreciate you sniffin' round for hand-outs on the lower decks. Come on! Cabins!"

"Sir!" Mr. Snelling, the Surgeon implored before Lewrie could make his escape. "Sir, I fear that this is all impossible. There are three stages of syphilis, and it is only the tertiary that can be discovered upon this sort of inspection, by which time no treatment will avail. I might just as well search for a *soul*!"

"All you can do is your best, Mister Snelling, sorry," Lewrie told him. "The last few years we've been lucky t'let the hands have shore liberty at Gibraltar, and what they caught there, out of sight and out of mind, well," he threw in a hapless shrug.

"Very well, sir," Snelling said, pulling a rueful face, "though I wish that the Purser could stock well-made cundums, and our sailors would use them."

"Just stand by for all the black eyes and bruises that they'll produce, once they run riot, sir," Lewrie warned him, then made his way aft into the quiet of his cabins.

"Ah, there is coffee warming on the sideboard, sir," Pettus offered, "fresh goat milk, and I've ground some sugar off the cone in your caddy."

"That'd be grand, thankee, Pettus," Lewrie said, tossing aside his new hat and boat cloak. "Where's Jessop?"

Pettus heaved a sigh before speaking. "Standing in line to pick himself a doxy, sir. There was no talking him out of it."

"Well, we all go to Hell in our own way," Lewrie said, sitting down at his desk to review the latest changes in the muster book, and the re-assignments of sailors to new duty stations for every possible evolution. Some men had been moved up from Ordinary to Able, some had been advanced to petty officer status; by now, the neat and orderly lists were full of cross-outs, over-writes, and mis-spellings, and it would soon be time to start from scratch. That would take some time, and kill some idle hours.

He was of a mind to write some personal letters, instead, and toss the mess into the First Officer's lap, but he had already written almost everyone he knew on-passage from Corunna. A good, long book, perhaps, he considered.

Somthin' that ain't *prurient for a change,* he told himself.

There were also the pages from Mr. Posey's report on all that the yard had done to replace the lower main mast, complete with a list of expenditures to be justified to the Navy Board, from new keelson partner blocks right to the truck of the new royal mast. He could easily kill an hour or more poring over those.

By three in the afternoon, he was done with all of those, and still had the fresh muster book pages to face. Thankfully, his cat, Chalky, wakened from one of his long naps and came to the desk looking for pets, and play, and Bisquit, who had been snoozing under the dining table in the coach, came out to join in with his perpetually soggy rope chew toy in his mouth.

That took at least a quarter-hour of idleness before the both of them were tired of the game, leaving Lewrie to scowl at the muster book, shrug, and go out onto the quarterdeck for some fresh air.

In his cabins, the sound of *Sapphire*'s crew at their revels had been muted, a distant background noise, but on deck, he could hear more clearly their laughter, the music from fiddles, flutes, squeeze-boxes, and womanly shrieks from the semi-drunken whores. Somewhere near the main hatchway, people were loudly singing, and he recognised the song, "Sandman Joe".

> *He stared a while then turned his quid,*
> *Why, blast you, Sall, I loves you!*
> *And for to prove what I have said,*
> *This night I'll soundly fuck you!*
> *Why then, says Sall, my heart's at rest,*
> *If what you say you'll stand to,*
> *His brawny hands her bubbies prest,*
> *And roaring cried "White Sand O!"*

"Good Lord," Lewrie muttered to himself, shaking his head as he recalled singing that in Cock and Hen clubs in the wee hours when he'd caroused with other Bucks of the First Head.

"Oh, my word!" he heard Midshipman Holbrooke whisper to Midshipman Chenery in shock. They had been appointed to the Harbor Watch by their senior mess-mates. "I never . . ."

"Then thank your lucky stars you never hear worse, young sir, like 'Captain Morris's Hymns in Plenipo'," Lewrie sternly told them. *Those* songs were reckoned the absolutely filthiest in the English language. Lewrie had sung those, too, in point of fact; lustily.

"It's all rather . . . bawdy, sir," Midshipman Chenery dared to say, as if in awe. A churchman's son might never have been exposed to such things in the flesh, in his *face*, had he lived the whole of his life ashore, even in London. Lewrie would have felt a tad sorry for his plight, but for the fact that at every school he had attended (and from which he'd been expelled) it always seemed to be the sons, and sometimes the daughters, of churchmen who'd made the greatest Hoo-raw Harrys . . . and the wenches with the roundest heels.

"Ehm, will this be going on long, sir?" Holbrooke dared to ask.

"The rest of the day and night, and 'til Noon tomorrow. After that, the hands'll run out of money and the doxies'll try their luck on other ships," Lewrie told them. "Avert your eyes if you have to go below for some reason, and don't tangle with the loudest drunks, male *or* female. If anyone accosts you, report it at once. Don't let anyone dis-respect you."

"Aye, sir," the two Mids mumbled as one, utterly daunted.

"I've the muster books to up-date," Lewrie said, scowling as he realised that there was no more putting it off. "Try not to get corrupted. Carry on."

"Aye aye, sir," they replied, as if that admonition would be an hellish-hard thing to accomplish.

CHAPTER TEN

*T*wo days after the revelry ended, *Sapphire* still swung to her anchors without orders. The last hangovers had passed, the last of the accumulated trash had been removed, the last exhausted doxies and the few actual wives had departed, and the lower deck berthing areas were put right. The weather turned a bit warmer, and it was not snow that whispered down, but several long spells of chilly, misty rains that swept in from the sea and the Channel, driven by winds that were "dead muzzlers" that penned every ship in port.

"How are they doing, Mister Westcott?" Lewrie asked the First Officer as they stood together on the quarterdeck, looking up to see the progress of their two newest Mids as they scaled the ratlines of the main mast, shepherded by two older hands appointed to be their "sea daddies".

"In over their heads, of course, sir," Lt. Westcott told him, and pulling a face he added, "they can barely box the compass, tie a secure knot of *any* kind, yet, and they've used up most of a quire of paper, trying to draw, and name the running rigging. Oops!" he exclaimed as Midshipman Chenery clawed his way from the futtock shrouds to the maintop, dangling for a heart-stopping second or so before gaining a firm grip and scrambling to a shaky footing in the top. After one or two "Whews!" both Mids began to scale the upper shrouds so they could start their introduction to the main course yard and the foot-ropes, arms thrown over the yard and the harbour-gasketed sail, with the foot-ropes shuddering and swaying under their feet.

"Watchin' 'em makes my 'nutmegs' shrink up," Lewrie said with a wince. "I always *hated* going aloft, shufflin' out to the tip of the yardarm, passin' the ring. Up to the cross-trees, to the royal truck? There's people who'll *stand* on the truck button, but I never did, no matter the dare, or the wager."

"Something to be said for holding a commission, aye, sir," Lt. Westcott replied with a laugh, "you can always send somebody else to do damn-fool things."

"Well, if one of 'em goes *splat* I'm certain I'll hear it," Lewrie said, turning away, unable to watch any longer. "I'll be aft."

Ycovill had prepared him a hearty breakfast of scrambled eggs, tatty hash, and several strips of bacon, with fresh shore bread in the barge, but there was still a slice or two of toast left. There was fresh butter from shore, though, and a barely opened crock of pear preserves, and Lewrie was tempted to sit back down at the table and polish it off, with a fresh cup of coffee. A bum-boat had come alongside bearing day-old copies of several London papers, and he'd bought a couple. It looked to be a grand day to stay inside, and dry, and while away the Forenoon with the latest news, even reading all the pre-printed outer pages which featured advertisements, with the news on the inner pages. After a while he moved himself to the starboard side settee to sprawl out and read on, with Chalky curled up beside him.

"Boat ahoy!" he heard one of the Mids shout, but could not make out the reply, dismissing it at first as just another bum-boat with goods to sell. He heard the thump, though, as the boat had been allowed to come alongside, and set the paper aside, preparing to get to his feet.

"Messenger t'see th' Cap'um, SAH!" his sentry shouted.

"Enter!" Lewrie called back, shooting to his feet in rising anticipation. A moment later and a Lieutenant entered the cabins with a despatch bag slung cross his chest, shaking rain from his bicorne hat before tucking it under his arm.

"Captain Sir Alan Lewrie, sir?" the officer enquired.

"I am, sir," Lewrie replied, itching to hold whatever the man had for him.

"Your orders, sir, just down from London," the officer said as he dug into his bag, sorted through several packets, and handed over one of them, wrapped in cloth against the weather and bound with blue ribbon, secured with a wax seal.

"You don't know . . . of course not," Lewrie said as he took it and broke the wax seal to remove the ribbons. "Sorry."

"No idea, sir," the Lieutenant said with a shrug, "just one of many I'm to deliver this morning."

"Well, I thank you, sir," Lewrie said as he crossed to his desk to remove the cloth wrappings. "Try t'stay dry."

"Aye, sir," the fellow replied as he performed a sketchy bow and saw himself out.

The letter inside the cloth wrapping was also sealed with wax, several sheets, it felt like. He sat down, broke that seal, and laid it out to read, discovering . . . "Well, just damn my eyes!"

> To Cpt. Sir Alan Lewrie, Bart, aboard HMS
> Sapphire, *now lying at Portsmouth,*
> Sir;
>
> The Lords Commissioners for Executing The High Office of Admiralty direct and require that you take upon yourself the Charge and Command of a Squadron intended for operations to interdict French efforts to supply their land forces by sea, into those ports under their Occupation upon the Northern coast of Spain, from Cape Fisterre East to San Sebastian, not limiting yourself from operations off the French ports of Bayonne or Archachon, as you may feel necessary to the Success of your Duties.
>
> To accomplish said Duty, you are appointed as Commodore of the Inferior Class, authorised to hoist a Broad Pendant representing that Grade, for which a Temporary Commission is enclosed.

"Christ, right back to where we came from," Lewrie muttered as he furrowed his brow and stroked his forehead. He was being shoved into "the sack" at the bottom of the Bay of Biscay, where every inch of the coast was a lee shore, and a rocky one, along the dreaded Costa de Morte, the "Coast of Death" round Corunna, and Ferrol, the Costa Verde, which might not be a whit better, the Costa de Cantabria, off the great port of Santander, and into the Golfo de Vizcaya, and the ports of Bilbao and San Sebastian, right up to the French border. The prevailing Atlantic Westerlies blew right down into that corner of "the sack", sometimes becoming Nor'westerlies against which ships could fight hard to thrash their way to deep water, and safety. He figured that a frigate could manage, but *Sapphire?*

Lewrie went back to the letter.

Pursuant to the Accomplishment of this Duty, the following ships, now lying available at Portsmouth, are assigned to you, viz. HMS Undaunted, *5th Rate 38, Capt. R. Chalmers; HMS* Sterling, *6th Rate 32, Capt. C, Yearwood; HMS* Blaze, *Sloop, 18, Commander G. Teague & HMS* Peregrine, *Sloop, 18, Commander H. Blamey.*

"Pettus, I'd admire did you pass word for the First Officer, and the Sailing Master," Lewrie said, taking only a moment to admire his commission document as Commodore, with all its official seals.

"Aye, sir?" Pettus said, surprised. He paused long enough to pinch his nose with his fingers, then snatched his watch-coat from an overhead beam peg, and dashed out onto the quarterdeck.

Lewrie opened a desk drawer for fresh paper to pen a quick reply to Admiralty confirming his receipt of his orders, and was in the middle of that task when the Marine sentry reported Lt. Westcott.

"We've orders, sir?" Westcott asked right off, looking eager.

"Aye, but ye may not care for 'em," Lewrie told him, intent on his penmanship. "Have we a second class broad pendant aboard?"

"Hmm, don't think so, right off hand, sir," Westcott told him, "but congratulations."

"Sailin' Master t'see th' Cap'um, SAH!" the sentry bawled.

"Enter!"

"God help us," Westcott muttered, pinching his own nostrils.

"Ah, you sent for me, sir?" Mr. Yelland, the Sailing Master, enquired after he had entered. He looked rumpled, as if a good, long nap in his sea cabin had been interrupted.

"Aye, Mister Yelland," Lewrie replied, looking up. "We are ordered back to the North coast of Spain, with a brief from Cape Fisterre to the French border, and off Bayonne and Arcachon, too. We'll be in command of *Undaunted*, the *Sterling* frigate, and the two brig-sloops that came with us from Corunna. That makes you the senior Sailing Master of the squadron, so I want you to dig out all the charts that you have, or go ashore and find all you can, then get together with the Sailing Masters, and the Commanders of the brig-sloops, and see that there are no discrepancies that might bring one of 'em to grief."

"Oh, I see, sir!" Yelland exclaimed, looking as if the responsibility was puffing him up with pride. "Fisterre to the French border, Bayonne and

Arcachon, too, right. At present, I don't have much at hand East of Corunna or Ferrol, but, if I may have a boat I'll go ashore and see what I can find, sir?"

"Aye, at once, Mister Yelland, if you'd be so kind," Lewrie agreed. "Take one of the cutters, and Crawley and his old boat crew. If you'll delay a few moments, I'd admire did you bear my letter to Admiralty ashore with you."

"Of course, sir," Yelland agreed, eager to be off. Whatever he did when allowed ashore didn't bear thinking about.

"And when ashore, request a broad pendant, second class, for me, too," Lewrie added, returning to his letter.

"He's not quite as fragrant as usual," Westcott japed once the Sailing Master was gone. "Must've scrubbed up for one of the doxies, the other day. The North coast of Spain, is it?" He sucked his teeth in dread. "A damned nasty place, altogether."

"My manners," Lewrie apologised, waving Westcott to sit down in one of his chairs. "Jessop, pour Mister Westcott some coffee."

"Thank you, sir," Westcott said, "black with sugar, please."

"We're ordered to hunt up French ships bringing supplies into all the harbours along the coast," Lewrie told him, looking up from his letter briefly with a grin of anticipation. "Waggons cross the Pyrenees can't manage a tenth of what their armies need."

"Praise God, *prize-money*!" Westcott hooted in sudden joy. "Bags and bloody bags of it, surely!"

"One can only hope," Lewrie teasingly agreed as he signed his letter, sanded it, blew on it, then began to fold it upon itself and dug into his desk for a stick of wax and his seal. A last dip of his steel-nib pen into the inkwell to address it properly, sand and dry that, and it was ready to be despatched. "Jessop," he said to the lad as he fetched the First Officer's coffee, "take this to the Sailing Master, if ye please."

"Aye, sir!" Jessop replied, looking eager, for once, to go on deck in raw weather, and Lewrie and Westcott shared a knowing look; what passed in the great-cabins or the wardroom was usually known to the crew within minutes. Jessop would surely drop a hint or two that they would be sailing, with fine prospects for lots of prize-money, in passing.

"So, who's to be in our little squadron this time?" Westcott asked after a sip of coffee.

"*Undaunted, Blaze,* and *Peregrine,*" Lewrie told him, "evidently Admiralty thinks that if we came in together, we're all old mates by now, and a Sixth Rate, the *Sterling*, a Captain Yearwood? Know him?"

"Not from Adam, unfortunately, sir," Lt. Westcott had to admit, "though the name strikes me as familiar."

"I'll be dining them in tonight, along with you and Mister Yelland," Lewrie told him, "pick a somewhat clean Midshipman for the bottom of the table, and pass word for my boat crew, and a *responsible* Midshipman, to deliver the invitations as soon as I scribble 'em out."

"Very good, sir," Lt. Westcott said, rushing through his cup of coffee as if he intended to rise and depart that instant. "For supper, I'd suggest Hillhouse." To Lewrie's puzzled frown, he added, "After he failed the Examining Board, he's been as sulky as a bulldog, yet he *is* the senior-most, and should show more leadership for the other Mids. Being included may perk him up, sir."

"And just why, again, do you not have your own ship?" Lewrie teased. "That's a very good idea, worthy of a Post-Captain, or a Commander at the very least. One of these days, you simply *must* stop hanging around t'watch me diddle, amusin' though that may be, and allow me to advance you into the next big prize we may take."

"Well," Westcott said as if seriously considering the offer, "I suppose I could use the extra pay. Sing out when your letters are done and I'll see them off. Uhm, any idea where the *Sterling* frigate might be anchored?"

"Haven't a clue, sorry," Lewrie replied, already digging around in his desk for fresh letter paper and his pen. "Hmm, best you pass the word for my cook, and give him advance warning of what's wanting."

"Doing it directly, sir," Westcott said with a cock-headed grin on his way out.

CHAPTER ELEVEN

*I*t was winter-dark enough by the supper's appointed hour, too dark to make out the fresh, new red broad pendant bearing the white ball that now flew from *Sapphire*'s main mast, yet Lewrie looked aloft for it as he turned out near the entry-port in his best dress uniform, new bicorne hat, and presentation sword, with the star and sash of his knighthood prominently displayed for a rare once. He could make out a line of rowing boats approaching, though, already sorted out in order of seniority, not quite within hailing distance.

"Hoy, *Sapphire*!" the leading boat's Cox'n called out at last, "*Undaunted*, arriving! Permission to come aboard?"

"Tell them to come alongside, smartly now, Mister Chenery," Lewrie said to prompt the Mid of the Harbour Watch into action.

"Aye aye!" Chenery began in his newly-acquired "tarry" fashion, "Come alongside, smartly now!"

Oh Christ! Lewrie thought; *What a twit!*

"The 'smartly now' was an admonition to *you*, Mister Chenery," Lewrie growled, "not for Captain Chalmers. 'Smartly' means 'quickly', and 'handsomely' means slow and carefully, and I'll thankee t'remember that in future!"

"Sorry, sir," Chenery managed to say, shrinking into his coat.

Extra lanthorns had been lit on deck to ease the arrival and departure of his guests, so Lewrie could see the displeased look on Capt. Chalmers's face as his hat and head appeared above the lip of the entry-port, and the stamp of Marine boots, the slap of hands on presented muskets, and the dual calls from Bosun Terrell and one of his Mates did nothing to make him any merrier.

"Welcome aboard *Sapphire*, sir," Lewrie said, going forward and doffing his hat, "Sorry about that. The newest of my new-come Mids," he apologised with a hapless shrug. "All's literal to him, yet. Not with us a Dog Watch."

Capt. Richard Chalmers was the epitome of the public's image of a Navy Captain, wide of shoulder, lean and tall, and almost rakishly good-looking. That worthy lifted one expressive eyebrow and gave Lewrie a chary look as he doffed his hat in salute. "And you've not yet had him flogged, sir?" Chalmers asked, making Chenery blanch.

"I'll mast-head him, if ye like that better, sir," Lewrie said, realising that Chalmers was jesting. "Put the Surgeon's leeches on him?"

"No no," Chalmers said, relenting and smiling, "thank you for your kind invitation, sir,"

Capt. Yearwood of HMS *Sterling* was next aboard, and the complete opposite of the immaculate Capt. Chalmers. Yearwood was a dour and heavy-set fellow in his late thirties, Lewrie thought, dressed in a coat with gold lace gone green from long exposure to salt air, with a white shirt and white waist-coat gone pale tan from long use and washing, and in a pair of issue slop-trousers crammed into Hessian boots.

Didn't shave too close, did he? Lewrie thought; *Or, is his beard so dense it doesn't matter?*

"Captain Yearwood, welcome aboard *Sapphire*," Lewrie offered as he doffed his hat once more.

"Captain Lewrie, sir," Yearwood answered in a deep, basso rumble as he lifted his older cocked hat in reply. "Heard of you for ages, and I'm delighted to make your acquaintance at last."

"Hope it was the good parts only," Lewrie replied.

"Oh, I'm sure it was, sir!" Yearwood rejoined, chuckling.

Commander Teague of the *Blaze* sloop was an up-and-comer in his late twenties, well-dressed and obviously someone's favourite to gain command of a ship so early, a fit fellow with a pleasant face, almost a book-end to Capt. Chalmers. Commander Blamey was older, in his late thirties or so, and Lewrie could almost make him a match to Capt. Yearwood, though he was much better-attired, barrel-chested, somewhat squat, with a hard and rather brutal face. His voice was higher than Yearwood's bear-like grumble, though, and almost had an Anglo-Irish lilt.

Lewrie led them aft to his great-cabins and did the introductions to Lieutenant Westcott and his Sailing Master, Mr. Yelland, whom Lewrie devoutly hoped had sponged some of his aroma off for the occasion. "Well then, sirs, shall we take our seats and have a glass of something before supper begins?"

Pettus and Jessop had set out place cards in their plates, putting Chalmers and Yearwood at the head of the table to his either hand, the two Commanders next down-table opposite each other, Yelland and Westcott further down, and Midshipman Hillhouse at the foot of the table.

"Shall we lift a toast to our gallant smugglers, sirs?" Lewrie asked as Pettus and Jessop filled their glasses with French champagne, which had been chilled in a wooden tub filled with seawater and what snow had gathered on the decks during the afternoon flurries.

"I heard that you were recently in London, sir," Chalmers said, smacking his lips after a sip of his wine. "What's new in the city?"

"Didn't have time for the theatre, but the political satires were amusing," Lewrie told him, describing what had struck him most, "the Prince of Wales is takin' a beating over his new style of wig. It's called a 'Jazey'. Puffed up on top and draping like a willow tree, down over the ears, the forehead, the back of the neck? Like an un-combed farm worker. Unfortunately, it's all the 'crack' now."

If the rest of them hadn't gone further from their ships than the the shops of Portsmouth, they had all devoured the latest newspapers, so they could converse on an host of safe topics before Yeovill came in with the first course, a tangy cockle soup, and a brimming barge of fresh shore bread. The hearty conversation continued over roast quail with pease porridge, and a nice Spanish white wine, then a fish course of breaded and grilled haddock over a rice pilaf. Lastly, the roast beef turned up, individual steaks with potato skins stuffed with bacon, horseradish, and mashed potato filling, some broad beans, and a very pleasant claret. Yeovill finished things off with eggy caramel *flan*, sweet bisquits, and a sherry to accompany them. Once the last plate and serving bowl had been removed, and the tablecloth had been whisked away, out came the cheese, nuts, and port bottle.

"A hellish-good repast, Sir Alan, thank you," Commander Teague commented as he began cracking walnuts for all.

"As delightful as one could expect in Mid-winter, aye," Capt. Chalmers agreed, dabbing at his mouth with his napkin.

"I suppose you've all received your orders by now," Lewrie began, looking round his guests. "Somewhat mystifying?"

"That we're to be under your command, aye, sir," Yearwood said with a firm nod of his head as he pulled an ivory toothpick from his vest pocket. "The where and why, though, no."

"Perhaps by the time we get where we're going, there'll be lashings of fresh fruit and vegetables available, and I can set you all a better table," Lewrie explained, shifting in his chair as the port bottle made its larboardly way to him.

They had done Fashion, the Arts, Music, Parliament and the Prime Minister, edging round Politics very carefully, then back to Horses and Racing, Boxers, and the new steel-spring suspensions now available for coaches. Lewrie thought it time for Business, and the un-heard of "Shop Talk".

"Back to Gibraltar, sir?" Commander Blamey enquired with a hopeful expression on his face.

"Oh, I was thinking Lisbon, instead," Lewrie broadly hinted with an impish grin. "I wrote Admiralty requesting a store ship to be stationed there for our use, placing us closer to the North coast of Spain. That's right, back where we just came from, gentlemen. Our brief is from Cape Fisterre to the French border, with permission to cruise off Bayonne and Arcachon when we think it profitable. There are French supply convoys landing goods all along that coast, and it's up to us t'stop all that, and gobble 'em up."

Supply ships full of goods and military stores meant prize-money, and that realisation made them gape, then pound the table with their fists and cheer their future good fortune.

"First thing tomorrow morning," Lewrie went on after the din had subsided, "I wish all your Sailing Masters t'get together with Mister Yelland, there, and lay your hands on every chart we can find . . . Lisbon, and on North up to Cape Fisterre, and everything existing about the Spanish and French coasts. Every map maker, every printer, special order what's lacking, and make sure that we all have charts as accurate as possible, and if there are discrepancies on some of them, we can pencil in fresher information so that we know where to find every rock, shoal, or old wreck."

All of them seemed eager and agreeable, though Lewrie got the sense that Capt. Chalmers might have thought that talking "Shop" at-table was on the crude side.

"The weather looks as if it'll continue miserable for a few more days," Lewrie went on, "which'll give us time to make sure that we find our charts and correct them . . . take aboard the last stores you think you'll need. For myself, I may take on a whole, spare main mast . . . never can tell when I get struck again, hey?"

"I can finally finally find out if my gunners can aim small," Commander Teague piped up, "now we know for sure that we'll encounter lots of targets."

"Aim small?" Lewrie asked.

"Well, perhaps not as well as you did at Corunna, sir," Teague said with a seated bow in Lewrie's direction, "the way you swotted that French battery away the last day of the evacuation, but . . . I've heard some officers wonder whether *aimed* fire at close quarters might be more effective than broadsides. Direct three or four guns at the enemy's quarterdeck, the base of his main mast, or right into the gun-ports to dis-mount his guns. I've had my nine-pounders notched on the bells of the muzzles and at the tops of the uppermost breeching re-enforcements, so my gun-captains could actually aim their pieces as one does a musket."

"Hmm, clear the quarterdeck with roundshot and grape," Capt. Yearwood mused aloud, "right from the start? Maybe double-shot the carronades and dis-mast the foe, right off?"

"Hit 'em where they're most vulnerable, aye!" Lewrie said with delight. "Take out the helm, the enemy captain, and watch officers at one go? Hmm! Suddenly, *I* feel very vulnerable!"

"Like using a surgeon's scalpel instead of a battle-axe, one might suppose?" Capt. Chalmers posed, sounding amused. "All well and good for the Army's artillery, all scientific and predictable so their heavy siege guns can strike the same section of a fortress's wall over and over to bring it down."

"Shooting from gun positions that don't pitch and roll, haw haw!" Commander Blamey grumbled dismissively. "Give me the battle-axe, or the sledge hammer, every time! The only way that'd ever work, Teague, is to be gunn'l-to-gunn'l with the foe, and anything beyond an hundred yards would still be by guess and by God."

"Well then, sir," Commander Teague rejoined with a wee grin, "let us place ourselves hull-to-hull and *see* if it works."

"My heartiest sentiment, sir," Blamey declared, "and will you have a glass with me?"

"That I will, sir!" Teague happily exclaimed.

"A general toast, sirs," Capt. Yearwood roared. "To good gunnery and smashed foes!"

We'll be slingin' 'em into their boats like water casks, they keep this up, Lewrie thought as his glass was refilled, just as eager to second Yearwood's words. Hardly had their glasses been tipped back to "heel taps" than Capt. Chalmers proposed "Confusion and Death to the French!" which required another quick refill all round, making Pettus and Jessop scramble to open a fresh bottle.

"Ah, gentlemen, before we're 'half seas over'," Lewrie interrupted, "a few last thoughts upon our endeavour. Once the weather lets us out to sea, I wish to sail directly for the coast of Northern Spain without any waste of time at Lisbon, at first. Let us get to grips at once, and trust that when we *do* re-plenish at Lisbon, we go there with a string of prizes in tow."

"Hear hear!" Yearwood roared, pounding the table with meaty fists.

"And, I think that we set a 'rondy' at five degrees West, about sixty miles out to sea from that coast," Lewrie went on, hoping that they remembered half of what he was saying in the morning. "First off, I think that you, Captain Yearwood, should pair off with Commander Teague's *Blaze,* and hunt West of the 'rondy'. You, Captain Chalmers, can pair off with Commander Blamey's *Peregrine,* to hunt together to the East, and have a squint at Bayonne and Arcachon. You've the strongest of our frigates, after all. For my part, I'll cruise alone from Gijon to Santander and back. You, sirs, have swift ships, while my poor old ship . . . plods. Once we separate, we'll give it a fortnight of prowling and raiding before we meet back up to compare notes and plan any future moves. All agreed?" he asked. Seven drink-reddened faces peered, or goggled, back at him, vociferously nodding and crying approval. "I'll send you all brief notes upon that head in the morning.

"Now!" he cried, raising a full glass. "Charge your glasses, gentlemen. I give you . . . Success to our Prospects!"

"Success to our Prospects!" they all yelled back at him, and drank their full bumpers back to "heel taps" again, laughing, cheering, and Yearwood burst forth in song in a deep and burly voice, surprising everyone that he could actually carry a tune and sing hellish-well, so well that they all joined in.

Wine, wine, it cures the gout, the spirit, and the colic.
Wine, wine, it cures the gout, the spirit, and the colic,
Hand it to a-all men, hand it to a-all men,
Hand it to a-all men, a very specif-physick!

"Good Lord, what's that?" Capt. Chalmers exclaimed, breaking off from the second verse.

"Oh, that's my cat, Chalky," Lewrie leaned over to tell him as Chalky, who had been fed in the starboard quarter gallery among all the stores, came to Lewrie for comfort from the loud noises, and had leapt atop the table, then into Lewrie's lap for a reassuring snuggle, trying to wriggle between his uniform coat and waist-coat. "They are awfully loud, ain't they, puss? I thought you'd be hidin' in my bed-space, by now," he crooned as he stroked the cat's chin and neck.

"So *that's* why they call you the 'Ram-Cat' is it, sir, haw haw?" Capt. Yearwood boomed once the song was done, reaching over with one huge paw to ruffle Chalky on the head, which made him lash out with his claws, and Yearwood snatched his hand back before any damage was done.

"Careful, sir," Lt. Westcott cautioned from down-table. "Like our foes have learned, the 'Ram-Cat' has sharp claws."

"Hah!" Commander Blamey laughed, "Like the McPherson clan's motto . . .'touch not the cat bot a glove'!"

"Toast, toast!" Commander Teague insisted, "I give you . . . May we *all* have sharp claws with which we draw *blood*!"

"Sharp *claws*, and *blood*!" they all chorused.

"See what ye started, kitten?" Lewrie whispered to Chalky, who tucked his tail round his front paws and hid his head in Lewrie's coat, uttering a long moan that might have signified fear, or anger.

This is goin' well, Lewrie could tell himself, pleased with his squadron mates' spirit; *Even if Chalmers is* still *givin' me chary looks. Maybe he's a dog person. Before he departs, I should introduce him to Bisquit!*

CHAPTER TWELVE

*W*ith all last-minute wants and needs loaded aboard, the squadron had fallen down to St. Helen's Patch near the Isle of Wight, where they had awaited a break in the weather and a decent slant of wind. A day later, and HMS *Sapphire* could finally hoist the signal for all ships to hoist anchors and make sail.

From that moment on, all five ships had enjoyed a blustery but brief passage, down the English Channel, and into the wide Atlantic, arrayed like beads on a string, with the brig-sloops in line-ahead of *Sapphire* by about a mile, and allowed to scout about if they spotted anything interesting, much like gun-dogs after pheasant. *Undaunted* and *Sterling* followed in the flagship's wake, trailing by about one cable's distance from her and one frigate from the other by a like separation. Lewrie was certain that *they* were having no fun.

Lewrie was tempted to play a "Captain Blanding", the squadron Commodore under whom he'd served in 1803, and a man in love with the Popham Code signal book, and un-scheduled orders to perform manoeuvres from pre-dawn to sundown, but no. It would be a rare thing for them to work together as a proper squadron, like the Third Rate 74s that plodded and wheeled on un-ending blockade duties. Besides, he didn't wish to be dubbed a man afflicted with the "flag flux", or one who ran off at the signal halliards like a gossipy old "chick-a-biddy" at a "cat lapping" tea party.

Their Southerly course cross the Bay of Biscay was over three hundred or more miles seaward of the French coast, so they rarely espied a sail on the horizon, and when they did it was always one of their own Navy's ships, making their way to or from the blockade. The home-bound convoys of British-flagged merchantmen, even with the comforting presence of naval escorts close at hand, stayed a careful two hundred miles further out into the Bay, well West of the 10th Meridian, down which Lewrie and his squadron sailed.

The days were filled with sail-tending, trimming, reefing then making sail, with live-fire gun drills to get *Sapphire*'s people up to snuff after several weeks in port, with cutlass drills, musketry and pistol practice, as well as the usual sluicing and scrubbing of decks, meals, rum issues, and the changes of watches, with Sunday Divisions and "Rig Church", followed by a few precious hours of "Make and Mend" before the start of Sunday's First Dog Watch.

At heart, Alan Lewrie, when left to his own devices, could be as lazy as a butcher's dog, a minor vice that the Navy had beaten out of him long before, but a vice that could arise on a long passage such as this one, now that there were no watch officers standing over him with a stiffened rope starter, and the necessary separation from his officers and crew left him, the Captain, with time on his hands.

He threw himself into weapons training, honing his skill with his hanger, shooting at passing flotsam targets with his pistols or his breech-loading rifled Ferguson musket, sometimes his Girandoni air-rifle. He paced the ship right round several times a day, from the flag lockers and taffrail lanthorns on the poop deck to the round house abaft the crowned lion figurehead, over and over. In his cabins, he hoisted wooden pails filled with various weights of shot over his head, swung them about, to keep fit, 'til he blew and puffed, short of breath. Despite his dread of it, he ascended the main mast right up to the cat harpings, now and then even essaying the futtock shrouds to the fighting top, then down the other side to maintain the strength of his arms and hands, and to test the soundness of his leg, wounded off Buenos Aires by a musket ball three years before, which had healed so slowly that for a time he'd feared that he would end up a gimp-legged cripple, putting an end to his naval career.

Even with all that, though, there were still so many long hours with nothing to do, and no demands upon his attention, that he *had* to retire to his cabins before he became a pest to the watchstanders, and began to be slurred as "old fussy". There, he had a small selection of new books to read, along with some of his older favourites, of the bawdier variety it here must be noted. There was Chalky to play with, though his cat was now of an age,—*Twelve years old, now?* he realised—and was no longer quite as eager to chase after things and fetch them back. Chalky was now fonder of laps, sometimes a playfight when Lewrie donned a thick leather glove and rolled him about and let Chalky bite and scratch and make aggressive noises.

Touch not the cat bot a glove, indeed, Lewrie thought!

There was Bisquit, who was more eager to play, thundering about the great-cabins to chase his soggy, thick rope, or his equally damp stuffed rabbit hide. Bisquit had begun as the Midshipmen's pet when he'd had the *Reliant* frigate in the West Indies, and still roamed the lower decks to call upon his many friends among the crew, especially at mealtimes, but a Winter spent in the country on Lewrie's father's estate at Anglesgreen in Surrey as Lewrie had recuperated made him more the Captain's dog, who assumed the freedom of the great-cabins as his right, and it was a rare night that Bisquit slept in his wee house under the starboard ladderway to the poop deck. By Lights Out every evening, Bisquit would be whining and scratching at the door to be let in, and the Marine sentry didn't even bother to announce him any longer, but simply opened the door so Bisquit could frisk through.

There was Lewrie's music, if one could call it that. Long ago his late wife, Caroline, had gifted him with an humble penny-whistle, and after all those years, Lewrie could tootle along right well, but for Bisquit's responses, his long whines and even longer howls as if the music pained his ears, or he tried to sing along, it was hard to tell which. The penny-whistle was best indulged in when the dog was elsewhere.

There were letters to write, of course, to be posted someday if they ever spoke a passing mail packet, or dropped anchor at Lisbon; long "sea letters" to family and friends, added to each day as events struck him as notable 'til they were several pages thick, filled in on both sides in the smallest writing he could manage.

He'd gotten some whose authors had penny-pinched, also written on both sides, but also written firstly horizontal, then vertical atop that, and the very Devil to decypher stacked atop each other, and as hard to figure out which direction the writer wrote first!

Lewrie could pore over his newly-marked charts of the Spanish coast, and usually spent a whole hour each day at that, making guesses as to which ports the French used more often for their coasting ships. Did they put in each night, as they did along the coasts of France itself when he'd prowled those shores? Or, did they employ larger merchantmen, and dash from Bayonne, Arcachon, or the Gironde River estuary straightaway, with escorts? And, what sort of escorts would the French put to sea, and of what strength? Frigates, *corvettes*, or the sort of armed *chasse-marees* that were employed as privateers or raiders in the Channel or in the Baltic, the plague of British shipping?

After all that, there was a lot to be said for the restorative powers of naps on the starboard side settee, or the cushioned tops of the lazarette lockers right aft, though they were a tad narrow.

The closer they got to Spain, nearing the 45th Latitude, there was a subtle change in the weather. It was still nippy, and sometimes raw and chilly, but at last the sash-windows in the stern transom could be lowered several inches from the tops, during the days, at least, to purge the long-pent stuffiness (and frankly some stinks) from the great-cabins. Lewrie longed for the day when the windows could be fully lowered, the door to his stern gallery opened, and the twine-strung screen door which kept Chalky from dashing out to chase sea bird, leaping atop the gallery rails and falling overboard, could let in all the fresh air that he wished. Why, with any luck at all, soon he could put a chair out there and read, and loaf, and snore, in full view of his subordinates!

And in the evenings, after dining in some of his officers and Mids, Lewrie could tap one of the stone crocks of American corn whisky that he'd found in London, savour a nightcap, then roll into his bed-cot, there to be rocked and lulled to sleep by the swaying of the ship and the scend of the sea. He thought it perverse, but while he loved the snug softness of a feather mattress in a shoreside bed, he still got his best rest in his almost-wide-enough-for-two hanging bed-cot and its thinner cotton batt mattress, and the sag of the heavy sailcloth support. Even if he did have to sleep in his shirt and slop-trousers under two blankets as long as it was cold, craving the time when he could strip down to his underdrawers and pull up one sheet in milder weather. Either way, there would be a cat tucked into the back of one knee, or the small of his back.

"Ah, so many hopeful faces," Lewrie quipped as he emerged from his cabins with his sextant case and his boxed chronometer. Awaiting him at

Noon Sights were all his watch-standing officers, the Sailing Master, and all of the Midshipmen with their own sextants and slates for calculations. The youngest of them looked anxious.

"Wouldn't get my hopes up too high, sir," Mr. Yelland growled as he cast a glance aloft at the overcast. "It looks like another dead reckoning day." The Sailing Master swept a hand in the direction of his sea chart, pinned to the traverse board of the binnacle cabinet. There had been very few semi-clear noons on-passage, so the track of *Sapphire*'s progress was littered with hourly notations of her speed, some with sarcastic question marks.

"It's a thin cirrus overcast, though, Mister Yelland," Lt. Harcourt pointed out. "You can see the sun ball through it, direct. You can look straight at it."

"Vague, though," Yelland replied, scratching his un-shaven chin. "Drag the iffy blob down to the horizon and make a wild-arsed guess?"

The younger Mids found that amusing.

Lewrie consulted his chronometer, then his pocket watch, to determine the exact time. He noted that his and the Sailing Master's were only two seconds out of agreement.

"And . . . time," Yelland said at last, just before the sand ran out of the half-hour glass up forward at the belfry, and a ship's boy began to strike Eight Bells. Up went the sextants to people's eyes, sure fingers drew the "blob" down to the horizon, then locked the angle with the set screws. Chalk began to screech on the slates as the mathematical formula drummed into them was solved.

Lewrie kept his mouth shut, waiting for whatever result could be announced. He had not brought a slate, or pencil and paper, and would be the first to confess that while the Navy had *thrashed* mathematics into him, it was best to wait for consensus, for sometimes his own estimates *were* "wild-arsed guesses", not quite as exact as others' could be, putting his own work within sixty or one hundred miles of the correct position on his worst days.

Close enough for "church work", he told himself with a secret grin.

"Hmm," Yelland announced with a shrug as he looked over what he and the officers had derived from their sums, "Fourty-four degrees, ten minutes North, or thereabouts, sir . . . five degrees, twenty minutes West . . . or so we *think*, mind." He leaned over the chart on the traverse board and ran a thick finger to those co-ordinates. "About here . . . ninety miles off the coast, round the longitude of Gijon."

"Good enough, then," Lewrie said, tracing the dead reckoning track from the last noon's guesstimate, and finding that their sights were close enough to corresponding. "Time for us to part, I think. Mister Kibworth, go to the flag lockers and make up this signal, if you please. Good Luck, Good Hunting, Be Here in a Fortnight. Got that?"

"Aye, sir!" the Mid answered, furiously scribbling on the back side of his slate, then scampering up to the poop deck. He paused, though, half-way up, and returned. "Ehm, if I may suggest, sir, that we use the single flag for Pursue the Enemy More Closely, *then* Good Hunting, and the 'rondy' point?"

"Ahem!" the Second Officer, Lt. Harcourt, barked, irritated that a Mid would dare make a suggestion to a Commission Sea Officer.

"Aye, that sounds more to the point," Lewrie breezily agreed. "Pursuin' the buggers is what we're here for. Do so, young sir."

"Has a nerve, sir," Lt. Harcourt groused close to Lewrie's ear.

"He has wits, more-like, Mister Harcourt," Lewrie told him. "He and the other lads. They're not the pink-cheeked children who came aboard two years ago. Somewhere along their way, they must be able to learn to think for themselves, and contribute."

Lewrie looked forward to where the other Midshipmen were gathering up their sextants, slates, and sticks of chalk, some of them looking pleased with their reckonings, and only the newest, Holbrooke and Chenery, getting cautioned by the Sailing Master, nodding dutifully, though looking sheepish.

"Well, most of 'em," Lewrie added with a jut of his chin in their direction, and a brief smirk. "I believe you have the watch, sir?"

"Aye, sir," Harcourt replied, looking un-convinced by Lewrie's words.

"Continue on this course to close the coast, somewhere round Gijon, however one pronounces that," Lewrie ordered. "The last cast of the log showed seven knots, so we'll be at it a good, long while. If the weather gets up, you may reduce sail at your discretion, but I'd admire being in-formed."

"Aye, sir," Harcourt dutifully said, nodding assent.

"We're in no great rush t'get in sight of land," Lewrie went on, cross-ing to the traverse board for another peek at the sea-chart. "With this ship, we *never* are," he japed. "Seven, eight knots . . . it will be round nine hours from now to fetch the coast, middle of the bloody night, really, when we change course Due East and stand off-and-on 'til dawn. Warn your re-placement."

"That I will, sir," Lt. Harcourt promised.

"Carry on, then, Mister Harcourt," Lewrie bade him, doffing his hat in a departing salute. He did not retire to his cabins, but went up to the poop deck for a better look round, just as the signal hoist soared up the halliards, bright, clean flags brilliant against the gloom of the day. Lt. Westcott was already there, indulging in one of his *cigarros*, a newly acquired habit.

"Sir," Westcott said, tapping the brim of his hat.

"Mister Westcott," Lewrie replied, nodding acknowledgement.

"What happened to your new bicorne, sir, might I ask?" the First Officer enquired with a taut grin, taking note that Lewrie had reverted to one of his older cocked hats.

"The bloody thing doesn't keep the rain off my ears," Lewrie confessed with a grin of his own. "I'll trot it out for formal, full-dress occasions . . . and to make Captain Chalmers happy, I suppose."

Lewrie looked down to the quarterdeck and at Lt. Harcourt.

Such a tight-arsed man, Lewrie thought with a shake of his head; *A good, conscientous officer, but a hard stickler. And a dullard. No imagination.*

When Lewrie first got command of *Sapphire*, the officers and her people had been split in support of her former Captain, a fierce disciplinarian, and her former First Officer, who had been opposed to some of the harsher practises, and Lt. Harcourt and his favourite Midshipman, Hillhouse, had been in the former Captain's camp. Thank God that those two officers had wounded each other in a duel, ending their careers, allowing Lewrie and Westcott to take her over and unite their new crew into a happier, more efficient concern.

"What in the world is *Undaunted* hoisting?" Midshipman Kibworth wondered aloud after *Sapphire*'s hoist had been struck, the signal for Execute. He clapped his telescope to his eye.

"Can you make it out, Mister Kibworth?" Lewrie asked.

"It's *Peregrine*'s number, sir, and P . . . S . . . A . . . L . . . M, Psalm, sir," Kibworth decyphered slowly, "number twenty-three, dash two."

"Captain Chalmers's little joke," Lewrie said. "He's telling Blamey t'lay him down in green pastures, and *lead* him to still waters."

"Now, *Peregrine*'s making *Undaunted*'s number, and . . . Psalm 23 dash 4!" Kibworth exclaimed.

" 'Yea, though I walk through the valley of the shadow of death, I will fear no evil; for thou art with me, thy rod and thy staff they comfort me'," Lt. Westcott quoted.

"Your bigger, heavier guns, *they* comfort me," Lewrie said with a laugh. "Well, I expect they *should*!"

Midshipman Hugh Lewrie stood near the flag lockers right aft of HMS *Undaunted*'s quarterdeck, reading the hoist from the *Peregrine*.

"Hah!" Capt. Chalmers exclaimed in delight. "I did not know that Commander Blamey would be such a biblical scholar. Better and better! Proof that we're not *all* heathens."

Chalmers cast a quick glance over at the flagship, wrinkling his nose before turning back to the matter at hand. "Alter course to East, Sou'east, if you will, Mister Crosley," he ordered the First Officer. "I wish to strike the coast somewhere near Santander by first light tomorrow, so we can begin scouring for prizes."

"Aye, sir!" Lt. Crosley replied, then began calling out his own orders to man the braces and swing the ship's head about.

"Jump to it, Mister Lewrie," Chalmers sang out with great cheer, "aloft with you, now. We'll show the Commodore how to Pursue the Enemy More Closely, hah hah!"

"Aye aye, sir," Midshipman Lewrie responded and going forward to the mainmast shrouds, wondering if *he* would have to learn how to quote chapter and verse in future, and what his Captain had against his father.

It was *a good signal he sent us,* he thought.

Wish I could send something personal, Lewrie thought as he saw *Undaunted* altering course, but he could not. *Damn your eyes, Chalmers, you better take good care of my boy!*

CHAPTER THIRTEEN

$\mathcal{H}$ ere we are, again, sir," Lt. Westcott said as he scanned the dawn's horizon for threats, or prey.

"Off Spain?" Lewrie asked, thinking that was his meaning.

"No sir, on our own with none of our ships in sight," Westcott replied with a snigger. "The last time we hoisted a broad pendant off Spanish Florida and the Carolinas, the other ships of our little squadron might as well have been on the other side of the Atlantic most of the time. Oh well, fewer to share in our prizes."

"If there's something to take," Lewrie said with a shrug as he raised his telescope to his eye for another long, sweeping look along the line of the horizon. To the East, the West, and the North from where they had come during the night after the squadron had separated, there was not a sail in sight or even a suspicious cloud to darken the morning, that might be mistaken for a sail.

The skies were still almost fully overcast, casting the seas a gloomy steel grey with no sunlight to glitter off wave tops in joyful sparkles, and the slowly churning white caps and white horses were a dingy sud's-water grey, which made Lewrie shake his head in disappointment that Noon Sights might prove to be as "iffy" as yesterday's, forcing them to depend again on Dead Reckoning. Which dependence might prove dangerous, for the Sailing Master had estimated that the rocky coasts of Spain lay only twelve or fifteen miles to the South.

Lewrie swivelled round to peer in that direction, hoping for a prominent cape or headland, or a mountain peak, that might reveal to them just where along that coast they might be, but the Southern horizon was even murkier, the overcast skies and clouds lower, shrouding the Costa Verde in enigmatic gloom. It even appeared darker down in that direction, as if they would sail into a coastal storm, a storm which Lewrie hoped was rolling inland ahead of them, not sweeping off the mountain ranges out to sea.

"Well Hell," Lewrie said at last as he lowered his glass. He looked aloft at the commissioning pendant which streamed to larboard almost at right angles to the ship. HMS *Sapphire* trundled along on a beam reach, and a slow one at that, pressed over a few degrees from from level by a weak wind that, at the last half-hour cast of the chip log, showed only five and a half knots.

'*Give me a fast ship, for I wish to go in harm's way*', *that American pirate, John Paul Jones, said,* Lewrie thought; *Harm's way, mine arse! He only wanted* t'get *somewhere before he died of old age!*

He scowled as the commissioning pendant began to curl and lazily whip even slower, its yards' long length beginning to droop as the winds turned weaker and more fitful.

"Change o' weather coming, sir," Mr. Yelland pointed out with a jut of his chin towards the Southern horizon, "Change o' wind direction, too. That yonder gloom may bring a gale of wind."

"Nothing for it, then, Mister Yelland," Lewrie replied, scowling even darker. "We can't risk closing the coast, for now. Let's come about to Sou'east 'til we know which way that storm's going."

"Both sheets aft, aye sir," Yelland gloomily agreed. On that point of sail, they'd have the prevailing wind on their starboard quarter, almost fully astern.

"At least it's warmer," Yelland pointed out. "Sort of."

"Small blessings," Lewrie agreed. "Carry on, Mister Westcott. Let's alter course."

"Aye, sir," Lt. Westcott said, going to the compass binnacle cabinet for a brass speaking-trumpet so his orders could be heard as far as the forecastle.

Lewrie went up to his favourite perch on the poop deck above his cabins to continue scanning the seas from a slightly higher vantage point, thinking that the morning, early though it was, *was* definitely warmer than it had been when they had left England. It was getting on for early Spring of 1809, and they were hundreds of miles South of sleet, snow, and icy winds. It still could be nippy and raw in the mornings when he was roused from his bed-cot in the dark, but he no longer needed both blankets and the quilt-like coverlet to sleep snug. The thermometer attached to the Sailing Master's sea-cabin bulkhead now usually registered in the 40s before dawn, and might get into the high 50s by mid-day. At the moment, fully-uniformed and with his boat cloak on, Lewrie didn't even feel the need to shiver!

Once the ship had been brought round to steer Sou'east, the winds did pick up a bit, again, coming from a quim-hair 'twixt Due West and West by North, and Midshipmen Griffin and Chenery reported that the last cast of the log now showed six and a quarter knots.

The decks had been sluiced and holystoned, the wash-deck pumps had been stowed away, and the galley funnel was fuming in promise of breakfast, even if it was a Banyan Day with no meat served. Lewrie's stomach was growling in protest by the time he went down to the quarterdeck for a last look round, to determine that everything was in good order, then retired to his cabins.

"You oughta play with him, Chalky," Lewrie said as he cast off his boat cloak and hat for Pettus to see to. The ship's dog Bisquit was frisking and prancing round Lewrie's now-made bed-cot, where his cat, Chalky, was taking refuge, fur on-end and hissing dis-pleasure to be "treed" so early in the morning. "Leave off, boy. Come here, Bisquit," he summoned as he sat down on the starboard side settee to give the dog some attention, and the dog gladly galloped over to him.

With nothing still in sight, the hands were piped to breakfast. It was traditional that officers dined later than the crew, sometimes by an whole hour, so Lewrie had plenty of time to devote to the dog 'til Bisquit was yawning and sprawled on the settee and plenty of time to go aft and mollify his nettled cat, too. Lewrie had Chalky purring on his back with his paws in the air before Yeovill breezed in with the brass barge. Chalky rolled over to all fours and dashed for Yeovill, with Bisquit prancing round him, too, their past animosity quite forgotten as Yeovill filled their bowls with warm oatmeal gruel, livened with shreds of sausages or dried jerky, and cut-up hard-boiled eggs.

"Makes their coats glossy, the eggs do, sir," Yeovill cheerfully said as he laid out Lewrie's breakfast in the dining coach.

"Might even work for me, Yeovill," Lewrie said with a laugh as he was presented with a bowl of oatmeal and a pair of hard-boiled eggs on the side. So soon out of port, there was still fairly fresh butter to stir in, along with liberal dollops of treacle, and Pettus had brewed a small pot of coffee on the sideboard, nowhere near as hot as he preferred it, but there was goat's milk and sugar to make up for the lack of scalding-hotness. Admittedly, Lewrie cheated on Banyan Days, for he had stowed away two hundredweight of sausages and jerky for the cat and the dog, and could always dig into that stash, as he did that morning.

He was done with his breakfast in a twinkling, and sipping on a second cup of coffee when the Marine sentry announced Midshipman Ward.

"The First Officer's duty, sir, and I am to report that the weather down to the South is clearing, and the coast can now be made out."

"Ah!" Lewrie replied, perking up. "My compliments to Mister Westcott, and inform him that I shall be on deck, directly." He polished off his cup of coffee, tore the napkin from under his chin, and rose to his feet, requesting only his hat in his haste to follow close on Midshipman Ward's heels, with Bisquit dashing out, too.

"Sir," Lt. Westcott said, tapping the brim of his hat, "we can make out the coast, now, though the capes and mountain peaks are still iffy." He nodded to Mr. Yelland to continue his report.

"It appears that what storm front there was preceded us ashore, sir," Yelland said, holding out a large book of sketches of the coast, flipping idly from one to the next. "As you can see, the mountains, the Picos de Europa, are completely shrouded by it as it makes its way inland. There appears to be mists and rain lingering along the shore, but I do believe that we are about ten miles off Candás-Carreño, a few miles West of the port of Gijon, roughly where we hoped to be."

Lewrie lifted a telescope from the binnacle cabinet and peered shoreword. He got impressions of very green meadows above the stony coast, with darker green pine forests above those, and winter-blasted deciduous forests further inland on the slopes that led to the mountains, which were merely to be guessed at; all his observations veiled in mists which swirled tantalisingly, revealing a bit, then closing to hide what lay over there, like a stage curtain.

"No sign of life," Lewrie said as he lowered the glass, and collapsed its tubes. "Who'd be a sailor on such a day, even a French sailor, or Spanish fisherman."

"That is odd, sir," Westcott pointed out. "Now the weather has blown inland, there *should* be some fishermen out at sea. Unless the French have prohibited them, of course."

"No, the French need fresh fish, too," Lewrie dis-agreed. "I'd imagine they're still allowed to fish, but they're kept on a short leash, much closer to shore, right under what guns the Frogs have put along the coast. *If* they've placed batteries every few miles, as they do on their own coasts."

"Wouldn't that tie up too many troops, sir, when they need them further down in Spain to complete their conquest?" Westcott asked.

"Napoleon's got more than enough to spare, I'm sure," Yelland spat, "what with all the so-called 'volunteers' he scrapes up from all the lands he's conquered, already. All Europe's his recruiting ground, whether they want to fight for the bastard or not."

"Deck, there!" the lookout at the mainmast cross-trees sang out. "I think I sees a sail!"

"He *thinks?*" Mr. Yelland scoffed, peering aloft.

"Where away?" Lt. Westcott shouted to the lookout.

"Two point off th' starb'd . . . it's gone!" the lookout began, then trailed off, standing on the cross-trees with an arm wrapped about the topmast, and trying to use his other hand to funnel his vision. "Two point off, no! *Four* point off th' starb'd bows, *and* one point off . . . Kee-rist!" he could be heard cursing in frustration.

"Blithering idiot," the Sailing Master decided.

"Mister Fywell," Lewrie snapped at the nearest Midshipmen at hand, "aloft with you and discover what he's about, smartly now."

Fywell patted a chest pocket of his jacket to assure himself that he had his own small telescope, then dashed to the mainmast stays to scamper aloft.

"It is awfully hazy over yonder," Westcott commented as he and the other officers on the quarterdeck lifted their more powerful day glasses to see if they could make out what was confusing the lookout.

"One point off, two points, then four points?" Lewrie muttered. "It sounds like a clutch of fishing boats putting out." He looked aloft for a moment, then returned to his telescope, straining to see through the mist and haze that thickened, then thinned mystifyingly.

"Can't really see much beyond five of six miles, sir," Yelland commented. "Not clearly, really. It's still raining along the coast, off and on. The seas aren't up as fierce as one would expect, so it may be that the local fishermen are indeed out. When I was reading up on conditions along this coast, I found that the Spanish fishermen go to sea in all but a hurricane."

"Deck, there!" the lookout shouted, sounding sure of what he saw, at last. "*Four* sail, off the starb'd bows, 'bout six mile off, steerin' West . . . small brigs or ketch-rigs!"

"Too big for local fishing smacks," Lewrie snapped. "Mister Westcott, alter course, steer directly for 'em, and beat to Quarters!"

"Aye aye, sir!" the First Officer happily replied. Lewrie left the quarter-deck to fetch the keys to the arms chests as Westcott began to issue orders for the course alteration. A moment before Lewrie's return, the Marine drummer began beating out the Long Roll, drawing *Sapphire*'s off-watch hands up from below to man their guns.

A quick scan with his telescope showed Lewrie all four of the vessels, small brig-rigged ships perhaps no longer than seventy-five feet, strung out in a ragged line-ahead. A look aloft showed him the commissioning pendant now beginning to stream more abeam to larboard as *Sapphire* came about.

Wind's from the Nor'west, and they're beatin' hard against it, Lewrie told himself, seeing all four of them almost bows-on as they clawed their way out to sea from that dangerous coast, bows rising and plunging, their sails slatting as they dipped into the troughs. And, they would *have* to stay on larboard tack half the day to make any progress Westward, only tacking about to close the coast sometime round dusk to enter one of the many wee fishing ports to shelter for the night. Lewrie began to grin, knowing that their only choice was to haul their wind and put about, then run back to Gijon or Candás-Carreño, and they would not make it, not all of them. *Sapphire* was already making at least seven knots, and had a much longer waterline. With any luck on this new course, she might even attain eight knots, and those strange ships would be run down.

"The ship is at Quarters, sir," Lt. Westcott reported, eager for a whiff of gunpowder smoke.

"Bisquit dashed below?" Lewrie asked.

"At the first drum roll, sir, aye," Westcott told him, his eyes twinkling.

"Load bow chasers, nine-pounders, and upper gun deck twelve-pounders," Lewrie ordered. "The twenty-fours and carronades would turn 'em into kindling, and worthless as prizes."

"French colours, sir!" Midshipman Fywell shouted as he ran to his station at Quarters. "They fly French colours!" he added as he ran down to the upper gun deck.

"Deck, there!" the lookout screeched with excitement. "They's haulin' their wind an' puttin' about!"

Sapphire had strode down upon them before the French ships put about, all of them falling off the wind to wear about, sails fluttering untidily, and slowing down as they did so. The winds were just too gusty for them to try to perform a riskier tack to close the coast. They were now roughly only four miles off, and at least ten miles from the shore, with even more miles needed to get into shelter.

"I think we have them, sir," Mr. Yelland opined.

"Many a slip, 'twixt the crouch and the leap, Mister Yelland," Lewrie cautioned. "Or, don't count your chickens, hey?"

It did look promising to Lewrie, in point of fact. The four French merchantmen looked to be badly handled, taking far too long to brace their yards round to take the wind on their quarters, and their foresails winging out as loose as bed sheets on a line in a stiff breeze before being sheeted taut. Three miles, he made it, now, and not one of them looked like an armed escort of any strength. Stern transoms cocked up like the asses of feeding ducks as they plunged on in their bid to escape.

"We take the trailing ship, the others might get away before we can send over a boarding party," Lewrie said to the First Officer. "I'd admire did you arrange for a file of Marines and a boat crew for the barge t'stand ready, and have the barge drawn up closer astern."

Ship's boats stored too long on the cross-deck boat tier beams dried out and developed wee gaps between their strakes, so it was necessary to tow them and let them have a good soaking to seal up those gaps, now and then. It slowed the towing ship, but they were handy at a moment's notice if a boat was needed.

"Mister Keane," Westcott shouted to the senior Marine officer, quickly relaying the Captain's wishes, then calling to Mr. Terrell, the Bosun, for him to tell off a boat crew and have them stand by. Lt. Keane picked Sergeant Clapper, Corporal Rickey, and six Marines. The Bosun quickly called for Crawley, the former Captain's Cox'n, and his old boat crew to muster with their arms near the starboard entry-port.

As *Sapphire* closed the coast, catching up the French vessels, she entered those bands of misty rain and haze that had partially hidden their prey, drizzling on the decks and wetting the sails, which was a wee blessing; wet sails captured more wind than dry ones, and in a long stern-chase, some warship Captains, and the Masters of the pursued ships, had buckets sent aloft to dampen their sails for even a quarter-knot more speed.

"A little over a mile to the nearest, I make it, sir," Yelland estimated. "Not quite time for a shot under her bows, hah hah."

"Why not?" Lewrie asked him with a grin. "Pass word forrud to the starboard bow chaser . . . quoin fully out, and fire a warnin' shot."

Midshipman Chenery scampered forward to the forecastle to tell the gun crew what Lewrie wanted, prompting some shifting with crow-levers to aim the whole carriage, removing the wooded quoin block to rest the gun breech on the truck carriage. A last peek down the barrel of the 9-pounder, a tautening of the flintlock striker line, a last look-see to the recoil tackle, and a warning to stand clear and mind where your feet were, and . . . *Bang!*

The bow chaser reeled back to the extent of the breeching ropes, snubbing, as a cloud of yellow-white gun smoke blossomed to life, to be quickly whisked downwind, and a wee black dot of iron could almost be made out as it soared off in a low arc.

"A *hit,* damn my eyes!" Lt. Westcott shouted as the nine-pounder shot struck, not under the bows as requested, but upon the larboard bulwarks just abaft of the anchor cat-head, flinging up a shower of splintered wood, paint flecks, and long engrained dust and dirt.

"A little under one mile, now, sir," Mr. Yelland told them.

"Serve her another," Lewrie ordered, and within a minute the chase gun barked again, flinging a round shot that punched a neat hole right through the wee brig's inner jib, a hole that rapidly turned into a long rent in what was surely old and worn-out canvas, right down to the bolt-ropes on the jib's foot.

"She's struck!" Lt. Westcott chortled. "Her colours are down!"

"Haul up the barge to the entry-port, Mister Westcott," Lewrie ordered, then shouted forward to the waiting boarding party. "Boarders, away, smartly now!" Which order raised a brief cheer from those men, and the hands on deck. "That was damned quick, I must say. Now, let's get on after another. Ready another boarding party, and be ready to draw the pinnace up, next."

"Aye aye, sir!" Westcott replied, about ready to rub his hands together over what value their prize might fetch.

"Seven and one-half knots, sir!" someone called out from the taffrails as the chip-log was nipped.

"Why, just *blisterin'* speed," Lewrie hooted in mirth, "so fast it'll take your breath away!"

He looked down overside to see how the boarding party was getting on. The barge was now up beneath the mainmast chain platform, its tow-line snubbed round a thick rope stay, madly tilting, rising, and falling into the suck of the ship's creaming wake, and sailors were carefully timing their jumps from the chain platform or the last battens, with the Marine party carefully clambering down to join them. At last, the barge was manned, and the bow-man cast her free. Former Cox'n Crawley put the tiller hard over to let the barge surge away on the fuming bow wave, even as oarsmen were lifting their oars from the barge's sole and poising them upright, waiting for orders to ship them in the tholes and begin the stroke.

Further away from his ship, Lewrie could see that the French prize brig had wallowed to a stop, her courses and tops'ls clewed up in untidy bights, subserviently waiting for her captors to claim her.

Forward, three points off the starboard bows, the second brig they pursued was being fetched up right smartly, temptingly almost within range for a warning shot. Lewrie's cabin-servant, Jessop, was hopping from one foot to the other in excitement by his un-used carronade, now and then looking aft as if pleading that his gun be employed, but the new one looked as fragile as the first one, and Lewrie shook his head in the negative.

Lewrie felt as if he could hop about in impatience, too, if he could get away with behaving so, as the long minutes passed before his ship could close the range to where a hit or two would be certain.

Beyond the second prospective prize, the other two French ships were striding off for the jutting headland West of Gijon, Luanco-Gozón, and Candás-Carreño, the lead ship, a ketch-rig, altering course to go closer inshore in hopes that the threatening British warship couldn't follow into shoal waters. The one in trail of her, third in the line, was much slower, which gave Lewrie hopes that they might be able to take her, too, before she got round the headland.

"Half a mile, I make it, sir," Mr. Yelland announced after he'd lowered his sextant and done some scribbling on a slate.

"Bow chaser!" Lewrie snapped. "Fire into her!"

The 9-pounder's gun captain did so much fiddling that Lewrie almost repeated the order, but at last, the crew stepped clear, the gun captain jerked the flintlock striker lanyard, and the gun erupted with a shrill bark. This time, the roundshot hit the sea close under the brig's forefoot, flinging up a shower of water, a feathery column of spray that drenched the brig's forecastle.

"It appears this 'un is more stubborn than the other, sir," the Sailing Master said with a scowl.

"Mister Westcott, open the ports of the upper gun deck and run out the starboard battery," Lewrie snapped. A moment later and HMS *Sapphire* rumbled to the sounds of truck carriages being run up to the gun-port sills to thump against the hull timbers.

If that don't put the wind up that Frog, nothing will, Lewrie told himself.

"Damn my eyes, but I do believe her master's lifting his coat and showing us his backside, sir!" Lt. Westcott said with a telescope to his eye.

"Very stubborn," Mr. Yelland said.

"The Devil with *that,*" Lewrie fumed. "Twelve-pounders, as you bear . . . fire!"

Sapphire's gunners had had copious amounts of live-fire drills in the two years Lewrie had had her, and they had honed their craft to a fine degree in action, as well. Barely had the order been relayed below than the first gun forward of the upper gun deck battery fired, slowly followed by carefully aimed shots from the other ten 12-pounder guns, almost as regular as a salute, each gun captain waiting for the ship to pend on the top of the up-roll before jerking his lanyard to spark the flintlock striker of his gun, which lit off immediately, not like the old loose powder poured round the touch hole fashion.

"How's your arse *now,* ye snail-eatin' bastard!" Lewrie whooped with joy as heavier roundshot ploughed the sea round the brig's hull, one or two striking home higher up to blast away lighter bulwarks.

God, but I do *love the guns,* Lewrie thought; *the roar, stinks, and all, even if I end up deaf as a post.*

No real engagement had been expected, so hardly anyone had gotten some candle wax to plug their ears, and most of the gun crews had merely bound the neckerchiefs over their heads.

"That's the second one struck," Westcott hooted. "Just needed a bit more convincing, was all."

The French brig's colours were lowered very quickly, cut away it appeared, in her master's haste to surrender. Sails were being clewed up to take the way off her, and her jibs were struck down as well.

"Away, the boarding party!" Lewrie shouted down to the waist, then took up his telescope to peer hard at the next French ship which lay off their starboard bows, three points off the bows, and looked to be within a little more than a mile off. She was altering course to point at that distant headland, trying to get into shallower waters where *Sapphire* could not dare go, hoping to shave the headland by the slimmest margin, then hug the coast to the nearest fishing port.

"The pinnace is away, sir," Lt. Westcott announced, jutting his chin at the third French ship. "I don't know as if we'll fetch her up before she gets into the shallows. The lead ship, that ketch, is sure to get round the cape, first."

"Well, three out of four ain't bad, Mister Westcott," Lewrie said with a grin and a shrug. "If we can convince her Frog master that his situation's hopeless, that is."

"Ehm, sir," the Sailing Master said near Lewrie's elbow. "Permission to put leadsmen in the forechains? We're only three miles off the shore."

"Aye, Mister Yelland, do so," Lewrie agreed distractedly, intent upon the third ship. It was minutes later, as *Sapphire* slowly stalked up on the French brig, that he heard a leadsman sing out that he had only five fathoms to his line.

"Ehm, sir . . ." Yelland cautioned, harumphing loudly.

"Aye, Mister Yelland," Lewrie replied, letting his disappointment show. "Mister Westcott, steer more Due East and get us some safer sea room."

"Aye, sir," an obviously disappointed Westcott said, groaning.

As the helm was put over, and the braces altered, that French brig swam over from three points off the starboard bows to a broad four points, and looked to be no more than half a mile off.

"Another point free, Mister Westcott," Lewrie ordered, feeling hope renewed. "That'll place her almost abeam of us. Ready the upper gun deck, load the carronades at maximum elevation."

Jessop whooped in glee, snapping his fingers at the waiting powder monkey to fetch his leather case up and hand over the serge cartridge bag inside it.

"If we can't make prize of her, I'll be damned if the French have any joy from her," Lewrie said in a growl.

Sapphire rumbled and trembled as her upper gun deck 12-pounders were re-loaded and run up to the port sills, again, as the weather deck 9-pounders were run in, loaded, and run out, too.

"All guns ready, sir," Westcott reported after a long moment.

"By broadside this time, give her fire, Mister Westcott. *Hull* the bitch!" Lewrie barked.

"By broadside . . . ready . . . on the up-roll . . . *fire!*" and the two-decker was wreathed in a bank of spent powder smoke, shuddering as the guns slammed back in recoil.

Tall pillars of spray erupted round the French brig where shot struck short to carom on into her, and everyone could hear the sounds of the parrot-shrieks as wood was punched clean through.

"Lower deck twenty-four pounders, too!" Lewrie demanded. "Swat her

like a fly!" and he was answered with the deeper rumbles and shudders of
the heavier lower deck guns being run out to the port sills.

"*All* guns . . . by broadside . . . *fire!*" Lt. Westcott bellowed.

Sapphire slowly wallowed, heeling to the press of wind on her sails and
the scend of the sea, coming upright to the top of the up-roll and hanging
there for a second or two. At that moment, the guns roared, wreathing the
ship in an instant fog bank of spent powder smoke, stabbed through by jets
of flame, with swirling firefly clouds of cartridge cloth and wadding flar-
ing, dying, and falling to the sea along her starboard side.

"Got her!" Midshipman Chenery screeched in awe and delight to experience his first full broadside. "Now, she *must* strike!"

As the winds blew the smoke clear, all could see that the brig had been
hit hard by a few roundshot, but, embarrassingly, there were far too many
pillars of spray from misses collapsing upon themselves short of her, or
wide off her bows and stern.

"Serve her another, and aim closer, Mister Westcott!" Lewrie snapped,
disappointed with his formerly stellar gun crews. He bit his lip in frustration. "She must strike, or face the consequences."

The French brig's Tricolour flag still flew.

"Weather deck guns ready . . . upper deck ready," the reports came in.
"Lower gun deck ready!"

"By broadside . . . fire!" Westcott yelled, with the fingers of his right
hand crossed behind his back.

Once again, *Sapphire* hung at the top of the up-roll, and once again, the
old two-decker shuddered, pushed a few feet to leeward by the force of
her guns' discharges, groaning and rumbling as the guns recoiled to the
extents of the stout breeching ropes and the iron ring-bolts in the ship's
side.

"This time we got her!" Lewrie crowed once the smoke had dissipated
enough to give him a clear view of the brig. There were star-shaped shot
holes all down her larboard side, sails torn to rags by shot that had soared
high, and there didn't appear to be anyone still standing on her small quarterdeck, or round her helm. But that damned French flag *still* flew! Lewrie raised his telescope for a closer look and saw a hopeful sign. There were
crewmen on deck, mostly gathered round the brig's boats which were
stored amidships. Lashings were being slashed, and hoisting blocks
were being fitted from her main course yard.

"Smoke, sir," Westcott pointed out. "Fire, sir!"

Up forward near the brig's forecastle and galley, grey smoke began to boil upwards, blown over her bows, and flames could be seen licking above the bulwarks.

"They're just jumping into the sea," Mr. Yelland said, "quite hastily, and to Hell with the boats. Wonder what . . ."

He was interrupted by a large explosion aboard the French brig, a blossoming cloud of grey and black smoke shot through with rolling flame that enveloped her foremast and throwing deck planking skyward.

A second later, and there was a second, larger explosion that ripped the entire brig apart, and this time it was shattered boats and sections of her mainmast that rocketed skyward.

"Good Lord in Heaven!" Lt. Westcott said, wincing. "No *wonder* her crew was so quick to abandon her. She must have been packed to the deck heads with gunpowder and ammunition."

"That the French army won't have," Yelland said with a satisfied sniff.

"Do you imagine that anyone survived that, sir?" Lt. Westcott asked, turning to Lewrie. "Should we send a boat to look for survivors?"

"Aye, I s'pose that'd be charitable," Lewrie decided after a long moment, "though I doubt we'll find many. Secure from Quarters and fetch the ship into the wind, sir. Haul up one of the cutters from towing astern, and pass word for my boat crew t'man her."

"Aye aye, sir," the First Officer replied, still stunned by the sudden destruction.

"Like I said, Mister Westcott," Lewrie told him with a wry grin, "three outta four's not bad. And, not bad by way of a beginning."

CHAPTER FOURTEEN

*H*MS *Sapphire* had loitered off Gijon for another two days before pressing on towards Santander, catching a large brig bound West with supplies for the French armies. Her master was most indignant that he had been captured, when just hours before he had been congratulating himself for successfully escaping the clutches of two British warships off Santõna, the only one of five to remain free, a happy confirmation that *Undaunted* and *Peregrine* were feasting well off to the East.

Lewrie could peer astern from the taffrails of the poop deck, and now and then when the weather moderated from his cabins' stern gallery, at the prizes that wallowed in his ship's wake. In addition to those three, *Sapphire* had come across yet another large brig bound back to Bayonne, sailing empty, which had been lured in close by the ruse of flying a French flag 'til it was too late for her to escape.

That ship was now a cartel ship, with the crews off all four transferred aboard her and placed under guard belowdecks, leaving the other three manned by *Sapphire* sailors under the command of the older, experienced Midshipmen. That was one Hell of a risk, for all the prizes were crammed full of wine, a harsh brandy called *ratafia*, and rum, and placing British sailors in close proximity to all that was sure to engender pilferage, and drunken riot and insubordination, so it took sharp eyes and harsh punishments to keep the prize crews somewhat sobre, and obedient, but the situation could get out of hand in a Dog Watch.

Some of that wine and rum had been brought aboard *Sapphire* to supplement her own stocks, along with foodstuffs other than salt-meats. Most of the French wine was almost as bad, vinegary and thin as Navy issue "Blackstrap" or "Miss Taylor", making most who partook of it wondering why the French *ever* had a reputation as a people who made fine wines. Rum, *Sapphire*'s people thought, was merely rum.

French bisquit was the same as British bisquit, though fresher and easier to chew than what was in *Sapphire*'s bread bags, with nary a crop of weevils, yet.

What excited the Midshipmen's berth, the officer's wardroom, and Lewrie's table were the large *litre* bottles, in the French measure, of broths, soups, and gravies, sealed with corks and the necks liberally dipped in wax or lead. Bean soup, pea soup, even an onion soup that, with an admixture of cheese and crumbled, water-soaked bisquit, was declared as good as any onion soup that they had ever tasted. Even salt beef or salt pork, far too long in cask, tasted better when slathered with broth or gravy.

Even more bottles had been found in the West-bound prize that contained pickled vegetables of all varieties; large jars of carrots, sweet and dill gherkins, tangy radishes, mushrooms, long green beans, even asparagus spears. Lewrie's cook, Yeovill, had almost wept over the sudden, unexpected bounty, and had sworn that he would create one feast after another, hinting strongly that Lewrie should host as many suppers for his officers as possible. So he could show off, Lewrie strongly suspected, but he was more than happy to oblige the man, since it would be *his* plate that would be filled with succulent, and fairly fresh, delights nightly.

"Whew! Talk about farting proudly," Lt. Westcott said to his compatriot, Lt. Elmes, at the change of watch at 8 A.M.

"Sorry, sir," Lt. Elmes replied. "All the beans, the sausages, and the sauerkraut we ate last night. Who knew that Napoleon has so many Germans in his army to feed."

"An excellent preventative for scurvy," Westcott japed.

"So is wine, or apples," Elmes carped, "and I'd much prefer either. Captain Cook *forced* his sailors to eat sauerkraut. Just because we have lashings of the stuff is no reason for our mess cook to keep shoving it on us."

"You'll miss it when it's gone," Westcott told him.

"No, I won't," Elmes declared. "Sir, I relieve you," he added, turning formal and doffing his hat in salute.

"I stand relieved, sir. The deck and the watch is yours," Lt. Westcott replied, doffing his own hat. "We are at present twelve miles off Llanes, the wind is from the Nor'west, the' weather mild and clear . . . there's a bloody wonder . . . and we steer Due East. The last cast of the log showed six and one half knots. No enemy in sight, dammit."

"Enjoy your nap, sir," Elmes bade Westcott as that worthy left the quarterdeck for the wardroom below. Elmes settled himself on the larboard, windward side of the quarterdeck and raised his telescope to scan the horizon to satisfy himself that there were no sails in sight to windward. After a moment, he crossed to the lee bulwarks to make an even closer search of the Spanish coast.

There was a playful bark behind him, followed, by the stamp of boots on the deck, and hands on a musket stock. "Cap'um on deck!" the Marine sentry announced.

"Good morning, Mister Elmes," Lewrie genially said.

"Good morning, sir," Elmes replied, trying to doff his hat, but Bisquit was greeting him with paws on his chest.

"Any trade this morning?" Lewrie asked, coming to the leeward side to raise his own glass.

"Nothing yet, sir," Lt. Elmes had to tell him, spieling off all that the First Officer had imparted just before going below.

"Hmm," Lewrie commented, making a face, "I wonder, if we've been *too* successful, we and the other ships. It seems as if we've scared the Frogs and run 'em into port. I expected that we might, but I did not think that would happen so quickly. No one's spotted any semaphore towers, have they?"

"No, sir," Elmes replied, "though one would imagine that the French would have built a string of them, by now."

"Well, word of our presence got passed down the coast somehow," Lewrie groused.

"Despatch riders, I'd think, sir," the Third Officer speculated with a shrug. "Heavily escorted, if the rumours about the doings of the Spanish partisans are true. Either way, sir, if the convoys are frightened into port, their supplies aren't getting where they're wanted."

"They've got them *into* Spain," Lewrie said, "maybe not where they intended them to be, but the French can round up waggons and draught animals . . . horses, mules, oxen . . . and carry them on from there. Puts no silver in our bank accounts, though."

"If word of our presence reaches Bayonne as quickly as it seems to have spread along the coast, sir," Lt. Elmes suggested, "no fresh supplies get sent by sea, not 'til we've left, and that's all to the good, surely. And if the Pyrenees mountains are as bad as what our army suffered on the retreat to Corunna, keeping the French army in Spain supplied by that route would put them on very short commons."

"Not 'til the French've looted the countryside of the very last turnip," Lewrie countered with a shake of his head and a wee laugh. "Carry on, Mister Elmes. It seems I've a dog to amuse. Come on, boy!"

Bisquit's new rope toy, a foot-long length of three-inch cable with a monkey's fist worked into each end, was not as filthy and continually damp with dog slaver as the old one, though that wouldn't last for long. He growled over it as Lewrie tugged one end, then went flying all over the poop deck to chase it down and fetch it back. After a time, Lt. Elmes and the watchstanders on the quarterdeck below had to duck whenever it sailed over, and the dog came bustling down after it. A very good throw even sent Bisquit to the ship's waist and back, before he finally tired of it and came to lay the toy at Lewrie's feet, and join him on the taffrail flag lockers, head and fore paws in his lap for a lazy petting.

Lewrie eyed the windward corner of the poop deck where he would have his collapsible wood-and-canvas deck chair lashed. The weather was almost warm enough, the last few days, to fetch it out from storage. Oh, other captains might think it idle, lazy, and lubbery, but Lewrie didn't give a fig what people made of his indulgence.

Not quite time, yet, he told himself; *give it a month or more. And where are the bloody French, anyway?*

He swivelled about to peer up to windward, off *Sapphire*'s larboard quarter, where his clutch of four prizes idled along under reduced sail, about five miles more to seaward. He wondered if their presence was a lure, or a hindrance. If French watchers ashore saw what appeared to be a convoy, would the ones in port feel confident enough to hoist sail and continue their passages?

Not as long as Sapphire's *in sight, they won't,* he thought; *Now, if I armed the damned things and used 'em as Trojan horses . . .*

He shook his head, rejecting that idea at once as he returned his gaze in-board. He already had far too many hands, and Marines as guards aboard the cartel ship, handling the prizes, and to send them close inshore flying false flags would require even more of *Sapphire*'s people, reducing his ship's efficiency even more. None of the French convoys they'd met so far had been under escort, but that might change, and if it came to a proper fight, he'd have trouble manning all of *Sapphire*'s guns, or have enough hands to repel boarders.

Well, maybe just one *of 'em,* he further mused, a small grin spreading on his face; *if there's need for a cutting-out. Ah, well.*

Bisquit's eyes were closed, having himself a wee nap after his exertions, looking so content that Lewrie regretted having to rouse him.

"Come on, Bisquit. Nap's over," he said, getting to his feet. "Wakey-wakey, lash up and stow. Don't forget your toy. It's almost time for cutlass drill . . . won't that be fun, hey?"

Lewrie and the dog went down to the quarterdeck, where he took another long look shoreward with his glass. "Last cast of the log, Mister Elmes?" he asked over his shoulder.

"Six and three-quarter knots, sir," Elmes informed him.

"Halfway 'twixt Llanes and Comillas," Lewrie speculated, "and at this rate, we'll be off Santander a little after Noon Sights. Take a long look in, perhaps fetch to . . . taunt 'em, see if anyone'd come out t'face us?"

"Get into a fight, sir?" Elmes said with a hopeful grin.

"Never can tell, sir," Lewrie told him, collapsing the tubes of his telescope. "The shore shoulders out, ahead. Call me when you feel it necessary to alter course to stay twelve miles off."

"Of course, sir," Elmes promised.

"Ehm, here, Mister Fywell," Lewrie said, holding out Bisquit's rope toy to him. "Keep him amused, if he's still of a mind."

"Uh, aye, sir!" Fywell exclaimed, though he took the toy with only one finger and thumb, suspecting that it had gotten very slobbered.

"I'll be aft," Lewrie announced, then went to his cabins.

Midshipman Fywell shared a look with the Third Lieutenant, one of silent amusement.

"Some Captains are quirkier than others, Mister Fywell," Lt. Elmes told him. "Carry on with the, ah . . . amusing."

CHAPTER FIFTEEN

ood Lord, it's an armada, sir! Just look at that!" Lt. Elmes cried with
glee as *Sapphire* and her prizes hove in sight of the other ships of the squadron at the "rondy" far out to sea from the coasts of Spain. "The others
have made a fine reaping."

"Well, we haven't done so bad, ourselves," Lewrie agreed as he counted
masts on the horizon. He could just make out his warships by the commissioning pendants that streamed from their mainmast trucks, but the rest . . . !
"Sixteen, seventeen . . . nineteen!" he marvelled half to himself. 'Til they
fetched them hull-up and determined their types, they appeared, for the
most part, to be two-masted brigs, their sizes a match, he imagined, to the
ones that *Sapphire* had taken. He looked astern to the six that now trailed
his ship, suddenly feeling like a piker to have not taken as many prizes as
Undaunted, Sterling, Blaze, and *Peregrine* had done.

That's what I get for having such a slow ship, he thought; *We couldn't catch
half of what we chased.*

He lowered his telescope and drew out his pocket watch, then did a quick
estimation in his head. Stowing it back away, he called to the nearest Midshipman. "Mister Chenery, go forrud and pass word for my cook. I'll be
dining our Captains aboard, round one in the afternoon, I'd imagine."

"Aye aye, sir," Chenery replied, tapping the brim of his hat and dashing off for the galley to hunt up Yeovill.

"Shaping well, sir," Lt. Elmes commented. "He and Holbrooke take to the life like ducks to water."

"Aye, they have," Lewrie agreed, "though what they *think* they know, and what's still to learn, is dumbfounding. I count nineteen prizes yonder. What count do your younger eyes make of it?"

After a long minute or two of scanning the horizon, Elmes lowered his own glass and rubbed at his eyes. "Close to that, sir, but they're all in a jumble, sailing close to each other under reduced sail, just idling along, and they overlap each other," he cautiously declared. "We'll know more when the other Captains come aboard, and crow about their 'bags'."

"I'll have t'trot out the good wine, then," Lewrie said with a laugh, "and by the third bottle, the numbers might even increase!"

"So much for *in vino veritas,* sir," Lt. Elmes sniggered.

"Leapt from the main top t'their quarterdeck, dagger in my teeth, sword in each hand, and slew a dozen in one blow," Lewrie pretended to boast. "Grabbed the nearest nine-pounder, fired it from the hip, and dis-masted 'em. And *then* . . . !"

"Tales *do* grow in the telling, aye sir," Elmes agreed, "especially when well lubricated with drink."

"Aye, don't they just," Lewrie said, looking forward down the length of the weather decks and the waist. *Sapphire*'s crewmen were crowded along the sail-tending gangways, on the forecastle, and halfway up the shrouds for a good look at the impending "rondy" with the other ships of the squadron. Someone had struck up a fiddle tune, and a fife joined in, and sailors laughed in glee to marvel over what a success the squadron had won. Everyone would soon be flush with prize-money, even if *Sapphire* had not been "in sight" at the moment that those French supply ships had struck their colours, and would have no share in *those* prizes. To match the festive mood, the weather had cleared, the days-on-end gloomy overcast had dissolved, revealing clear blue skies and vast expanses of white cloud banks, and the sea had calmed to only five- or six-foot waves of a steely blue colour, with cheerful, non-threatening white caps.

At the moment, *Sapphire* did not quite appear as a dreadful man o' war, either, for sailors' clothing, soaked by rain and spray, was now hung out to dry, at least everywhere one looked.

Truth be told, Lewrie's stern gallery was strung with a clothes line on which several shirts and pairs of slop-trousers flapped in the wind. It would all have to come down by Noon Sights, and be well out of sight by the time the other Captains were welcomed aboard. Lewrie only hoped that the long soakings in fresh rain water would have gotten the salt crystals out, so he, and the rest of *Sapphire*'s people, would not develop salt-water boils from the constant chafing irritation. That would cut into the Ship's Surgeon's, Mr. Snelling's, fees for lancing and salving them, but that was his lookout.

Lewrie glanced upward and aft to the poop deck. If the weather improved, he *would* have his deck chair rigged, but not quite yet.

"I'll be aft 'til Noon Sights," Lewrie announced, then went to enter his cabins.

"The pickings were so good off Ferrol and Corunna that I had to end up *burning* more than I cared to," Capt. Yearwood of *Sterling* boasted after his third glass of a pleasant Spanish *tempranillo*.

"Aye, eight we took, all told," Commander Teague of HMS *Blaze* stuck in, "and we could have fetched out even more, but after a time, we just ran out of hands to man the prizes, *and* work our ships in the proper numbers."

"Oh, Blamey and I found a way to man ours," Capt. Chalmers of *Undaunted* said with a satisfied smirk. "Much easier when we allowed the French to row or sail ashore. No need for guards."

"The big one we took," Lewrie said at the head of the table, "we turned into a cartel ship. She was bound back to Bayonne, empty and on her own. Your prisoners, Captain Yearwood, can be transferred to her, if you've a mind."

"Glad to see the back of them, thank you, sir," Yearwood said with amusement. "Even if she evaded us, more's the pity."

"By the by, Captain Chalmers," Lewrie went on, "we snapped up the next biggest near Santander, one that got away from you."

"Oh, aye?" Chalmers replied, frowning a little as if suspecting that he would be twitted, or chastised for not taking her.

"Her master was just *spluttering* indignation," Lewrie told them, "that he'd been the sole survivor, got away by the skin of his teeth, and *still* got caught. He thought it *most* unfair."

"Well, a clean sweep was made of that little convoy, after all, for which I thank you, sir," Chalmers replied after a blink or two to decide how to take that news.

"Aye, she must have been the one that got into a thick squall whilst we were fetched-to taking possession of the others," Commander Blamey boomed out in good cheer. "Good to know that she didn't get far, haw haw."

"That ship's cargo of pickled vegetables liven our dinner," Lewrie boasted. "Damned clever, the French."

"Hear, hear!" Capt. Yearwood roared, lifting his glass.

"I wonder, though . . . ," Lewrie said after everyone had drained their glasses, and refills were being poured. "The next time we close this coast, it may not be rich pickings. Surely, the French will provide escorts, in future. As a matter of fact, I'm surprised that they haven't, yet."

"I hope they do, sir," Chalmers declared, "so we can have a proper fight." That sentiment was heartily seconded by one and all.

"More prize-money, taking a national ship, than a merchantman," Commander Teague agreed.

"Speaking of prize-money," Lewrie told them, "it's about time we shape course for Lisbon, and turn our prizes over to the Admiralty Court that's been established there. I think we've all more than earned a little run ashore . . . some welcome liberty for our sailors, and ourselves?"

That decision was cheered with another glass-draining toast.

"You don't know if we have a prison hulk at Lisbon, do you, sir?" Capt. Yearwood asked. "Or, will our prisoners be turned over to an army prison?"

"I don't know," Lewrie had to confess. "There was no mention in my orders, or my last letters from London, when I requested that a store ship be placed there. Admiralty confirmed that, at least. Hmm . . . the cartel ship's empty of anything of value to the French. We could set 'em free to sail her into Vigo, on our way to Lisbon. Or, transfer them all to one of the least value, and let 'em sail her into Vigo . . . as far from France, and a quick return as possible."

"With nought but their sea-chests, and pocket money, aye, and let them be a drain on the Vigo garrison," Commander Blamey laughed.

"And, the main course, sirs," Yeovill announced as he lifted the lid of a large serving tray, "a suckling pig, gentlemen, done to a turn, with apple sauce, cheesy potato halves, and pickled carrots," he boasted as Pettus and Jessop set out the various bowls.

"Commander Blamey, might I prevail upon you to carve?" Lewrie asked.

"My pleasure, sir!" Blamey replied, getting to his feet and taking up the large knife and fork. "Now, who shall have this particularly fine slice? Captain Chalmers, if you will pass me your plate? Plenty to go around, sirs, a gracious plenty, hah hah!"

"D'ye think this *tempranillo* will serve, or should we break out a claret?" Lewrie asked them.

The *tempranillo* would go down quite well, the others assured him as their plates were passed down, filled with slices of pork and passed back.

Lewrie awaited his own plate's return with a pleased grin on his face, thinking that his *ad hoc* little squadron had gelled together quite nicely, so far, and had been so successful that there was not a one of those officers that he could find even a wee fault with. Their first cruise together had worked most wondrously.

And soon, they would be in Lisbon. And he could send for Maddalena.

CHAPTER SIXTEEN

*T*here were no anchorages anywhere close to the Praça do Comercio or the fashionable centre district of Baixa, for the Tagus River was jam-packed with shipping to support the British army that still held the city and its environs. The closest to the city that Lewrie's squadron and impressive clutch of prizes could find room to anchor was near the South bank of the river, near Almada and Barreiro, making for a long row to thread through busy harbour traffic to the North shore, and the piers.

Sapphire had fired off a gun salute as she led the squadron into port, though to whom Lewrie had no way of knowing, for no one had a clue to the ranks of the officers of the warships they could see; there were a couple of Commodores' broad pendants visible on two 74-gun two-deckers, solid red pendants declaring that those Commodores were of the senior variety, with their own Flag Captains, but no one could discover an Admiral's flag. Lewrie had ordered fifteen to be fired, and hoped for the best, sure that someone's superior nose was going to be out of joint, and he'd hear about it, sooner or later.

Their latest copy of Steel's list was several weeks out of date, anyway, and though he had hoisted the numeral flags to declare which ship he commanded, not one of the Navy vessels present thought to make their own numbers back in reply.

"My, but you're turned out smart," Lt. Westcott teased as Lewrie came to the quarterdeck in his best-dress uniform, with the star and sash of his knighthood, his presentation sword on his hip, and his new bicorne hat on his head.

"Ye never can tell, Mister Westcott," Lewrie japed in tune to his First Lieutenant, "I might impress *somebody*. I'll try the Prize-Court, first, then the Post Office. Someone at either *must* know who I should report to. My boat alongside?"

"Aye, sir, and the crew scrubbed up in their finest, too," Westcott told him.

"Very well, then, sir," Lewrie said, "you have the ship. And if anyone sends a complaint aboard, or comes t'curse us out, himself, my apologies for you havin' t'be the goat."

It was quite a bundle that Lewrie had to bear ashore with him, all the pertinent documents off the French prizes, their registries, their bills of lading, manifests, and muster books of masters, mates, and sailors captured, then released at Vigo. In addition, he carried another packet of personal letters and his comprehensive reports of their cruise from Portsmouth to the Spanish coast, the doings of all the ships under his command, and a separate list of the prizes they had taken; tonnage, cargoes, lengths, and estimates of their material conditions.

As his cutter was stroked towards the vast commercial piers, a second boat under Lt. Harcourt set out for the store ship with another list of things needed to replenish.

Maybe the master of the store ship'll know who t'salute round here, Lewrie thought.

Soldiers, my God . . . bloody Redcoats! The quays teemed with troops from the Quartermasters, the Artillery, and not one of them had the first clue where anything was. Even the Provosts who policed the city were struck dumb by Lewrie's request as to where the Prize-Courts could be found. "Dunno, sir . . . Admiralty Court, ahn't it on a ship out there? . . . Think it moight be way uphill, sir . . . Post Office? For letters d'ye mean, sir? 'Aven't any idear, sir."

There were wholesale lots of Portuguese soldiery present, but Lewrie's poor language skills were of no avail, either. Every time he began with "*Bom dia, falar Inglese?*" he got back enthusiastic shouts of "*Viva l'Inglaterra!*" and not much else. At least the Portuguese soldiers looked as fine as British troops.

That could not be said for the loosely organised mobs of "volunteers" who idled in front of cafes, wine bars, taverns, or street corners, some of them engaged in laughable parodies of "square bashing drill", armed any-old-how, with everything from hatchets and butcher knives to boar spears, lances, fowling pieces to rusty muskets. At least they seemed eager to fight, and were full of appreciation for anyone British.

Lewrie ended up following many false leads, up narrow cobbled streets that were rather steep, and hard on the ankles if the cobblestones were too loose or too irregular. The lower Baixa district was laid out in a proper grid, but above and to either direction along the Tagus turned positively medieval, narrow and winding. After an hour or two, he felt that he had been led on a wild-goose chase, or a snipe hunt. At last he wound his way back downhill to the quays fronting the Baixa, continually pestered by begging children, his feet hurting, and his leg muscles crying out for a long sit-down. Trooping up such steep streets, then down again, nigh a mile or two of walking, Lewrie reckoned by then, was simply too much to ask of a sailor!

He reached a tavern with its large double doors spread wide in welcome, almost limped in, and sat himself down at a rickety table, free of beggars or too-cheerful volunteers, at last.

"*Bom dia, senhor,*" an aproned waiter said.

"*Bom dia. Cerveja, por favor?*" Lewrie replied, fanning himself with his bicorne. A moment later and a pint mug of beer was placed before him, costing only five *centimos*. He handed over his usual sixpence coin, which delighted the fellow into more "*Viva l'Inglaterra!*"

"*Viva Portugal,*" Lewrie replied, then drank deep.

Hmmph! he thought after a second deep swig; *At least the town's not mounded with filth and garbage any longer.*

The last time he'd been in Lisbon, just after the French surrender and evacuation, some streets were clogged with vast piles of trash, offal, and garbage, swarming with flies, mice, and rats, some streets appearing as if a good rain had sluiced an avalanche downhill to where it clogged up like a log jam, leaving a long, foetid slug-trail in its wake. Some said it was because the French had shot all the stray dogs which usually dealt with any edible garbage, forcing the new-come British to think that Lisbon was the filthiest city they ever had seen, and the Portuguese even lazier and more used to dirt than the Spanish!

He could almost see the lemony facades of the Praça do Comércio and all the mansions built on the centuries of wealthy trading from the Portuguese empire, the vast plaza with its neatly trimmed decorative bushes and flowering plantings, the stately trees that shaded it all, and . . .

"Oh, my Christ!" Lewrie gawped aloud.

Just up the street which followed the course of the quays and the river sat a neat pale-yellow-fronted building with a signboard that declared that the offices of the Falmouth Import-Export Company were inside. That had been the false front that Foreign Office's Secret Branch had used at Gibraltar, and what were the odds that someone in the skulking-spying trade hung his hat there, too! Perhaps Thomas Mountjoy, their chief agent at Gibraltar, had removed to be closer to the scene of the action.

"Just damn 'em all," Lewrie muttered under his breath.

Lewrie finished his beer at a slow, deliberate pace, steeling himself to call upon those offices. Long ago, 'tween the wars when he'd still been a Lieutenant idling about on half-pay, Secret Branch had roped him in on an expedition to India and Canton in China, then a romp all over the China Sea and the Philippines, a neck-or-nothing, dangerous business, run by a cold, sneering, top-lofty throat cutter and back-stabber, one Zachariah Twigg.

Secret Branch had found Lewrie to be a useful gun-dog, and over the years, he had gotten dragged back into dealings that, had he one minute's warning, he would have run from, screaming. He and *Sapphire* most recently had been given Independent Orders to serve as Thomas Mountjoy's one-ship Navy in 1807 for raids along the Andalusian coast, and the delivery and retrieval of spies and their messages.

It was understandable, therefore, that the prospect of going in to call upon whomsoever was the chief agent in Lisbon made Lewrie a tad bilious, or made his bowels feel a little looser than normal.

"Hang it," Lewrie said at last, "nothing for it." He got to his feet, tossed the waiter a "thankee", and crossed the street.

There was a thin and gangly young fellow manning a desk in the outer office who looked up as the bell over the door tinkled when he opened it. "Good morning, sir. I fear you have the wrong place. We are a commercial trading company, not a chandlery."

"Who's the chief agent, Thomas Mountjoy, or Daniel Deacon?" Lewrie asked. "Some other sneaky fellow? Please inform whoever it is that Captain Sir Alan Lewrie has come to call."

"I'm sorry, but I don't know what you mean, sir . . . Sir Alan," the young fellow stammered, looking shocked that anyone other than another Secret Branch spook saw through the facade. "The manager of the firm *is* Mister Mountjoy, but . . ."

"Just announce me, lad," Lewrie insisted. "I promise that I won't prowl through any classified documents while you do so."

Very reluctantly, and scanning the innocuous outer office as if to fix it all in his mind should anything be pilfered or dis-lodged, the young man opened the door to the inner offices a mere crack, and edged through the narrow gap sideways, like a house-breaker. The door was not only firmly shut, but Lewrie heard the clank of a key turning in a lock.

"Damn my eyes! Who?" someone shouted inside. A moment later and the lock was turned again, the door flung open wide, and Thomas Mountjoy came bustling out. "Well, just damn my eyes!" he said once more, offering his hand, "Captain Lewrie! Where the Devil did *you* spring from? Hellish-grand to see you! Come on in!"

Lewrie was quickly shown into the inner sanctum, as bland and innoc-uous as the outer offices, then up the stairs to the first storey where Mountjoy kept lodgings. Like his former "digs" at Gibraltar, there was a wide and spacious gallery overlooking the street, the quays, and the river, topped with a shading awning. In one corner sat Mountjoy's powerful tele-scope on a tripod stand.

"Wine, first," Mountjoy decided, "a lovely rosé *vinho verde*. Now, where did I lose the cork-puller this time? Saw you sail in . . . no clue it was you. The Commodore's pendant put me off. A squadron, is it? Good for you. And such a swarm of prizes you fetched in, too. Where did you get them all?"

"French convoys all along the northern Spanish coast, Corunna to San Sebastian," Lewrie told him, finally getting a word in. "They were just cruisin' along, fat, dumb, and happy, with no escorts about. Ah, thankee," he said as he got his first glass of the fruity, sweet *vinho verde*. The bottle glistened with water, fresh drawn from a tub to cool it, and it went down marvellously well. "How are you?"

"Oh, doing just topping-fine," Mountjoy happily stated as he took a seat across from Lewrie in one of the well-padded chairs that Lewrie recalled from Mountjoy's Gibraltar aerie. "London decided I should remove here, now that it's determined that Britain will hold Portugal, and have another go in Spain. Gibraltar's become a backwater for now, unless the French march down and lay siege. Deacon's still with me, but London's placed an-other man in my place at Gibraltar, with his own team of agents."

Thomas Mountjoy had, long ago before, been Lewrie's clerk at sea when he'd had HMS *Proteus*, before Mountjoy had been beguiled by Zachariah Twigg to go into his line of work.

Mountjoy didn't look like the popular image of a spy; but then who truly did? He was most un-remarkable, which was probably an asset; brown-eyed, brown-haired, a very average-looking fellow now in his mid-thirties or so, soberly dressed, mostly free of revealing or dangerous vices, and to most observers a mild, adequately educated, and inoffensive sort, easily dismissed.

After Lewrie's experiences with the likes of Zachariah Twigg, James Peel . . . " 'tis Peel, James Peel" . . . Mountjoy's second, Daniel Deacon, and a few others who'd served the aforementioned, most especially that murderous maniac, Romney Marsh, who might still be roaming about Spain or Portugal with his pet dagger, Thomas Mountjoy seemed tame in comparison, an organiser, not a cut-throat. Though Lewrie always suspected that he *must* have a dangerous side, a well-disguised one. *Mean t'say,* he thought; *What was trainin' in spy-craft for?*

"And you were sent to call upon me?" Mountjoy puzzled, shaking his head. "No one's told me about it. Secondary orders, for us . . ."

"Good God, no, Mountjoy," Lewrie hooted with glee. "I've spent half the morning stumbling round Lisbon tryin' t'find the Post Office and the Prize-Court, saw your signboard, and thought you'd know where the Hell they are, if anyone did!"

"Oh! That's simple!" Mountjoy exclaimed, looking relieved. "I'll show you the way, after we've polished off this *vinho verde*. This time round, my brief is more oriented to the land, anyway, working with the army, cobbling up decent maps of the countryside, which General Sir John Moore didn't have, sadly. Finding where the French are garrisoned, and in what numbers, that sort of thing."

"I was at the evacuation of Corunna," Lewrie told him. "It *was* a damned shame that Moore had no idea how rough and trackless the interior of Spain was before he set out. What happened to his army was simply pitiful."

"You say we're goin' back into Spain? This spring?" Lewrie asked. "With what?"

"Well, there's strong rumours that General Sir Arthur Wellesley will be coming back to command the army, after the good showing that he made at Roliça and Vimeiro," Mountjoy told him, squirming about in his chair and leaning forward to impart his news, as if it was secret. "For the last six months or so, General Cradock has held Lisbon with about ten thousand British troops, and the Portuguese, some of our remnants of Moore's army that got evacuated from Vigo, and the garrison that Moore left here, originally. General Beresford, remember him? He's been whipping the Portuguese back into shape, recruiting, training, weeding out the chaff of the Portuguese officer corps . . . Do you know, there's some of their generals in charge of fortresses that have never *seen* them, just loaf about Lisbon? He's stiffened them with British officers and senior sergeants, and they look about as good as any British soldiers, now, fully armed, shod, provisioned, given everything they need. There's about twenty thousand of them, by now, foot, horse, and artillery.

"Speaking of fortresses," Mountjoy happily went on, "there's one at a place called Badajoz, on the border with Spain, that was just in *awful* condition, and Beresford's having it rebuilt and strengthened."

"Badajoz," Lewrie mused over Mountjoy's semi-native Portuguese pronunciation, "sounds like a bad sneeze."

"Oh, don't it, just," Mountjoy gaily agreed. "It's like a magnet for all those eager volunteer sods. I wish the ones loafing about in Lisbon would move on there. Can't even stick one's head out of the door without being mobbed with *Viva l'Inglaterra!*"

"At least they seem to like us," Lewrie commented.

"Immensely," Mountjoy agreed. "So, what brings you to Lisbon? Is this your new base of action?" he asked as he topped up their wine glasses.

"Aye, for now," Lewrie told him, "though it is rather a long trip to the coast of Northern Spain and back. I was hoping to work closer, from Oporto, say."

"Oh, that's out, for now," Mountjoy objected, pulling a face. "The French have it. Marshal Soult crossed back into Portugal and took the city. God, what a massacre he made! Portuguese soldiers and volunteer militia slaughtered, civilians too. It didn't signify to *him*. There was a bridge of boats cross the Douro River, simply packed with fleeing townspeople. Broke under the weight, Soult shelled it, either way it broke and *thousands* were drowned.

"Now, Marshal Ney, he's in charge of your new patch, Galicia and Cantabria provinces, and having a very hard time of it from the Spanish partisan raiders, the *guerreros*. From the reports I have gotten so far, they're finally making an impact. So, too, are Portuguese partisans round Oporto. The French hold the territory where they stand, within a long musket shot, and no further . . . have to travel in large units, because the smaller units are found stripped, looted of their arms and such, and most *appallingly* dead.

"As for their other armies, Marshal Victor's last position we think is round Mérida, stretching down toward Madrid, and there is another large army under a General Laplisse near Ciudad Rodrigo . . . oh, but that's all soldiers' doings, none of interest to you."

"Well, takin' ships that feed Marshal Ney do interest me," Lewrie said with a laugh. "That vainglorious bastard. Deprivin' him of his horse shoes and nails might slow his famous cavalry down."

"And that's always a good thing," Mountjoy heartily seconded. "From all I've read about him, Ney is either the bravest cavalryman in history, or simply too stupidly daft to see the dangers. Hmm . . . much like you, perhaps?" he added with a sly look.

"I don't go *courtin'* death like he does," Lewrie objected, "but I will fight if I have to."

"But so *often!*" Mountjoy said with a roll of his eyes. "Ehm . . . have you heard from Maddalena Covilhā lately?"

Damned spies, Lewrie thought; *I'll bet he has, knows all about what's happened at Gibraltar.*

"I wrote her, soon as we got back to England," Lewrie told him, "and wrote her again before I hoisted my broad pendant and set sail, saying that I'd be working out of Lisbon, but if she wrote me back, her letters haven't caught up with me, yet. I imagined that she'd be excited about it. I sort of promised her that she'd see Lisbon someday, like she's always wanted. Do you know anything about her? She hasn't taken up with an army officer in my absence, has she?"

"She called upon me, just before I sailed here," Mountjoy told him, refilling their glasses yet again and peering owlish to see how much was left in the bottle. "Worried about you, all that . . . and about her own prospects if you didn't come back, or went down with your ship. It was a stormy winter when you set out for Corunna, remember."

"How well I know it." Lewrie nodded agreement, thinking it time to trot out the tale of his lightning strike.

"I assured her that you'd be back, eventually," Mountjoy went on. "And if you didn't, you'd left her in decent prospects, so she'd not have to find herself another protector for some time. Her lodging paid for another six months or so, some funds at the garrison bank?"

"Aye, I did," Lewrie said. "More than enough for passage here if she wished."

"Recall that I once considered putting Maddalena on my payroll," Mountjoy reminded him. "She'd've made a grand listener in the markets, the chop-houses, and no one would ever suspect her. Then, there are her linguistic skills . . . Portuguese, Spanish, English, some Italian, maybe even French by now, I don't know," Mountjoy said with a shrug, and a chuckle. "On the strength of those talents, I recommended her to my replacement, to spy for him and serve as translator, perhaps aid him with our forged news accounts."

"Still doing those are you?" Lewrie asked. When the French had marched into Spain, just after conquering Portugal, early on he and Mountjoy had cobbled together drawings from Lieutenant Westcott and Midshipman Fywell depicting French atrocities which, strictly speaking, hadn't yet occurred, along with fake newspaper articles to infuriate the Spanish people into rebellion against their useless old king, and becoming a British ally. They had kept the *Gibraltar Chronicle*'s presses busy, and well paid, to boot.

"Of course we are," Mountjoy replied, beaming. "War by the printing press is all the 'crack' these days, and London has taken it up, wholeheartedly. Earned me creditable notice and approval from my superiors, too, thank you very much."

"And I got no credit for it?" Lewrie groused, or pretended to.

"Of course *not*, sir!" Mountjoy hooted. "Credit for such subtle skull-duggery can't go to a tarry old sea-dog!"

"Just a simple sailor, me," Lewrie frowned. "Ah, well. So . . . did your replacement take her on?"

"Haven't a clue, sorry," Mountjoy said, "though, if you wish her to remove to Lisbon, I could use him to aid her along, claiming that Maddalena is needed on my staff here. I really *could* use her."

"I may take you up on that, Mountjoy," Lewrie was quick to accept, "if she's still of a mind, and wishes t'stay under my protection. We'll see what the next mail brings."

"Speaking of mail," Mountjoy said, finishing his wine in three quick slurps, "I still have to direct you to the Post Office, and the Prize-Court offices. Show us 'heel-taps' and we'll be off."

Lewrie quickly drained his glass, tilted it upside down with an appreciative sound over the wine's fresh taste, and shot to his feet, ready to go. Even if his feet in his best Hessian boots still complained after his hour or so of thankless prowling the streets of Lisbon.

CHAPTER SEVENTEEN

*T*he visit to the Post Office took very little time, but going to the Prize Court was a bother. Those beady-eyed officials were all but drooling to have such a large bit of business drop in their laps, but of course they pretended that it was rather a bother to adjudge, assess, and certify so many prizes at once. And, it was a given that Admiralty Prize-Courts proceedings moved forward much like "church work", or cold molasses; it was *damned* slow! Even with the best of efforts, the squadron might not see a penny of profit two years hence!

"It may be necessary, you see, Sir Alan," one of the senior Proctors told him, all but rubbing his grubby hands together, or fingering his coin purse in expectations of how much might *stick* to those hands, "for all the Captains of your squadron to call upon the Court before we may even begin to assess the matter at hand. All together, or separately, hmm? Perhaps some time in the next week, hmm?"

Lewrie finally escaped their clutches round sundown, feeling badly in need of a sponging down to remove the oiliness that he imagined clung to his skin.

Mountjoy had scarpered back to his own offices and lodgings hours before, after directing him to the right place, intent upon his own business, so Lewrie found himself a streetside coffee house, and lingered in the rare luxury of solitude away from the demands of his ship and squadron, enjoying cups of fine Brazilian coffee just arrived by ship from the Vice-Royalty of Brazil, and some sweet and tasty cinnamon-dusted *pastéis de nata* before going to the quays to search out a boatman to ferry him back to *Sapphire*.

"Anything go smash in my absence?" Lewrie asked Lt. Westcott after the welcome-aboard ritual had been performed.

"All quiet, sir," Westcott reported. "The hands are at their supper, a welcome one if you cock an ear."

The sounds rising up from the gun decks certainly resembled the good cheer usually associated with holiday messes.

"Fresh *porco preto,* what the Portuguese call 'black pork'," Lt. Westcott informed him, "roughly an eight-pound shoulder for each mess, already smoked and ready for slicing, boiled winter potatos, fresh-baked shore bread, and the usual pease porridge. The Purser, Mister Cadrick, says that beef on the hoof is rather thin on the ground, but pork's plentiful. Winter vegetables, well. The next time we enter harbour here, I expect that will change for the better. How was the Prize-Court?"

"Unctuous, greedy, liars," Lewrie gravelled. "No better than one can expect. They wish all Captains to attend them. Probably to dis-abuse us of any hopes for penny on the pound, as usual. What of the store ship?"

"Mister Harcourt reports that they have all we require, and all we must do is submit a list, sir," Westcott said, leaning over the compass binnacle lanthorn to ignite one of his *cigarros*. "Mmm, now the New World trade is back up and running, I expect I can get some fresh *cigarros,* too. I'm running short of my Spanish lot. Oh! Mister Harcourt also fetched off the mail bag the store ship had held for us! Your clerk, Faulkes, has yours, sir, all sorted out."

"Sorted 'til Chalky gets his wee paws on it," Lewrie scoffed. "Fresh pork roast, is it? I'll be aft, then, smackin' my lips 'til Yeovill has my supper ready. Carry on idle, Mister Westcott."

"Idle I'll be, sir," Westcott replied, blowing a smoke ring.

"Welcome back, sir," Pettus said as Lewrie hung up his sword, hat, and dress coat. "A glass of something?"

"Some of that Spanish white," Lewrie told him as he seated himself at his desk, with Chalky leaping from the deck to the desk to his lap. "Hallo, ye old rascal. Haven't eat my mail yet, have you?"

It took a few minutes of stroking, scratching, and rubbing to settle the cat down, stretched out cross his lap; then Lewrie could address his mail. Faulkes knew the drill; official Admiralty letters first, bills from purveyors second, then personal mail, last. That was a lesson that Lewrie had painfully learned as a Midshipman, bent over a gun to "kiss the gunner's daughter" for not obeying that stricture.

Thankfully, there was nothing urgent from Admiralty, just the usual "to all ships" notices of new-found hazards to be marked upon what charts the ships carried, promotion lists, and such, quickly and easily breezed through. He had cleared all his debts in London and Portsmouth before he sailed, so there were no bills to be paid, either.

He flipped through the much smaller pile of personal letters, setting aside one from Governour Chiswick, sure that it was a report on his daughter's, Charlotte's, deportment, and yet another hint that she should have a London Season where she might catch herself a suitable husband. There was one from his father, also to be read dead last. Aha! There *was* a letter from Maddalena Covilhā, and he broke the seal in a rush.

Great relief that he was healthy and safe, delight that her fervent prayers had been answered, expressions of how much she had missed him, then a rather amusing description of all that had transpired at Gibraltar since he had sailed away, what she had done during the Christmas holiday, New Year's celebrations, Three King's Day, and Epiphany, and how difficult the populace had dealt with the dreadful news of General Sir John Moore's death, and the cruel conditions that his army had suffered on their long retreat to Corunna. She had been extremely relieved to get his first letter from Portsmouth about the evacuation, then his second letter telling her that he would be coming back to Lisbon.

> Meu amor, *does this mean that you will never be returning to Gibraltar? If that is so, I am heartbroken, for you have been such a kind, endearing protector to me that I had, in my imagination, hoped that our mutually pleasing arrangement might continue for as long as possible. Ah, silly, hopeless me, clinging to dreams that might come to nothing! Even if you are in Lisbon for only a few days in a whole six months, I yearn to be re-united with you, and be there for you when you are free!*

"Well, it don't *sound* like she's found herself another keeper," Lewrie muttered half to himself, immensely pleased that she still had a yen for him. He found himself missing her, too, of a sudden, eager to take Mountjoy

up on his offer to smooth her way to Lisbon, even if the man really didn't
employ her in his shady line of work. He felt her absence so strongly that he
felt a tightness in his groin, gladly summoning up memories of their lovemaking. Hell *yes*, he'd send for her, that instant! Leaving the rest of his
mail un-read, he opened his desk for pen and paper, dipped into the ink-
well, and wrote her an invitation to take ship and join him, assuring her
that Mountjoy could help her find lodgings if he was at sea when she arrived, with a hint that Mountjoy might even offer her gainful employment!

Barely had he signed his name—"eagerly awaiting your expeditious
arrival, I am your most humble servant and fondest admirer, Alan"—
then folded it over and sealed it when Yeovill came breezing in with the
brass barge.

"Your supper, sir!" Yeovill cheerfully called out as he swung the barge
atop the sideboard in the dining coach. "And Bisquit, as usual," he added
as the ship's dog pranced in at his heels, whining and licking his chops.

"Well, serve it up, my good man!" Lewrie roared in eagerness as he
rose and went to his dining table. "Is it that Portuguese *porco preto*? Grand!
I haven't had that yet, and the First Officer said it was toothsome. I think
a red wine'd go well with it, hey, Pettus?"

"There's a nice Spanish *rioja* already decanted, sir," Pettus assured him.

There was Bisquit to calm down and coddle, a re-awakened cat to stroke,
before Lewrie could seat himself, tuck a napkin under his chin, and take
a first bite of anything, but the pork *was* heavenly, as were the boiled
potatoes, the medley of pickled carrots and peas, the fresh butter and shore
bread, right on to the sweet orange tarts bought off a Lisbon bum-boat.

It was only after a post-prandial glass of Lewrie's rapidly diminishing
cache of American corn whisky that he scooped up the last of his personal
mail off the desk and stretched out on the settee to read the rest. Lewrie
felt a vague disappointment that his eldest son, Sewallis, had not written;
he hadn't for some time, which was worrying.

"Father, solicitor, Lock's . . . better be an advertisement, I *paid* for that
new hat . . . *who*?" he muttered to himself, then sat up with a start. He had
a letter from Mistress Jessica Chenery. "Hope she don't think her brother'll
get preferential treatment," he said further as he tore open the plain green
wax seal and unfolded it. He would be immune to "petti-coat influence"
or personal pleas.

*My youngest brother, now your newest Midshipman, sent us a final letter
just before your ship set sail, Sir, reassuring us all that he would be in the*

best of hands to begin his naval Career, and that, from what little he had gleaned from his conversations with his Fellows, and divers members of the Crew, Charlie stated that he was Delighted to discover the Fame and Successful Repute of his new Captain.

"Aye, piss down my back, buss my blind cheeks, before ya plead for little Charlie's petting," Lewrie grumbled, sure that he was being cozened.

Indeed, Sir, Charlie related that you and your Ship had been attached to our Army in Portugal and Spain, that you had aided the evacuation from Corunna, and that you had been ashore to witness Gen. Wellesley's Victories at Roliça and Vimeiro.

I trust that you will not find my Plea for information Importunate, or too silly or trivial a Waste of your Time, but—there was a young man of our Parish, Lt. John Briscoe Beauchamp, of the 9th Regt. of Foot, with Genl. Wellesley's Army, then with Genl. Sir John Moore's in Spain, a promising fellow much beloved of his Parents, our Parish, my Family, and Myself. Though no promises were made, he and I hoped that, upon his Victorious Return, John and I might have become Affianced.

Sadly, John is listed among the Fallen, though his Regt. cannot, or will not, say under what circumstances that he Perished, and his family has not received any of his Possessions, or even one last Letter, and, needless to say, we are all most distraught at his Loss. Though you are not in the same Service, do you, or could you, write me and advise us how we may learn the details of John's demise?

"Beauchamp, Beauchamp," Lewrie whispered, seeking a face to go with that name, one out of thousands lost from an entire army. "Oh, God! Yes!" he blurted as it came to him. "What a damned small world. Poor chit."

He rose from the settee, crossed to his desk and lit the candle in an overhead lanthorn, then sat down, re-read her letter, and took out pen, ink, and paper to pen her a reply, taking a moment to admire her neat and economically small penmanship.

My Dear Miss Chenery,

Allow me to express to you my Sympathy for the Loss of One Dear to you, your family, and your Parish. As unimaginably implausible as you find this to be, it was my Pleasure to have met Lt. Beauchamp twice; firstly at Maceira Bay when my First Officer and I went ashore after the

Battle of Roliça. We were in search of horses; sailors are infamously Lame ashore, and were confronted by a young Lt. who accused us, all in jest, of being French spies due to our blue uniforms, then guided us to the Re-mount station, further giving us a tour of the encampment, and a lively description of the fight the day before, none other than your Lt. John Beauchamp of the 9th!

Lewrie went on the describe how jolly yet knowledgable that young man had been, how striking his person was, and how pleased that he and Lt. Westcott had been with their tour.

The morning of the Battle of Vimeiro, I went ashore once more, before dawn, upon Sureties from your young man that there would be a Battle, which I wished to witness, and went well Armed just in case. After a ride to the vil-lage of Vimeiro with an Irish carter, I obtained a mount and travelled along the long Nor'east ridge which did prove to be the site of the French attacks, against which I took more than a few shots. It was about eleven in the morn-ing, two hours after the first French assaults, that I met Lt. Beauchamp again, this time in the role of galloper, seconded to General Sir Arthur Wellesley's staff. This was quite a vote of confidence upon him from his regi-mental commander, and a signal honour to be singled out for such a duty, a sure sign that Lt. Beauchamp was a young fellow with a lot of promise. Not everyone can be trusted to bear the general's orders or wishes reliably, quickly, and accurately.

We joshed with each other, he in the gayest and most confident airs, 'til Sir Arthur spotted me and said, and I quote, "Leftenant Beauchamp, stop that prittle-prattle with that naval person, I have need of you!" Lt. Beau-champ was handed a message to the regiments at the furthest Nor'east end of the ridge, and the last I saw of him, Beauchamp tipped me a wink, then galloped off. All in all, I found him to be a fine young fellow, personable, charming, yet efficient and dedicated to his Career, the very sort that I would wish aboard one of my ships.

Lewrie paused, wondering if he should relate what he'd heard of the awful conditions of the retreat to Corunna in the blizzards, on the ice-slick roads and arched bridges, the drunken indiscipline, the looting, hunger, utter exhaustion that had forced many brave men to just lay down beside the road and freeze to death. No, that'd be too gruesome and horrifying to express to a young lady of a proper up-bringing. Lewrie made a brief reference to the accounts in the newspapers, which Jessica Chenery had surely read.

A friend of mine, Colonel of a Light Dragoon Regt., lost a third of his troopers and most of his horses on the retreat to Corunna. We spoke briefly on the quays as boats from my ship bore his wounded and sick out to the transports, then he had to turn what little he had left to the defence of the roads into Corunna during the last French assaults, and I have no idea if he survived to be evacuated, either.

"This'll be an expensive letter," Lewrie muttered as he began a second sheet of paper, having done both sides of the first in the tiniest script he could manage, and thank God for steel-nib pens. "I hope she thinks payin' the postage is worth it."

He had to write that it was possible that, in all the confusion of the long and hasty retreat, Lt. Beauchamp's camp gear, possessions, and such had been abandoned, or just lost, perhaps even left to the French at Corunna to make more room aboard the transports for those who had managed to get aboard, one way or the other; wounded, sick, or whole. Perhaps her borough's Member of Parliament could put pressure upon Horse Guards, or Beauchamp's regiment, now that they were back in England in their home barracks, he suggested; surely, his fellow subalterns in the 9th would know how, and in what circumstances, Beauchamp had perished.

"Maybe she *don't* want t'know," Lewrie muttered, well aware of just how many ways even strong and healthy young men could die, most of them having nothing to do with honour or martial glory, and mostly messily prosaic. "A mystery might be better."

Frozen to death, starved, puking, fouling one's breeches in a raging fever, even murdered by rebellious, drunken soldiers denied the looted stores of village wine or brandy? Such happened.

Let me once again express to you, Miss Chenery, my sad Regrets for the loss of such a decent young man, one whom I would have wished to have known better.

On a happier note, I trust, allow me to relate to you that your brother, Midshipman Charles Chenery, is well and progressing nicely in his learning of nautical and "tarry" skills. We have just returned from a raiding cruise along the North coast of Spain which resulted in the Capture or Destruction of over two score French supply ships, Eighteen of which lay at

Lisbon as Prizes. Should the recently established Prize Court here ever get round to Certifying them, a lengthy process, believe me! your brother may be in the way of a tidy Sum, as all the ships of my Squadron will. They've made me Commodore, of all things! Should you be able to determine the ultimate Fate of Lt. Beauchamp, feel free to write me.

A little braggin' on myself never hurts, Lewrie thought with a grin on his face as he finished the letter, folded it, and got out his wax and seal . . . the one with his crest of knighthood, this time. As the stick of wax heated over a candle's flame, he looked over the girl's letter one more time, admiring once more the neatness of her copper-plate hand, and the direct nature of her writing, the intelligence behind her words. No shrinking violet was she, but a very sensible young lady with a mind of her own. Lewrie *wanted* to impress her, he suddenly realised, and half-way hoped that she *would* write him back. For whatever reason!

"Oops, oh damn!" he exclaimed as he dribbled a line of wax cross his desk-top and the cover sheet of the letter. He managed to make a large blob where it was needed, pressed his seal into it, then used a pen-knife to scrape off the drops of excess, chidding his instant of stupidity and in-attention.

"A glass of something before bed, sir?" Pettus asked with a barely stifled yawn.

"Hmm, a dram or two of whisky, thankee, Pettus," Lewrie said as he rose to go to the wash-hand stand to brush his teeth, first.

Damme, but Midshipman Chenery has an incredibly *handsome and fetchin' sister!* he thought; *A smart'un, too, and talented t'boot.*

As he scrubbed his teeth with flavoured pumice powder, he found that he could recall quite distinctly how she'd looked when he'd met her at her father's parish manse, the tone of her voice, and how she had gestured as they had talked.

After rinsing, he looked at himself in the small mirror, turning his head from side to side to see if he looked his true age, or still appeared younger than his fourty-six years, wondering if an unmarried lady in her late twenties might find him interesting.

Oh, you sorry bastard, he chid himself; *You're like a hound that chases carts. What'd I do with her if I did catch her fancy? Utterly ruin her good name, most-like. Jessica Chenery ain't for the likes o' me!*

He got his glass of whisky, a lit candle, and entered his bed-space, ready to retire, wishing Pettus and Jessop a goodnight.

"Come on, Chalky," he called out, "Beddy-by!"

CHAPTER EIGHTEEN

$\mathcal{H}$as everyone had a good run ashore?" Lewrie asked the officers of his squadron, summoned by the Captain(s) Repair on Board hoist the third day in port. "Good. No problems with the Army Provosts, or the Portuguese? Also very good," he amiably said, looking down the length of his dining table where Chalmers, Yearwood, Teague, and Blamey sat, sipping tentatively at glasses of Lewrie's cool tea, a novelty to them.

"The Prize-Court, sir," Capt. Yearwood grumbled, "have you any idea when they'll get round to certifying our captures?"

"When pigs fly, is my guess, sir," Lewrie said with a shrug. "We all know how slowly they go about their business, as bad as the Court of Common Pleas back home. The only way I know to spur them is to swamp them with even more work. Are we all provisioned, and ready for sea in all respects?"

"Common Pleas, sir? Oh, please!" Commander Teague hooted, "More like Chancery Court!"

"Aye, I'm ready," Capt. Chalmers spoke up, looking eager, which prompted agreeing sounds from the others.

"Then let's set sail tomorrow's dawn, and take advantage of the ebb in the Tagus," Lewrie announced, which raised another roar of agreement, and some fists thumped on the table. "Now," Lewrie added as the din died away, "I suppose you've all heard that the French have taken Oporto? It's good odds that their Marshal Soult is at the far end of the supply lines leading from the North coast of Spain, lines which are very vulnerable to partisan raiders, and through very rough mountain country, too, so . . . it's also good odds that Oporto might be supplied by sea up the Douro River mouth. If no other ships of our Navy are blockading Oporto, we should take a long look at the place on our way North, and do the same off Vigo, before we get back to our proper patrol stations."

"Ehm, sir," Commander Blamey said, raising a hand, "what if there are good prizes off Oporto and Vigo? Might we have to part with one of the squadron to see them back to Lisbon?"

"Hmm, good point," Lewrie replied, mulling that over for a bit. "If we meet with rich pickings, we may have to, though I would prefer that we all keep together 'til we're off Northern Spain, *then* break up into pairs, as we did before."

"We could sail what prizes we take off those ports close in so all the Frogs could see them, and set them alight, sir," Yearwood suggested. "Let them know who rules the seas, and who controls their victuals. When they're reduced to eating rats and such, hey?"

"Well, if they're not *worth* much," Capt. Chalmers gruffed.

Yearwood's suggestion was a sly'un, but it evidently cut raw to see valuable ships and cargoes go up in flames with nary a penny awarded for their taking. Tossing away perfectly good prizes was an anathema to aspiring naval officers!

"Well, it's only a possibility the French would dare supply their armies by sea, that far from Bayonne," Lewrie allowed, "but if they are, for the moment, a few prizes paraded under their noses, set afire or not, will make 'em think twice about tryin' again. And, if there are ships in harbour, I'm certain the French have taken over the shore forts, or erected new batteries to protect them, so they'd be un-reachable. We'll simply have to see, sirs.

"Once off Galicia, I intend that we split up into the same pairs we had before." Lewrie went on. "*Undaunted* and *Peregrine* will take the Eastern sector, as you gentlemen did before, and Captain Yearwood and Commander Teague patrol to the West, off Ferrol and Corunna, then work your way East along the Costa Verde, reap what you can, then meet me out to sea at the same 'rondy' and report all you've encountered. I'll cruise 'twixt Avilés and Santander, should any of you meet up with opposition."

"There's a good possibility of that, sir," Commander Teague said, sounding as if he relished the idea. "I don't know how many ships the French employ, but we took a substantial bite out of them, so it stands to reason that they'll *have* to provide escorts from now on, or give up on supply by sea altogether."

"Hmm, it may be that you're right, Commander Teague," Lewrie replied, idly stroking a patch of beard he'd missed when shaving that morning, "all the more reason to work in pairs, this time. On our third return, we may have t'sail all together, spread out to the limit of signalling. Hah!" he added as an amusing idea sprang up. "Then, I can truly justify flying a broad pendant, instead of just cruisin' by myself, with no one to impress!"

Most were polite enough to laugh, though Capt. Chalmers gave him another of those odd looks of his, as if Lewrie's idea of wit was a trifle unseemly.

"Up-anchor by dawn, then," Lewrie summed up the meeting of his Captains, "and I'm sure that all of you have last-minute things to see to, so I won't keep you from them a moment longer. By dawn, my hands will be sobred up, at least, as I trust yours will be. That'll do it, gentlemen, you're free to go."

"Thank you, sir," Commander Blamey said, shooting to his feet. "Must say, the cool tea was refreshing." Blamey was the only one to have finished his glass, Lewrie noted.

Must think me a miser, t'not trot out wine, Lewrie thought.

"Sailing tomorrow, are we sir," *Sapphire*'s First Lieutenant, Geoffrey Westcott, idly enquired after the last honours had been rendered to the departing captains, and their boats were stroking for their own ships.

"Aye, Mister Westcott," Lewrie agreed, "round dawn, to take the ebb down to the mouth of the Tagus. Pass word to the Bosun and his Mate, and the petty officers, Purser . . . I'm sure everyone'll wish to send ashore for last-minute lacks."

"I'll see to it, sir," Westcott vowed, then yawned hugely.

"Had a good run ashore, did you?" Lewrie teased.

"I did indeed, sir, and thank you for asking," Westcott said with a beamish smile. "You give me cause to boast. I learned that a grand lady, lately refugeed from Oporto, a day or two ahead of the French, had opened her grand house for the ease and comfort of British officers. Didn't know quite what that included, but it sounded most intriguing, so I went. Outnumbered by the Army, of course, but there was music, dancing, excellent service, and good wines and things to nibble on. *And*, best of all, the house was simply awash with young Portuguese ladies . . . unfortunately *not* available for my . . . ahem . . . interests, but most gracious and charming, from good families.

"My hostess, I gathered, is *huge* in the port and sherry trade," Westcott went on, "and as wealthy as the Walpoles, a hellish-handsome widow by name of Georgiana Beauman."

Oh Christ, them again! Lewrie thought.

"Let me guess," Lewrie interrupted, "ash blond hair, pale green eyes, tall and slim?"

"Uhm, aye. How did you know?" Westcott had to ask.

"I stole a dozen Beauman slaves on Jamaica, got tried for it *in absentia*, and pursued to London with a sentence that would've gotten me hanged," Lewrie explained. "When I finally *did* go on trial in Eighteen Oh-One, she and her husband, Hugh Beauman, had scampered off to Lisbon before *they* got tried for framin' me and riggin' the first trial with false evidence and a packed jury. Their ship foundered just offshore, Hugh Beauman drowned, and she inherited everything."

"Well, I did think it odd that she asked about you, sir," Lt. Westcott said with his head cocked over in puzzlement.

"She did?" Lewrie gawped.

"As I was introduced, I named my ship and Captain, and she went all squinty," Westcott went on. "Said she knew you of old, she did, that you were well known to the Beauman clan from long before in the West Indies."

"Hmm . . . still fetchin' ye say?" Lewrie pondered.

"Oh, ravishing, sir!" Westcott assured him. "Though, I did get warned off by an Army Major that the widow Beauman was a 'fireship' . . . rumoured to be poxed, and *not* one to mount without *three* cundums, haw!" After a long moment, he just had to ask, "Did you really steal those slaves, sir?"

"Aye, I did, and I'd do it again," Lewrie declared, "just to put the Beaumans' noses out o' joint. Her husband's long dead, and she's poxed to her eyebrows, so . . . to Hell with 'em. They deserved each other, most-like, and deserve their lots."

"She did wish me to offer you an invitation to call upon her, sir," Westcott slyly told him, with a quizzing brow up.

"An invitation I'll ignore, Geoffrey," Lewrie laughed off. "People who grew up in the West Indies know the best poisons, learned 'em from their slave nannies and maid servants. 'Oh, Sir Alan, *do* try the she-crab soup, it's a secret family receipt!' and the next I know, I'm heavin' up black bile, *and* my last breath. No thankee!"

"Perhaps she meant it in gratitude, sir," Westcott surmised. "After all, she ended up with a fortune."

"Still as arch and mannered as an empress, was she?" Lewrie asked.

"Aye," Westcott replied.

"Her sort *have* no gratitude in 'em," Lewrie scoffed. "They're supposed t'have what they want when they want it, and whoever fetches it matters no more than a footstool. Like I said, to Hell with 'em.

"Hmm," Lewrie went on, looking Westcott over with, a sharp eye, "ye surely had more sense than t'top the bitch after bein' warned, and all the young Lisbon ladies were pure and high-born . . . so, why d'ye say ye had a grand time?"

"There's more than *one* grand mansion in Lisbon open to provide ease and comfort to British officers, sir," Westcott said, smirking, "and more than enough frisky courtesans grateful the French are gone, and in need of fresh income, hmm?"

"Don't tell me where they are, whatever you do," Lewrie told him. "My life's complicated enough. See you in the 'early-earlies'."

"Goodnight, sir," Westcott bade him, doffing his hat.

*   *   *

"No, I don't think *Blaze* will catch her before she gets under cover of the French guns," Sailing Master Yelland stated, telescope to one eye, stifling a curse that a rich prize would escape.

Lewrie had ordered the squadron to stand well out to sea, and pass beyond Oporto's latitude before turning to steer shoreward level with the coastal town of Póvoa de Varzim, so the French would not see them coming, and possibly intersecting the course of any French ship bound South, sailing close to the Portuguese coast.

"*Are* there French guns?" Lewrie wondered aloud, using his own day-glass to scan the coast, and the hills either side of the mouth of the Douro River. Much closer inshore, HMS *Blaze* raced shoreward, with a bone in her teeth, under a great press of sail. Tantalisingly just out of gun range, a modestly-sized French brig was racing for her very life, and looked to be near enough to the Castela de Foz to make her turn into the mouth of the Douro and make her escape.

He turned about and looked astern to see what HMS *Peregrine* was doing with the first prize taken, and found that they were fetched to close alongside each other, and a British ensign how flew above a French Tri-colour.

Only two wee brigs, hmm, Lewrie thought; *And that'uns not worth all that much, by the look of her. Come t'think on it . . .* He turned again for a look up the Douro to see if he could make out masts in harbour, but the hills were still blocking his view.

"Guns, sir!" Lt. Harcourt snapped. "In that castle!"

Distant bursts of yellow-grey smoke, followed seconds later by faint door-slamming thuds, and even longer seconds before tall pillars of water arose well short and wide of HMS *Blaze.* Sure enough, that French brig *would* make her escape, for she was already altering her course and show-ing her transom as she began to enter the river mouth.

"Signal to *Blaze,*" Lewrie snapped, slamming the tubes of his telescope shut, "Dis-Continue the Action."

"Aye, sir," Midshipman Fywell called back from the taffrail flag lock-ers and signal halliards.

Lewrie paced down the larboard bulwarks of the poop deck, head down in thought, then looked seaward to his two idling frigates, and had to smile.

Chalmers and Yearwood, he thought; *They must be cursin' me, or grindin' their teeth in frustration that I didn't send* them *after those brigs. Maybe I should've . . . they've longer waterlines, and they're a tad faster. Wouldn't've mattered. Small loss.*

Sapphire was slowly coming level with the Castela de Foz and the river mouth proper, prompting Lewrie to extend the tubes of his telescope once more. This time, he could begin to make out the city that sloped down from the hills to the North bank of the Douro, and the long quays of the wine shippers, but Lewrie's flagship was still over five miles off, and there was little detail that he could make out at that distance.

"Signal to *Undaunted* and *Sterling,* Mister Fywell," Lewrie called out to the signals Midshipman. "Form line astern of me, and follow my movements."

He then descended the ladderway to the quarterdeck where Lt. Har-court temporarily held the post at the larboard bulwarks, making that wor-thy swing away from his own study of the city.

"We will alter course, Mister Harcourt," Lewrie told him. "I wish a close look at the place. Come about to Due East, and shorten sail. Mister Yelland? Get out your slate, and inform me when we're three miles off, where I wish us to turn North and let the French get a good look at us."

"Aye, sir," the Sailing Master said, louder than normal so he could be heard over Harcourt's orders sending men aloft to reef sail, and preparing hands to man the sheets and braces to take the wind on a new angle.

Despite it being Harcourt's watch, and *Sapphire* had not been called to Quarters, Lt. Westcott and Lt. Elmes were on deck and up against the larboard bulwarks with their own day-glasses extended. Indeed, so were half the Mids who should have been off-watch, and a parcel of curious sailors.

Back up to the poop deck Lewrie went for a look astern for what his brig-sloops were doing. *Blaze* was sulking her way out to sea, and further off to the Nor'east, *Peregrine* and her prize were just getting under way.

"Another signal to the brig-sloops, Mister Fywell," Lewrie called aft. "Form line, astern of *Undaunted* and *Sterling*."

"Aye aye, sir!" Fywell shouted back, as he and men of the Afterguard dug into the flag lockers one more time as the two-decker began to sway and heel a bit to starboard as she slowly came round to her new course, sails rustling and slatting, yards groaning as they were re-angled, and blocks squealing as the squares'ls were drawn up to the first reef points.

"Due East, sir!" Lt. Harcourt reported. "Almost square-on to the mouth of the river."

"Hmmph! I wonder, Mister Harcourt, if the French fancy that we're goin' t'sail right in and lay waste to 'em?" Lewrie japed.

"Could we, sir?" Lt. Harcourt asked, looking up at him with his head laid over in consideration of the idea.

"No, sir," Lewrie told him, "we'll just parade past and take a good, long look at how things stand."

Temptin', Lewrie thought, though; *Rash, pointless, sure t'end in tears, but . . . it* might *be hellish-fun!*

As *Sapphire* got her way off, the two frigates were cracking on sail and catching her up, beginning to form line, both of them already near the required one cable distance from each other. The two brig-sloops were racing to cross *Sapphire*'s stern, timing the right moment to wheel about and fall in line-astern of the frigates.

"A mile more, I make it, sir," Mr. Yelland announced, "before we have to come about North."

"I leave it up to you and Mister Harcourt, Mister Yelland," Lewrie replied, leaning far out to see anything that wasn't masked by the foresails. "General signal, Mister Fywell . . . Prepare to Alter Course in Succession. Due North."

"Aye, sir!" Fywell replied, and the lids of the flag lockers slammed open once more.

The closer to the mouth of the Douro the squadron got, though, the less-appealing the idea of a seaborne attack right up the river appeared. The mouth of the river was nowhere near as wide and welcoming as was the Tagus at Lisbon, and once past the Castela de Foz on its tall, steep headland on the North bank, and the village of Afurada on the South bank, the Douro narrowed to only a few hundred yards' width, too narrow to sail in, firing, and turn about in succession.

Lewrie could make out the famous wine shippers' warehouses and shops on the South bank opposite the city proper, the Villa Nova de Gaia, and what was left of that infamous bridge of boats which had broken, somehow, drowning thousands as they had fled the French invasion of their city. As for shipping, Lewrie could espy the same sort of boats he had seen harvesting seaweed at the Spanish town of Ayamonte the year before . . . *molicieros* he recalled they were named . . . and large wine barges to bring the great casks of fresh wines down from the Alto Douro vineyards, where the great export houses would blend them with brandy to stop the fermentation process and retain the sugars that made ports or sherrys sweet. He wondered if his London club, the Madeira Club, would run short even of ruby port, much less the aged vintages, the tawny, aged tawny, select vintage, or the precious "Rainwater Madeira".

Lewrie licked his lips without thinking.

"Three miles off, sir!" Mr. Yelland called up from the quarterdeck. "Time to turn North."

"Very well, Mister Yelland. Alter course, Mister Harcourt," he ordered, raising his telescope again for a good long look.

Once *Sapphire* was settled on her new course, with her yards re-angled to take the offshore wind abeam of her larboard side, Lewrie spotted the small French brig that had escaped them, now anchoring close to the Cais de Ribiera under the city's quays on the Northern bank, stern-on to his view to breast the flow of the river, the last sails being handed and harbour gasketed.

"I don't think we'll have to linger off Oporto," Lewrie announced to his officers below on the quarterdeck. "But for her, there aren't any other ships of worth in sight. I don't think the French get supplied by sea, here."

"Well, there's always Vigo, up North, sir," Lt. Harcourt said with a whimsical shrug. "Maybe the French dare send their cargoes that far."

"Hmm, perhaps," Lewrie replied, though he was not all that sure of that, either; Vigo was too far from Bayonne, or other enemy harbours, too, and it would take a major effort for the French to provide proper escorts that far from home.

He looked aft to see his squadron strung astern like pearls on a rope, one cable's separation between them, with *Peregrine* and her lone prize brig just attaching herself at the very end, having cut a corner and idled for a time 'til the other warships had crossed her bows. All in all, Lewrie thought that his ships made an impressive, and implacable, display to the French watchers ashore, proof that the Royal Navy would be there to isolate and starve the bastards, and that there was nothing they could do about it, even if the French Navy finally found the nerve to sortie. That thought made him grin.

He heard a tentative *woof* near his left leg, and there was the ship's mascot, Bisquit, raising a paw to stroke at his boot to prompt *somebody* to play with him. In Bisquit's mouth there was a new chew toy, a foot-long length of three-inch rope with Turk's Heads worked into either end.

"Oh, who's a good boy?" Lewrie cooed, bending over to pet him. "Yes, you *are*, Bisquit! Got a new toy? No dog slobber on it, yet? Want t'chase it, fetch?"

Bisquit's bushy tail whipped like a flag in a stiff gale, and he dropped the toy, beginning to prance. A snatch, a toss aft, and Bisquit was off in a furry brown streak, pouncing on his toy, giving it a fierce shake, growls, and a chase round the poop deck ahead of pursuit, running far enough away to lower his fore end in invitation.

Lt. Harcourt, the Sailing Master, and the Quartermasters on the helm exchanged faint smiles. Lewrie was sure that they were doing so, but didn't care a fig. Once he caught up with the dog and snatched the toy away, he tossed it down to the quarterdeck, plop into the compass binnacle, which got the watchstanders into the game, too, and it was a fine scramble before Bisquit pranced back to the poop deck with his prize in his mouth, eager for more fun.

And when Bisquit's played out, I think I'll give the French a bit o' fun, too, Lewrie decided.

Once the morning parade past the mouth of the Douro was done, and the squadron had made their way further out to sea, Lewrie had the signal made to *Peregrine,* and Commander Blamey, for him to Repair on Board for a conference. Instead of taking to his gig for a long, slow crawl up the line to *Sapphire*, Blamey cracked on sail and brought his ship almost within hailing distance before getting into his personal boat and getting rowed across.

"Good morning, Commander Blamey," Lewrie bade him once the man attained the deck. "A nice piece of work, this morning. My congratulations."

"Ah, thank you, sir," Blamey replied, doffing his hat with a proud grin on his face. "Though she's not all that much t'speak of."

"Let's go aft so I can offer you a glass of something, sir," Lewrie bade him. "*Vinho verde,* or would you prefer a *tinto?*"

"Oh, the *vinho verde,* sir, and thank you, again!" Blamey said as he followed Lewrie into the great-cabins, got pointed to a seat by the settee, and got a glass of wine in his hands.

"Lovely stuff," Lewrie commented, once he'd taken a sip from his own glass. "After sampling Spanish and Portuguese wines, I may find claret and burgundy too dull."

"Oh, there's Spanish *tempranillo,* and Genoese *monte pulciano* to make up for those, sir," Blamey said with a twist of his mouth, "though I had hoped that we might find a way to obtain some port, as long as we're off its source."

"I would, too, sir," Lewrie agreed, "but, there's little that we can accomplish on that head, so long as Marshal Soult and his Frogs hold Oporto. Now, Commander . . . have you had a chance to take the measure of your prize, her cargo and such?"

Blamey screwed his harsh face into a fierce scowl and made a faint growling sound of disappointment. "She's shoddily maintained, both her running and standing rigging as thin and worn as charity, sir, her sails all but patches, and full of filth, so I doubt if she'd fetch two thousand pounds at the Prize-Court. Her cargo, well, sir . . . salt-meats that, frankly, smell a bit 'off' to me, cheap, raw *vin ordinaires* no better than paint thinner, and about one hundred kegs of gunpowder. The best items aboard her are the bottled soups and such, and the pickled vegetables."

"So, you wouldn't cry if we burn her, sir?" Lewrie asked him. "Once the bottled soups and gravies, and the pickled vegetables are removed and shared round the squadron?"

"Well, not really sir," Blamey said after a long moment, with another harsh scowl. "There's better pickings off the North coast of Spain. Though, there are kegs of apples and potatoes, as well, along with flour, salt, sugar, molasses, and dry pastas that should be got off her first."

"Good!" Lewrie said with good cheer, "If you would be so good as to hoist the good stuff up from her holds, boats from the other ships can be alongside t'go 'shares' of what we wish to keep, we can set her alight by dusk, I'm hopin'."

"Dusk, sir?" Blamey asked, waving his empty glass at Pettus for a re-fill.

"Dusk, and fire, go hellish-good together, sir," Lewrie told him with a wink.

The squadron returned to the mouth of the Douro just as the sun was low in the Western skies, most aptly painting the horizon and the clouds a grand, or ominous, amber and gold as they rounded up into the winds and fetched-to, beginning to turn into stark silhouettes of warships loitering just out of gun range from the Castela de Foz.

The prize brig had possessed two ship's boats, two dowdy and scabrous twenty-footers, now manned by her former master, mates, and her small crew, laden with their few miserable possessions, and slowly stroking for the headland.

"If so few French ships put in here," Midshipman Chenery was chortling with his new mess-mates, "those poor sods will have a long journey home, over the Pyrenees, walking all the way, hee hee!"

"Where did you pick up the word 'sods', Chenery?" Midshipman Kibworth teased him.

"The prize shows two lanthorns, sir," Lt. Westcott pointed out. "She's ready to go."

"Show two lanthorns back, Mister Westcott," Lewrie ordered, back on the poop deck to enjoy the show.

The winds off the Atlantic that evening were moderate, out of the West by North. The prize brig's forecourse and tops'ls spread to cup them, hauled down loose and let fall, and she began to gather a bit of way, steering directly for the river mouth. Sailors off *Peregrine* tumbled down into their rowing boats, oars hoisted aloft, waiting for the last officer to lash and secure her helm, then join them, the last hands who set piles of spare canvas and rope alight, then dashed to the bulwarks to scramble over and leave her.

"What was her name, I wonder?" Lt. Elmes asked Harcourt on the quarterdeck.

"Hmm, don't know," Lt. Harcourt had to reply.

"It don't matter worth a damn," Lewrie called down to them, then muttered, "Oh, damn!" The prize brig's crew, slowly rowing into port, began pointing and gesticulating at her, then put their helms over as if they would go alongside their former ship whilst it was going so slowly, and re-take her.

But no, after only a few oar-strokes in her direction, flames began to wink above her bulwarks, and dark smoke began to waft aloft, and the French sailors turned hastily away and began to row shoreward as if the Devil was raking his talons on their transoms. They *knew* what cargo they had carried, and wanted nothing to do with the casks and kegs of gunpowder if the hated *l'Anglais* had left them aboard!

There was the gloom of the land ahead of the brig, the lights of Oporto and Villa Nova de Gaia sparking to life for the evening, and there was the brig, well aflame now, sailing into the river mouth, beginning to veer a bit to starboard, towards the village of Lavadores on the South bank of the Douro.

"Charts show a shoal, there," Mr. Yelland commented, "and it's noted that the Portuguese were building a mole atop it, before the French put a stop to it. She may take the ground, there."

There were a *lot* more pinpricks of light ashore, lanthorns and torches lower down the slopes and steep streets of Oporto, as if many watchers were streaming down for a better view of the burning brig, which was now a bowl to contain a conflagration that shrivelled her sails into momentary sheets of flame, before disintegrating into flittering firefly embers borne away and ahead of her by the wind. Her masts and yards, her tarred and slushed rigging, afire from deck to mast-trucks, made eerie, glowing geometric patterns, as if a spider web could glow yellowish-red.

"Ooh!" was a collective sigh from many hands, "Aah!"

The fire belowdecks finally reached the gunpowder kegs, and the brig went up like a *feu de joie,* a brief but brilliant pyrotechnic display that shot skyward like a royal fireworks, planking and bits and pieces of her soaring up and outward in ballistic arcs, and the thunderclap of the explosion was so loud and forceful that men on the squadron's decks could feel it rattling their chests, feel the stiff gusting of wind, and see the bristly wee wavecrests radiating outward from the wreck as if God himself had slapped the sea.

"Whee!" Midshipman Holbrooke crowed. "Magnificent!"

"I wish we'd caught the other," Midshipman Ward tittered, "so we could do it, again!"

Satisfied with the show and the probable effect it had on the watching French, Lewrie slowly clomped down the ladderway to the quarterdeck, and bent to reassure Bisquit, who was no fan of loud noises.

"Well, that'll put the wind up them, sir," Lt. Harcourt said with a triumphal grin on his face. "Quite clever."

"Clever? Me, Mister Harcourt?" Lewrie scoffed. "I believe it was Captain Yearwood who first proposed such a show, in jest, and in his cups, too, if memory serves. I'll have t'send him a thank you note."

"A damned good show, anyway, sir," Mr. Yelland crowed.

"Aye well, I must admit I always liked t'see things go boom," Lewrie confessed, still more attentive to the dog's distress.

"Perhaps we could do the same off Vigo, sir?" Lt. Elmes asked, tongue-in-cheek.

"We'll see, we'll see," Lewrie replied, then stood back up to turn sobre. "I'd admire that we signal all ships, while they can still *see* a flag hoist, for the squadron to get under way, course North by West, to clear the coast for the night."

"Aye, sir, general signal, make sail and way, Course North by West," Lt. Harcourt repeated, then called out for the Master Gunner. "Mister Boling!" he bellowed, "load two six-pounders for a general signal!"

"You have the watch, sir," Lewrie told them, "I'll be aft in my cabins . . . cackling over my witches' cauldron t'see what fresh mischief we can conjure. Bisquit . . . want t'come aft where it's safe and quiet? Bring your toy, mind. Come on!"

BOOK THREE

To be sure I lose the fruits of the earth,
but then I am gathering the flowers of the sea.
-ADMIRAL BOSCAWEN, PRIVATE LETTER, (1756)

CHAPTER NINETEEN

Conditions at sea off the North coast of Spain might have become warmer than the weather during the squadron's first foray, but milder temperatures did not signify a Spring-like lull in the winds, or the boisterousness of the ocean. One day out of three, the prevailing Westerlies piped up, the seas turned steep, and when IIMS *Sapphire* was within sight of land, the on-rushing waves roared and smashed ashore in tumbling white breakers that almost could be heard from five miles off, forcing Lewrie to tread carefully in the search for prizes, with many looks over his shoulder to see if the weather would turn so foul that his ship might be unable to wear about to face it, and be driven to ruin on that battered coast.

The Sailing Master and the Lieutenants all agreed that conditions were marginally improved since their last outing, even so, so . . . if things were better, where were the French? It had been at least a fortnight since the squadron had quit the coast and sailed for Lisbon to re-plenish. The French surely would have noticed their absence, gotten over their initial panic, and gotten back to the business of supplying their armies, yet . . . where were they?

After despatching the rest of the squadron to their operating areas, *Sapphire* had made her appearance six or seven miles off from Aviles and had slowly prowled Eastward under reduced sail as far as Santander, sometimes closing within four or five miles off the small fishing ports and fetching-to. Her presence had terrified many of the Spanish fishermen, robbing them of a day's catch, sending what looked like racing regattas dashing into the shelter of their home ports, but there was no sign of French convoys, or escorts, or much of anything.

"We'll have t'think of something else, then," Lewrie growled as he sat in his collapsible wood-and-canvas deck chair on the poop deck, staring intently, frowning rather, at the little seaport town of San Vicente de la Barquera, and the wide and deep notch of an inlet on which it was situated. He levered himself to his feet and clomped down the ladderway to the quarterdeck.

"Mister Harcourt," Lewrie said to the watch officer, "I'd admire did you fetch the ship to, and haul one of the cutters alongside, then muster a boat crew."

"Aye, sir?" Lt. Harcourt replied, so taken aback that he made that sound more like a question.

"Mister Fywell," Lewrie turned to one of the Midshipmen, "do you pass word for Mister Roe. He speaks decent Spanish as I recall."

"Aye, sir!" Fywell said with a quick doff of his hat, then a dash below to the officers' wardroom.

"I'll be aft for a moment, Mister Harcourt," Lewrie went on. "I'll fetch you the keys to the arms chests, just in case, and some money."

"Sir?" Harcourt asked.

"With any luck, Mister Roe can buy us some fresh fish for our supper, Mister Harcourt," Lewrie said with a grin as he went aft to his cabins.

Should've thought o' this sooner, Lewrie chid himself as he unlocked the bottom drawer of his desk where he kept a stout ironbound chest that held his passage money and personal funds, took out a wash-leather purse, and sorted out some coins, lamenting the fact that His Majesty's Government sent so much silver to support their so-called "allies" that private banks, large employers, and stores minted their own coinage, and that mostly brass or copper.

He did have a goodly pile of thruppence, six pence, and even some older silver shillings, all nice and shiny, and . . . tempting? He dug out a spare purse, dumped those coins in it, and drew the strings to secure them. With that, and the keys to the arms chests, he returned to the quarterdeck, just as Marine Lieutenant Roe, in his shirtsleeves, came to the quarterdeck.

"You sent for me, sir?" Roe asked, puzzled.

"Aye, Mister Roe, I did," Lewrie replied, a sly smile on his face. "Once we're fetched-to, I wish you to take this purse of coins and go buy us some fresh fish from any Spaniard who doesn't run off screamin' at the sight of you. While you're doin' that, I wish you to enquire, casually mind, where the French supply ships are. Hang the cost if they wish t'haggle. Hmm, you might forego your red coat, and all, so they don't think you're there t'press 'em. You'll go armed . . . pistols and cutlasses . . . but keep 'em out of sight 'til you really have need of 'em."

"Ehm . . . aye, sir, I see," Lt. Roe replied, looking as puzzled as Harcourt for a moment, then breaking out a grin of agreement, and some amusement. "Fresh fish it will be, sir!"

"I've told off Crawley and his gang to man the boat, Captain," Lt. Harcourt said, more intent on fetching a brass speaking-trumpet so everyone as far forward as the foc's'le could hear his commands to round the ship up into the wind and fetch her to.

But of course ye did, Lewrie sourly thought, striving not to roll his eyes; *You and the old Captain's Cox'n are still thick as thieves.*

"All hands!" Harcourt bellowed. "Stations to wear ship and fetch her to!"

Lewrie went back to his solitary perch on the poop deck once the ship had rounded up into the wind, with squares'ls backed and the fore-and-aft sails trying to drive her forward. He took a telescope with him so he could scan the dozen or so scrofulous fishing boats between *Sapphire* and the shore, hoping that just one of them would not panic and dash into harbour with the rest.

This could take a while, he told himself, and wondering why the Spanish, who were now not only British allies, who were living under the boots of the occupying. French, *would* run from the sight of a British warship.

Lewrie thought of returning to his deck chair, but Bisquit the ship's dog had usurped it for a good, yielding place for a nap, and regarded him with one eye half-slit to see if he'd have to jump down. Lewrie walked past the chair, giving Bisquit a head rub on his way aft to the flag lockers and the taffrails, where he would have an un-interrupted view, now that the ship was cocked up into the wind with her stern facing the shore.

There were two or three fishing boats within a couple of miles of *Sapphire,* close enough for his telescope to make out ant-sized Spaniards pointing at his ship, ignoring their nets for the moment. Farther off, one or two boats looked as if they would give up on a catch, hauling their nets in empty as if they would flee.

Surely, the French don't put guards aboard, do they? he had to ask himself; *That'd be a good way o' getting' their throats cut.*

Hard as he looked, he saw no sign of anyone on the nearest boats in uniform, or under arms, making him think that the French might be closely watching the fishermen from a shore promontory, and would punish anyone who might dare to have "truck" with a British ship, them and their families as well, with the loss of their boats and livelihoods the least of it.

It had worked for others, seeking information from fishermen, even cajoling them into passing and delivering messages back and forth from British agents or *partisanos*. When Lewrie had had the *Savage* frigate, blockading the mouth of the Gironde River in France, he had developed good relations with French fishermen who'd sell him fish, sausages, and fresh bread for solid coin, and information on the two shore forts, later, both of which he'd assaulted and blown sky high, at last.

Looking closer aboard, Lewrie could see that the cutter was well under way with her loose-footed sail bellied out, slowly making way towards the nearest fishing boat, whose crew was at least still hauling in their latest cast of their nets, perhaps more intent upon one last haul *than* a quick escape. There was Crawley at the tiller right aft, and Marine Lt. Roe next to him, in waistcoat and shirtsleeves with his collar spread *sans* neck-stock. Roe had put his hat on, but that was as militant and threatening as he went.

After a time, Roe stood up with one hand on Crawley's shoulder, and waving his hat with the other. *How d'ye say it*, Lewrie thought; *Hola, senores? Hav-ee fresco pescados? Or, something like that. Damn all foreign tongues!*

The lugs'l was handed and the cutter coasted quite near the fishing boat while the fishermen strained to haul aboard what looked to be a promising weight of catch. They didn't look up or pay Roe much attention 'til the last yard or two of their net was aboard, then stood up, merely looking curious.

Now's the crux, Lewrie told himself, even more intent on his telescope, seating himself on the flag lockers with his day-glass resting on the taffrail cap-rail, wishing he could hear what was being said even if Spanish wasn't in him, wishing he was closer so he could detect any treachery, any ambush by Spaniards currying favour with their occupiers, like the *anfresados* in Madrid who had kissed Bonaparte's arse and had sold out their wretched people.

The better part of an hour passed, before *Sapphire's* cutter could complete its two-way journey and return near the ship. At last, Lewrie closed the tubes of his telescope and stood up, thinking that it would be best if he did not appear *too* eager to hear the results. He trotted down to the quarterdeck and entered his cabins, quickly finding a half-read book, flung himself on the settee, and pretended to be engrossed and above it all.

"Boat ahoy!" a Midshipman shouted, as if a Viking dragon boat had popped up, as if it was not plainly evident that it was theirs.

"Returning!" he could hear Crawley bellow back.

Navy ritual, my God, Lewrie thought, shaking his head.

Sure enough, the Marine sentry at his door stamped boots and musket butt on the deck and shouted to announce Midshipman Fywell.

"Enter!" Lewrie called back, striving for "unconcerned".

"Mister Harcourt's duty, sir, and I'm to inform you that the cutter is coming alongside . . . with fresh fish, sir!"

"My compliments to Mister Harcourt, and inform him that I'll be on deck, directly, Mister Fywell," Lewrie replied, fulfilling his own part in the ritual. "A *lot* of fish, is it?" he asked, marking the last page he had "read", and getting to his feet.

"Rather a lot, aye sir!" Fywell said with an impish grin.

"Very well, you may go," Lewrie bade him, snatched his old hat off a peg, and followed the Midshipman out to the quarterdeck.

Lt. Roe had just scampered up the boarding battens and man-ropes to the deck, looking as pleased as punch.

"Ah, Mister Roe, how did your negotiations go?" Lewrie idly asked him.

"Quite well, sir . . . swimmingly well, if you will pardon the pun," Lt. Roe boasted, "though my schoolboy Castilian Spanish gave me a bit of a problem, at first. The locals speak a Galician dialect, and one of them even spoke Basque, which is *totally* incomprehensible, another tongue entirely. I spent all your coin, sir, sorry, but I obtained quite a lot. Sea bass, I think some of them are, a basket of sardines . . ."

"The French, Mister Roe?" Lewrie pressed.

"There are three French merchantmen far up the bay between San Vicente and Comillas, even as we speak, sir!" Lt. Roe crowed. "The Spaniards say that they only put to sea just after sundown, and sail as far as they can before dawn, then put into shelter before we *Anglais* pirates snatch them up! It seems that *someone* frightened them out of their boots, hah hah!"

"What sort o' ships?" Lewrie gruffly pressed.

"Uhm, I gathered that they were all brig-rigged, sir," Lt. Roe replied, "and the Spanish fishermen said that they were not all that big. They say that large ships are rare along this coast since Spain got invaded."

"Hmm, about what we saw on our last cruise," Lewrie surmised, rubbing his chin. "No escorts?"

"None that they've seen putting in anywhere along this part of the coast, so far, sir," Roe told him, then blurted out, "They asked for arms, sir, anything we could spare. The French have gone through all the coastal towns and villages and rounded up all the weapons they could find, but the Spanish still find ways to ambush them or cut lone soldiers' throats. I sense they'd rise up if they had the means."

"Well, arms'd do these poor Devils no good, Mister Roe. The French would slaughter them, and their families, if they did rise up, and that in short order," Lewrie dismissed quickly. "There are organised bands inland who fare better, 'cause they can dash back into the mountains, but this lot . . . they wouldn't stand a chance.

"*But,*" he said, perking up, "we can always recommend the idea to Mister Mountjoy back in Lisbon, and see what he can make of it. As for us . . . hmm," Lewrie said, looking up at the commissioning pendant, then out to sea to ascertain the weather and sea state. "We need to encourage those three brigs to set sail this evening, and to do that, we should sail on East, out of sight, first. Mister Harcourt? Get way on the ship, if ye please, course Due East, under easy sail."

"Very good, sir!" Lt. Harcourt piped up.

"Well done, Mister Roe," Lewrie said, "and I trust there's a fine, fat fish in your 'catch' for my supper?"

"Thank you, sir, and I'm certain that there is," Roe replied, doffing his hat in salute, visibly pleased to be praised.

Now, how to catch me three brigs, Lewrie thought as he went back to the poop deck and his collapsible chair as Lt. Harcourt issued orders for getting *Sapphire* under way.

Sapphire sailed on, slowly edging seaward 'til she was ten miles off Santander, then altered course Nor'easterly as the sun declined that late afternoon. Once at least twelve miles off the coast, she came back on the winds, bound West, on starboard tack, slanting back to where she had started, so that by half-past seven of the evening, swallowed by the darkness and with all lanthorns doused, she was off Comillas once more.

Should've asked about semaphore towers, Lewrie fretted as he paced the poop deck, now and then stumbling over ring-bolts and the odd protuberance; *The bloody French just* love *the bastards, and if Santander warned ports up and down the coast. . . .*

Sapphire's re-appearance off Santander after a respite of at least a fortnight surely would have forced what French merchantmen were in that port to stay put for that night, but would the three brigs up that inlet near Comillas be that wary, or would they feel safe enough to put to sea and try to make it all the way to Gijon before dawn?

Santander and Gijon, Viviero and Ortigueira were good places to land their supplies, before Cape Ortegal and the ports of Ferrol and Corunna, he reckoned; perhaps they didn't have that much farther to go before reaching the end of their voyage. What if they were unloading that very hour up near San Vicente de la Barquera, and would not have to come out?

Lewrie's fingers flexed on the hilt of his everyday hanger. He ran a hand over the brace of double-barrelled Manton pistols in the band of his breeches. HMS *Sapphire* had gone to Quarters a bit after full dark, and the arms chests had been unlocked and opened. Gun crews stood or slouched at their pieces with the gun-ports still shut, and the red battle lanthorns lit. Lookouts were aloft, long after they should have descended to the deck, and more lookouts were posted along the bulwarks, peering into the darkness.

Lewrie looked aloft, but the night was too dark to make out the commissioning pendant, or much of anything else. There was no moon, and an overcast had blown in from the Atlantic that masked the starlight, so that the only illumination was the tiny glim-like lights ashore in the small seaports, fishing villages, and farmhouses that lay between them.

"Well, if we can't see them, they can't see us," Mr. Yelland the Sailing Master said in a stage-whisper to Lt. Westcott below on the quarterdeck. "There's a hellish-small blessing, hah."

"On a night this dark, they *must* be at least twelve miles off the coast," Lt. Westcott sourly grumbled in a matching loud whisper. "Where away now, Mister Yelland?"

"By dead-reckoning, we must be off Llanes or Ribadesella by now," Yelland told the First Lieutenant, between yawns. Over the sounds of the ship working and the wind in the rigging, Lewrie could make out their footfalls on the oaken deck, and the squeak of the First Officer's new boots.

"Ehm . . . somethin' out there, sir," a larboard side lookout near the main mast shrouds spoke up, sounding hesitant. "Somethin' 'tween the shore lights, seven points off th' larboard beam!"

Several night-glasses snapped open, sweeping back and forth from the bow to almost amidships, looking for something that might occlude the wee lights ashore, for something darker than the night.

"I think . . ." Lewrie muttered, cursing the night-glass for its tendency to show everything upside-down and backwards. "I've got one, two points abaft amidships! And *close*, by God!"

The watch officers swung their telescopes abaft to confirm, and after a long moment, Lewrie could hear grunts of surprise.

"No more than two cables off, I think, sir," Lt. Westcott announced, "two points off the larboard quarter. The trailer? And, there's another, seven points off the larboard bows. Black as my boots, but they're there. Now, where's the third one?"

"Crack on a bit more sail, Mister Westcott," Lewrie snapped, "I wish to fall down on the one almost abeam, and cut her off."

"Aye aye, sir!" Westcott eagerly said. "Pass word aloft to shake out the reefs in the fore and main tops'l's!"

Slowly, slowly, *Sapphire* began to gather a bit more speed over the ground, edging ahead of the leading shadow, out-footing it and laying it one point, then two points aft of abeam.

"Helm up, Quartermasters," Lewrie called down to the men at the helm, "ease us down on her. Mister Westcott, pass word to the gun decks to be ready to run out. I want t'hammer this'un, and put the fear o' God in 'em."

Once one knew that they were there, they were easier to make out, those two brigs, darker-than-night blobs. One could almost slap one's forehead and go "Duhh!" for being so blind before.

"A cable, I make it, sir," Westcott reckoned at last after a long look with his night-glass, "two points aft of abeam."

"Order the ports opened and the guns run-out," Lewrie snapped, grinning evilly at how the French would react when two rows of reddish light suddenly appeared like the eyes of a pack of demons.

"Upper deck ready . . . lower deck ready!" was shouted up from below.

"By broadside . . . fire, Mister Westcott," Lewrie yelled, and quickly shut his eyes to preserve his night vision.

Twenty-two guns, 12-pounders and 24-pounders, erupted with a titanic

roar to shatter the peace of the night, amber jets of flame stabbing outward through fire-lit clouds of powder smoke and swirling bits of burning lint from the cartridge bags and wadding. Above all that, a second or
two later, came the welcome sound of shot striking wood, punching holes
into the French brig with the shrieking sounds of terrified parrots.

The guns were sponged out, gun-captains' leather thumb-stalls placed
over the touch-holes to prevent air entering the gun tubes to make a flash
burst among the smouldering remnants of wadding, cartridge bags, and
any remaining powder. Once done, fresh cartridges were fetched up and
inserted, then wadding, then roundshot, then more wadding. Before
HMS *Sapphire* could start to rumble and shake as the carriages were
run back up to the port sills, there was a new parroty screech off their
larboard side, a longer, wrenching sound of wooden agony, and the
dim shape of a blackened ship against the lights ashore changed, losing
part of itself. Her foremast had been shot clean through, and was falling
into the sea alee, slowing her so quickly that it seemed that *Sapphire*
dashed past her like a race horse.

"Hold fire!" Lewrie yelled, looking for the trailing ship, but could not
find her. He swung his telescope back in search of their first victim, just in
time to see her taffrail lanthorns and deck lamps springing to life, enough
light for everyone to make out the large white sheet being stretched from
her mainmast shrouds as she struck.

"Helm up, give us three points alee," Lewrie ordered, "ease sheets and
braces!" and *Sapphire* turned shoreward, sweeping past the bows of the
crippled brig by at least a full cable, leaving her to wallow astern.

"There she is, sir!" Lt. Westcott shouted, pointing off the larboard quarters. Yes, the suddenly bright lights of their first target's taffrail lanthorns
threw just enough light to make her out, frantically wheeling about off the
wind to perform a panicky wear-about to get shoreward, perhaps get into
Rebadesella before the terrible *Anglais* "Devil ship" got her.

"Two cables off, d'ye make it, sirs?" Lewrie demanded.

"About that, sir," Mr. Yelland opined.

"Give her *fire*, Mister Westcott!" Lewrie ordered, his blood up.

"Aye, sir. Pass word below," Westcott snapped to the Mids waiting
nearby, "tell them to aim small, and fire as they bear, bow to stern. Run,
lads!"

"Another point alee, quartermasters," Lewrie called out as the second
brig began to become indistinct once more, wearing out of what light there
was. "Thus! Steady!"

"As you bear . . . *fire!*" Westcott howled.

Blam-Boom! First the upper gun deck 12-pounder would fire, quickly followed by the lower deck 24-pounder below it, marching the full larboard broadside down the ship's side, and Lewrie just had to trust that his gunners were taking time to aim and adjust their elevation with the quoin blocks in their own eagerness to hit the foe.

Almost like firin' blind, Lewrie despaired, slamming a hand on the caprail of the larboard bulwark; *Shootin' at spooks!*

The night winds were not all that strong, though as any night wind was, it was steady, which meant that the vast bank of powder smoke took *ages* to blow clear, a fog in which the French brig might yet escape, lost to view completely.

"Lights, sir!" Westcott yelled. "She's lit her taffrail lanthorns! She's showing a white flag of some kind, and she's lowered her Tricolour! By God, she's struck, too!"

"Secure the guns, Mister Westcott," Lewrie called down to the quarterdeck, ready to titter with glee despite the damage it might do to his dignity. "Get the way off the ship, fetch us to, haul up boats for boarding parties, quick as you can. Let's light all our lanthorns, too. Before the bastards think to change their minds!"

"What did you say the last time, sir?" Lt. Westcott called up from the quarterdeck. "Two out of three ain't all that bad, was it?"

"Birds in the hand, sir," Lewrie chortled, "birds in the hand."

CHAPTER TWENTY

*A*ll in all, it's quite a haul, sir," Lt. Elmes said as he reported the results of his search of the captured ships' manifests. "The *Arabelle*, yonder, is full of foodstuffs, salt-meats, bisquit, flour, and the usual bottled soups and sauces, along with tentage, blankets, leather goods, and several thousand pairs of boots and shoes."

"Let the bastards hobble in their stocking feet," Lewrie said with a firm nod of his head.

"Barefoot, more like, sir," Lt. Elmes cheerfully told him, "for there are bales and bales of stockings aboard her, as well. Shirts, trousers, uniform coats, winter greatcoats . . ."

"Naked *and* barefoot, hah!" Lewrie chortled. "Better and better!"

"The other brig, sir," Elmes went on, "the *Cheval Rouge,* has a dozen twelve-pounder artillery pieces, their limbers, caissons and gun-tools stowed below, along with two armourers' forges, uhm . . . several sets of spare wheels," Elmes added, consulting the captured ships' papers for a second, "dozens of sets, rather, and the bodies of six field waggons, along with all the harnesses."

"And gunpowder?" Lewrie asked.

"Ah, no sir, nothing kegged," Elmes told him, "though there are at least two thousand muskets in crates, and about eighty thousand rounds of pre-made paper cartridges. And, there's tobacco. At least three tons of cake, twist, shag tobacco for pipes, and cases of *cigarros* . . . uhm, marked as American or Spanish exports."

"*Cigarros*, did you say, sir?" Lt. Westcott piped up, looking delighted at the un-looked-for chance to replenish his thin stock of smoking materials. "I doubt the Prize-Court would miss a box or two."

"Three tons!" Lewrie marvelled, "that'll make the Purser a very happy man. Even the dead men will be pleased."

British sailors were not big on *cigarros*, but a fair number of any ship's crew would have clay pipes, and aboard *Sapphire*, even the ship's boys chewed when they could afford Mr. Cadrick's prices. And Pursers were always suspected of padding the accounts of men who were Discharged, Run as deserters, or Discharged, Dead with spurious purchases to skim a few more shillings of profit.

Hmm, which to burn, or sink, Lewrie thought as he strolled off a few paces with his hands in the small of his back; *Our Army, or the Portuguese, would find both cargoes useful. Fetch a pretty penny at the Prize-Court, too. They'd snatch everything up in an eyeblink!*

Keeping both prizes, though, would rob *Sapphire* of at least two dozen hands, several senior petty officers, and two Midshipmen.

This early into the cruise, one of them would have to go.

Lewrie looked aloft then seaward to gauge the weather and the sea state, then gave both prizes a long look.

"Mister Westcott, we're going to sink the prize with all the artillery and such aboard," Lewrie announced, turning back to face his officers. "Before we do, though, I wish some of her cargo to be shifted to the other prize, the muskets and cartidges . . . and, all of the tobacco. Most especially the tobacco. I wish some of it, the shag, and the chewing tobacco, brought aboard *Sapphire*. Send for Mister Cadrick."

"Ah, some of the *cigarros*, too, sir?" Westcott hopefully asked.

"Aye, some of the *cigarros*, too, Mister Westcott," Lewrie allowed with a false frown, "so you may indulge your beastly habit, and corrupt the rest of the wardroom with the damned things."

"I'll see to it directly, sir," Westcott vowed, then sent one of the Mids scrambling below to summon the Purser.

"And the Bosun, Mister Westcott," Lewrie added of a sudden. "We'll be needin' some of his paint store."

⚓

With the cargoes shifted aboard *Sapphire,* and into the other prize, the ship's crew was ordered to a series of mystifying tasks; a towing bridle was afitted from the *Arabelle* to the *Cheval Rouge,* long enough for a full cable's separation; the French crews off both prizes were ordered into their own lifeboats with their scant personal possessions, and set free to sail or row ashore on the rocky coast of Spain; and lastly, squares were painted along the sides of the *Cheval Rouge* that vaguely resembled gun-ports, using whatever hue that Bosun Terrell had in stock—white, red, black, and blue, which looked rather comical, in all.

Finally, Lewrie ordered that All Hands be piped, and he took his place at the filled hammock stanchions at the forward edge of the quarterdeck as *Sapphire*'s sailors and Marines gathered along the gangways and in the waist, some spryer sorts even sitting on the massive cross-deck boat-tier beams above the waist.

"Lads, we're going t'have ourselves a contest," Lewrie began, looking down on his crew. "Since I took command at the Nore, you've proven to me that you just may be the best gunners in the Fleet . . . now, we're goin' t'find out just how good you are.

"See those blotches of paint on that prize yonder?" he asked, pointing to the *Cheval Rouge,* she of the shot-through foremast. "Let us call 'em gun-ports, and let's see how close you can come to hittin' 'em."

He explained that one prize would tow another, and that their own ship would come up alongside the trailing prize brig at about one cable's range, at first, and each gun crew would take careful aim and fire as they bore, one at a time, with the results noted, first with the upper gun deck 12-pounders, then with the lower gun deck 24-pounders.

"Those gun crews that come closest, or score direct hits, get free to-bacco, *and* full measures at the afternoon rum issue," Lewrie told them, "with no 'sippers' or 'gulpers' owing. Are you game to try? Penny a pitch?"

Hell, it's captured tobacco, and didn't cost me more than ten shillings, he thought; *and damn Mister Cadrick's pinch-penny soul he charged me that much!*

Sapphire's sailors had gotten used to the idea that some prize money had to be thrown away for the lack of hands to man them, though it did cut rough, but—the idea of firing their guns in practise, and making a con-test of it like a game at a fair, roused them to raise a great, agreeable cheer. Besides, shooting things to match-wood was always lively, if noisy, fun!

"Right, then," Lewrie shouted, "let's be at it. Sound the Beat to Quarters! Mister Westcott, signal *Arabelle* t'get a way on."

⚓

The lead prize could only tow her consort slowly, not much over four knots, and without a helmsman aboard the target brig to "steer for the bollard", *Cheval Rouge* wallowed and strayed to either beam like a willful pig on the way to market. HMS *Sapphire,* under much-reduced sail, crept up on the target brig only one knot faster. At last, the first 12-pounder's crew, after much fiddling with the crow levers and quoin blocks, fired.

"A miss . . . over!" Midshipman Hillhouse shouted down from his perch on the starboard gangway. "Number Two, try your eye!"

That shot was short, but the ball did skip up from First Graze to smack into the target just above the waterline.

And so it went, all down the upper deck, with only one of the 12-pounders scoring a hit within a few feet of the after-most "gun-ports".

"Check fire!" Lewrie ordered, "We'll fall astern then sail up to her again before the lower deck guns have a go."

Christ, and I thought they could shoot! he thought, grimacing.

At one cable's range, the lower-deck 24-pounders did no better, certainly scoring hits but nowhere near the painted squares. Lewrie had the ship fall astern of the towed target once more, ordering the range to be halved to half a cable, and gave the upper deck 12-pounders another chance.

"Hmm, rather disappointing, sir," Lt. Westcott said, close to Lewrie's shoulder to make his comments private. "Was it Commander Teague who told you that he'd had notches filed in his guns so his men could actually aim after a fashion?"

"Aye, it was," Lewrie answered in a low voice. "Damme, should have thought o' that. No time, now. We'll just have t'carry on the way we are, and hope for the best. In my enthusiasm, I put the cart before the horse," he said with a groan, almost feeling an urge to slap his forehead.

By Six Bells of the Forenoon Watch, round eleven A.M., the range was cut down to a quarter-cable, sixty yards, or only 180 feet, and *Sapphire* surged up from astern for yet another attempt.

"Number One, fire as you bear!" Midshipman Hillhouse, now most thoroughly bored with the whole endeavour, shouted down to the upper gun deck. A long minute passed as that gun's captain made his last-minute adjustments, then . . . *Blam*!

"Hit!" Hillhouse shouted, sounding more surprised than congratulatory. "Top left edge of the white square! Number Two, stand ready!"

Boom! and that gun's shot smashed into the top of the bulwark a few feet above its intended target. Number Three gun quickly followed, and people cheered when a red-painted "gun-port" was hit fair and square, leaving a ragged star-shaped hole, dead-centre! Four more of the eleven 12-pounders managed to score direct hits, or hits that nibbled at the edges of the painted squares.

The lower gun deck 24-pounders tried their eyes at that range, and five of eleven guns managed to score hits worth their tobacco and rum.

"More, sir!" Midshipman Chenery cried as he came to the base of the ladderway to the quarterdeck. "The men want to keep at it, now they have their eyes in!"

"No, that's enough for now," Lewrie decided. "We've winners enough. Pass word to *Arabelle* t'let go her towing bridle. Mister Westcott . . . serve her a full broadside, six-pounders, carronades, the whole lot, and finish her off."

"Aye, sir. All guns, by broadside, this time!" Lt. Westcott shouted, shooing Chenery back below to his post at Quarters.

With the towing bridle cast free, *Arabelle* almost shot away ahead, now she was free of her burden, and *Cheval Rouge* wallowed to a crawl, quickly shedding way, beginning to yaw.

"Guns ready . . . by broadside . . . fire!" Westcott shouted.

After the slow pace of single shots half the morning, the roar of every piece of artillery going off at once was staggering, wreathing *Sapphire* in a great, stinking cloudbank of spent powder smoke. Beyond that sudden blanketing cloud, the sound of a ship being riddled and smashed with iron roundshot was almost as loud as the roars of the guns. As the smoke drifted down onto the mangled prize, then beyond her, the *Cheval Rouge* was revealed as a wreck, her main mast gone, her hull punched in in myriad places, with several holes shot into her waterline, but she was still on the surface.

"Hell, serve her another!" Lewrie snapped.

That second massive broadside did the trick. The target brig had taken more damage along her waterline, and she was slowly heeling over to larboard, showing details of her ravaged decks. Slowly, she filled with seawater, the air in her holds and belowdecks steaming out, and the many shot-holes along her waterline foaming with the in-rush, heeling and groaning her death-cries as she rolled onto her beam-ends, then began to settle lower and lower, foot by agonising foot, 'til suddenly she was gone, leaving loose gear and shattered bits of her as flotsam amid the last white-foaming gouts of trapped air wheezing upwards.

"Secure from Quarters," Lewrie ordered, "and I'll have our successful gun crews mustered under the quarterdeck edge once they have seen to their pieces. Ah, Mister Hillhouse, you've your list of 'marksmen'? Good. And I'd admire did you have a box of tobacco fetched from my cabins."

And once the hands were gathered, Mr. Cadrick the Purser and his Jack-in-the-Breadroom, Irby, saw to the distribution. There was some joshing and boasting, some longer faces among the gun crews that had not quite hit the mark, but the free tobacco was welcome.

"Lads, you did rather well, for a first stab at close aiming," Lewrie told them, "and with any luck we'll find another target for you t'practice on. The idea is to be able to aim and fire at any part of an enemy ship that'll kill Frenchmen quicker, and surer than just blazin' away by broadsides. Smash in their ports, dis-mount their guns, and kill Frogs . . . take down the people on their quarterdecks, the helmsmen and the wheels, even have three or four guns aim at the base of their masts and bring 'em down early on. It'll be at close quarters, since it looks as if it only works at long musket shot, but . . . when we *do* find a Frog that'll fight us, we'll give him such a drubbin' that he'll yell 'Mon Dieu' and wish he'd never tangled with *Sapphire*, right?"

Even the less-successful gun crews roared agreement loudly.

"Dismiss, and get ready for 'Clear Decks and Up Spirits'," he concluded, and the crew raised another cheer for the morning's rum issue.

"Ah, Mister Westcott," Lewrie said to the First Lieutenant as the hands dispersed. "Pass word for the Master Gunner, his Mate, and Mister Turley, the Armourer."

"An afternoon of filing, is it, sir?" Westcott asked with one brow up. "You wish the guns notched?"

"Aye," Lewrie replied with a sheepish smile and a shrug of his shoulders. "Something I should have ordered done beforehand."

"I'll explain it to them, sir," Westcott promised, "and set them to it."

"Deep V notches, muzzle swells, and in line with the top-most of the breech rings," Lewrie agreed. "I'll be aft."

"Aye, sir." Westcott said, touching the brim of his hat in salute as Lewrie entered his cabins, where he found things tidy and being prepared for his mid-day meal. Pettus was back from the orlop, where he usually went with Chalky and Bisquit, laying a table setting, and Jessop was there, opening a bottle of Portuguese white wine.

"Ah, there's my lads," Lewrie cooed as he hung up his hat and coat, kneeling to cosset the cat and the dog, who were still upset by the loud noises. "Yes, Chalky, you're alright now. And there'll be no more loud bangs today, Bisquit, there's a brave dog."

"Weren't fair, sir," Jessop sulkily said as he brought Lewrie a glass of wine.

"What wasn't fair, Jessop?" Lewrie asked.

"Ya never let us on the 'smashers' have a go, nor the lads on the six-pounders, neither," Jessop carped. After a time in Lewrie's service as a cabin servant, the lad had eagerly volunteered to learn more of a seaman's trade, learning his knots, boxing the compass, going aloft with the top-men of his own age, and serving in a crew manning one of the 24-pounder carronades in action. He'd also gotten a desire to be more a sailor than a servant.

"We're seein' to that, me lad," Lewrie told him as he got to his feet. "Cuttin' aimin' notches in all the guns, like the sights on a musket or pistol. The next spare prize we take, I'll expect you t'pick your target and hit it bang on the nose."

"Oh, well then!" Jessop perked up. "Here's yer wine, sir!"

"Thankee, and I think I've earned it this morning!" Lewrie said with a laugh.

CHAPTER TWENTY-ONE

*F*or several days after the first experiment with aimed gunnery fire, the weather along the Costa Verde and the Costa de Cantabria turned foul, with heaving seas, continual rain squalls, and limited visibility, forcing HMS *Sapphire* to quit her close prowls along the coast and seek deeper water, many miles offshore, for her own safety.

The notch-sights were filed onto all her guns, from the puny 6-pounders to the carronades and lower deck 24-pounders, and Lewrie delighted in inspecting all of them, squatting down behind the cascabels and breeching ropes and squinting down the sights at imaginary foes, assuring himself that every filed notch was cut into the metal at absolute top-dead-centre, and in perfect alignment.

He was both enthused yet frustrated at the same time, eager to give his gunners another chance, and more practice, but in this weather, there was little to do in that regard. *Sapphire* trundled along with her topmasts struck down, heaving, rolling, and pitching, so slowly that Lewrie could conjure that the ship could not pursue a migrating sea turtle with any hope of success.

Then . . . wonder of all wonders, a lone French merchant ship, separated from her convoy by the weather, and seeking safety from wrecking onshore, had swum up out of the swirling, misty rain, suddenly just *there,* at two cables' range! A quick hoist of the Union Jack, a single discharge from a 6-pounder—remarkably accurate by the way!—and she was forced to strike her colours, fetch-to, and accept a boarding party.

For a time, Lewrie hoped that once the weather cleared, she could serve as the next target for his gunners, but, once Lt. Elmes reported back with her manifest, Lewrie had felt so frustrated that he could have kicked furniture. Food, clothing, muskets and ammunition, tentage, blankets, boots and shoes, winter greatcoats, and kegs of gunpowder by the hundreds. She was just too *valuable* to shoot to pieces!

Dammit, I want t'smash *something!* he growled to himself.

"All more than welcome to our army and our Portuguese allies," he said, instead, as calmly and deliberately as he could sham such. "Do place her crew below, well secured and guarded, 'til we can set 'em ashore once the weather clears, Mister Elmes."

"Very good, sir," Lt. Elmes replied, and departed the great cabins.

"Shit, shit, *shit!*" Lewrie fumed once he was gone.

Thankfully, the weather did clear, and *Sapphire,* with her two prizes in trail, could close the coast once more near Aviles, send the latest captives ashore in one of their own boats, and take up her prowling once more, just about ten miles seaward, and Lewrie's hopeful mood returned. In point of fact, he was much like a boy who'd gotten a set of bow and arrows for Christmas; there would be no pleasing him 'til he had a chance to play with them!

To that end, he summoned Mr. Boling, the Master Gunner.

"Aye, sir?" that worthy, a thick-set fellow in his fourties with greying hair, and a paunch over which a red waistcoat was stretched, said as he doffed his hat.

"French gunpowder, Mister Boling," Lewrie began, "is it worth a damn? There's rather a lot of it aboard the latest prize, and we could use it in lieu of ours, for practice shooting."

"Hmm, well, sir," Boling replied, scratching at several days' worth of stubble on his cheek, "that'd depend on how long it's been in cask, in storage, and in what conditions. Damp, d'ye see, Cap'um. There's no way of knowing unless we could test it in a *prouviette.*"

That they did not have. At Woolwich, the quality of powder was tested in what looked like a mortar mounted on a wooden block, a *prouviette,* with a fixed amount of powder flinging a fixed weight of shot—usually a twelve-pound roundshot—at 45 degrees, to march off and measure how far the shot was thrown down range. The better the gunpowder, the farther the shot would end up.

"Hmm, if we loaded one of the forecastle six-pounders with British powder," Lewrie contemplated with his head laid over to one side, "and the second with French powder . . . both guns set at the maximum elevation with the quoin blocks fully out, would that do for a proper test?"

"Well, it might, at that, sir," Boling replied, though he did look squinty over the idea.

"Excellent!" Lewrie cried, all but clapping his hands, then turned to the officer of the watch, Lt. Harcourt. "Mister Harcourt, I'd admire did you summon a boat crew, send the launch over to the latest prize, the . . . what the Devil is she called?"

"The *Mouette*, I believe, sir," Harcourt supplied, "the *Seagull*."

"Right, have 'em fetch us, say, ten kegs o' French gunpowder t'practise with," Lewrie finished. "We'll test it alongside our own and see if it's up to snuff."

"At once, sir," Harcourt replied, then bawled for the former Cox'n, Crawley, and his gang.

Lewrie paced the poop deck in rising excitement, and more frustration over how long it took for the launch to be led up alongside, manned, and rowed over to the *Mouette*, secured alongside her, the kegs hoisted out of the prize's holds into a cargo net, hauled up by brute force with the prize crew and Crawley's people, using the foremast main course yard as a crane, lowered into the boat, secured, and the launch stroked back to *Sapphire* so the whole hoisting aboard of the kegs, with the net affixed to a line from the ship's mainmast course yard, could be repeated. Finally, with the boat secured, Mr. Boling saw the kegs taken below to the magazine, where he would fill 6-pounder cartridge bags with the proper amount of French powder, mark them with a dash of paint to distinguish them from preloaded English powder cartridges, then whistled up some ship's boys who served as powder monkeys on the forecastle guns, and announced that the test could begin.

All this activity attracted the attention of the on-watch seamen, and a fair number of off-watch hands who came up to watch the show. Lewrie fetched his telescope and left the quarterdeck to go forward to amidships of the larboard sail-tending gangway. Lt. Westcott, who was off-watch with nothing better to do, ambled up to join him.

"All ready?" Lewrie shouted to the forecastle gunners and the Master Gunner. "You may begin!"

"Think the damned stuff will squib, or go *pfft?*" Westcott japed.

"If it does, I may have t'end up buyin' powder with my own funds," Lewrie growled. "The Navy'd say I'm wastin' our stock."

"English powder first, sir!" Boling shouted back. "Ready? Fire!" *Blam!* went the 6-pounder, jerking back to the extent of the breeching ropes, smothering the forecastle in a cloud of smelly, spent powder smoke. Lewrie eagerly looked seaward to spot the fall of shot, and found a small, quickly dissipating pillar of spray.

"Half a mile?" Westcott guessed aloud.

"Here's the French stuff, sir! Ready? Fire!" Boling shouted.

Blam! went the other larboard forecastle six-pounder, creating a fog of smoke that was quickly blown away. Lewrie could barely make out the wee circle of disturbed water from the fail of the first shot. Seconds later, a pillar, a feather of spray, leaped aloft for a quick second before it collapsed, leaving another round patch of foam.

"Hmm, just a tad short of the first'un," Lewrie groused, but not completely disappointed. "Were both fired at the peak of the up-roll, Mister Boling?" he demanded.

"Both, sir, aye," Boling shouted back.

"One more time, t'be sure!" Lewrie ordered.

"Fire them together, sir?" Boling suggested.

"Aye, together!" Lewrie agreed.

"Left-hand gun'll be the French powder, sir," Boling said.

As *Sapphire* pent herself at the top of the up-roll, where she paused for a long second or two, both guns went off together, almost as one. Lewrie's and Westcott's telescopes were whipped up to spot the fall of shot, and . . .

"Almost alongside each other, sir," Westcott hooted. "Not a ha'penny's difference, really."

"We're in business!" Lewrie crowed, and his evident pleasure with the results of the experiment raised a cheer from the crew.

"Secure, Mister Boling," Lewrie said as he went to the forecastle. "I'd very much admire did you have cartridges made up for *all* gun calibres, about six rounds per gun, and mark them, and all of the French kegs, for practice only."

"Aye aye, sir," Boling replied, touching the brim of his hat with the fingers of his right hand, carefully concealing how much of a chore that would be, and how he felt about it.

"Disappointing in a way, though, sir," Lt. Westcott said as they made their way aft to the quarterdeck once more.

"How so?" Lewrie asked him.

"Well, French-made gunpowder," Westcott said with one of his fierce, quick grins on his face, "one'd think that it should smell more like lavender than rotten eggs."

"We could sprinkle 'em with *eau de cologne*, once we're back in Lisbon," Lewrie said. "That'd make ye happy?"

"Oh, immensely!" Westcott laughed. "We'd even make the French happy . . . to be shot at with such elegant and cultured stinks!"

CHAPTER TWENTY-TWO

*H*MS *Sapphire* did reap a few more prizes, even one upon which the new gun sights could be tested, but Lewrie's hopes of being in "business" were pretty-much dashed. Still seemingly without escorts, the French convoys, sent out in penny-packets of three, four, or five ships to reduce the odds of them all being swept up by the dozens, seemed to spend more time huddled fearfully in ports all along the coasts during the daylight hours, and if any strange tops'ls were spotted by shore watchers, that was where they stayed.

If they did slink out of shelter round sundown, they ran without lights, making them almost impossible to spot, and put into harbour at the first alarm only twenty-odd miles further along on their voyages. If they *were* detected, and *Sapphire* gave furious chase, most of them managed to enter port long before the plodding, heavy two-decker could catch them up within gun range, making Lewrie imagine that even if he still commanded a swift frigate, they would have still escaped.

His officers and Sailing Master tried to console themselves, and him, with how much delay in the delivery of supplies that they were causing, even if they didn't capture anything, how their very presence was freezing the process, creating one gigantic bottleneck, and starving Marshal Ney's army in Northern Spain of everything needful, slowing their operations, perhaps even forcing them to remain in place in large garrisons awaiting the largesse that Paris promised them, but receiving only dribbles.

"It's possible, sir," a hopeful Lt. Elmes suggested, "that we are forcing them to land their goods in all these little fishing villages, and have to cart them inland from there. Think on it; long baggage trains using up all their waggons and draught animals, with thousands of troops drawn off to guard them. Would not that give the *partisanos* more opportunities to raid and bum the supplies, and kill more Frenchmen?"

"Mister Elmes has a point, sir," Lt. Westcott contributed to the gloomy conversation over supper in the great-cabins. "The French planned to use the large port cities, Corunna, Ferrol, Gijon, and Santander, Bilbao . . . nice, sensible, easily protected, but now? Little land convoys scattered all over the lot, each one needing a squadron of cavalry, or a battalion of infantry to keep the Spanish off them!"

"You're makin' it sound like *blockade* duty, sir," Lewrie petulantly replied as he idly shoved pickled vegetables round his plate. "Boring, excruciating, eye-glazing, *dull* blockade duty. We need to be *after* them, not loafin' along and just *watchin'*'em!"

"Well, sir, if they won't come out, perhaps we must go in," Lt. Keane of the Marines suggested. "I will own that the last few weeks have proven to be stultifyingly dull to me, as well. What if we found an occasion for some cutting-out raids? Even if we don't fetch the enemy ships out, we could set them alight and plant new fears in them."

"There's nothing I'd like more, Mister Keane," Lewrie quickly agreed. "Hear, hear! A glass with you, sir! But . . . ," Lewrie said after they had drunk each other's health, "we've five prizes, with sixty-eight hands, and half our Mids aboard them already. There are two with their crews still aboard, and two files of your Marines off t'stand guard over 'em. Perhaps, if the French continue with their skulking practices on our next cruise, we'll start off with cutting-out raids."

"And, if the French have erected batteries to protect all the little fishing ports, we can get in some more gunnery practice, sir," Westcott told him with a wink. After serving as Lewrie's second-in-command for six years and more, he knew his Captain's delights, and his frustrations; most especially his need for meaningful action.

"We'll give it one more day, then," Lewrie announced, "before we sail for the pre-arranged 'rondy'. Hopefully, the other ships of the squadron've done better."

"To the 'rondy'!" Lt. Elmes proposed, lifting his glass high, which demanded a refill all round.

"To the 'rondy'!" they chorused once everyone was topped up, and drained their glasses to "heel-taps".

Damme, I'll bet the others have had more fun! Lewrie thought in unrelieved gloom, despite his cheerful demeanour.

It didn't look as if the other ships had done much better, though, as they slowly loomed up over the horizon at the meeting point, seventy or more miles out to sea. Captain Yearwood's *Sterling,* and Commander Teague's *Blaze* trailed in from their watch off Corunna and Ferrol with only four prizes, half the "bag" of their first cruise. Hours later, the masthead lookouts announced the arrival of Captain Chalmers's *Undaunted,* Commander Blamey's *Peregrine,* with four more sail following in their wake, fresh from their hunting grounds from Bilbao to San Sebastián and Bayonne.

"Signal to all ships, Mister Elmes," Lewrie ordered, "with two guns t'make it a General. '"Form column on *Sapphire.* Prizes to form column to seaward'."

"Aye, sir," the officer of the watch said, shouting aft to Midshipman Griffin to make up the flag hoist, and forward for two 6-pounders to be loaded, run out, and fired.

That'll take at least two hours, Lewrie estimated; *more than time enough t'shave and get presentable. And have Yeovill kill the fatted calf, so I can dine 'em in.*

"Once the signal's repeated, Mister Elmes," Lewrie said as he turned to go aft to his cabins, "Shape course Due West. We'll keep on under reduced sail, t'make it easier for the rest to catch up."

"Due West, aye aye, sir," Elmes repeated.

"I'll be aft for a bit. Send for me when you are ready to go about," Lewrie added at the door to his cabins, then entered, calling out to Pettus and Jessop to lay out the good tableware for a feast.

It'll have t'be a good'un, he thought; *For sure, they'll all be disappointed.*

Sundown was a rare'un, all red, lemony, and amber, painting a mild sea to the West, and highlighting the thin clouds. The taffrail lanthorns had been lit for the night, just as dusk gathered. Lewrie stood on the poop deck, awaiting his guests, freshly shaved and sponged down, watching the boats making their way to the starboard entry-port. *Sapphire* slumbered along at only six knots, making for an easy row for the oarsmen, with *Undaunted*'s cutter in the lead. As she came close alongside, Lewrie gave Bisquit a final pet or two and descended to the quarterdeck to greet Capt. Chalmers and the others, giving the side party a final look-over. After a quick peek overside, Bosun Terrell lifted his silver call to his lips and began to tootle a long, trilling welcome as Chalmers made his way up the man-ropes and boarding battens.

"Welcome aboard, sir," Lewrie said, doffing his hat once that worthy had gained the deck, looking a tad stern. "Oh, Bisquit, don't sniff his 'wedding tackle'!" for the dog, thinking himself one of the side-party, was trying to "identify" the new arrival.

"Oh, no matter, sir!" Chalmers replied, bending down to give Bisquit some pets. "I adore dogs, and ain't you a fine one, hey? How do, fellow. You're a *good* dog, yes you *are*!"

I knew *I should've introduced him to the dog, long ago,* Lewrie thought, congratulating himself; *They're nigh-slobberin' over each other!*

Next aboard in seniority was Capt. Yearwood, acting less affable, as though his lack of success was a bit of gristle to chew over. Commander Blamey, then Teague, came next. Blamey seemed in better takings than Teague.

"Hmm, it seems the pickings aren't as good this time as they were on our first endeavour," Lewrie commented, eliciting a grunt from Yearwood in agreement.

"Well, actually . . ." Chalmers said. He and Blamey looked at each other like "sly boots" ready to chortle. "We did have one bit of success, sir. See that three-master in the middle of our column?"

"She's the French National Ship *Le Caprice*!" Blamey crowed.

"One of their *corvettes*?" Teague gawped.

"Well, damme," Yearwood gravelled, irked that he and Teague had not had the fortune to cross hawses with one, too. "*Much* of a fight, was it?" he sourly asked.

"Not really," Chalmers said, looking as if he'd polish his fingernails on his coat lapel. "we ran into her off San Sebastián, escorting six merchantmen. *They* managed to scuttle off, more's the pity, but she offered a fight. When she did, we doubled on her, and after a couple of broadsides into her from either beam, she struck her colours, right quickly and sensibly, too."

Damn the both *o' you lucky bastards!* Lewrie thought, feeling robbed of glory; *Of* course *the convoy got away, 'cause you were too eager t'make more o' your names! Why not us, I ask ye!*

"God in Heaven, how grand for you, sirs!" he said, instead. "My heartiest congratulations! It's a good thing that my cook laid on a cool champagne punch for us. Let's go dip into it to celebrate your success."

Worst of all, I wasn't "in sight", so Sapphire, *and I, can't share one wee* scrap *of the prize-money,* or *the credit!* he futher thought as he saw his supper guests into his great-cabins.

And, once supper was served, the less successful had to endure a long and lively tale of how the *Le Caprice* was taken, how few casualties they had suffered, how heavy the loss of life aboard the French *corvette* had been, and how they'd disposed of their prisoners.

"We took this horrid little cockleshell, the shabbiest barge you ever did see," Commander Blamey regaled them, "filled with the usual cargo of food and such. We hauled her out of sight of land, dumped most of her cargo overside, then transferred our Frenchmen into her and told them to make the best of their way into a port, and bedamned to them, and if her Captain survives his court-martial for her loss, I'd be very much surprised."

"I've heard that the Frogs don't take kindly to any more failures at sea, any more embarassments," Chalmers sniggered. "Trafalgar was bad enough. Bonaparte may be a great soldier, but he knows nothing of the sea, and can't understand how or why his Navy loses so often, or sits idle in port, for all the money he's thrown at building it back up."

"Their gunnery was horrible, too," Blamey sneered, "as if they were firing live for the first time in their miserable lives, hah!"

"Speaking of gunnery," Lewrie said, happy to interrupt the tale of derring-do, "I find myself in your debt, Commander Teague. All of *Sapphire*'s guns, even the carronades, now have notched sights cut into them, and we've had a couple of opportunities to practise aimed fire. Well, *somewhat* aimed fire. It's still early days."

"Bless me, sir, but I really can't take complete credit for the idea," Teague modestly replied, all but ducking his head. "Two years ago, I dined with several other officers, one of whom was a Captain Broke of the *Shannon* frigate, who first mentioned the idea of aimed fire, and targetting specific parts of an enemy ship, to kill her officers and crew faster. You've actually practised, sir?"

Then it was Lewrie's turn to expound on sacrificing a poor prize as a target, the painted "gun ports", the rewards of tobacco or full measures of rum issue to more-accurate gun crews.

"We took aboard some French gunpowder, and it's almost as good as our best, for practise use only," Lewrie told them, "there's plenty of it still aboard one of our prizes, and you're welcome to it, if you've a mind."

"Pity that you couldn't retain the target ship's cargo, though," Capt. Chalmers said. "Our Portuguese allies could have used those guns, and waggons."

"Well, French shot isn't quite the same calibre as British shot," Lewrie brushed off, "so sooner or later, the Portuguese would have run out."

"Windage, too, sir," Teague reminded Chalmers. "Too loose a fit down the barrel, and God only knows where your shot lands."

They all agreed that the new French practise of sailing by night, only, and in short legs from one little fishing village to the next, was making their hunting more difficult. It was also agreed that the French would have to organise dozens of vulnerable road convoys from those wee ports, eating up troop strength from the field, forcing them to scour Spain for oxen, mules, and horses to do the hauling, and if the armed partisan bands could deprive them of those, the French would be in a cleft stick; eat or fight.

"For my part, I just hope that the French at last realise that un-escorted convoys just ain't in the cards," Capt. Yearwood gravelled. "If they need supplies so badly, they must go through the largest port cities. Larger convoys, larger baggage trains to their troops, with fewer troops drawn off to guard them. Bonaparte's generals are surely giving him an earful, begging for more of everything. Surely, he'll order his Navy to do something about it, and the next time we prowl these coasts, we'll find a chance for *real* combat."

"Pray God!" Commander Teague heartily seconded him.

"Unless the French send out some of their two-deckers, and chase *us* off," Capt. Chalmers quipped.

"Then we act like privateers and sneak in to pluck prizes under their very noses," Lewrie japed back. "When there's a will, there's always a way, hey? Perhaps stay together as a proper squadron, for once, instead of hunting in dribs and drabs? I might enjoy that, the opportunity to fly my broad pendant, flaunt my authority, and drive you all to distraction with flag signals, hah hah!"

"Just so long as we dine this well, at your expense, sir," Chalmers quickly rejoined, with a laugh.

"Hear, hear!" Lewrie agreed. "Yeovill, Pettus, Jessop. Pour yourselves some port, to congratulate this fine supper."

Once they'd been toasted, the tablecloth was whisked away, and the port bottle, the shelled nuts, and cheese were set out, along with grapes and oranges taken aboard at Lisbon.

"These walnuts," Capt. Yearwood marvelled, "they're *sugar* glazed? Delightful."

"With a touch of cinnamon, sir," Yeovill told him as he gathered up the plates at the sideboard for washing, later.

"I envy you, Capt. Lewrie," Yearwood said, "your cook is a marvel."

"He's been telling *me* that for years, sir," Lewrie replied.

"Meant to ask," Lewrie said to Capt. Chalmers as they stood on the quarterdeck awaiting the various ship's boats. "How's my son doing?"

"Quite well, sir," Chalmers told him. "He's in command of the prize *corvette* this very night, and keeping it in good order. Young Hugh is all that one could ask of a professional seaman, and more. Dependable, bold, and fearless. When he stands his examination for promotion, be assured that he will go with my heartiest recommendations. And pass, the first try, I'd wager."

"I'm delighted t'hear it," Lewrie said, pleased to his toes, "though once back at Lisbon, I'd admire a few hours of his time. In the same squadron, but 'so near but yet so far', what?"

"I shall see that he'll have some free time with you, sir," Chalmers promised. "Ehm, where's that dog of yours?"

"Following my cook to the galley for his own share of our supper, I'm sure, sir," Lewrie told him. "If he hasn't made a pig of himself, beggin' off the crew, below."

"Pity," Chalmers mused. "I've a mind to adopt a pup once back at Lisbon."

"Thin pickings, I'm afraid," Lewrie told him. "I was ashore there, just after the French evacuated. They'd shot them all."

"Lord, what a monstrous people!" Chalmers said with a shiver. "Well, I shall say goodnight to you, Captain Lewrie."

"And a good night to you, Captain Chalmers," Lewrie bade him.

CHAPTER TWENTY-THREE

*L*isbon's waterfront quays, and the nearby anchorages, were full of shipping, as was the wide and deep bay on the South side of the Tagus River, where they had anchored before. *Sapphire* and her consorts, and their prizes, had to advance a few miles up-river to find room to swing, under the looming hills of the ancient Alfama district, near the far end of the Avenida Infante Dom Henrique, and a long row or walk from there to the Baixa, the heart of the city.

That made it a little harder to secure the first provisions, the usual firewood and water, and a long row for a ship's boat over to the naval stores ship, where the squadron's long-delayed mail was saved pending their return.

Fresh water! Hogsheads of it! After the first fortnight on the North coast of Spain, the rainwater collected in canvas sluices and kegs had been depleted, and the weather had given them but a rare sprinkling, putting all ships dependent upon their stored water, too long in casks, and going a tad brown, with all for cooking and for drinking from the scuttlebutts, with none for bathing or washing of clothing. *Sapphire*'s Surgeon, Mr. Snelling, had made a pretty penny at lancing salt water boils and daubing salve on irritated rashes, but everyone's daily wear, from Captain to the "duck fucker" who over saw the forecastle manger, was full of dried saltwater crystals that rubbed them all raw and raised those painful boils and itches.

A long, hot bath! Lewrie thought; *And shirts, underdrawers, and bed sheets that don't scratch . . . or stink!* Pettus and Jessop had bound up a young bale-sized bundle of clothes, bedding, and even tablecloths and napkins ready for the washerwomen of Lisbon. For the moment, though, Lewrie itched, and would for at least one more day; there was too much to do aboard ship before he could be rowed ashore and seek out a *bagnio* for a long, hot soak and a vigourous scrubbing.

Personal hygiene and relief aside, he was anxious, too, for a word with Mr. Thomas Mountjoy, or his assistant, Danial Deacon, the Foreign Office's Secret Branch agents in Lisbon, to see how the war was going. And to see if Maddalena Covilha had arrived.

Would she come to Lisbon? Had she done so, yet? It felt like the better part of a year since he had sailed away from Gibraltar the last time to evacuate General Sir John Moore's battered, starving army from Corunna, and a lot of things might have changed. Oh, he'd gotten one letter from her that *sounded* fond and longing, but after writing to prompt her to come to Lisbon and take lodgings, back he'd gone to sea with not one word more on the subject.

It was simpler at Gibraltar, he told himself.

Out and back on specific raids, gone for only a week, or a fortnight, then right back to anchor off the Old Mole, and there were her lodgings up behind the long fortifications, overlooking the bay, and Maddalena standing on her balcony to wave a tea towel or a scarf in greeting as *Sapphire* ghosted into port, barely hundreds of yards away. If she *had* removed, he only hoped that Mountjoy had arranged lodgings in the planned and gridded streets of the Baixa district; anything further uphill was an incomprehensible rat's maze of twisting, narrow streets, and too steep a hike for a sailor's legs! Some rented rooms on the flat land round the Praça do Comércio would be best of all, he reckoned; there trees, gardens, and parks!

For now, though . . .

"Yards are squared, sir," Bosun Terrell reported.

"Ship is securely anchored bow and stern, sir," Lt. Harcourt, the watch officer, announced, "six fathom depth, with five-to-one scope."

"Boat's returning from the stores ship, sir," Lt. Westcott told him, "with mail, I hope. And Bisquit badly needs a bath."

"Oh, that'll be jolly," Lewrie replied, casting an eye on the ship's dog, who sat and panted, giving Westcott a brief, wary look at the mention of "bath". At least at sea, once bathed, there were no mud puddles or dusty spaces for him to roll in to get his accustomed scent back.

"Once we've fresh water aboard, see that some of the ship's boys take care of that."

"Boat ahoy!" Midshipman Chenery shouted to the approaching cutter.

"Returnin'!" came the answering hail, and everyone leaned out eagerly for signs of sacks of mail, and news from home. Lewrie was just as eager, and smiled with delight to spot one very full canvas sack next to the boat's cox'n.

"Yes, by God!" he whispered.

Everything was ready for the morning. His reports to Admiralty were completed and wax-sealed, the registries and manifests from *Sapphire*'s most recent prizes were sorted in order and ready for presentation to the Prize-Court; he and the other squadron captains would go as a group. Lewrie's washing bundle sat ready to be dumped into his boat, though at present Chalky lay sprawled atop it, snoozing. Lewrie's out-going letters, written in the idle hours at sea, were ready to be sent off to the British Post Office. And lastly, his shopping list of personal needs and desires had been handed over to the Ship's Purser, Mr. Cadrick, along with a purse of solid coin.

Lewrie had another shopping list that he would carry ashore himself, though most of the next day would be taken up with official duties, and a visit to Thomas Mountjoy's offices. As much as he wished that he could dash off to find Maddalena, first thing, there was too much to see to, just as there had been too much that had needed doing aboard ship before sundown. Awnings had to be rigged, some running rigging spliced or replaced, fresh water fetched off the quays or the barges to fill her novel iron tanks, and fresh meat and baked bread taken aboard, along with lashings of fruit and vegetables to give the crew a welcome break from salt-meat junk and oak-hard issue bisquit.

So, it was with a satisfied sigh of completion that Lewrie could at last sit on the padded cushions of the transom lazarette lockers and savour the sunset that painted the mouth of the Tagus, and the Atlantic, with tinges of roses. The upper halves of the transom sash windows were open, as were the windows in the quarter-galleries, and the glazed wooden door to the stern gallery was open to let a light, cooling breeze into the cabins. The string-mesh screen door was in place, though, so Chalky did not get out to the gallery and tumble off the railings in his pursuit of a bird.

He had a pint piggin of his lemoned and sugared cool tea in one hand and the first of his official letters in the other, now that he had the time to open and read his mail which Pettus and his clerk, Faulkes, had sorted out earlier.

"Bilgewater, bilgewater," Lewrie scoffed as he quickly went from one to the next, "*more* bilgewater . . . aha, Notice to Mariners entering or leaving Galway . . . and etcetera and etcetera *reeking* dead *rat* bilgewater!"

Well, he might file that'un away in the chart space off the quarterdeck; calling at Galway *might* come to pass . . . someday.

Wish somebody'd send me some newspapers, he thought, starved for word of what was acting in the world. Newspapers were high on his personal shopping list, but they would have to wait 'til the morrow. *Maybe I can cadge some free'uns off Mountjoy.*

"Oh, just damn my eyes!" he burst forth after opening one from his London solicitor. "Mine arse on a band-box!"

On-passage to Gibraltar two years before, escorting a small troop convoy along with an old friend's smaller frigate, they had been intercepted by two French *corvettes* who had mistaken all the ships for merchantmen. One *corvette* had been taken, the other had managed to scamper off, and the Prize-Court was *still* wrangling over the division of spoils, for the very good reason that the troopers' masters and crews had declared that they'd been ordered to hoist the Blue Ensign and pretend to be National Ships, so they had earned a share. The soldiers, too, posing suddenly at the rails to pretend to be Marines, and overawe the French, had laid claim to the prize-money, too, since Army troops *had*, in past, been posted aboard warships in *lieu* of Royal Marines! His solicitor, Matthew Mountjoy and kin to the local spymaster, advised that the fees their hired Advocate charged to argue *Sapphire*'s case had now risen to the sum of £185, with no end in sight, and Mountjoy had taken the liberty of dipping into Lewrie's London account with Coutts' Bank to pay him.

Lewrie tossed that letter to the deck, feeling a sudden need for a large measure of his American bourbon whisky!

The next official letter, from the Prize-Court at Gibraltar, he was almost *afraid* to read.

He had taken a pair of lateen-rigged *feluccas* that the Spanish garrison at the massive fortress of Ceuta had been using to feed its soldiers, following them from the Moroecan *entrepôt* of Tetuán in the night. Then, using those two as subterfuges, he'd raided the docks at Ceuta, right under those hundreds of cannon, and had cut out another pair, setting fire to the rest, and putting an end to fresh food for their re-enforced gunners and soldiers.

The *feluccas* had been exceedingly shabby, badly maintained, and filthy, so Lewrie wasn't expecting much from the Prize-Court. He was mildly surprised to read that they had been bought up rather quickly by local

Gibraltarian merchants, and had fetched the sum of £6,800. It was not all that much, but it would be welcome to his officers and crew.

His share was two-eighths, with nothing owing to a senior flag officer, since *Sapphire* had been sailing under Independent Orders at the time; an additional two-eighths would go to his officers, petty officers, and four-eighths to the sailors, non-commissioned Marines, and Marine privates, right down to the ship's boys.

"Pity they changed the rules," he muttered under his breath, longing for the old days before 1808, when the captain's share was three-eighths. "Now, what about the frigates? Ah."

Their last raid with a hired transport to carry two companies of soldiers in addition to his Marine complement and an equal-sized party of armed seamen had been interrupted before the troops could be landed by the appearance of two big Spanish frigates, 38-gunners, and sister ships, as alike as two peas in a pod, the *San Pablo* and the *San Pedro*. Fine ships, but badly handled and their guns just as badly served after idling at anchor at Cartagena or Barcelona far too long. Lewrie had sent his transport haring for Gibraltar, had clawed *Sapphire* up to windward of the pair, and had forced them to pursue so he could engage them one at a time. One had been so badly mauled that she had sunk with appalling loss of life; the other had taken so much damage from *Sapphire*'s lower deck 24-pounders and carronades that she had finally struck her colours.

Two years, now, since he'd fetched the survivor into harbour, and the Court was *finally* issuing its judgement?

> *Trusting that the number of guns in the surviving frigate's armament, and the number of men aboard her when she set sail, represented the true numbers for the frigate which sank, we have determined in the case of the San Pedro frigate that she had aboard a total of 325 officers, naval infantry, and sailors, and was armed with 28 18-pounders, two 12-pounders, and eight 9-pounders at the time of her sinking, resulting in a sum in Head & Gun Money the value of £1,815.*

Lewrie rose and went to his desk to do his own sums; £1,700 from the *feluccas*, and roughly £453 and 15 shillings for the sunken frigate for him.

> *Unfortunately, sir, in regards to the San Pablo frigate which you brought in to Gibraltar for judgement . . .*

"What the bloody Hell d'they mean, 'unfortunately'?" Lewrie growled, on his guard like a hound with its fur stood on end. He had a damned dim view of Prize-Courts and their venal officials, already, and was firmly convinced that those wretched weasels' corruption could make the crookedest Purser appear a saint in comparison.

. . . lay in-ordinary for almost two years, her condition deteriorating and her severe damage, inflicted in her taking, only partially repaired due to the needs of our own ships at H.M. Dockyards, Gibraltar, until Spain abandoned her alliance with France and became an ally of Great Britain. At that point, it was determined the San Pablo should be fully restored and returned to Spanish service as a gesture of good will. Following a Foreign Office request, it was determined that the prize would be declared Droits of The Crown, not Droits of Admiralty. Accordingly, the value of the prize due to HMS Sapphire can only be Head & Gun Money for her taking, amounting to another £1,815 . . .

"You bloody, fucking *thieves*!" Lewrie roared. "Pettus! Whisky! A full bumper . . . now! Droits of the damned . . . Mine arse on a band-box!"

"Something amiss, sir?" Pettus dared ask as he went to the wine cabinet to fetch out the stone crock of whisky.

"We've been robbed, coshed on the head, purses stolen, and our pockets turned out," Lewrie fumed. "Damn the Prize-Court! Damn their blood, ev'ry one of 'em!"

He got his whisky and tossed back a large swig, grimacing as the bourbon stung all the way down from his gums to his gut, still pacing the cabins ready to lash out, or kick furniture. If he sat, he would end up becoming so enraged that he could gleefully strangle someone.

It took half the bumper to calm him down, when he could trust himself to throw himself into his desk chair and grumble. Once more he scribbled with a pencil. The sums were pitiful.

What o' my people? What do I tell those poor buggers? Sorry, but ye've been robbed by your own government?

And what would it do to the morale of his crew, he wondered.

Fame, glory, high adventure, and lashings of prize-money were not the things that sprang to mind in connexion to a slow, plodding two-decker like *Sapphire*; one had to volunteer aboard a frigate for those, those swift greyhounds of the ocean.

If he had taken command of *Sapphire* fresh from the graving docks, even with his repute in the Fleet as a fighting Captain, he doubted if he could have recruited a quarter of the hands needed to take her out beyond a breakwater.

No, he'd gotten command by default in the middle of an active commission when her former Captain and First Lieutenant had fought a duel for some damn-fool reason or another, and ended up wounding each other . . . physically and in their careers. He had read himself in to a chary crew who imagined that they would continue their un-ending dull convoying in the North Sea and the Baltic, with never a chance for the thrill of the chase, a fight, or any excitement whatsoever.

He'd promised them, though, that first morning, that he would seek out opportunities to make *Sapphire* a true fighting ship. And, he had done so. There was a swagger to them, now, pride in their ship, pride in themselves and what they had accomplished with such a slow barge, able to boast when on shore liberty of their battles, their raids, and their gunnery.

They *knew* that there was prize-money due them, and those who could do sums would spin fantasies of how much that might be, already spending it, sending money home to their families, starting businesses once out of the Navy . . . in their minds, anyway.

Now this slap in the face! Oh, there was *some* prize-money, but it wouldn't be in their hands 'til *Sapphire* paid off, perhaps one or two years later, and all they would have would be chits, not real money, even then.

He tried figuring out how much each sailor, ship's boy, and private Marine would get, but he tossed his pencil down in frustration; it was just too depressing to contemplate. He heaved a sigh, imagining how sullen they might turn, how many times people would be at the gratings for insubordination, fighting, drunk on duty, and how many might feel so cheated that they would try to desert!

What, fourteen pounds and a bit, for all they've done? Lewrie thought, taking another deep sip of his whisky; *That's pathetic, not even a whole year's extra pay for each man and boy.*

Still, he considered, looking for any scrap of cheer, the last two cruises along the Northern Spanish coast had resulted in quite a few captures, mainly small vessels, but they *were* full to the deckheads with military stores, weapons, ammunition, all of which was more than welcome when dispensed to the Spanish and Portuguese armies. Their contents would sell quickly, and the ships themselves might go for at least £5,000 apiece.

That must *cheer 'em up!* Lewrie hoped to himself.

He drained the last sips of his whisky, rose from his desk, and retrieved his abandoned cool tea, then idly shuffled through his personal mail which was always read last. Father, brother-in-law, Governour, brother-in-law Burgess, nothing from his eldest son, Sewallis, which in itself was troubling; he hadn't written in some time.

Lewrie was sure that his father, Sir Hugo, would be passably amusing to read. He was equally sure that Governour's letter would be pressing him to consent to sending his spiteful daughter, Charlotte, to London for a "buttock-brokering" Season, or full of his boasts over his elevation in rural Anglesgreen's society.

There *was* a letter from Percy Stangbourne, and he contemplated opening that one, but another caught his eye.

"Hello?" he muttered. "Jessica Chenery? What more does she have t'write me about?"

"Light the lanthorns an' glims, sir?" Jessop asked, drawing Lewrie's attention to the fact that it was almost fully dark by then.

"Aye, admire it if ye would," Lewrie said off-handedly as he broke the seal of her letter and spread it out. There were two pages, written front and back, contained in a larger outer sheet of heavier paper, which he found was a remarkably accurate sketch of his own likeness.

Hmm, rather . . . idealised, ain't it? he thought, grinning; *I was only in her presence, what, half an hour? Damned quick study, done from memory!*

> *Please allow me to offer you this humble effort to make Amends for how icily I behaved towards you when you came to gather Charlie up and bear him away to a dangerous career in the Navy. While I, father, and the rest of our family continue to pray for his good Health and Safety, quite understandibly, his latest letters have greatly eased our minds upon his choice. Indeed, he regales us with tales of how Adventurous his time under your command has been, how many Grand things he has done and seen, so far, and how Merry are his Mess-mates, for the most part.*

The young lady had a fine and legible copperplate hand, and he was impressed by how easily and fluidly she expressed herself, framing her sentences as if conversing face-to-face.

Miss Chenery described what a fine Spring had come to London, except for an excess of rain, and perkily told of how she had to don pattens to do her shopping, errands, and calls upon potential clients for her portraits, elevating herself, and the hems of her gowns and cloak above the mud, ordure, and the wet, making her feel as if she clomped about on iron stilts like a performer in a raree show. She'd gained a commission for a portrait from a prominent Bond Street merchant just recently, and had been approached by a book printer to do the illustrations for a childrens' book.

Sadly, though, upon your suggestions on the matter, we and the late John Beauchamp's family have discovered the manner of his passing. John became deathly ill on the long, cruel march to Corunna. In the mountain village of Bembibre, he became so stricken that he could no longer go on, and had to be left behind with the other sick men.

The regimental surgeon related that there was no hope for recovery, and John and the rest were left, in hopes that the French would care for them, though we also heard dire tales that the French had no mercy in them, and, indeed, were rumoured to practise the utmost cruelty on the sick, wounded, and those too utterly exhausted to carry on. How can a just God, I ask you, suffer such beasts to walk the earth? Were I not a Christian, I would blaspheme, and and curse them to the nether pits of Hell!

"Think ye just did, my girl," Lewrie muttered, wondering if she had submitted her letter to her father for approval, first, as most young ladies did, or had sent it off without doing so. That showed Lewrie that she was a young lady of modern spirit, despite being the daughter of a sobre churchman.

The rest of her letter was more cheerful.

Once again, in closing, do accept my Apology for how brusquely I responded to your presence in our house. Though you may find my pitiful attempt to limn you merely passable, and may not have time to correspond with a goose-brained young woman, given the demands of your duties, our family and I would truly appreciate hearing how my youngest brother progresses, and we pray for your shared Success.

Yr most humble & obdt. servant,

Mistress Jessica Chenery

Lewrie took a sip of his tea and determined that, aye, he would write her back. He closed his eyes, summoning up a mental image of her, and was amazed at how vivid his memory of her was, from such a short meeting.

There was a tautness in his crotch.

Damme, am I besotted? he had to ask himself.

CHAPTER TWENTY-FOUR

Lewrie's, and pretty-much everyone's dealings with the Prize-Courts, always left him, and others, with their hackles up and a bad taste in their mouths, and this encounter was no different.

"Cavalier?" Lewrie spat. "Cavalier, mine arse!" He re-iterated as he and the other squadron Captains left the chambers a little after mid-day, after a whole morning's wrangling.

"The idiots have no concept, sir," Capt. Yearwood of *Sterling* commiserated, "they ain't seafarers, or Navy men. Just jumped-up store clerks and penny counters, with no idea of what it is we do."

"So we shifted some cargo before we sank or burned our lesser prizes," Capt. Chalmers scoffed, "*then* nailed the hatches shut, and fetched them in all proper, discarding the dross. But those . . . ah, people," that prim officer said, as close as he might come to casting aspersions, or cursing, "want it *all*, for their side-profits or to make themselves more comfortable. Bah!"

"You'll join us for a toothsome shore dinner, sir?" Yearwood asked as they neared the edge of the great, paved, and shady square of the Praça do Comércio, and the quays where their boats waited.

"I fear I must beg off, sirs," Lewrie told them. "There are some government officers I must call upon . . . if only to beg for some newspapers.

Do allow me to foot the bill for a later supper ashore, though, once I've discovered the best restaurant or chophouse."

Free of his compatriots at last, Lewrie made a quick way to Mountjoy's offices. Across the street from it, he took note of some rather shady-looking sorts entering or leaving, with hats pulled low over their faces, some positively skulking.

Looks like spyin'₂ a goin' concern, he thought, grinning.

He crossed the street, took hold of the heavy iron door handle, and stepped inside, with the little bell over the door tinkling as it had the first time he'd entered the so-called "Falmouth Import & Export Company Ltd.". And there was the same thin and reedy younger clerk, busy at his quill-pushing, as if doing legitimate sums.

"Ah, Captain . . . Sir, ah," the young clerk stammered as he got to his feet, struggling to recall his name.

"Sir Alan Lewrie," Lewrie supplied.

"Of course, sir . . . Sir Alan!" the clerk replied, relieved.

"This still where Mountjoy hangs his hat? I'd admire to see him," Lewrie asked, taking off his new bicorne hat.

"He's in, ah . . . conference, Sir Alan," the clerk told him, gesturing towards a faded padded chair. "If you don't mind waiting for a bit? I will tell him that you are here."

At least there was a fairly recent London paper to occupy his time whilst he waited. The clerk emerged from the door to the inner offices, trying to slink through a six-inch gap as if opening that door fully would jeopardise the nation's most closely guarded secrets, and seated himself behind his ledgers, as quiet as a mouse.

A moment later and the door was opened fully, revealing a man with a swarthy complexion, in what looked like farmer's garb, a man who shied as Lewrie shot to his feet. The strange fellow looked as if he'd seen a spook! He was quickly, stealthily, out the door to the street.

"Ah, Captain Lewrie!" Thomas Mountjoy exclaimed with seeming joy, coming forward with a hand outstretched, "Back from the wars, are you? Come in, come in. I've some sparkling wine cooling in a water tub."

"Don't suppose I should ask who that fellow was," Lewrie said after sitting down in a much cleaner club chair, and crossing his legs.

"Oh, best not," Mountjoy said with a snigger as he poured them both glasses of wine. "He scouts cross the Spanish border for us, so the less said of him, the better. Isn't that wine delightful? I suppose you've come to enquire about *Senhora* Covilhā."

"She's here, in Lisbon?" Lewrie perked up, eagerly.

"Just arrived a week ago, and is busily establishing her new lodgings," Mountjoy said with a knowing wink, "not *too* far uphill from here, a place with a balcony overlooking the Tagus. There is a decent place to eat up that way, if you're feeling peckish at the moment. I can show you where it is."

"Well, that's one worry off my mind," Lewrie said, letting out a sigh of satisfaction. "What I really came for is news of what's acting in the world, first."

"Ah, well!" Thomas Mountjoy said, all but rubbing his hands to do what his sort did best; knowing what one did not, and relishing a chance to expound. "I've plenty of papers from home, and the local English-language papers, of course, and you're more than welcome to them. Where do you wish to start?"

"How's the war going here, first-off," Lewrie suggested.

"Hah!" Mountjoy tossed back his head in joy. "To everyone's delight, General Sir Arthur Wellesley was appointed Supreme Commander in Portugal and Spain. He arrived here, the twenty-second of April, whilst you were at sea, looking like a Drake or Raleigh, gathered up all the effectives that General Cradock had re-organised, along with the rump of poor old Sir John Moore's reserves, all the Portuguese troops that General Beresford had recruited, armed and trained, and set off for Oporto before the music at the welcoming balls had died down. We think he's up above Coimbra, already, and moving fast."

"I'd love it if he took Oporto," Lewrie said, enthused by the prospects. "That harbour'd be much closer to my assigned area. Who's he up against?"

"Marshal Soult," Mountjoy told him with a grimace of dislike, "the same bastard who chased our army to Corunna, and butchered so many people when he took Oporto earlier this year. Hard as I have tried, my informants can't get hard numbers. The French don't dare come too far South of the Douro River, except in large numbers . . . else the partisans get them. We're all hoping that Wellesley has an equal number of troops, or a slight edge. I expect we'll hear, one way or another, soon."

"Over the border in Spain?" Lewrie asked, taking a deep sip of that sparkling wine, and finding it so sprightly that he wished that he had two cases of it aboard, that instant.

"Oh, God, the bloody Spanish," Mountjoy sneered. "One would think they'd learn not to *boast* before they try to bring the French to battle, 'cause it always ends in tears and embarassing defeats, but . . . with the help of Almighty God, the recent discovery of some saint's bones, or *El Cid*'s toenail clippings borne to the forefront, their *immensely* amateurish generals send their half-clothed, poorly armed, un-paid, and starving soldiers into *impossible* situations . . . then abandon them and run for the rear once the French crush them. It's like setting kittens into the dog-fighting pit!"

"Then of course it's England's fault, one way or another?" Lewrie snidely concluded.

"Of *course* it is!" Mountjoy scoffed. "We ain't fast enough with the arms, cannon, powder and shot, or too niggardly at getting it where it's needed, and where's all that silver and gold that we promised them?

"Where's it all *gone,* is my question," Mountjoy went on with another sneer. "Down near Cadiz, there's a spanking new manufactury for the production of muskets, oh, just a *grand* edifice, makes one think of a ducal palace . . . cost umpteen *thousands,* and it took forever to run up, yet it hasn't turned out a single musket! And it's sitting right next to other gigantic, empty buildings the Spanish could have bought for a lot less, and could have been arming their troops for the whole last year, 'stead of begging and demanding of us for our Tower muskets!"

"Makes one long for the old days, when we had Hessians on the payroll," Lewrie sniggered, holding out his glass for a refill. "It is delightful, and where do I get some?"

"I'll show you," Mountjoy promised, topping both of them up. "What is your bag, this time?" he asked with a twinkle.

"A round dozen," Lewrie told him, explaining the change in how the French carried out their supply deliveries, and their use of smaller vessels that could enter almost every wee fishing port on the coast, and his suspicions that the enemy was organising smaller road convoys inland, which took more front-line troops away from availability in the field. "*Undaunted* and *Blaze* potted themselves one of their *corvettes.* Pity I wasn't 'in sight', or a flag officer, due a share!" he laughed.

"Hmm, hate to disappoint you, but what information I've gotten, and reports from other sources further afield, is that the French in Northern Spain aren't suffering for lack of supplies as much as we'd wish," Mountjoy had to dis-abuse him. "Oh, you're making them pinch, but only for so long as you're on the coast, and the large seaports are still doing a thriving business, and Marshal Ney is loath to fritter away his soldiers at every little inlet village."

"Well, if Wellesley gets us Oporto, our time in port'd be much shorter," Lewrie replied, shrugging that off. "Out and back, with the stores ship moved there, maybe even a small Prize-Court office. Those idle bastards'd most-like working there, with first pick of all the ports and sherries, hah hah."

"Or, might you need more ships?" Mountjoy hinted with a speculative brow up. "Two squadrons, handing off from one to the other, *or . . .* I imagine it'd not be as profitable, or as much fun, but, might it not require a proper blockading *fleet?*"

That turned Lewrie grumpy and defensive at once. "Why, what've ye heard? Someone sayin' we're not doin' enough, is what you're implyin'?"

"No complaints yet," Mountjoy said with a dis-arming smile and spread-open hands, "you've done hellish-well, so far, but . . . there's that *corvette* your ships took. Ney needs supplies, and he already holds the major sea ports, with as many garrison troops as he can take from his army in the field. Sooner or later, the French navy must come out and try to run you off; and *then* where would you be?"

And here I thought I enjoyed *talkin' to Mountjoy,* Lewrie told himself, feeling peevish. He realised, though, that the Foreign Office spy, a fellow years younger than he, and one who had long before been his *clerk,* was, despite all that, the closest thing to a direct voice of His Majesty's Government at Lisbon.

Christ, the prat might even be smarter *than me!* he thought in uncomfortable disgust; *Next thing I know, me and my ships'll be just a little part of a fleet, ploddin' about under an Admiral. Damn his eyes, Mountjoy's right.*

"Maybe Admiralty will send you Admiral Gambier," Mountjoy said in jest.

"Gambier?" Lewrie snorted in derision. "Dismal Jemmy, the mournful prophet? No thankee! His sailors don't dance hornpipes or jigs on his ships, they're on their knees, prayin!, and all their chanteys are hymns!"

"He'll soon be free of his current command," Mountjoy said as he rooted through a pile of newspapers and shoved one at Lewrie. "Read this."

"Good Lord," Lewrie exclaimed, half-way through the article, "A proper cock-up. The miserable idiot."

First off, Admiral James Gambier's temporary absence from the blockade had allowed a French squadron of eight ships of the line and four frigates to escape from Brest, bound South to meet up with even more warships from Lorient and Rochefort for some nefarious venture—the article only speculated that they might be bound for the West Indies—which venture had been scotched, and they had all taken shelter in the well-protected anchorage of Basque Roads near Rochefort, and behind the Ile d'Aix and its fortress guns.

Perhaps to make amends for letting them escape in the first place, Gambier took his eleven ships of the line to blockade them, but could not discover a way to get at them. He had requested fire ships to go in and burn them out, and Admiralty had sent him both fireships and explosive-packed bomb vessels, under the command of the illustrious Capt. Thomas, Lord Cochrane, a *very* un-conventional and pugnacious man who, reputedly, could drive his superior officers to distraction by going his own way, and bedamned to orders.

Cochrane and 'Dismal Jemmy'? Lewrie thought in amusement; *One* bad *combination! Did he ask Cochrane if he was saved, right off?*

Cochrane and his frigate, *Imperieuse,* had bulled his way in, using the bomb vessels to blast away a stout log-and-cable boom at the mouth of the Roads, sent his fireships swarming forward, driven by a stiff breeze. Cochrane had been one of the last men to leave one of the bombs, lighting the fuses himself, then had gone *back* aboard . . . to rescue the ship's dog! As some of the fireships got through the hole in the boom, panic had ensued as eleven ships of the line and four frigates cut their cables.

Cochrane signalled Gambier that success was in the offing. Inexplicably, Gambier did nothing, and kept *on* doing nothing for hours, ignoring Cochrane's repeated signals before *finally* sending frigates and lighter warships to aid him, long after dark.

Two French ships of the line had struck their colours, two more and a frigate were set on fire and abandoned, burned to cinders, and the rest had been driven onto the shoals or the mainland. They *all* could have been gobbled up, if only Gambier had acted! Once the tide had risen, the grounded ships had been floated off and had taken safer shelter in the mouth of the Charente River which leads to Rochefort, and the whole grand scheme had been a bust. The newspaper gloated over how many French flag officers and captains had been put on trial and shot, imprisoned, or cashiered, but, all in all, it was not the Royal Navy's finest hour.

"Christ," Lewrie said at last, letting out a sigh.

"Know what Gambier said of it?" Mountjoy sneered. " 'It is all simply too bad'."

"I'd love to attend the court-martial," Lewrie sniggered. "I'd vote for death by firing squad. They shot Admiral Byng for less."

"Ah, but we live in *such* enlightened times, now," Mountjoy drolly countered. "I doubt if the old Bible-thumper will get much more than a slap on the wrist, or put on half-pay for the rest of his natural life. What does the Navy call it?"

"Being 'yellow-squadroned'," Lewrie said with a laugh. "There's the Blue, lowest of all, then the Red, and very senior flag officers are atop in the White. Fools, poltroons, and village idiots are in the Yellow . . . barred from goin' within twenty *miles* of the sea for the good of the Service!"

"Feeling peckish?" Mountjoy asked, lifting the bottle to see how much was left, and using the last of it for a final top-up for both of them. "If you are, I've found a grand restaurant just re-opened . . . the French trashed and looted the place on their way out when they evacuated Lisbon. Spite, I suppose, for better cooking than a Parisian establishment. Our army officers adore the place."

"Sounds good to me," Lewrie happily agreed. "I promised that I'd lay on a shore feast for my Captains."

"It will suit you admirably," Mountjoy promised, tossing off the last wine in his glass and rising. "Here. You're welcome to all these newspapers. They ought to catch you up on things."

"You are the epitome of Christian kindness." Lewrie laughed.

"But Lewrie," Mountjoy teased. "Are you *saved*?"

CHAPTER TWENTY-FIVE

Hope she's happy t'see me, again, Lewrie thought as he shot his cuffs, tugged down his waistcoat, and fiddled with the set of his neck-stock outside the lodging house that Mountjoy had pointed out to him just before he'd set off to return to his "lair".

It was a rather nice place of pale tan and white stone, with a double door entry, three-storied, with many large balconies bound with ironwork, all shaded with dark green canvas awnings that had faded in the bright sunlight, the only shabby touch to the building's finery.

He also had to ask himself just how much these fine lodgings were costing him, as he entered, at last, discovering an entry hall much larger than a house foyer, with a large Turkey carpet on the tiled floor, sparsely filled with casual rattan furniture, and with potted plants spotted in the corners. There were some big paintings on the walls, dog hunting scenes in gilt frames, too. Along one wall by the stairwell stood a stout wooden counter, behind which a round older fellow with a cherubic full white heard puttered, sorting out letters in a rack of mail slots, much like a clerk in a hotel.

"Ah, *bom dia, Senhor,*" the fellow said with a smile.

"*Bom dia,*" Lewrie replied, grinning back. "*Fala Ingles?*"

"*Sim, Senhor,* I do," the stout fellow said with a hearty laugh. "The English has always been useful in Lisbon, and the English and Portuguese have been good friends for ages. It is even more useful now, with your soldiers protecting us from the detestable French." He looked as if he would spit on the floor when he said French. "I can help you, *Senhor*? You need lodging?"

"I'm looking for *Senhora* Covilhã's rooms," Lewrie told him.

The clerk, manager, whatever he was, squinted, losing his helpful, cheerful demeanour, and stiffly said, "The *Senhora* is in Number Four, one floor above, in front, *Senhor*," He then brusquely returned to his sorting.

"*Obrigado*," Lewrie said, heading for the stairs with his bundle of newspapers. *Ouch*, he thought; *Should have known*.

This wasn't Gibraltar, where officers who could afford to kept mistresses, where courtesans brought their clients, filled with thousands of rollicking sailors both naval and merchantmen, and off-duty garrison troops roaming about eager for drink and the services of the doxies. At Gibraltar, prudity was rarely observed, and mostly was scorned by all but the senior officers, and their prim wives who nagged them to do something about it.

No, this was a conservative Catholic city in a conservative Catholic country. Lewrie suspected that Lisbon, and Portugal, were just as sinful as any other place—they were full of humans, after all—but here, people *pretended* to be scandalised a *lot* stronger than they did in London.

As he ascended the stairs, Lewrie cautioned himself to take care, perhaps *not* sleep over, else the owners might deem Maddalena a whore and kick her out. With a secret grin, he also wondered if he must bite on a pillow in "the melting moments" to stifle his usual exuberance when they made love!

He found her door, took a deep breath, and rapped.

"*Sim*?" from within, an exasperated sound. "*Quem é*?"

"The bloody Royal Navy!" Lewrie called out with a laugh.

"*Alan*?" she cried back. "*Fantastico!*"

The lock clacked, the door was flung open, and there she was, flinging herself upon him and drawing him inside her rooms.

"Oh, at last, at last!" Maddalena crooned between deep kisses. "It has been so long! Ah, *meu amor*!"

Lewrie lifted her off her feet and danced her round the room, oblivious to the surroundings, admittedly stumbling here and there on the odd piece of furniture or the carpet. He nuzzled her neck and breathed in the scent of her hair. "At last, indeed, *meu querida*," he whispered in her ear. "Did ye miss me *that* much?"

"Desperately . . . horribly," Maddalena told him, leaning back for a moment to gaze at him, then pressed herself close once more with a girlish squeal of delight. "You find me when I am such a mess."

"You look grand," he assured her.

Smells a touch high, *though,* he had to admit to himself.

"In the middle of cleaning and un-packing . . ." she said.

"You still won't take on a maid?" he asked, finally taking the time to look about her new set of rooms. And Maddalena, Lewrie at last took note, wasn't exactly dressed for company, but wore one of her oldest peasant shifts, a pair of woven reed slippers peeking out from below its hem, with a long apron atop the shift, and her long, lustrous dark hair pinned up and covered with a kerchief like a maid-of-all-work, or a scullery maid. At Gibraltar, she had been just as frugal, preferring to do as much as she could for herself.

"The *gerente* . . . the manager, offers to send maids to change the bedding once a week," Maddalena told him, "and to sweep, mop, and clean, but is fifty *centimos*, and I . . ."

"Maddalena, *meu querida,* I can afford it," Lewrie assured her. "Take them up on it. The manager. Is he that bearded fellow at the desk?"

"No, that's Rubio, the morning clerk," she said, "He imagines that he runs it all, and thinks that the standards have slipped too far since the French came. I don't think he likes me," she confided with a twinkling grin.

"Happy here?" Lewrie asked.

"Now that you are, *meu amor,*" Maddalena replied. "Let me show you the view!"

The deep balcony spanned all three of her rooms, with glazed doors leading out to it. South-facing, the canvas awning would be more than welcome as the season advanced into Summer. Below lay the city, marching down to the flatter land and the Praça do Comércio and its parks. Beyond was the wide Tagus River estuary, all of the shipping, and beyond to the South bank towns and villages of Almada, Cacilhas, Seixal, Barreiro, and Montijo, all in all a most impressive vista.

"It comes mostly furnished," Maddalena explained, showing him the rattan seating and side tables on the balcony, then leading him back inside. Off to the left of the parlour was a dining area with kitchen with a four-place table and chairs, a waist-high cooking grate set into a stone chimney, and a battered old sideboard to store things and serve as a work counter.

To the right of the parlour was the bedroom, dominated by the tall bedstead and a large *armoire* to supplement the two large chests that Maddalena had fetched from Gibraltar. Her white-and-tan cat, Precious, lolled on one corner of the colourful coverlet, and her red warbler was flitting about and singing to itself in its cage.

"Still cook for yourself, too?" Lewrie teased.

"Oh, Lisbon is so much nicer than Gibraltar, Alan," she told him, excitedly, "there are so many cafes close by, so many *pastelerias,* and so many places to buy fresh food for cooking, or shops where I can pick up whole meals to bring home! Oh, so many wonderful things that I haven't tasted in *years*, the *alentejana, pataniscas de bacalhou,* and all the *cheeses!*"

"Home, are you?" Lewrie japed, with not a single clue as to what dishes she raved about; his Portuguese was even more limited than his poor command of French.

"*Sim,* I feel so," Maddalena quickly agreed, looking dreamy for a second, "I feel I am becoming a *Lisboêta,* happily so, and may never wish to live anywhere else. Would you like something to drink, Alan? I have some *vinho branco,* and some *espumante.*"

"Think I'd favour the *espumante,*" he told her, gathering up all the newspapers he'd spilled and heading for the settee. As Maddalena busied herself in the kitchen, he had time to look all round her new lodgings. She had not brought much from Gibraltar, due to the shipping costs, so most of the furnishings and decor had come with the rooms, though there were some familiar tablecloths, the bed coverlet, and some throws over the settee; things that could be folded or rolled up in a chest or crate. Her clothing would have been her major concern, along with her cat and her bird. When she came back with the wine, Lewrie saw that the glasses were new to him, too.

"You had to re-furnish almost everything?" he asked after a sip of the sparkling wine. "Just sell up and take ship? Sorry for making you rush."

"I was *delighted* to," Maddalena assured him. "Getting a chance to come to Lisbon, at last? To be with you, again? What I sold off was easy to replace, just . . . things, and what is not furnished here was much less costly than things were at Gibraltar, and with a much greater selection. I had not been aboard a ship in years, not since I left Oporto, but that was not that costly, either, and it was *fun.*"

"Mountjoy said something about offering you some work?" he asked her. "Has he?"

"Ah, yes!" Maddalena said, growing excited, again. "He has me translating from Portuguese, Spanish, and some of the few items he gets from the French, or from one to the other. It is all so mysterious, what he and Mister Deacon do. If what little help I give them drives the French from my country, and from Spain, then I am proud to help them, and I will make five pounds a month for doing so, too! Maybe I will buy *you* supper?" she teased.

Christ, women workin' for a living! Lewrie thought; *Her and that Jessica Chenery, both! She keeps this up, she won't need me or my money!* Wait. *Now she's learnin' French?*

"So many newspapers," Maddalena said, reaching over him to pick one out of the pile. "*Bom,* I can use them when I clean all of the glass panes." To Lewrie's puzzled look, she added, "I think it is something about the ink that helps cut the grime."

"You can do that anytime," Lewrie told her.

"No no, it must be done today," Maddalena insisted. "I need more pails of water. You will help me, *meu querido?*"

Work? Lewrie gawped; *Cleanin'? Domestic . . . ? Damn!*

Such was the *last* thing he'd come ashore for!

"Behind the building, in the old stableyard, there is a pump," she explained. "It might smell, but for the fact that no one can afford horses after the French ravaged the city, and what beasts there were before, they took with them when they surrendered and left. It will not take long. I'll show you where it is."

"Ehm, for the windows," Lewrie hedged, "not for a hot bath? Surely, the house helps with that, the cleanin' maids?"

"Oh no," Maddalena laughed, leaning her head over to pretend to sniff herself, "though I will need one before we go out to dine. There is a women's *bagnio* one street over, very discrete and secure. And a man's bathhouse across from mine. Come. It will only take a moment, and then you can read your papers, sip your *espumante,* as I clean." She batted her lashes and almost put on a pout.

"Oh, very well," Lewrie grumbled as he stood, took off his sword belt and coat, and went to pick up a pair of wooden pails.

"And, as I clean the windows, you can read the articles to me, and we can talk," Maddalena said most perkily and encouragingly.

Oh, how holly jolly! he thought. His late wife, Caroline, had never roped him into housewifery, though she'd never thought it beneath her own dignity as the lady of the house to work alongside their few maids at the more-demanding chores, herself, but . . . !

He was an English gentleman, for God's sake, a Post-Captain only slightly under God in the Royal Navy; people like him simply didn't *do* "domestic", or chores!

The things I do for King and Country, he told himself; *Or for a chance to roger a woman 'til I'm cross-eyed!*

In the end, though, reading interesting articles aloud whilst sipping the sparkling *espumante*—and watching someone else work—wasn't all *that* bad an afternoon, and Maddalena's acute comments to the papers' contents proved all over again how shrewd and intelligent a young woman she was, besides being so fetching.

The *bagnio* Lewrie visited afterwards was a welcome treat, too, nothing like his dubious expecations. Instead of a wooden tub used by dozens before him, there was a copper tub, fresh-scoured, rinsed out, and set in a private room where he could keep an eye on his belongings and clothing. Cheerful attendants kept pails of hot, clean water coming, the soap cake was finely-milled and pleasantly scented, and the towels provided were dry, clean, and smelled of lye and sunshine, fresh off a line. After a splash of Hungary Water (only five centimos extra), he left the *bagnio* a much happier and cleaner man, with no more salt-crystal itches, even if the presence of a British army had raised the bath prices from six pence to a whole shilling.

Maddalena met him in the street, fresh from her own ablutions, and dressed in a pale green gown she'd carried with her, a white lace shawl, and a perky bonnet, daintily twirling a yellow parasol, with a welcoming grin on her face.

She steered him to a *pasteleria* for *travesseiros,* sugary egg and almond pastries and marvellous Brazilian coffee with thick and sweetened cream, lingering and idly chatting in emulation of the other Lisboêtas. Later, on their way back to her lodgings, they visited a well-stocked wine shop, where Lewrie bought more *espumante* and some rosé *vinho verde* for her pantry.

And then it was time for supper, and a leisurely stroll down to the same restaurant where Lewrie and Mountjoy had earlier dined, savouring the slightly cooler air of dusk, and the—dare he call it romantic?—aura that Lisbon took on as the sun slanted lower to the Atlantic, casting the city's stone buildings golden, and as the lanthorns before shops and houses sprang to life. In the Tagus, nigh an hundred ships' taffrail lights twinkled, and their reflections danced and rippled on the flowing river like a fairyland,

and Lewrie felt it a crying shame that the restaurant did not have an outdoor patio where he could gaze down at the magical city and the Tagus, mesmerised.

Oh, God, after weeks of deprivation, there were fresh salad greens, razor-thin cucumber slices, tiny wedges of tomatoes, heaps of lettuce and spinach, all dripping with vinaigrette. Fresh bread rolls with butter instead of stale, weevily ship's bisquit. Lashings of a *vinho branco*, *Gazpacho*, a Portuguese version of chilled tomato and garlic bread soup, redolent of olive oil, vinegar, and oregano.

And then, most toothsome of wonders, came that *alentejana* she had enthused about for Maddalena; diced pork and cockles spiced with olive oil, garlic, and paprika in a savoury sauce. She allowed him a taste or two, but his own order, the *acorda de camarãoes*, sent Lewrie over the moon; prawns, lobster bits, with garlic and cilantro, thickened like the *gazpacho* with bread crumbs.

Something sweet for after were *queijadas limao*, perfect following such spicy dishes; cheesecake-like lemon pastries. They lingered over port, *queijo da Serra*, a creamy, soft cheese, and sweet bisquit.

At last, sated, stuffed in point of fact, and after a final cup of that strong coffee, and with Maddalena bestowing upon him fond, yet dreamy, gazes Lewrie essayed his slim Portuguese to their waiter, saying *"Queria a conta, por favor."*

"Sim, the bill. At once, *Senhor,"* was the prompt reply.

"Oh, you were close, *meu amor,"* Maddalena told him with a teasing smile, "but it's not *conta*, it's *congta poor favor*. When you try to speak *Poor-toogesh*."

"Then I'll never get the hang of it, I suppose," Lewrie replied with a sheepish grin, and a shrug of his shoulders. "Ready for me to see you home?"

"Yes, *meu querido,"* she slowly said, "but only if you promise to stay the night."

"Wild, sword-wavin' Turks couldn't *drag* me away," he vowed. "Let's go, ah . . . *vaamoosh para a caa-ma*. Did I say that right?"

"Perfectly, *meu amor,"* she agreed, with her eyes full of promise. "Let us go to bed."

CHAPTER TWENTY-SIX

Mountjoy's right, damn him, Lewrie thought once back aboard and seated at his desk in his day cabin; *playin' pirate is all well and good, but . . .* He heaved a sigh as he opened a drawer and took out a sheet of good bond paper, opened the ink-well, and began to compose a letter to Admiralty requesting more ships. There were only three ways that his superiors in London could take his request; as an admission that the task was too big for him to handle and that he had bitten off more than he could chew; as a sly way to promote himself to the status of an Admiral in all but name; or, as a legitimate plea for more help. Knowing full well the Navy's jealousies and penchant for back-biting—A Band of Brothers, bedamned!—he was certain that his request would *not* redound to his good credit, but it would be necessary, if the task was to be done properly.

He threw in a little boasting, of course, citing the numbers of prizes taken in only two brief cruises, and the capture of a French *corvette*, but admitted that those successes were but a pittance of the volume of trade, and that once his ships had to quit the coast for lack of prize crewmen, and sailors to fight their own ships if the French ever sortied to offer battle, the enemy had all the time in the world to supply their armies during their absence.

He sketched out what he *might* be able to accomplish if given enough ships, even going so far as to suggest that he could emulate his cruises along the Andalusian shore in 1807; landing soldiers and Marines from transports to raid French semaphore towers, gun batteries, and the smaller seaports' garrisons and sheltering convoys, laying out the needed boarding nets, extra ships' boats, and light guns required.

Chalmers, he considered, idly tapping the wooden end of his steel-nib pen against his teeth; *He's senior-next to me, and a second squadron could be built around him, maybe a third under Yearwood.*

That would deprive Lewrie the chance to see his son, Hugh, as often as he wished, but it would spare him from those dubious, "stink-eyed" glances that Chalmers shot his way, now and again!

That long letter at last finished, Lewrie considered a second tack, going round Admiralty and writing the senior-most officer in Iberian waters, or the Commander-in-Chief of the Mediterranean Fleet. If he could put a flea in someone else's ear who could see the opporunities and second his idea—or find himself and his favourites a place to reap profits and find more excitement than plodding on a dull blockade—and write to London supporting the scheme, the better.

Lewrie was just laying out a fresh sheet of paper to do just that when he heard someone on deck hailing an approaching boat, followed by a loud response, asking for permission to come aboard.

And, when the senior Midshipman of the Harbour Watch called for a side-party to be mustered, Lewrie rose to go satisfy his curiosity. He got to the quarterdeck just in time to recognise *Undaunted*'s gig approaching the starboard entry-port.

"Speak of the Devil," Lewrie said as he greeted Capt. Chalmers once the welcoming ritual was completed. "Believe it or not, I was just thinking of you, sir,"

"Were you, Sir Alan?" Chalmers said, somewhat surprised by that statement. "Your pardons for calling aboard without a proper request, but there is a matter which has been nagging at me, and I wished to discuss it with you."

Of course, being greeted by his Commodore dressed in his shirt sleeves without a neck-stock drew forth one of Chalmers's dubious, "whatever are you up to, now?" glances.

"Come aft, then, and tell it me," Lewrie offered, waving him towards the door to the great-cabins. "Will you have cool tea, or a glass of local *espumante?*"

"Well, I've heard of your cool tea," Chalmers said, sounding as if that beverage was either heathen or un-British, "but the wine sounds refreshing."

Lewrie steered Chalmers to the settee, chairs, and the large, round brass Hindoo tray-table, calling for the sparkling wine, and Pettus went to the wood bucket hung from the overhead where the wine was cooling in water.

"From India?" Chalmers asked, tapping the table.

"Aye, pretty-well banged up after all these years, from when I was there in the eighties, 'tween the wars," Lewrie admitted.

Chalmers looked round the cabins as if he'd never seen them before, taking in a glimpse of Lewrie's almost-wide-enough-for-two hanging bed-cot in the bed space, (and most-like finding it sinful!) just before Chalky came to sniff at his boots and brush round his ankles. Then their wine was there.

"Ah! Cooled!" Capt. Chalmers marvelled. "Where did you discover the ice, Sir Alan?"

He's pissin' down my back with all that 'Sir Alan' stuff. He must really need *something,* Lewrie thought.

"A trick I heard of in the West Indies," Lewrie told him with a grin. "They hang a large clay jar, an *olla,* filled with water and place it where it can catch a breeze, in the shade, of course. Keeps things cool enough. You've something on your mind you wished to discuss, you said?"

"Aye, Sir Alan," Chalmers replied, shifting in his chair like a travelling chapman ready to start his sales pitch. "As successful as we've been up North, we're only able to stay there for so long, and then the French have a fortnight or longer to play 'silly beggars', and . . ."

"And we need a second squadron up there, threatening them in rotation," Lewrie finished for him, "or, we need enough ships to keep the coast under constant watch. Is that your thinking, sir?"

"My concern to a Tee, exactly, sir!" Chalmers said, appearing somewhere betwixt pleasure to be so agreed with, or having his idea, and his argument for it, shot to pieces.

"I just finished a letter to Admiralty expressing that very problem," Lewrie told Chalmers, secretly enjoying the look on the man's phyz. "Had I not already sealed it, I'd show it you. I also was just about to write the senior officer in the Med, requesting ships, or support in London, but for your timely arrival."

"Ah, I see, sir," Chalmers said, looking glum that Lewrie had beaten him to the punch.

"In that letter, I put forward your name, Captain Chalmers, as the best officer on scene to command that second squadron, should it be formed. Would that suit you?"

"Me, sir?" Chalmers gawped. "Well, of course, sir, I would be delighted if such came to pass. Mean t'say, doing the duty's the only thing."

Oh, horse shite! Lewrie thought; *You came here* angling *for it!*

"If you get command of the second squadron, you'd need two more frigates and three more brig-sloops," Lewrie went on, "and I'd need a frigate to replace *Undaunted,* and one more sloop to work with me . . . the pairing of a frigate strong enough to face any French escorts, and a sloop to aid in the hunting, seems to work well, so far, and three pairs can cover the Spanish coast well, too."

"It seems to, so far, aye, sir," Chalmers agreed, looking up at the overhead as if in deep thought; or seeking his own broad pendant. "The fewer pairs, though, the greater glory, and prize-money, what?" Now that the matter seemed to be settled in his favour, he was merrier.

"That *corvette* you took," Lewrie asked him, "I did not enquire if she put up much of a fight. How did it go with her?"

"Well, her Captain *did* fulfill his duty to protect his convoy," Chalmers explained, shrugging and making a deprecating gesture. "She covered their retreat into San Sebastián, which was only fifteen or so miles to their lee, anyway, and the *Caprice* a mile seaward of them when we spotted them. She came out to face us, bows-on to Blamey's ship 'til *Peregrine* was within a mile's range, and ahead of me by two cables. It was then that she hauled her wind to lay herself cross *Peregrine*'s bows and fired off a broadside . . . for honour's sake more-like, then altered course to run into San Sebastián, herself, hoping to keep ahead of us and spin out a long stern chase into shallower coastal waters where we'd be forced to break off."

Capt. Richard Chalmers took great, but properly modest, delight in describing how sloppily the French ship had been handled, and how quickly Commander Blamey's *Peregrine* had caught up with her, and had engaged the *corvette*'s larboard side which had not initially been manned or the guns ready for action. Then, minutes after the French realised that they were in a real fight, up *Undaunted* had surged to engage her starboard side, and one broadside from Chalmers's frigate had forced her to strike.

"You can't imagine how *weeded* she was, sir," Chalmers hooted with glee, slapping his knee, "nigh as green as her Captain's face when we boarded her. The poor devil told me he'd *begged* the yards at Bayonne for a careening, or fresh coppering, but his superiors told him that there wasn't enough time, nor material available, to delay his sailing. That's another reason she was so slow at running away."

"Hmm, and they only sent one *corvette* to escort the convoy," Lewrie mused, stroking his jaw. "Did you press him on the matter, Captain Chalmers? Are we goin' t'see more of that, in future?"

"I did probe, sir," Chalmers said with a sly smirk. "I dined him in and 'liquored his boots' . . . *in vino veritas,* what? . . . and he boasted that he'd saved an important shipment of troops, artillery, and cavalry remounts for Marshal Ney's army. I gathered, though, that only vital convoys would be given escort, for now, and that the trade we've seen so far, the brigs and coasters, will have to soldier on on their own devices, 'til the French manage to shift more ships South from Bordeaux and ports North past the inshore squadrons of our blockade.

"And, when deep 'in his cups', sir," Chalmers went on with a sly tap alongside his nose, "he complained that France is robbing Peter to pay Paul, as it were . . . taking hands from their navy to flesh out their armies, and using seasoned timber, and copper for new construction of frigates and ships of the line, instead of properly maintaining their lesser ships, like his *Caprice.*"

"Still, she'll fetch you and Blamey a pretty penny," Lewrie congratulated him, "even if she's badly in need of a hull cleaning."

Lucky bastard, Lewrie sourly thought; *there'll be no Droits of the Crown for you!*

"I fully expect so, sir," Chalmers gloated, tilting his glass to request a refill, and Pettus was there to pour him back up.

"I've discovered a good place where I can dine you all in," Lewrie told him. "Dined there the other night and found it grand. Unless there's a reason to preclude, shall we hold it tomorrow night?"

"Sounds delightful, sir," Chalmers agreed.

"Then I'll make the reservations, and send invitations round to all," Lewrie said. "I'm told that our army officers favour the place, but Wellesley, the new Commander in Chief, has taken most of them off to Oporto with him, and has limited idling in Lisbon, so we won't have to deal with too many of their sort."

"Even better, sir," Chalmers said with a laugh. "Ehm, I say. What *is* your cat doing?"

Perhaps Chalky took to boot blacking like catnip, for he had been twining and brushing round Chalmers's boots since he had seated himself. Now, to mark the man completely, the cat was quivering his rump and tail against them.

"He must be taken with you, Captain Chalmers," Lewrie said in secret glee. "He's marking you as his."

"Well, I wish he wouldn't," Chalmers rejoined, tucking his heels and knees together very primly. "Shoo, you. Scat."

To that command, Chalky turned to look up at Chalmers's face, then leaped into his lap!

"Uh, could you, ah?" Chalmers gawped.

Cats just know who don't like them, Lewrie thought; *and what to do to* vex *'em!*

"Come here, Chalky, you pesky scamp," Lewrie cooed, reaching over to lift him off, then sit with the cat cuddled in his own lap. "Bad cat! Bad boy!" Which only made Chalky purr.

CHAPTER TWENTY-SEVEN

*L*ater that afternoon, Lewrie had that *rencontre* with his son, Hugh, that Capt. Chalmers had promised, though it was more by accident than arrangement. He had finished reading his personal mail, had penned some replies, and had gone ashore with his letters to the Post Office. It was in the vicinity of the Post Office that he espied Hugh, on the same mission, and hailed him.

"Hallo, father . . . sir," Hugh said, grinning broadly, but doffing his hat in proper salute to a senior officer.

"Mister Midshipman Hugh Lewrie, is it?" Lewrie teased, returning the salute. "You *sort* of resemble him, but damned if I know where my little *boy* has gone. Just *look* at you, nigh a man full-grown, and a tarry one, at that! It's been too long, me lad, even with you not a stone's throw away from me! Why, we could've conversed by *letter* more easily, the last few months!"

"It's good to see you, too, father," Hugh replied, beaming as they shook hands, and Lewrie Senior seized his shoulder for a second.

"You've come ashore with the mail? So have I. Do they need you back aboard all that badly, or can I treat you to some pastries so we can catch up?" Lewrie eagerly asked.

"Well, perhaps for a *few* minutes, sir," Hugh allowed. "There is my boat crew waiting."

"Let's get all this posted, then find us a *pasteleria*. Lisbon is famous for them, *and* damned good coffee." Lewrie tempted.

"Of course, sir!" Hugh was happy to agree.

Once free of their errands, they found a *pasteleria* nearby, one with an awninged outdoor seating area, and took a table, ordering wee cups of strong coffee and *pastel de natas,* creamy, flaky custard tarts.

"Umm, my Lord, I haven't tasted anything this good in *ages*!" Hugh raved, after his first bite of his tart.

"That's the Navy for you," Lewrie said with a laugh, between bites of his own tart. "Nothing but deprivation, years on end. Have you and your mess-mates had many chances for a run ashore in Lisbon? The food here is a marvel."

"Not all that much, really," Hugh admitted. "Captain Chalmers keeps us rather busy, and doesn't think that shore liberty is good for our morals. The hands, aye, but young gentlemen?" He made a face at that statement.

His sort would, Lewrie thought.

"Actually, when I was aboard my first ship, with Captain Charlton, we never *saw* a foreign port," Hugh further confessed, looking up and around in appreciation. "Lisbon is my first exposure to the wider world."

"And . . . ?" Lewrie posed.

"I like it!" Hugh enthusiastically stated. "A lot!"

"Well, there's a lot to like," Lewrie told him.

"The only port we've been allowed ashore was Valletta on Malta," Hugh expounded, returning to his custard tart, "and that was mostly working parties, and perhaps one quick ale before rowing back to the ship. Our Chaplain, Mister Wickes, gave us a tour or two . . . fine if one likes museums, churches, and architecture . . . with a shore meal after . . . *and* with his keen eye on our wine consumption."

Chalmers carries a Chaplain? Lewrie thought; *Of course*!

"Perhaps your Captain thinks that his young gentlemen should be exposed to *cultural* experiences, if they're destined to become proper representatives of Great Britain when they make 'Post', *if* they do," Lewrie said, putting a charitable slant on such doings.

"Perhaps, father," Hugh replied, "but it makes for *very* dull going. Our Jacks have all the fun."

"Depends on what sort of fun you have in mind," Lewrie said, with one brow significantly raised in query.

"Oh, music, dancing, wine, and ale," Hugh replied, laughing at the prospects, "meeting foreign young ladies and polishing our linguistic skills? The proper sorts, of course," he added, rolling his eyes to mock his intentions.

Well, they say that acorns don't fall far from the tree, and he is *a Lewrie,* Lewrie thought, surprised by how much his son *had* grown up these last few years. He was just about to suggest that his boy should invest in some well-made cundums!

"Just be careful," Lewrie said, instead. "Young foreign girls have strict male relatives with sharp knives, and the 'commercial' sorts could be 'fire-ships'."

"Oh, grandfather sent me a packet of, ah . . . protections," Hugh told him, blushing a tad. "And a five pound note, which was more than welcome."

There we are, then! Lewrie thought; *He's a Lewrie* and a *Willoughby, God help us!*

"Used both in the same place, did you?" Lewrie wryly asked.

"Ehm . . . not yet, father, no," Hugh admitted. "Do you think I could get another of these tarts? They're heavenly."

"Of course, and I'll have another coffee," Lewrie agreed, and summoned the waiter to try out his limited Portuguese. As they waited, he thought to ask, "Heard from Sewallis, have you?"

"Not the last two months, no," Hugh told him. "I've written him at least twice, but . . . perhaps I put his nose out of joint with too much boasting about all the action we've seen, and how many good prizes we've taken. Poor Sewallis!" Hugh said with a mirthful snort. "Six years in the Navy, and he's yet to hear a gun fired in anger, nothing but dull plodding off-and-on some French port. Not what he expected when he ran off to sea. I'd wager he thought that he'd have the same sort of adventures that *you've* had, father."

Hugh was none too sympathetic for his older brother; the few years that Lewrie had spent ashore on half-pay, he had seen how the two had competed with each other, but he'd always thought that it was harmless.

"I haven't heard from him, either," Lewrie said, "and in his last few letters, he sounded as if he was becoming a bit of a rake-hell."

"Sewallis?" Hugh exclaimed, then laughed aloud. "Father, you must
be *joking*! Why, one *couldn't* get his nose out of a book, and a *hymn* book,
at that! Mister 'sobre-sides' . . . hah! What has he been up to, then?"

"Well, the few times his ship's put in for provisions, he says he's attended
subscription balls, danced and flirted with the girls," Lewrie related, "gotten 'half-seas-over' with his mess-mates, and says he's the best dancer
aboard . . . so good that he's been playin' 'hop master' to the other Mids.
Hmpf . . . rather short letters, too, with little said of doings at sea, or his
prospects for promotion."

Sewallis was twenty-one, and only had one more year at sea to go
before he could qualify to stand before a board of Post-Captains' oral
examinations to gain his Lieutenancy. Yet . . .

"His first Captain, my old friend, Benjamin Rodgers, said he was stu-
dious, and sopped up skills and sea lore like a sponge, navigation and
all," Lewrie mused. "I expected him to be made 'Passed' and gain his
Lieutenancy first try, but now . . ."

"Perhaps he's lost interest, father," Hugh speculated as their fresh
order arrived. "I always thought that he'd read for the law, or attend university, even become a churchman, anyway. He's the eldest, after all. That's
what elder sons expect to do. Inherit the estate, learn to manage it properly, beforehand."

"Well, I hope he hasn't . . . lost interest," Lewrie said as he stirred sugar
into his strong, black coffee.

"Have you heard from Charlotte, father?" Hugh asked him.

"Oh, Lord no!" Lewrie said, scowling. "What I learn of her, I get
second-hand from your Uncle Governour, or Aunt Millicent. I *have* written her, but I might as well drop stones down a well for all the good that's
got me. Have you?"

His only daughter was a touchy subject, one that Lewrie hoped his boys
learned the least about. Charlotte was his late wife's, Caroline's, darling,
who had absorbed all of Caroline's spite and vitriol over his dissolute ways.
Yes, he'd been unfaithful when half-way round the world, and years from
home, even though, in his own defence he could call his dalliances "serial
monogamy", quite unlike his "buck-of-the-first-head" youth. Yes, he'd
fathered a bastard—at least he *thought* there were only two!—one with a
wealthy Greek widow, heiress to a currant export fortune. Unfortunately,
Theoni Cavares-Connor didn't care to be dropped, and had written a

series of scathing letters, providing Caroline a litany of his affairs, some invented, but the most of them alarmingly well-informed and detailed. Why, it was as if the jealous bitch had better sources than John Peel or Thomas Mountjoy of the Foreign Office's Secret Branch!

Charlotte was utterly convinced that Lewrie had been the one to drag her mother to Paris on their reconciliation "honeymoon" which had resulted in her mother's death at the hands of the French police, too, and could not be dissuaded by anyone. By now, the girl was hateful in the extreme, arch, sneering, and dismissive of her father, and her grandfather, too, when her blood was up, barely able to behave in a civil fashion when she and Lewrie were in the same vicinity.

"Aye, I have, father," Hugh told him with a rueful shake of his head. "She wrote me about a month ago, or so. On and on about how deprived she was, and how beastly you are to deny her a proper allowance, the promise of a dowry, and the funds for a London Season, so she can make her entry into *Society*," Hugh sneered, grimacing over the word. "Snag herself a rich husband, before she wastes away back in dull old Anglesgreen, where there are so few prospects?"

"Oh, Lord," Lewrie said with a groan. "What does she expect, t'be presented at Court, meet the bloody Prince of Wales, and marry a titled twit? That's far above our lot, and my meetin' the King was a fluke. Just like my baronetcy's a fluke 'cause the King was havin' one of his bad days. I've written Governour and told him I'd put an hundred pounds out there for the 'buttock-brokers' . . . two hundred if that's what it takes, but damme if I'll lay out more as long as Charlotte treats me like a red-headed, cack-handed leper!"

"She really is spiteful," Hugh commented. "Pity, 'cause she was so sweet and biddable when she was little. A very lovable sister . . . as sisters go," he quipped. "What's her rush, anyway, father? She isn't even twenty, yet. Far too young to marry anyone. Oh, upon that head, she wrote that she *has* been squired about by the Oakes' son, and Sir Harry Embleton's middle son."

"Never met either of 'em," Lewrie grumbled. "Does Harry's boy resemble an otter like his father?"

Old Sir Romney Embleton had been a distinguished-looking man, but Harry had not inherited a noble profile.

"No future in either, I expect," Hugh said, sounding surprisingly mature for his years. "Charlotte would need five hundred pounds to tempt the Oakes family, and, isn't there bad blood 'twixt you and Sir Harry?"

"Of long standing," Lewrie said, laughing as he repeated that bit of family lore. Harry had sort of "set his cap" for Caroline, and had been wroth when a nobody half-pay Navy Lieutenant and friend of the Chiswick brothers had turned up as a house guest and had won her heart. Harry had made such a scene at one morning's fox hunt that Caroline had lashed him cross the face with her reins and had made Harry's nose "spout claret"! He'd not attended their wedding day, either, though Sir Romney had.

"God, I wish I'd been alive to see that!" Hugh said, laughing along with him. "We'll never drink at the Red Swan, none of us."

"The Olde Ploughman is good enough for the likes of us," Lewrie agreed. "And their beer is better."

"I'm just beginning to realise that we live in a 'rotten borough'," Hugh said. "Not twenty men who hold the franchise, and most of them go to the Red Swan, where they're beholden to the Embletons, and send Sir Harry to the Commons time after time."

"Aye, perhaps it's best we aren't there full time, else we'd *not* vote for Harry, or your Uncle Governour for Magistrate, and the whole borough'd be howlin' for our blood."

"Ah, that was tasty," Hugh said as he laid his spoon aside and drew his pocket watch out to determine the time. "I'm sorry, but I must get back to the quays. I've left my hands idle much too long."

"I'll walk you back," Lewrie said, summoning the waiter for the bill, and pronouncing *queria a conta, por favor* the right way.

Good Christ, he's taller than me! Lewrie realised as they walked towards the waterfront; *He tops me by two inches, at least!*

Whilst Sewallis had gotten Lewrie's mid-brown hair and his mother's amber eyes, Hugh had gotten Caroline's lighter near-blond hair and Lewrie's grey-blue eyes. And, somewhere along the line, his youngest son had developed into a wide-shouldered, lean and muscular near-adult, one whom Lewrie could admire and be proud of. Sewallis, his eldest . . . well, the jury was still deliberating on that'un.

"Damme, another bloody funeral procession," Lewrie carped as their way was blocked by the emergence of an array of saintly statues borne on platforms, an ornate coffin, and a train of mourners, with a grim-faced priest leading the way, and robed acolytes carrying the censors and crosses. "They do a lot o' dyin' in Lisbon, I suppose."

"Captain Chalmers says that we should show respect," Hugh said as he took off his hat and laid it on his breast.

"Can't hurt, I suppose," Lewrie said, emulating his son. They both low-ered their heads as the coffin passed by.

Upon looking back up, however, Lewrie felt his bowels shrivel. They were almost directly across the street from Mountjoy's offices, the innocent-sounding Falmouth Import & Export Company Ltd. And who should be right by the doors, crossing herself like a properly respectful Catholic lady, than Maddalena!

This won't end well, Lewrie told himself; *Maybe Hugh won't . . .*

"Ehm, father . . . doesn't that woman there by the doors look the spit-ting image of that Miss . . . what's her name that you introduced me to back at Gibraltar?" Hugh asked.

"Uhm . . . possibly," Lewrie waffled.

"It is!" Hugh blurted. "Miss Margaret? No. Maria? Covee-something or other."

"Maddalena Covilhã," Lewrie confessed. "Yes, it is her."

"My *word*!" Hugh exclaimed. "Dare I ask you . . . congratulate you, rather, on just *how* you managed to bring her here, sir?"

"You're *not* scandalised?" Lewrie marvelled.

"Mother's gone, the last seven years, father," Hugh said with a worldly shrug, "and you're a man of the world, not a tonsured monk in a dank cell. Expecting you, any widower, to shun that part of his life is foolishness."

Damme, he is *my little acorn!* Lewrie gratefully thought.

"It'd be best did you not tell Sewallis or Charlotte of it," Lewrie cau-tioned. "Or your Aunt and Uncle. Or your Captain. I'm sure he thinks me an un-redeemable sinner, already, and he's quick with the dis-believing glance."

"Mum's the word, father," Hugh promised, grinning. "Oh, she's spot-ted us. It'd only be polite to cross over and say hallo."

"S'pose it would be," Lewrie hesitantly agreed, waving at her and cross-ing the street.

In for the penny, in for the pound, he thought, plastering a a warm smile on his "phyz" to make re-introductions.

CHAPTER TWENTY-EIGHT

*D*uring the shore supper that Lewrie hosted, Commander Teague had raised the subject of shore liberty for the squadron's sailors, and Lewrie had said that he would consider it, once re-provisioning had been completed. The more he thought of it, though, shore liberty looked less appealing, even if his Sapphires had grown used to that freedom, and might turn sullen at its lack. He had ordered the Easy Pendant be hoisted to put all ships Out of Discipline, but only for one day. As enjoyable as he found Lisbon, and time to be with Maddalena, he felt an anxious urge to be back at sea.

"You leave tomorrow?" Maddalena exclaimed, drawing back from his embrace, looking a tad startled.

"First light, weather permittin'," Lewrie told her.

"But, you just got here only a few days ago," she complained, turning pout-ish.

"I know, m'dear, but I have to," Lewrie said, enjoying a view of her bare body as she propped herself up on an elbow. He'd waited 'til after their lovemaking before breaking the news, hoping that she might take it better. "Blame it on your employer. He told me that the French are ma-kin' hay in the days we aren't on the coast, and we have t'cut our time in port short and get back up there, soonest."

"Making . . . hay?" Maddalena puzzled. "For their horses?"

"It's an expression," Lewrie had to explain. "One makes hay in the sun-shine, quick as one can, lest it rains before the crop's in. As soon as we quit the coast, they scuttle out like roaches and make the most of the time we give 'em."

Maddalena Covilhā was a bright and intelligent young woman, multi-lingual and well read, but casual English speech idioms now and then tripped her up, despite her formal grasp of the language.

"But, you will be back soon?" Maddalena cooed as she slinked back to cuddle close once more, most enticingly.

"Well, I really can't say," Lewrie had to dis-abuse her notions once more. "We have t'stay on station as long as we can, and that'll be weeks and weeks. With decent winds, it's three days there and three back. Three or four days at Lisbon, that gives the Frogs almost a fortnight free of in-terference. And Mountjoy also told me that even when we *are* there, there's only so much that five ships can do, and they're still gettin' their supplies, ready as clockwork."

"Oh, I wish that we were still back at Gibraltar," Maddalena said with a long sigh. "You were never gone very long."

"Sorry ye came, girl?" Lewrie asked in a fond whisper.

"No, *meu amor*, of course not," she replied, her face hidden against his shoulder. Her denial, though, did not sound heartfelt, more rote than sin-cere. "I missed you so much after you sailed off to Corunna, never know-ing if, or when, you would return . . . I . . . I had hoped for more time with you."

"Well, that's my dearest wish, too, Maddalena," Lewrie was quick to assure her, shifting about in the bed to look her in the eyes. "Else, I'd never have sent for you. But I did, didn't I, hey? Didn't hunt up some other young woman here, some *Lisboêta*. No, I sent for *you*. 'Cause I *wanted* to. Wanted *you*, no matter how short our time together might be. I *thought* we'd have longer between voyages, but . . . it's the war, and the Navy, and my duty."

"Oh, Alan," she cooed, melting, and pressed close once more, kissing him deeply. Even if he could feel faint tears on her cheeks.

⚓

There had been time for a last bath at the *bagnio,* one last supper together, then it was time to part, and Lewrie made his solo way to the quays and a hired boat out to HMS *Sapphire.*

To the war, to the Navy, and his Duty.

And, once the squadron had a way on, falling down the Tagus to the open sea, Lewrie stood by the starboard bulwarks of the poop deck with his telescope extended to seek out Maddalena's balcony. In the past at Gibraltar, he could rely upon the sight of her whenever his ship set sail, or returned to port, bidding him goodbye, or welcoming him back with a gaily-waving tea towel.

He counted the tiers of buildings upwards from the flat land and the broad thoroughfare that ran along the Tagus's banks, up past the town blocks of the Baixa district as his ship came level with it, seeking out the lodging house with the green awnings, finally found it, and . . . nothing. Nothing waving, no sign of her, the glint of dawn reflecting off the glazed double doors, and perhaps he could make out a hint of her warbler's brass cage, and a flutter of red as it flitted . . . but no Maddalena.

Damme, does she go t'work for Mountjoy this *early? Or, is she out to break-fast?* he asked himself, made a face, and let out a long, disappointed sigh. He lowered his telescope and slowly collapsed the tubes, feeling let down somehow.

Woof, and there was Bisquit, sitting on his hindquarters by Lewrie's side, giving him a playful nudge for attention on the back of his knee.

"And a fine mornin' t'you, Bisquit," Lewrie said, reaching down to give the dog some petting. "At least I can count on you, hey? Oh, yes! Ye beat 'working' women all hollow, ye do."

Off the Costa de Morte, the *Sterling* frigate and the *Blaze* sloop departed the squadron to return to their hunting grounds, but Lewrie kept *Sapphire* with *Undaunted* and *Peregrine* to have a look at the enemy-held harbours to the East, and the French ports of Bayonne and Arcachon, mostly out of sheer bloody-minded curiosity, and on the chance that, with their operating area closest to French naval ports, Capt. Chalmers and Commander Blamey might need backing if the enemy had decided to provide escorts to their precious convoys.

Of course, the weather in that corner of the Southern-most Bay of Biscay was squally one day out of three, with lashings of early Summer rain. With iron water tanks or traditional casks full, and fresh from Lisbon's abundant washing facilities, there was little need to rig the canvas sluices to funnel rainwater into storage, or for the ships to sprout laundry, yet. When the weather did pipe up, it was necessary to take in the royals and t'gallants, gasket them and lower the yards, and reef the tops'ls, sometimes even taking a reef in the main course, but so far the winds did not rise to a full gale which would have demanded striking top-masts.

It was on one of those rainy, somewhat blustery mornings that Lewrie left the comfort, and dryness, of his great-cabins and went out to the quarter-deck, swathed in a tarred canvas knee-length coat and one of his oldest hats. He paused under the relative shelter of the poop deck overhang, readying himself for a long, slow soaking.

"Stayin' dry, Private Quiller?" he asked the Marine sentry who guarded his entry door, who had sprung to rigid attention.

"Ehm, aye, sir . . . mostly," the sentry replied, darting a half-glance in Lewrie's direction, and speaking from the corner of his mouth, sure that his officers, sergeants, or corporals would give him Hell if they caught him at it.

Lewrie stepped out round the Quartermasters manning the helm, took a peek into the compass binnacle to note the course steered, and put his hands in the small of his back to pace forward to the cross-deck hammock stanchions so he could look down into the ship's waist.

"Bowline on a bight," Midshipman Hillhouse was demanding of the youngest lads, Fywell, Chenery, and Holbrook below in the waist. "Pass-able . . . now, sheet bend, quick as you can. *Sheet* bend, not a marling-spike knot, *Mister* Chenery." Beyond them, several of the ship's boys were emulating the lessons with lengths of small-stuff instead of one-inch ma-nila. Hillhouse looked up for a moment with an exasperated expression to deplore his newest students.

Lewrie paced back to the helm, eyes aloft on the set of the sails, the com-missioning pendant, and the weather, blinking away the rain. He stopped short as he beheld the odd sight of his First Officer and Sailing Master, both hard-handed "tarpaulin men", sheltering like shopkeepers. Mr. Yel-land was standing half-in the open door to his starboard-side sea-cabin with a mug of something in his hand and looking out as if regretting a loss of trade on such a day. On the larboard side, Lt. Westcott stood in the open door to the chart room, idly puffing away on one of his *cigarros,* and *not* looking sheepish to do so.

"All's well, Mister Westcott?" Lewrie asked with a teasing brow up as he neared him.

"Simply fine, sir," Westcott said with a tap of fingers on the front of his hat. "Just pencilling in dead-reckoning of our postion . . . and considering fumigating the chart room," he added, wiggling his *cigarro*.

"Pests?" Lewrie asked. Every now and then, ships had to be scoured with vinegar then smoked with burning faggots of tobacco to rid them of accumulated stinks and insects.

"Mister Yelland, sir," Westcott said in a whisper with a grin on his phyz. "He spends so much time in here I can smell his aroma on the paper charts. How his sea cabin reeks can only be imagined," he said with a mock gagging. "I wish you could *order* him to bathe."

"It may be against his religion, or something," Lewrie had to tell him. "One when you're born, one when you're wed, and one just before they put you in the ground?"

With so many un-bathed men aboard, and their dirtied clothes, their wet wool, and the reeks rising from salt-meat casks on the orlop, ships couldn't *help* but stink.

"Pity, 'cause he's so very off-putting at meals in the wardroom," Westcott groused, blowing a large cloud of smoke back into the chart room. "But, at least all the flies and such gravitate to *his* end of the table."

Lewrie ducked out from under the overhang to look at the sky for a moment, then ducked back. "We'll not see the sun today, and we dasn't close the coast 'til we do, so . . . show me where we are, or where you think we are."

The rich and mellow aroma of Westcott's *cigarro* really did alleviate the nigh-foetid odour of the chart room as they bent over the slant-top desk to follow the hourly-taken marks of course and speed recorded by the chip-log.

"By this reckoning, I'd say we're fourty miles Nor'west of Santander," Westcott said, tapping the brass dividers at the last X along the pencilled track, "and making an average of five and a half to six knots. At this rate, assuming the winds stay steady, we can expect to be almost level with Bilbao round noon tomorrow. If the bloody skies clear and the sun comes out . . . ?" Westcott said with a huge iff-ish shrug.

"And if it don't, we'll *have* to alter course and close the coast," Lewrie said, "before we run aground somewhere North of Bayonne, in France."

"Maybe we'll find some trade there, for there's none out this far from the coast," Westcott said, tossing the dividers aside. "Is it true that we're only getting Head and Gun Money for our Spanish frigate?"

"'Fraid so," Lewrie admitted. "Droits of the Crown, mine arse."

"At least it's something in my bank account," Westcott sighed. "Something for my 'hope chest', hah hah?"

"But, Geoffrey . . . what is it you're hopin' *for*?" Lewrie asked.

"A month entire in London's most expensive brothel," Westcott sniggered.

"Then we'll just have to snatch more prizes from the French," Lewrie told him. "We're doin' main-well, so far, and if our army gets us Oporto, we can spend even more time at it, without havin' t'sail back to Lisbon."

"Pity, that," Westcott said. "I rather *like* Lisbon, and I've established good relations with a couple of willing young things . . . as I gather you have, as well?" he leered.

"Miss Covilhã has removed from Gibraltar, yes," was as far as Lewrie would confess. "Even making a living on the side, translatin' for Mountjoy and his lot."

"Ah, the things this war will make us do." Westcott laughed, stuck his *cigarro* in one corner of his mouth, left the chart room with one more "cleansing" puff, and stepped aside so Lewrie could precede him to the quarterdeck.

Whilst Lt. Westcott resumed his post as Officer of the Watch, Lewrie drifted over to the starboard side to speak with the Sailing Master and confer on the course and position.

"About right, sir," Yelland said, agreeing with Lt. Westcott's guesstimate. "What I'd give, though, for a clear Noon Sight of the sun."

"Is that . . . cider in your mug, sir?" Lewrie had to ask.

"Ginger beer, sir," Mr. Yelland was happy to announce. "Found a keg in a wine shop at Lisbon, and God only knows how *they* got it. Didn't know what to do with it, really, once the army marched off, and there weren't many with a taste for it left. Got it for a song, I did. Always was partial to ginger beer, And it goes well with a dollop of rum."

"Spanish bowline . . . go!" Midshipman Hillhouse cried to his students up forward in the waist.

"Meant to ask," Lewrie hesitantly enquired, "how has Hillhouse taken to his charge over the newer Mids?"

"Surprisingly well, sir," Yelland told him. "Not at first, oh no, but he's come round to being a hellish-good schoolmaster. I think it takes his mind off his failure at his last attempt at the examinations. Teaching others what he knows may have focussed his mind and loosened his tangled tongue, to boot. So, if he stands for the next exams, he just might pass this time."

"I'm delighted to hear it, Mister Yelland," Lewrie said with genuine feeling.

Lewrie left the Sailing Master to sip the last of his ginger beer and paced along the windward bulwarks of the quarterdeck, right up to the sail-tending gangways, and back, head down in thought most of the time, pausing at the end of each lap to peer aloft and out to sea, frowning.

The cats are away, the mice will play, he thought, fretting that the French were using his absence to their advantage, using this bout of foul weather as a mask to scuttle out to sea like so many roaches and land their mountains of supplies for their armies in Spain, this very minute.

"Damn the risk," he muttered at last. "Mister Westcott?" he bellowed.

"Aye, sir?" the First Officer replied near the helm.

"Two guns for a General Signal, and bend on a hoist," Lewrie ordered. "Alter Course Sou'Sou'east. We'll close the coast and see what we can see!"

"Very good, sir!" Westcott crisply snapped, as if a move toward action suited him right down to his toes.

CHAPTER TWENTY-NINE

*E*ven on their new point of sail, the squadron of three ships could only wallow along at about six knots, sure that sooner or later they would fetch sight of the Spanish coast, but unsure of exactly where that might be. The brig-sloop *Peregrine* led, at least three miles ahead of the *Undaunted* frigate, which preceded *Sapphire* by another three miles, all within decent signalling distance from each other, given the rain and heavy overcast which now and then swept between them in sheets.

No matter the incessant rain and damp, the crew lined up as the midday rum issue was piped at Seven Bells of the Forenoon Watch, as the gilt-trimmed red rum keg was brought on deck with music and drum.

A few minutes before Eight Bells, and the change of watch, Lewrie came back to the quarterdeck with his chronometer and sextant, in hopes that *something* could be determined of their position at Noon Sights, but, after the last double-chime of the ship's bell echoed away, everyone's boxed instruments had to be put away. The overcast was simply too thick to make out even a ghost of the sun. The watch changed, Lt. Elmes, the Third Officer, replacing Lt. Westcott.

"A word, if I could, sir?" Westcott asked as the officers and Mids departed the quarterdeck off-watch, or to take up their stations of the Day

Watch. "Won't take a minute. Changes in messes, changes in duties in the muster book?"

"And a warming cup o' my fine coffee, hey?" Lewrie japed.

"That would be welcome, too, sir," Westcott admitted.

"Aye, come aft with me," Lewrie bade, re-entering his great-cabins and stripping off his foul weather coat and hat for Pettus to deal with. They went to his desk in the day-cabin, where he fetched out his muster book, and they began to cross out and write in who was to be where in both larboard and starboard watches, and when the ship went to Quarters.

"These two ship's boys . . . powder monkeys so far . . . wish to serve on the forecastle six-pounders. Moss and Rorie," Westcott said. "They're getting too old to be rated as boys, and there's two younger lads, Bandy and Vannoy, who can replace them, when they're not servants. And, there's Posey, he's fifteen now, who's been going aloft and wishes to be a topman."

"Fine with me," Lewrie said as he made those corrections. "If we keep this up, though, we might have to entice some likely lads at Lisbon, whether they can speak English or not."

"Hmm, who did this?" Westcott asked as he twirled Lewrie's portrait round atop the desk, where it had been left.

"A good likeness, d'ye think?" Lewrie asked.

"Very good," Westcott, who was a dab-hand artist himself, said. "Rather . . . flattering, though. It makes you look at least five years younger."

"Don't remind me," Lewrie groaned.

"Odd for a portrait," Westcott said, picking it up to peer at. "Not straight-on, more like a side-view. You sat for it whilst you were up in London? Who's the artist?"

"Not a bit of it," Lewrie told him. "Midshipman Chenery's sister sent it me, and that after I collected him and coached down with him. She did it from memory, after a half-hour in their house, at best, and that in the wee hours before dawn, when most people can't keep *both* eyes open."

"Then it is quite remarkable," Westcott marvelled, setting it back on the desk. "A most talented young lady. Pretty, is she?"

"Oh, don't leer, Geoffrey," Lewrie chid him. "Pretty? Aye, I believe so, though not in the contemporary sense of a *great* beauty. Miss Chenery is . . . striking. Memorable. Pity she's a professional artist and portraitist . . . or wishes to be, to the utter horror of her father, I gather."

"Pity, indeed, sir, for she's talented enough, in spades. To draw you so accurately . . . if flatteringly," he japed back, "would do any artist great credit, in such a short time, from memory of a brief encounter. She could be an artist . . . if Society allowed."

"She wrote that she's been offered a chance to illustrate some children's book, and has a commission for a Bond Street merchant's portrait," Lewrie told him. "I saw some of her other work, and they were amusing, and *accurate* depictions. March Hares, hunting hounds, children flying a kite, and a portrait of her sister and her child that was so realistic I could've sworn they were right there, posin' behind a framed hole in the wall.

"She did tell me that she made almost an hundred pounds last year," Lewrie said. "So I suppose she already *is* a professional."

"Hmpf, well," Westcott commented, "one would suppose that if women wish to enter the world of men's affairs, they'd best restrict themselves to the arts. What they're taught on how to be well-bred . . . drawing, playing some musical instrument, perhaps even writing *novels*," he seemed to scoff his own expression, drawling "novels" out in scorn of the Gothic thrillers that most women seemed to read, and fluttered over.

"I promised you coffee," Lewrie said, all but slapping at his forehead. "How remiss of me. Pettus, coffee for both me and Mister Westcott."

"Yes, sir," Pettus replied, going to the sideboard in the dining coach, but everyone froze in place when the Marine sentry yelled to announce Midshipman Kibworth.

"Signal from *Undaunted*, sir," Kibworth blurted out as soon as he was in the cabins, "*Peregrine* is showing Enemy in Sight!"

"Keys to the arms chests, Mister Westcott," Lewrie said as he hastily unlocked his desk and handed over those keys. "My brace of Mantons and my hanger, Pettus, then see the lanthorns and candles are snuffed, then get you and the beasts below."

He snatched his own foul weather coat from the overhead beam peg, clapped on his wet hat, and dashed to the quarterdeck, followed by a cheering Jessop on his way to his station at Quarters on one of the starboard carronades.

"Where away, Mister Elmes?" Lewrie asked.

"Ehm, no idea, yet, sir," the Third Officer confessed. "Just the first signal to go on. We can just barely make out *Peregrine* from the deck, out beyond *Undaunted*, and she . . ."

"New hoist, sir!" Midshipman Carey reported from the poop deck above them. "From *Undaunted*, her number . . . Enemy . . . *Convoy*, Course East, Many Sail."

That meant that the frigate's lookouts could also see what the brig-sloop had first reported, out there in the gloom and swirling banks of rain, not merely repeating *Peregrine*'s signals.

"Due East, is it?" Elmes pondered, with one eye pressed hard to his telescope's ocular to see for himself. "Empties, most-like, sailing in ballast back to France."

"Do you imagine the French would waste escorts on a convoy of empty ships?" Westcott scoffed.

"They would, if they wish t'keep enough bottoms for further voyages," Lewrie said as Pettus came from the cabins with his sword and pistols and helped him strap everything in place. Chalky was in his wicker cage, ready to be transported to the safety of the orlop, and making his annoyance at being rained on very loud. "Off ye go, my lad," he bade Pettus, sure that *Sapphire*'s crew would take the sight of his steward, the Captain's cat, and the ship's dog making their way below as a sign of action to come, and quite possibly, new prizes and more profits.

"Deck, there!" the mainmast lookout bawled. "*Peregrine* makes Numeral Ten . . . Sail! Ten Sail in th' offin'!"

"Oh, please let us scoop them *all* up!" Lt. Westcott cheered, rubbing his hands most greedily. "I could use the money!"

"Gentlemen, Beat to Quarters, and take your proper stations," Lewrie ordered. Leaving the quarterdeck to Westcott, he went up to the poop deck for a better view. His first eager scan of the horizon showed him only *Peregrine* and *Undaunted*, with curtains of rain beyond. Disappointed, he lowered his glass and looked forward to watch as his ship prepared for action. Marines making their way to the sail-tending gangways, and up the ratlines to the fighting tops with their muskets and swivels. Weather deck, forecastle, and carronade gun crews casting off lashings of their guns, plucking tompions from the muzzles, and fetching up loading scoops, rammers, sponges, and crow-levers to load and aim their pieces. Mast captains and topmen scurrying aloft to rig chain slings on the yards to prevent their being shot away and crashing down to cause damage, and injuries. Slowly, the din and the rush died away as the ship settled down, with everyone at their duty stations, and all preparations for battle were completed.

"The ship is at Quarters, sir," Westcott shouted up to him.

"Very well, Mister Westcott, stand by," Lewrie replied, lifting his telescope for another try.

There was no point in searching for the Spanish coast, not in such weather, even if they were in their usual ten or twelve miles offshore.

Twenty or better's more like it, Lewrie thought; *Even after a few hours on Sou'Sou'east at around six knots. Yes, I can see 'em! Sort of.*

There was one there, two there, then there weren't, but a moment later, he could make out at least five or six. He felt like he was trying to count fireflies. He was sure that he saw brig-rigged ships, and one or two that might be three-masted.

"Make up a hoist!" Lewrie called aft to the signals Midshipman by the flag lockers, turning his head just long enough to see that it was Mr. Harvey. "Pursue the Enemy More Closely, first, along with Make Sail, Mister Harvey."

"Aye, sir . . . Pursue More Closely, and Make Sail!" the gangly Midshipman echoed.

"Sic 'em!" Lewrie muttered to himself.

"What's taking him so long?" Capt. Chalmers fretted as he looked aft to the Commodore's flagship, then ahead at the enemy ships. "Surely, he can see them by now!"

"No idea, sir," *Undaunted*'s First Officer answered, shrugging.

"Don't tell me the 'Ram-Cat's' gone all house tabby on us, hey?" Chalmers scoffed, taking no notice of Midshipman Lewrie's return to the quarterdeck. "Thought he was full of *dash*!"

"Signal from the flag, sir!" Hugh Lewrie took delight in pointing out as a stream of colourful bunting broke open on *Sapphire*'s signal halliards. "It is . . . Pursue the Enemy More Closely, and . . . Make Sail."

"About time," Chalmers grumbled. "Crack on sail, sir, and let's go hunting!"

"Even if we enrich the Commodore, sir?" his First Officer said with a soft chuckle. "*Sapphire* will be 'In Sight' of all our captures, and due a share for that."

"Then we'd best take them all, sir!" Chalmers shot back, none too pleased by that prospect.

"They'll run right over the horizon before we get engaged," Lt. Westcott grumbled as he watched *Peregrine* and *Undaunted* surging ahead of them, mustachios churning under their bows, the sea creaming down their sides, and spreading wide bridal trains in their wakes. He and Lewrie looked up as one to see *Sapphire*'s courses and top'ls wind-full, reefs shaken out, and the t'gallants had been hoisted back in place. Yet their two-decker was *so* slow to accelerate, then only plodded, no matter what they could do to spur her progress.

"At least she's slow but sure," Lewrie hopefully said.

"Sure, aye," Westcott snorted. "Sure to be last to the party. God, do I miss our days in frigates!"

"Amen," Lewrie heartily agreed, lifting his telescope again. "Chalmers and Blamey work well together. You note how Blamey's goin' more shoreward to cut off the convoy's escape, whilst Chalmers is hot on the head of their left-hand column?"

"Hmm, looks like a gaggle to me, sir," Westcott said, "more of a batch of colliers trying to land their coal first at Wapping Docks."

"No National Ship in sight," Lewrie pointed out. "None of the three-masters look to be warships, so . . . damn my eyes, what *are* the French thinkin'? If they're in-ballast, we wouldn't touch 'em? That we'd let 'em pass 'til they head West with full cargoes?"

"Empty and less valuable they may be, sir, but they'll still fetch something at the Prize-Courts," Westcott shrugged off.

"Pass the word," Lewrie said. "If we do manage to get close enough to some of them, there's free tobacco to the most accurate gun crews."

Getting to grips with one of the fleeing merchant ships began to look even more improbable as the day wore on, and Lewrie felt his jaws tighten, ready to grind his teeth in envy, as first *Peregrine* then *Undaunted* overhauled the slowest, lagging ships, fired warning shots, and sent boats filled with armed boarding parties to take them as prizes, whilst *Sapphire* flogged away, falling even further and further astern, no matter how much sail was flown. As the faint sounds of warning gunfire grew even fainter, their long stern-chase went so boresome that Pettus and Bisquit, along with the Ship's Cook, Tanner, came up from their shelter below on the orlop for some fresh air. The Cook's presence out of his hidey-hole was a sure sign to all hands that there was nothing dangerous to be feared; Tanner was a perfect poltroon when it came to battle, or loud noises. He'd *had* his fights, had lost half a leg, thank you very much, and wasn't required to be a sturdy Heart of Oak any longer.

"Oh, 'give me a fast ship, for I intend to go in harm's way'," Lt. Westcott quoted with a roll of his eyes. "They keep this up, and they'll all be hull-down to us in an hour."

"At least we aren't *in* the fast ships' way," Lewrie quipped, though his heart wasn't in it. "Cast of the log, there!" he turned to shout aft, hoping for the best results.

"Eight and one-half knots, sir! Eight and one-half!" one of the Afterguard shouted back after a long moment.

At least the dismal rains had blown on by, rolling shoreward, and the skies were clearing; all could *clearly* see what they were missing out on.

Lewrie went up to the poop deck for a better view with his telescope. *Sapphire* was nearing the first two prizes left behind to sort themselves out, and would soon pass them. Beyond, the fleeing French merchantmen now stood out clearly, scattered cross half the horizon, with *Peregrine* and *Undaunted* coursing at their heels like a pair of wolves, their large Union Jacks and commissioning pendants colourfully streaming in the glimmers of afternoon sun that shafted through the breaking cloud layers.

If it wasn't such a grand sight, it'd be depressin', Lewrie glumly thought, ruing, and not for the first time, how he had been so eager for a fresh active commission that he'd leapt at *Sapphire*, fully expecting yet another fast frigate to command. *A pig in a poke, indeed, dammit!* he groused, wondering if Mr. Pole, the First Secretary of the Admiralty, was *still* laughing *years* after gulling him into taking the two-decker's command.

"Deck, there!" the mainmast lookout shouted down. "The coast is in sight, one point off the starboard bows!"

Lewrie lifted his glass to peer forward, and sure enough, he could make out a strip of grey and green, now that the weather had cleared. Not the coast itself, but the steep mountains behind the coast, all forbidding rock and forests.

He felt *Sapphire* lurch under his feet, a crippled hitch in her steady, metronomic hobby-horsing and rolling. Lewrie looked down to the quarterdeck to share a worried glance with Lt. Westcott. He then turned to look aft, as if searching for some un-charted shoal or rock ledge over which they had sailed, and touched bottom for a second.

No, it was the sea. Following the passing of the rains, the seas were working up under the press of a rising, clear-weather gale. Far out to sea, at the edge of the horizon, the waters were wrinkling and chopping, folding and spuming blown foam in a confusing welter of white-caps and white-horses. The infamous *Costa de Morte*, the Coast of Death, was awakening.

"Cast of the log!" Lewrie demanded, again, then peered upward to the masts and sails, wondering how long he dared wait before striking top-masts and reefing tops'ls and courses. Already, long before the full force of the winds could reach his ship, the commissioning pendant was veering more directly towards the bows. Soon, instead of sailing with the winds large on the quarter, they'd be "Both Sheets Aft", with the wind right up the stern.

So much for prizes, this day, he thought with a groan.

"Mister Westcott!" he called down to the quarterdeck. "Haul up abeam the winds, hands to the sheets and braces! Topmen aloft to brail up the t'gallants and royals, smartly now! We've a blow coming!"

"Aye aye, sir!" Westcott replied, going to the compass binnacle cabinet for a brass speaking trumpet so his orders could be made out all the way to the forecastle.

"Mister Griffin," Lewrie bade the Midshipman in charge of the signals by the taffrail flag lockers, "bend on a hoist to *Peregrine* and *Undaunted* . . . their numbers, Beware, Gale, and Reduce Sail!"

They won't love me for that, Lewrie told himself, looking ahead with his glass, again. The brig-sloop and the frigate were already level with two fresh prizes, with soundless gusts of powder smoke as warning shots were fired, and boat crews and boarding parties looked to be ready to be despatched.

Would Blamey and Chalmers heed his warning? Were they too intent on prize-money to pay attention to his signals? He looked up as the hoist soared up the halliards to break open; the flags were flying directly downwind, their flies pointing right at the other ships and only to be guessed at. And, at *Sapphire*'s distance from them, even a two-gun General Signal might go un-heard and un-seen!

HMS *Sapphire* slowly wheeled to larboard as the first moans and keens of the rising winds arose in the rigging, alerting even the newest lubbers to the urgency, but she was coming about, slowing and taking those winds more abeam. Her t'gallants and royals were brailed up, and those yards were being lowered to their rests lower down the masts.

"Steady on East by South, for now, sir," Lt. Westcott reported, halfway up the larboard poop deck ladderway. "Damn my eyes if the wind hasn't veered into the Nor'west quicker than you can say 'knife'!"

"Those greedy bastards yonder don't seem to see our signals," Lewrie griped, eye glued to his ocular. "Fire off two of the starboard six-pounders t'get their attention. Else, they'll think that we gave the game up for no good reason."

"Aye, sir!"

Lewrie looked for the first two prizes taken, and found that the British crews aboard them, thin as they were, had reduced sail to cope with the blow, pitching and rolling as the rising seas reached them, but they were coping, so far.

"Come on, come on, come on!" Lewrie muttered under his breath, "look aft, damn yer eyes."

At least six miles separated *Sapphire* from her consorts, and they still seemed more intent on their captures than upon the rising weather. There! At last, *Peregrine* and *Undaunted* were coming about, presenting their larboard sides, and reducing sail, as were the two ships they had just taken. Lewrie let out a tentative sigh of great relief. The Spanish shore was in sight from the poop deck, by now, not just the mountains, but the lower coastal plains, towns, and rocks, and the other fleeing French ships. . . . ! They were still thrashing off the winds to run into the dubious shelter of the coastal shallows, on a slant to try and reach Santander, perhaps Bilbao farther East.

"Cuttin' it *damned* fine, if ye are," Lewrie grumbled, wondering if the French masters had even noticed that the pursuing warships had broken off the chase, or had given a thought to the sudden change in the weather. Without hot pursuit, they *should* be bearing up into the winds, to keep a wary distance from the dangers of that shore.

Even as he peered hard at the French merchantmen, Lewrie felt *Sapphire* heeling to starboard a few more degrees, re-setting her shoulder to the wind and sea, pressed over.

"Alter course, Mister Westcott," Lewrie ordered. "Harden up to Nor'east. We may have to *claw* our way seaward! And I'll have one reef in the main course! Pipe Secure from Quarters, as well!"

"Begging your pardon, sir," the Sailing Master said, coming up the starboard ladderway to the poop deck, "but we may end up going 'full and by', and I'd suggest taking one reef in the tops'ls, too, and break out the middle and main top-mast stays'ls for more drive to windward, and steady her. Never *saw* the like, the weather on this bloody coast!"

"Very well, Mister Yelland, let's do so," Lewrie agreed, and went down to the quarterdeck to speak with Westcott, with one hand on his head to save his oldest cocked hat from sailing off alee.

With the guns' tompions re-inserted and the carriages bowsed and lashed to the port sills, more hands were available to go aloft and take in those reefs, their clothing fluttering in the breeze, skittering out along the yards with their feet on the swaying foot-ropes and their arms locked over the yardarms. The courses and the tops'ls were heavy in their own right, made even heavier by the winds pressing against them, and it was slow, hard labour to haul them up and gather them in, foot at a time 'til the first reef lines were in hand. *Sapphire* by then was close-reaching off the coast, easing her angle of heel only a fraction, but widening the distance from the rocks and shoals. As the excess topmen descended the ratlines, Lewrie could spare some attention to what was transpiring with his other ships, their prizes, and the fleeing French.

"What the bloody Hell are they playin' at?" Lewrie yelled in astonishment. "Harden up, you idiots!"

Two more captured prizes were rising and plunging, their sails shivering wind-full . . . wind-full and more, dipping their bows deep in showers of spray, their jib booms almost level with the sea, then rising so high above the water that the merchantmen looked as if they would launch themselves free of the ocean and soar off like rising terns as they fought their way up to windward, and away from that deadly shore, foot by agonising foot.

They weren't of much concern to Lewrie; it was what his other warships were doing. Instead of hardening up to the rising gales to claw their own way to safety, both *Peregrine* and *Undaunted* had only altered course enough to sail parallel to the coast, taking the winds abeam, and reducing sail, as if they would not give up the pursuit of the remaining four French supply ships!

Damn you, Chalmers, Lewrie furiously thought; *you can't be that greedy! Gone to his head, it has . . . a squadron of his own, too long sailin' independent, with Blamey t'boss about. Is he waitin' for the gale t'blow itself out, so he can still fall down on the French and take 'em?*

If he hoisted Discontinue the Action, he doubted if Chalmers, or Blamey, would obey him, so intent they seemed to be on their prey! They were acting like Nelson at Copenhagen, ignoring Hyde Parker's signal to quit.

"Sir! Captain, sir!" the Sailing Master shouted from the foot of the poop deck ladderway, "Another reef's needed in the courses!"

"Hands aloft, then," Lewrie agreed.

"What, sir?" Yelland cried, a hand to one ear.

"I said . . ." Lewrie began, suddenly noticing how loud the wind had gotten, how his 1,100-ton ship was pressed over about twenty degrees from upright, and how hard it was to stand upright with his own clothing turning into madly fluttering sails, forcing him to stumble forward to the edge of the poop. "I said hands aloft to take in one more reef line!" he all but screamed in Yelland's face.

"Aye aye, sir! Topmen! Trice up, lay out, to *reef*!" Yelland howled forward, and he and Lt. Westcott waved both arms in lifting gestures to urge the Bosun and his Mate to get the men aloft.

Where in Hell did such a gale come from? Lewrie wondered to himself, in awe, and a bit of fear, for he had never experienced the like in nigh thirty years at sea. Bracing himself against the iron hammock-filled stanchions at the fore end of the poop, he struggled to hold his telescope steady to see what was happening inshore.

It could have been his own dreadful imagination, but the Spanish coast suddenly looked a lot closer than it had before, with even the smaller details standing out more starkly, even though *Sapphire* was slowly clearing the coast, or seemed to be. Lewrie had to scoff at the notion that *any* ship her size could make that much leeway so quickly. But, there were the rocky beaches and headlands with wind-driven waves beginning to break in great, crashing explosions of foam and spray. There were the great rollers, ranks of them, crested with white spume, marching ashore in steeper and steeper waves, and 'twixt his ships and the shore, the seas were clashing in grand, mounting confusion.

Undaunted and *Peregrine* had reduced sail even more, but were still not coming about to point their bows seaward, still sailing on the same heading . . . no; Lewrie thought they appeared to be slowly edging *shoreward*. *What the Devil?* he thought, again: *Oh!*

Beyond them, even closer to that maelstrom shore, the French supply ships were struggling, heeling far over and baring their verdigried copper bottoms as their sailors tried to reduce sail, having a hard time of it. British transports and supply ships hired on by the Transport Board were very thinly manned, to save money on wages, and it appeared that whatever agency of the French Ministry of Marine arranged these convoys were just as parsimonious. Add to the fact that Napoleon Bonaparte's ever-expanding armies conscripted sailors from their own Navy and merchant marine, and it was no wonder that those French merchantmen were struggling, with too few experienced hands aboard, and too few crew overall.

"He's *herding* them!" Lewrie howled down to the quarterdeck, grinning fit to bust. "They're 'twixt the Devil and the Deep Blue Sea! Strike or die! Chalmers, you knacky bastard!"

One of the trailing vessels, within a few miles of the coast, but astern of *Undaunted*, made a move to escape. Her helm was put down and her bows swung up into that gale of wind, jibs flogging madly, and her squares'ls swinging as her crew hauled on the braces to bring them round. Her bows met an oncoming wave that struck her so hard that Lewrie imagined that he could hear the wet, booming impact, and the three-master was staggered in spray as high as her tops.

"She's 'in-irons'!" Lt. Westcott hooted, "She's missed stays!"

"Goner . . . whoo!" Mr. Yelland crowed.

The ship's fore course and fore tops'l were flat aback, with her bows dead-on into the gale, slammed to a stop and quickly gaining sternway, before falling off the wind and rolling heavily onto her starboard side. Then, as the French ship rolled back upright for a moment, her foremast parted, taking the tops'l and its yard down in ruin, and her upper masts bent over to hang loose. She *was* a goner, and there was nothing her crew could do to save her from being driven ashore to be smashed to kindling.

Lewrie went down to the quarterdeck for a moment to confer with the Sailing Master, and to get out of that cheek-fluttering wind.

"The coast, Mister Yelland," he yelled almost in the man's ear, "it shoulders out Nor'east, from Santillana del Mar to the peninsula and the headland where Santander sits, am I right?"

"As I readily recall, sir," Mr. Yelland assured him.

"If they can't claw off, with our ships pressin' 'em closer to shore, they may *all* take the ground," Lewrie said, looking wolfish.

"Aye, they may very well all be wrecked, sir," Yelland said back, "but Chalmers and Blamey'd best be looking to their own safety, and that damned soon. You will recall them, sir?"

Lewrie gave that a long thought, then shook his head.

"I think not, Mister Yelland," he said, instead. "Chalmers is clever enough t'weigh his moment, and I will trust his judgement. In any case, it's a very economical way to destroy enemy shipping, with nought expended in shot and powder. That'll please the Admiralty!"

"Kinder, though, sir," the Sailing Master objected, "for them to strike and live as prisoners. It cuts rough to watch sailors of any nation drive ashore and drown, poor Devils."

"If they won't, they won't," Lewrie said with a shrug, then returned to the poop deck with his telescope. With *Sapphire* sailing away from the coast, his best vantage point was the larboard corner of the poop deck, by the taffrail lanthorn.

He looked for the crippled three-master; she was drifting onto the shore, not a mile off the rocks by then, and doomed. Far out in the lead, beyond *Peregrine*, two of the leading French brigs looked as if they had managed to come up onto the winds high enough to gain sea-room to avoid the coast as it shouldered out to the Nor'east, beyond any British ship's gun range. The others . . . a three-masted ship was trying to come up into the wind far enough to emulate the leaders, but she *was* in *Undaunted*'s extreme gun range, and was being fired upon.

Oh, you ruthless *bastard!* Lewrie thought.

Chalmers must have drawn his roundshot from his guns, and was firing high with star-shot and bar-shot to rip through her sails and yards, to part running rigging and cripple her. It was not just the gale that made that ship's sails pucker and quiver, or for her main tops'l to suddenly split right down the middle, then fly free of all control, wrapping itself round the mast.

She did not strike her colours, though. Almost meekly, she fell off the wind to her original course, with men aloft frantically clearing away the damage and hoping for the best when she got past Santillana so she could skirt the edges of the shoals and survive to enter harbour.

Inshore of her, and with her master despairing that she had been so quick in the lead to run alee before the winds had risen, one of the French brigs suddenly lurched, her bows shooting skyward for a moment as she ploughed onto an out-stretching rocky shoal. Both of her masts came crashing down forward in a twinkling. With *Sapphire* secured from Quarters, many of her crew not strictly on-watch or tending to the sails, lined the rails and gangways, roaring out great, mocking cheers to see her wreck, and lay wagers on which one would be next.

"Merciful God, is there nought we can do to save those poor men?" Midshipman Chenery wailed.

"Not without wrecking ourselves, Mister Chenery," Liam Desmond told him, putting a steadying arm round his shoulders for a moment. "Aye, 'tis a great pity, lad," Desmond went on, looking the lad in the eyes, "Frenchmen they may be, our greatest enemies, but sailors like us, for all that. All we can do is have a prayer for 'em."

The jeers and whoops of glee became more muted when yet another French ship ran aground only two or three hundred yards shy of a sandy beach. If she had made it onto the sands, her crew might have been able to scramble out her jib-boom and bowsprit, then jump down to solid ground. But, between the ship and the beach there was a churning, roaring, smashing maelstrom through which no hatch grating, keg, or jury-rigged flotation device could pass safely. Great, towering waves smashed into that unfortunate ship, lifting her stern, driving her further onto the rocks or shoals, and heeling her far over to one side.

And when a third ship, this one a full-rigged three-master, slewed to a sudden stop with her masts toppling in a flash, there were only mutters and groans from *Sapphire*'s crew, and some tears brushed aside with horny, calloused hands here and there. It could have been them yonder, praying to be saved yet knowing how impossible survival would be.

In the end, only two of the ten French ships managed to get round Santander's headland, covered at last by cannon fire from the old Spanish forts, now manned and occupied by French artillerists. Their shot came nowhere close to *Peregrine* or *Undaunted*, who stood on for a bit before altering course seaward, at long last, showing the enemy their sterns, with two miles to spare.

As they came off the coast, *Undaunted* broke out a signal hoist, a long one spelled out letter for letter, for the Popham Code didn't cover impromptu messages outside the scope of duty.

Clean Sweep, Lewrie slowly read with his telescope.

To make his point even further, Capt. Chalmers had a broom hung from the ear-ring at the larboard tip of *Undaunted*'s main course yardarm.

Who knew that Chalmers had a sense of humour? Lewrie mused to himself: *I thought he was too high-minded for it. And for a prude, he's a* blood-thirsty *sort o' prude!*

He grimaced as he contemplated whether he would have to sport Chalmers and Blamey to a celebratory supper!

CHAPTER THIRTY

It was two more days before the fierce clear-air gales ebbed, forcing the squadron to stand well out to sea, rolling and pitching under storm try-sails for their own preservation, with their four prizes wallowing in their wakes, and it was a constant dread of what might go wrong aboard any one of them when so thinly-manned by their overworked, sleepless prize crews. Unladen vessels would make leeway like toy boats made of paper, would roll from beam to beam furiously, threatening to dis-mast themselves. If anything disastrous happened aboard one of them, there would be little the ships of the squadron could do to aid them, or even manage a successful rescue if one of them foundered. All that *Sapphire*, *Undaunted*, and *Peregrine* might do was keep an eye on them, hope for the best, and pray that their fellow sailors and Marines would live long enough for the winds to die, and the uncertain life of sailors might return to normal.

Lewrie spent a lot of time on deck, without sleep, and like his crew, going without hot meals with the galley fires cold, concerned for the safety of his own ship, first and foremost, but with a fear that his son, Hugh, might have been sent aboard one of the prizes that *Undaunted* had taken, and was now "on his own bottom", responsible for his own life or death. Capt. Chalmers *seemed* to favour the lad for such tasks, and Lewrie hoped that Hugh would prove up to the task, but he still fretted, continuously eyeing the prizes in the moments that he could spare, for any sign of pending disaster.

Would one of the captured French crews scheme to rise up and re-take their ship, murder their captors, or heave them over the side then dash back towards the coast? Was Hugh keeping a chary eye on his prisoners? Had he taken enough Marines to guard against that, or was it necessary to put the "lobsterbacks" to pulley-hauley to save their ship, leaving the French un-watched belowdecks?

"Sir? Captain, sir?" someone was saying.

Lewrie roused from a bleary cat-nap, sprawled in his collapsible wood-and-canvas deck chair, swaddled in his foul weather gear and his boat cloak. For a moment he had trouble recalling how he had gotten to the shelter of the poop deck overhang, or how long ago it had been since he had closed his eyes.

"Aye," he grumbled, swabbing his stubbled face and gritty eyes with his hands. "Mister Harcourt?"

"Permission to make sail, sir?" the Second Officer asked. "The winds have greatly moderated."

"Uhm . . . aye, do so, Mister Harcourt," Lewrie allowed, rising and stretching, stifling audible groans as his body protested. "How long have I been asleep?"

"Perhaps half an hour at best, sir," Lt. Harcourt told him just before turning forward to bawl orders to send topmen and sail-tenders aloft. The door to Mr. Yelland's sea cabin opened and the Sailing Master stepped out, looking mussed and untidy.

"Ah, you're awake, sir," Yelland commented. "Not much of a nap. Just long enough for me to change shirts and have a nip of my ginger beer."

The mention of that beverage made Lewrie aware of the dryness of his own mouth, and the musty taste of long sleeplessness.

"Care for a bit, sir?" Mr. Yelland offered, and Lewrie was quick to take him up on it, swizzling his first deep sip round to cleanse his mouth, then drinking the rest of the tangy mug right down.

"Ah, that's better, thankee, Mister Yelland," Lewrie said as he went up to the poop deck for a long look about. Bisquit, the ship's dog, emerged from his shelter under the starboard ladderway, sniffed at the odiferous Sailing Master, then trotted up to join Lewrie.

Lewrie heaved a sigh of relief; all four prizes were still with them, just beginning to make more sail, no longer heaving and rolling about like flotsam. *Peregrine* and *Undaunted* were within a mile of his two-decker, too, in-line-ahead off *Sapphire*'s larboard side, and with hands aloft in the rigging, re-roving strained lines and manning their yards to free brailed-up canvas.

"Oh, how heavenly!" Lewrie said, looking down at the dog. "Do ya smell that, boy? Know what that smoke means? The galley fires're lit, and there'll be a hot breakfast, at last."

Bisquit whined and licked his chops, as if he understood, shuffling his front paws in eager anticipation.

Or, is it supper? Lewrie asked himself, pulling out his pocket watch to find the time, discombobulated by his too-brief nap, and his mind-numbing lack of sleep. To his delight, he discovered that it was nearly six in the morning, and it *would* be breakfast. Upon that discovery, his innards growled so loud that Bisquit jerked his head up.

"Mister Spears," Lewrie called aft to the Midshipmen by the taffrail lockers. "Make up a signal to all ships . . . Make All Plain Sail."

"Aye aye, sir," Spears replied.

And after breakfast, Lewrie thought, *I'll send two more. One to alter course right back to the coast, and the second for a Make and Mend Day.* And, if the weather stayed clear and calm, he'd have his deck chair shifted back to the poop deck, too.

As ravenous as he felt, he could not take the time to delve into his personal stores for a wee sausage or two. There was still too much to be seen to; the charts for a guess at their position by Dead Reckoning, overseeing the hands making sail to his satisfaction, *then* a welcome quart of hot water for a sponge-off and a shave, *then* a hot and hearty breakfast, before retiring to his bed-cot for a long, long sleep. He felt his head drooping and his eyes glazing over, and shook himself all over. He had to do *something* productive.

"Hoy, Bisquit, want to play?" he offered. One of the dog's toys lay abandoned nearby and he picked it up and waved it back and forth. Yes, Bisquit was up for fetching!

Yelland'll tell me where he thinks we are, Lewrie thought.

With no one important to worry about, Lewrie allowed himself a loud belch after his last bite of breakfast, as he dabbed his lips and contemplated another cup of coffee. His cook, Yeovill, had done him proud, producing a cheesy three-egg omelet riddled with onion and sliced mushrooms, with hashed potatoes and fried sausages taken from his stash of finger-sized

links usually reserved for Chalky and the dog, and with the last of the stale
shore bread slices dipped in egg batter and drizzled with treacle.

"Another cup, sir?" Pettus offered, nodding towards the saidboard.

Lewrie felt his eyes getting heavier, and his head nodding.

"I think not, Pettus," he told him. "Unless something comes up, I intend t'try and catch up on my sleep. You and Jessop try to putter quietly
once I turn in."

One last chore, he told himself, getting to his feet and going out to the
quarterdeck. The watch had changed just minutes before, so Lt. Westcott
had the deck.

"Good morning, sir," Westcott said, tapping the brim of his hat in a
casual salute.

"Good morning, Mister Westcott," Lewrie replied, "and it is a good'un,
ain't it. Course and speed, and Mister Yelland's best guess?"

"We are on Nor'east by North, with the winds out of the West,
Nor'west, and the last cast of the log showed seven and a quarter knots. Mister Yelland reckons that we're about seventy miles Nor'east of Santander, or
thereabouts."

"Hmm, at that rate it'll take at least ten hours or more to fetch the coast,
again," Lewrie surmised. "I'd admire did you hoist a signal to all ships to
put about to the Sou'east and maintain all plain sail. No tearin' rush," he
added with a shrug. "After we've all come about, show them Make And
Mend. If our ship's anything to go by, I'm sure most of our sailors'll go
for a long caulk. Laundry and hobbies, bedamned."

"Aye, sir," Lt. Westcott said, agreeing. "Once my watch is up, I'd be
glad to do the same."

"Carry on, then prepare to put the ship about," Lewrie bade, going up
to the poop deck for one last look about before he could retire to his bed-
space.

It's almost too *nice a day t'sleep through it,* he thought.

The rains along the Spanish coast they'd encountered before discovering the French convoy could almost be fancied to be a good, hard
washing, and the fierce clear-air gales could also be deemed a final
cleansing. This morning, the skies were a lovely azure, only broken by
a few fleecy clouds, and the sea glittered as it heaved in peaceable slum-
ber, with the waves no more than three or four feet high, and long set
between. It was the sort of morning that he would normally take his
ease in his deck chair here on the poop deck, with a book to read, and
the dog to pet, now and again.

"The signal is acknowledged, sir!" Midshipman Ward reported to the First Officer.

"Very well, Mister Ward," Westcott shouted aft. "Bosun, pipe hands to stations to come about. Ready about? Strike the signal, Mister Ward. Helm up, wear away!"

Hauling down the signal was the Execute, and Lewrie took idle pleasure in watching how efficiently the other warships came about, then how his own ship fell off the wind, the yards wheeling round to keep way on as she took the wind more and more on her quarters, then across the wind to starboard tack. The spanker whooshed from one beam to the other over his head, and he paced to the forward edge of the poop deck to be out of the way of the Afterguard's work.

"Steady on Sou'east, sir," Westcott reported from the quarterdeck.

"Very well, Mister Westcott, you have the deck," Lewrie said, fetching up another tasty belch, then allowing himself a wide yawn. "I'll be aft. Send for me just before the change of watch."

He entered his great-cabins, stripping off his coat and his waistcoat, undoing his neck stock, and sat on a chest to tug off his boots. It would be a warm day, but for now the breeze through the transom sash windows was pleasantly cool. He rolled into his bed-cot, plumped up his pillows, and let out a grateful sigh. Chalky hopped up to join him, sat down near his pillows, and gently pawed for some attention. All Lewrie could spare before swooning was some stroking down the cat's back, some cheek rubs, and his hand dropped away as he fell into a deep sleep. Chalky pawed a time or two more, leaned in to touch noses, and uttered a few wee *meeps*, then realised there was nothing for it. He turned away, padded down to Lewrie's thigh, and stretched himself out against him for a nap of his own.

A little more than three hours' sleep before Noon Sights, and another three hour nap after gunnery drill and cutlass drill, exercises of a loud nature, and Lewrie felt restored enough to welcome his supper guests aboard. Captain Chalmers and Commander Blamey were in good spirits, despite their own lack of sleep during the days of gale winds, though Lewrie noticed that Blamey was a bit more subdued than Chalmers, who was still clapping his hands and crowing over his destruction of the bulk of the convoy.

"A toast with you, sirs," Lewrie posed once all had been handed glasses of *espumante*, "To our gale of wind . . . may we never see its like again."

"Amen to that, sir," Blamey quickly agreed after draining his glass.

"Oh, I don't know," Chalmers countered, looking puck-ish and amused, "it *was* God-sent, and saved me a deal of shot and powder! Death to the French, I say . . . however it is achieved."

"Pity, though," Blamey opined, studying his empty glass. "Now, were they French warships driven ashore, I'd dance you all a little jig. They signed aboard on their own and knew the risks, didn't they? Merchant sailors, though. Probably paid as little as our civilian mariners, or less, well. I doubt they got a bonus for hazard pay. I feel no joy in drowning the poor beggars."

"Perhaps when word reaches their brother *matelots,* the others will think twice before risking a voyage along this coast," Chalmers said with a whimsical shrug, "or, strike for better wages? That might be a thing to see . . . Bonaparte's police and soldiers would *have* to read them the Riot Act, then gun them down if they still refused. And that would put the lie to all that Froggish bumf about Liberty, Equality, and Fraternity, haw! No more rights than an Ottoman Turk!"

"After supper, Blamey," Lewrie said, "I've a penny whistle. I'd admire to see your dancing skills."

"You liquour me well enough, Captain Lewrie, and I just might, at that!" Blamey brightened up. "Ah, more *espumante,* please do."

"Ahem, sirs," Yeovill said from the door to the dining coach, "your supper is ready to be served."

That'd be a sight, Lewrie thought as they went to their places at the table; *almost as entertainin' as a dancin' bear.*

Chalmers and Blamey had not been frequent supper guests aboard *Sapphire,* so the chicken broth soup with shredded quail, heavily laced with tarragon, was a surprise to them. So too was the roast rabbit *ragout* drizzled with a mustard sauce sweetened with honey, potato halves laden with cheese, bacon, and green onion shoots, with boiled carrots on the side. Even the beef course, come straight from one of the salt-meat casks that afternoon, had been turned into a thin-cut delight served over a seasoned rice pilaf, with boiled green peas and green beans, and with a gravy made with flour, drippings, and beer to aerate it, one of Yeovill's trade secrets.

After an orange marmalade dowdy laced with crushed walnuts, it was time for cheese, sweet bisquit, the port bottle, and conversation more specific to their cruise than before. Oh, Chalmers was "cherry-merry", and a grand conversationalist, with a wealth of information gleaned from the latest London papers; dramas, music, doings of the royal family, and a novel or two.

In point of fact, it might as well have been Chalmers's table for most of the supper, with Blamey contributing little, and Lewrie mostly asking questions to steer things along, eliciting Chalmers's opinions . . . which he had by the dozens, and all of them firm.

"Right after we anchored at Lisbon, Captain Chalmers came to speak with me, Commander Blamey," Lewrie casually mentioned. "Has he spoken to you of his concerns about how short a time we seem to have on station?"

"A bit, sir, aye," Blamey replied, slicing himself some of the soft Portuguese cheese.

"Those ships that wrecked," Lewrie said, with his port glass held up to the swaying overhead lanthorn for study, "it's given me an idea . . . though it may prove unwelcome."

"Hmm?" Chalmers prompted with a mouth full of sweet bisquit.

"Perhaps we should sink, scuttle, or burn more than we carry back to the Prize-Court."

"Oh, I say!" Chalmers objected, as much as he dared.

"I've written Admiralty, requesting more ships," Lewrie said, explaining how he'd proposed that one more squadron, perhaps two more, were necessary to keep the Spanish coast under constant surveillance, the French in constant fear, and the supplies to their army in Spain cut to the bare bones. "The task is far larger than Admiralty imagined when they gave us our sailing orders, admittedly larger than I imagined. Five ships can't manage it, so long as we have to pack up and sail back to Lisbon after a fortnight for lack of prize crews. Even two squadrons in rotation could only do so much, for pretty-much the same reason. Until more ships arrive, we have to find a way to stay on-station for as long as the water, firewood, and rations allow."

"Well, if Wellesley takes Oporto for us, that would shorten our voyages here and there by several days," Chalmers said, sounding confident that such an event was in the cards.

"Even then, we'd *still* have to abandon the coast, sooner or later, to escort our prizes, re-provision, and allow the French to play silly buggers in our absence," Lewrie told him. He noted that Chalmers almost winced at the word "buggers", as if Lewrie had let go a fart. "We might be able to move our stores ship there, but would Admiralty agree to set up another Prize-Court at Oporto?"

"Well, they would if it was profitable enough," Blamey sneered. "So long as we keep fetching in captures, they'd follow the money."

"True enough, I suppose," Lewrie agreed with a chuckle, "but, as you said earlier this evening, Captain Chalmers . . . putting fears into the French sailors? If we burn prizes instead of tying up our hands manning them, we could pick and choose which ones to retain. Which ones I can loose my guns upon, and hone my people's accuracy, too. Burn them right offshore from the ports where others are sheltering. How eager would they be, then, to up-anchor and make sail?"

"We could bring about your labour stoppages, sir," Blamey stuck in with a snorting laugh to Chalmers. "Aye, burn them like the one that we torched off Oporto?"

"Keep the biggest, with the most valuable cargoes," Lewrie urged, "and torch the least valuable, and the homeward bound empty ones. *Most* visibly."

"Hmm, what about prisoners, though, sir," Blamey asked, looking as if he would scratch at his scalp. "Do we move them all to a prison ship and take them to Lisbon or Oporto or wherever, or do we continue to turn them loose on Spanish soil?"

"Yayss, it would seem that freeing them keeps the supplies flowing," Chalmers drawled, busying himself with the port bottle as it was passed to him. "They just sign aboard another. If we sling them into a hulk at Lisbon, we'd be denying the French their labour."

"Might be doing them a favour, Captain Chalmers," Blamey said. "That way, they can't be dragged off into the French army, hah hah!"

"Pity we can't just drown them, or shoot them," Chalmers said with a sneer between sips of port.

"Can't take the risk," Lewrie said after a moment of thought. "Do we put too many of them aboard a cartel ship, they just might overpower the guards and the prize crew."

Shoot or drown 'em, Chalmers? he thought; *My, you are a bloody minded sort, ain't you? You should be workin' for old Zachariah Twigg, cuttin' throats with a dull knife!*

"As it is, we're makin' 'em hurt," Lewrie went on. "They lose their pay, half their sea kits, and get landed in *Spain,* where odds are the *partisanos*'d murder 'em. If they do manage to make it to a French garrison, it takes weeks before they can take ship back to France, as un-paid hands. And, once back in France, it might take 'em even longer to find a new ship to join . . . if, as you say, Commander Blamey, their army doesn't press-gang 'em, first. Any French sailor we turn loose ends up dead-broke, and the families that depend on 'em end up beggin' in the streets. That's hurtin' 'em *sore,* in my books."

"Continue to let them row ashore in one of their ship's boats," Blamey summed up with a firm nod. "I like it."

"And, as long as that gale forced us to quit the coast, let's shift further East," Lewrie suggested, grinning. "Prowl your old hunting grounds round the French border, up to Arcachon or Bayonne. I've not seen them, yet. First thing in the morning, once we've sorted out the prizes you took, and be shot of their crews, of course. If you gentlemen don't mind, we could sacrifice one of them, paint gun-ports on her hull, and let my gunners get some more practice."

"Close aiming?" Chalmers said with an amused brow up. "Well, we all have our hobbies, I suppose."

"Speaking of hobbies, sir," Blamey prompted. "You said that you've a penny-whistle?"

"Oh, you don't want t'hear how bad I am at it, surely," Lewrie begged off, and wondering if he was slyly being twitted, but at the others' urging, there was no way to avoid, so he went to fetch it. He sat back down and after a few warm-up tootles and finger flexes, he launched into "Pleasant and Delightful".

Beyond the great-cabin door, Bisquit was curled up in his shelter beneath the starboard ladderway to the poop deck, having himself a post-supper snooze after a substantial bowl of leftovers from the Captain's table. True to form whenever Lewrie tried to amuse himself on his penny-whistle, the dog sprang out, stood at the door, and began to bay and howl.

Lewrie stopped and changed to "One Misty, Moisty Morning" in hopes that a faster tempo might silence the dog, but it only made it worse, for Bisquit began to scratch at the door with both paws most frantically, howling away . . . curiously, almost in time with the tune.

"Sorry, gentlemen," Lewrie said with a sigh, setting his humble instrument aside. "The critic has weighed in . . . critics, rather," he added as the laughter from the watchstanders on the quarterdeck, and his Marine sentry, could be heard.

Woof! as if to say "don't do that anymore!" Then one more warning *woof!* as Bisquit went back into his shelter, followed by some jowl-lifting, grumbling *whuffs* as he circled round on his old blanket to settle back down.

"I don't suppose we dare sing, then," Blamey said in a hammy whisper, which made them all burst out in loud laughter.

CHAPTER THIRTY-ONE

*L*ewrie wished that they could have landed all their prisoners further West than Tregandin-Noja, if only to deny the French their services longer. From there, though, it would be a fairly short walk to the larger port of Santoña, where they might take passage back to France, assuming that roving Spanish *partisanos* didn't get them first.

For a time, it seemed that their own people would do them in, There was a four-gun battery just outside the small fishing harbour, and the sight of three British warships fetched-to within a couple of miles offshore, launching five boats as if staging a raid, stirred the French artillerists to action, peppering roundshot all round the boats. Fortunately for the prisoners, they were miserable shots, but it was hugely amusing to the crews of all three warships to see the frantic antics of the prisoners, waving shirts or anything white for a call for truce, and one or two more fearful even jumping into the sea to swim the last quarter-mile without being shot at.

"Let's go see what France has to offer, then," Lewrie said, after a final chuckle.

From Santoña to Bilbao, then on to San Sebastian Donostia, in Basque country, the Spanish coast remained rocky and fir-treed, with the Picos de Europa a snow-capped backdrop, an introduction to the massive Pyrenees mountains. Military goods landed anywhere along the coast faced dauntingly steep and difficult road journeys to feed and arm the French armies further South and inland. Those mountains made Lewrie wonder how the Emperor Napoleon Bonaparte ever thought to maintain his troops so far from France. To his mind, after looking at one of the few atlases which depicted Iberia, and measuring off the distances, the whole endeavour seemed vastly improbable.

Damn fool's bitten off more than he can chew, Lewrie thought.

Yet the French strove to fulfill their Emperor's wishes, and that meant even more "trade" plying the seas closer to France proper, where supply convoys had shorter voyages, and shorter exposure to any raiders. Chalmers and Blamey had always reaped the lion's share of prizes because of their being assigned a richer hunting ground, which made Lewrie think of swapping *Undaunted* and *Peregrine* with Capt. Yearwood's *Sterling* and Commander Teague's *Blaze*, the next time they sortied from Lisbon, if they weren't re-enforced by then, just to share the wealth.

Four prizes became six, then seven, the last taken a dowdy old brig which had been the slowest of a clutch of six that they had sighted off Zumaya; again, all of them returning to France empty.

"I'll have that'un," Lewrie declared. "We need the gunnery practice. Take her crew off, Mister Westcott, and make a signal to *Peregrine* to take her in tow."

Her crew, now prisoners, were brought aboard *Sapphire*, well-guarded by Marines as Commander Blamey paid out a full cable's length of tow line, regardless of what he thought of the whole thing. Once *Peregrine* and the prize were under way at a slow four knots, Lewrie ordered the ship to Quarters, and had the word passed that tobacco would reward the best shots.

"What's that all about, Mister Westcott?" Lewrie snapped as he heard a commotion in the waist. There was some palaver with the French captives, and Midshipman Harvey reported to the quarterdeck.

"A couple of the prisoners, sir," he said, beaming, "they say this is the second time we've taken them, and their Master, yonder, says he can't guarantee their pay. They'd like to scrag him if we let them! They say it's just too unfair!"

"Shouldn't have signed on, if they can't take a joke," Lewrie quipped. "Thankee, and carry on, Mister Harvey."

⚓

"The Commodore will amuse himself, I suppose," Capt. Chalmers drawled as he watched the preparations. "Lord only knows that his gun crews hardly ever fire a single shot under anyone's bows to make them strike, as slow as is *Sapphire*."

"Must be a trial, sir," *Undaunted*'s First Officer simpered in agreement, "commanding such a lumbering barge."

"Spare *us* that fate, Mister Crosley, for as long as possible." Chalmers sniggered. "Aha, she's working up on the target, now. About two hundred yards . . . a wee short of a cable's range?"

"About that, sir," Lt. Crosley agreed once more, lifting his own telescope to one eye.

Boo-boom! as *Sapphire*'s forecastle chase guns, carronades, and her first pair of starboard 12-pounders and 24-pounders went off almost as one. The prize ship's jib-boom was shot away, her crudely-carved figurehead was blasted to scrap, and overlapping holes were blasted into the brig's forward larboard scantlings. *Boo-Boom!* and another pair of holes appeared further aft. *Boo-Boom!* and the brig's foremast shrouds and channel platform got shattered.

On down *Sapphire*'s side the firing went in twin blasts as the upper and lower gun deck fired almost as one. There were some shots wider of the mark, striking closer to the target's waterline, and one or two blasted through her thinner upper bulwarks, but the accuracy of *Sapphire*'s gunners was impressive, even to a sceptical Chalmers.

The last great-guns roared, along with the quarterdeck 6-pounders, and carronades tore through the target's helm, took bites from its mainmast trunk, and shattered the larboard quarter gallery and the hull, right where the master's cabins and the mates' wardroom would be. The prize brig looked as if a horde of gigantic rats had been at her, and *Sapphire* wasn't through.

The two-decker weaved away, off to larboard for a bit, then crossed the target's stern to allow her larboard guns to have a go. Once more, the stuttering. *Boo-Boo-Booms* rang out, bringing down the foremast, punching roundshot into the brig's hull, sending planking soaring, shivering the weakened main mast, and once again sweeping the quarterdeck clean. The target shook like a rat in a terrier's jaws as the last roundshot took the upper stock of her rudder away, and she began to yaw to either beam. Down came the main mast, and *Sapphire* hoisted a signal for *Peregrine* to slip her towline and leave the brig to sink or wander on her own.

"Oh my," Lt. Crosley said as he espied a broom making its way up one of *Sapphire*'s larboard signal halliards.

"It does appear as if there's a method to his madness," Capt. Chalmers said with a taut grin on his face, wondering if Lewrie was jibing his earlier boastful broom hoist. "That was . . . impressive."

"Against an un-armed, lightly built merchantman, sir, which cannot shoot back," Lt. Crosley commented. "Heavy twenty-four pound shot against two-inch thick oak, perhaps cheaper pine?"

"But he wasn't firing just to hit anywhere, was he?" Chalmers countered, rubbing his chin in thought. "Gun-ports, masts, the helm and quarterdeck . . . where officers would stand. Hmm. There may be something to it. Don't know if we'll be cutting sights on our guns, yet, but . . . it's a thought."

Further East, and the sight of snow-capped mountains became a memory, beyond the Western-most shoulders and foothills of the Pyrenees and the Picos de Europa. The coast became a plain, as the three-ship squadron approached France. Biarritz, mainly a whaling port, hove into view along the low, featureless shore that consisted mostly of beaches, dunes, scrub pine forests stretching far inland, un-inhabited and forever shifting low barrier islands fronting lagoons populated only by myriads of sea birds. The vista was even bleaker than Lewrie recalled from when he'd had the *Savage* frigate off Royan and the mouth of the Gironde River which ran to Bordeaux.

North of Biarritz and Bayonne, the coast ran as straight as a knife blade to Cap Ferret and the Bay of Arcachon, unbroken by even one wee fishing port worthy of the name, a dour and dangerous lee shore down which all the French supply ships would have to run, as risky as the Spanish coast, in its own way.

"There's some astoundingly good wines back behind all this, somewhere," Lt. Westcott commented. "Aquitaine's famous for them. If only we could get *at* them."

"We'll send Mister Cadrick up the Gironde with money," Lewrie quipped. "Who knows? As 'skint' as this part of France appears, the locals might not mind havin' some silver shillings in their pockets!"

Six prizes worth keeping became nine, and on their short cruise they set alight at least seven more, but, try as they might to man the prizes with as few spare hands as possible, it became impossible after a time. If they encountered French warships escorting the convoys, or an enemy squadron out to protect their supply lines, all ships would be too short of sailors to fight.

We've had our fun, Lewrie gloomily thought as he was forced to the admission that they would have to quit the coasts, both the French and the Spanish, and return to Lisbon. *Christ, if I only had more ships! Pray Jesus, there's good news from Admiralty when we get back.*

BOOK FOUR

Ye gentlemen of England
That live at home in ease,
Ah! little do you think upon
The dangers of the seas.

                  –MARTIN PARKER (1600-56)

CHAPTER THIRTY·TWO

*H*MS *Sapphire* and her consorts came to a stop in the same anchorage under the towering Alfama hills, dragging in a total of fourteen prizes. Sails were taken in and brailed up, lashed snug to the yards in harbour gaskets, and the yards lowered to rests. Bosuns from all ships rowed about to see that all yards were square, and that all rigging was snugged to geometric precision.

Once that was done, boats from all ships stroked to the quays to fetch fresh provisions; firewood and water casks, first, and fresh bread next.

Pursers from all five warships chafed at the delay, eager for first shot at the chandleries and the store ship, and Bosuns and their Mates checked and re-checked their lists of supplies with which to keep their ships ready for sea. Captains and officers had their own wants, but would have to wait 'til the basic necessities were seen to before they could go ashore. And, there was a steady stream of boats rowing prize crews from their captures back to their own ships, and men from the Prize-Court rowing out to replace them and take the prizes into custody. At last, as a sop to impatience, ships' boats fetched the mail sacks from the store ship to be distributed to all who could read.

In the midst of all that, a small *moliciero*, one of the oddly shaped boats used to harvest seaweed, came alongside *Sapphire*, and a Portuguese messenger managed to convey the fact that he had a letter for "*El Capitão* Loonie", to the great amusement of all on deck who heard it.

"Captain 'Loonie', mine arse," Lewrie growled as a Midshipman scrambled down to collect the letter and fetch it to the quarterdeck. "I swear, I doubt there's a single foreigner who *ever* gets my name right! Ah, thankee, Mister Chenery."

"Aye, sir," the cheeky young'un replied, trying to keep his face set, and not titter.

It was from Thomas Mountjoy, and Lewrie eyed it warily before breaking the seal and opening it.

"Yes, by God!" he shouted after a quick scan. "Wellesley's got Oporto. That French Marshal, Soult, has been beaten like a rug, and General Sir John Moore's been avenged!"

"That's grand, sir," Lt. Westcott cheered, "welcome news. Did he say how it was done?"

"No details, no, Mister Westcott," Lewrie told him, "though I'm promised all the juicy bits over a shore supper. Mister Chenery, is that seaweed barge still alongside?"

"Aye, sir."

"Can the messenger speak *any* English?" Lewrie demanded.

"Ehm, hard to say, sir," Chenery said, shrugging.

"*Hola, senhor!*" Lewrie cried, going to the larboard entry port to shout down to the boat. "*Falar Inglese?* Damn! Of course not. Do you tell *Senhor* Mountjoy *sim*, I will be happy to dine with him at the appointed hour."

"*Senhor Montahna?*" the messenger said, scratching his scalp in confusion. "*Não comprender, Capitão.*"

"*Carregar um carta* to *Senhor* Mount-*Joy?*" Lewrie pressed.

"Ah, *sim, Senhor Capitão!*"

Lewrie dashed into the chart room, scribbled a quick note, and handed it to Chenery, who bore it down the battens to the messenger.

Christ on a crutch, Lewrie fumed; *why can't foreigners speak even a little English?*

"No sense in trusting the newspaper accounts," Thomas Mountjoy told Lewrie as soon as they met that evening. "They always get things wrong. Do take those back numbers, though, for other news."

"And who's responsible for that, hmm?" Lewrie pointedly said, raising a brow. "War by print and ink, hey. Isn't that what you call it?"

"Well, I have my moments," Mountjoy replied, buffing his nails on his coat lapel. "There's a lovely little wine bar near here, in the Rua de Prata. Pretty girls, *fados* and entertainment, and simply luscious appetisers."

"*Far* uphill, is it?" Lewrie asked, casting a glance up from the lowest level of the Baixa district to the towering city above.

"Just a wee stroll," Mountjoy confidently assured him, so they set off uphill from Mountjoy's "false front" offices. The wine bar was on a wider major street, not tucked away in one of the many cobblestoned narrow side streets, a very inviting place with an outdoor seating area under a gay striped canvas awning, already busy with diners, drinkers, and music *aficianados*. It was just dark enough for the bar's many candles and smaller lanthorns to make it seem a lot more enticing than it might appear in daylight. They were led to a table just inside the wide, glazed double doors, and quickly supplied glasses and a bottle of *espumante*.

"Ah, that's lovely," Mountjoy said with an appreciative sigh after his first sip. "Must have a cellar, where they keep it cool. I must say, Portuguese *espumante* is growing on me."

"Anything other than French champagne, which is un-patriotic to drink, I s'pose, "Lewrie agreed. "Now, Oporto. When, and how?"

"Middle of May," Mountjoy said, squirming on his rickety chair with delight in the telling, "Wellesley kept flanking Soult's troops South of the Douro River . . . not very many of them, it appears, since Marshal Soult trusted the river as an impassable barrier, and French soldiers out in small packets are dead meat. The Portuguese partisans, you see," he said with a shrug.

"Mid-May?" Lewrie said, scowling. "Mean t'say, nigh a month ago? I wish somebody'd told me!"

"Well, I did leave a letter at the Post Office for you . . ."

"Which I didn't get 'til today, dammit," Lewrie groused.

"Anyway, Soult pulled all his troops back to the North bank of the Douro on May twelfth," Mountjoy went on, un-fazed, "burned the new bridge of boats, pulled anything that would float to the North shore, and figured that with the river in spate from all the snow melt in the mountains, he had all the time in the world to watch a British army diddle. Been to Oporto, have you?"

"Seen it from the sea," Lewrie told him, between sips of wine.

"Just like Lisbon, steep," Mountjoy said, "but, unlike Lisbon, it's steep on *both* banks, and the Douro might as well be at the bottom of a canyon. Now, earlier on, a General Hill had gathered up some of those seaweed

harvesting boats, the *molicieros,* and had used them to flank the French
through some lagoons, and Soult must have known that we still had them,
so he moved most of his army down near the mouth of the river to prevent a crossing there . . . the damned fool."

"*Pesticos, senhors?*" a waiter asked, and the tale had to wait while they
ordered grilled sardines, shrimp, cheese, and thin toast points.

"So there sat Soult, smug as only a Frenchman can be, cocking his nose
at Wellesley and daring him to try anything," Mountjoy said with delight,
"but he didn't keep any troops in the city proper, or on the Eastern side,
upriver . . . God only knows why. Wellesley's men found one half-sunk
boat, bailed it out, and ferried a brigade over to an un-guarded convent
or seminary on the outskirts of town, only thirty or fourty men at a time,
if you can imagine it, got a lodgement, and then they found some bigger
wine barges further inland, and moved even more men across. By the time
the French noticed, it was mid-day, and we beat off three attacks on the
seminary, and Wellesley's guns on the South bank just *swamped* them with
shrapnel shell.

"Soult got winkled out of town, retreating so fast that he left over fifteen hundred sick soldiers behind in the hospitals, and a retreat turned into
a rout," Mountjoy told Lewrie, almost cackling with glee. "The French
under Soult, another pack of them under a General Loison, had to flee
Northeast, into the rough country of the Minho. They left seventy pieces
of artillery behind at Oporto, and along the way out of Portugal, they lost
all their wheeled transport, baggage, artillery, and most of their cavalry
and draught animals. Our men found a lot of them ham-strung so we
couldn't use them. Hah, some of our soldiers made themselves rich from
the pickings they found at the bottom of a ravine and bridge over the
Calvado River. Portuguese silver coins, belts of gold coins, silver
plate . . . all looted from Oporto. The ravine was just piled with dead
horses and soldiers. Their retreat was as ghastly as Sir John Moore's
retreat to Corunna in December . . . less all the ice and snow, of course."

"So, Wellesley's avenged Sir John," Lewrie said. "Good! Just bloody,
bloody *good*!"

"Pity the Portuguese who got in the way, though," Mountjoy sobred,
"farms and villages along the retreat route pillaged, churches despoiled
and burned . . . the French really go out of their way when it comes to
churches. Townspeople and peasants massacred just for the fun of it, young
and old, and the women raped *then* murdered? It was as bad as anything
we invented at Gibraltar when the French invaded Spain."

Lt. Westcott and Midshipman Fywell had provided drawings for Mountjoy's spurious newspaper accounts of French depravity which had gone a long way towards rousing the Spanish people, and their turning from a supine French ally to a fierce British ally, the year before.

"To Sir John Moore," Lewrie proposed, raising his full glass, "May he take joy in Heaven of a French . . . humiliation."

"And to General Wellesley, and Oporto," Mountjoy seconded, which caught the notice of the *Lisboêtas* in the wine bar, who raised their glasses and voices in celebration, as well.

"Anything developing after Oporto?" Lewrie asked.

"Oh, there's a report I just saw that yet another French army under a Marshal Victor has crossed the frontier round Castelo Branco, making a try at Lisbon," Mountjoy related, "but nothing much came of it. After getting fresh supplies, Wellesley crossed the border into Spain to keep them on the hop, and off-balance. I've *heard* that he's to join up with the Spanish, under some twit named Cuesta."

"Good God, *that'll* be a disaster," Lewrie growled. "Ye can't rely on the Spanish for a slice of bloody *bread*!"

"Well, we'll just have to see," Mountjoy said with a deep sigh. "Hope for the best . . . all that? Wellesley's the best we've got, and has some nasty surprises up his sleeve for the Frogs. And, frankly, Lewrie?" He leaned forward to impart with a grin. "Even if Bonaparte comes back to Spain to save his Marshals' bacon, I have the feeling that General Wellesley could beat the stuffing out of him, too!"

"Well, I certainly hope you're right," Lewrie said, though in more dubious takings. "We'll just have to see."

"Now we've Oporto, you'll be moving your squadron there, like you had planned?" Mountjoy asked as he topped up their glasses.

"Definitely," Lewrie was quick to assure him. "It saves time spent going there and back, though I don't know if the Prize-Court would move with us. Might have to keep fetchin' prizes into Lisbon, but work out of Oporto. Move my store ship there, for certain, and at least get my mail delivered there. When I've time t'read it," he added with a grimace. "I still haven't heard from Admiralty about gettin' me more ships. Christ, it's like muckin' out the Augean Stables. We've taken over thirty prizes, burned nigh that many, and the coast is still swarmin' with French supplies! It's like swattin' roaches with only one shoe."

"But, it's a rich, rewarding mucking out," Mountjoy said. "If it continues." To Lewrie's puzzled look, he added, "I've word that Marshal Ney has left Galicia and moved down close to Léon, so there may not be as great a demand for supplies delivered by sea, Ney can count on whatever comes cross the Pyrenees. As a matter of fact, if he didn't leave large garrisons behind him, might you be amenable to making some arms deliveries to the Galician and Basque partisans? I have a fellow up North who has been making contacts."

"Do I know him?" Lewrie asked, ready to cross the fingers of his right hand for luck.

"You do," Mountjoy said, sighing.

"Romney Marsh?" Lewrie guessed.

"The very one," Mountjoy confirmed.

"Still cuttin' French throats?" Lewrie pressed, scowling.

"Revels at it," Mountjoy said with a grim nod. "Still good at languages, though. He even sent me a note in Basque. Couldn't find anyone, Portuguese or Spanish, who could make heads or tails of it, but . . . there it is."

"Seems even the blood-thirsty and totally *insane* have their uses," Lewrie gravelled. "Just so long as I don't have t'deal with him, just land muskets and such on some beach in the dead of night, I could help you."

"I'm glad to hear it," Mountjoy said, sounding relieved. "Ehm . . . I'd suppose that if you move your base of operations to Oporto, you might think of establishing *Senhora* Covilhã there?"

"It's her hometown, after all," Lewrie said. "I should imagine she'd be delighted. How's she doing, by the way, working for you and all?"

"As I told you long ago at Gibraltar, I would have recruited her to spy for me then and there," Mountjoy said, before popping one of the grilled and spiced sardines into his mouth. He chewed for a bit before continuing. "She's bright, intelligent, circumspect, the very last person our enemies would suspect. Pity the fieldwork in my line is so far off and, frankly, so damned dangerous for any woman on her own. Anywhere the French stand in the Iberian Peninsula, no one is safe from rape or murder, just to relieve their boredom, or get some of their own back when the *partisanos* ambush some of their chums. It is more in Marsh's line of work. The reports I got from our army . . . any French soldiers caught on Soult's retreat got stripped, nailed to barn doors, emasculated, skinned alive, and left with their pricks in their mouths, so you can understand how barbaric it might be for anyone suspected of spying for us."

"Thank God for office work, then," Lewrie said, though he was delighted to hear how the despised French might suffer. "What do you have Maddalena doing for you?"

"Oh, translations, for the most part," Mountjoy told him, "the odd false newspaper account to send over the border into Spain, or up North to the Portuguese. She's been teaching herself French, as well, with my, and Mister Deacon's, help, and has been cobbling up *faux* news items for enemy soldiers to read. Food shortages back home, women rioting for bread, graft and corruption accusations laid against civil authorities, and rumours to undermine Emperor Bonaparte's image. We've been able to obtain copies of the *Moniteur*, and several regional French papers, and we've been copying them, right down to the advertisments, with our false articles inserted.

"She's damned clever at it," Mountjoy admitted, "*much* sharper at it than me, to be truthful. I'd hate to lose her services."

"Hmm, no chance you'd open a branch office of the good old Falmouth Import and Export Company in Oporto, is there?" Lewrie asked.

"That's doubtful," Mountjoy had to tell him, "and the decision would be up to my superiors in London, anyway. Oh, I'm certain that an host of English traders will flock back to Oporto, now the French are gone, but General Wellesley didn't leave a garrison to hold the city . . . doesn't have a big-enough army for that . . . so the city's future security will be up to the Portuguese, and if the French come back, well . . ."

"Damme, if he didn't garrison it, I may not be able to count on Oporto being a safe harbour for my ships!" Lewrie almost yelped. All his hopes suddenly seemed dashed, his plans in a shambles.

"That might be so," Mountjoy sadly agreed, shaking his head in commiseration for a moment, before flagging down their waiter. "Feel peckish for something more solid, Lewrie? Ah, *senhor. Tem comida* the *caldeirada de peixe hoije a noite? Maravilhoso! Para dois*, Captain Lewrie?"

"Hmm . . . do you have the *açorda de camarãoes?*" Lewrie asked the waiter. "*Bom*, I'll have that . . . *eu quero aquilo.*"

"You've become a linguist, hah hah," Mountjoy japed. "At last."

"Hah-bloody-hah," Lewrie growled back. "So long as you're having the fish stew, and I the shrimp, let's get a bottle of *vinho branco*. Your treat, I believe you offered?" he said with one of his best shit-eating grins.

"But, of course, my dear fellow!" Mountjoy loudly assured him. "Anything for the conquering hero."

As they poured the last of the *espumante* into their glasses, a singer struck a chord on his twelve-string *guitarra*, then began to pick out a melancholy tune in a minor key, with many flourishes, and the other diners hushed to hear him. The fellow began to sing, baying out a mournful, groaning cry of utter sadness that descended the scale, trailing off to a pitiful whimper. Oddly, drinkers came into the tavern from the outdoor area with smiles of anticipation on their faces, and those already inside grinned and pointed to the stage, as if saying "now you'll really hear something."

The entertainer began a long, sad *fado*. Despite his ability to order supper, Lewrie's grasp of Portuguese was slight, so he only caught about one word in five, but it made no difference. The song was, like all *fados*, about something miserable; utter heartbreak, lost love, exile far from home, or mis-spent or long-lost youth. It was the very last thing he needed to hear, the mood he was in.

Lewrie looked cross the table at Mountjoy, who was swaying in time to the music, a silly grin on his face, and his eyed closed, lost in some personal rapture.

Gawd, Lewrie thought; *but where's Bisquit when ye really, really need him?*

CHAPTER THIRTY-THREE

*A*s much as he wished to dash off uphill to Maddalena's lodgings, there was the Prize-Court to attend, first, with his subordinates, and all the paperwork taken off their captures. That, unfortunately, took the better part of a day, with all the hemming and hawing and pointed questions from the Proctors, their seeming sense of being put-upon by such a volume of paperwork all at once, along with their dis-approval of how many prizes had been torched and *not* brought in, even if burning prizes *saved* the Court their very precious time!

It was as if they begrudged losing commissions on the cargoes described in the burned ships' papers, goods which could have been awarded to the Portuguese army, used by the British army in lieu of precious imports, or sold (on the sly) on the Lisbon market. And, of *course*, the Prize-Court could not yet even make a guess as to the value of their previous captures, which were still going through an exhaustive evaluation!

"If I may, sirs," Lewrie said once the long, boring meeting broke up, "I would like to discuss something with one of the senior Court members."

"I fear that they are much too busy, Captain Lewrie," one of the Proctors told him. "Perhaps if you wrote them a letter about the matter?"

"I could, but," Lewrie pressed, "now we have Oporto, is there a way that I might move my squadron there, save time in transit from Lisbon to the coast? Or, would I still have to despatch our prizes to the Court here at Lisbon? No way to open a branch office there?"

"To Oporto, sir?" the Proctor said with a dis-believing sniff, followed by a wee chuckle. "For my part, I do not see a way to do so. Admiralty does not establish Prize-Courts 'will-he, nill-he', and we only were established here after a lengthy debate back in London. To open a . . . branch office . . . as you term it, at Oporto for your convenience I expect would be completely out of the question. It was a matter of some import to open offices at Lisbon, instead of requiring you to conduct all your business at Gibraltar."

"Well, damme," Lewrie said, groaning, "it was a thought."

"I would suppose, sir," the Proctor went on, in a drawling air of amusement, "that you could write my superiors, but what they would make of it? What London would make of it?" He concluded with a huge hand-spread shrug.

"Thankee, anyway, sir. Good day to you," Lewrie said, teeth gritted in a dutiful smile, one he didn't mean. "I shall write your superiors, and we shall see."

"Good luck with it, sir, and good day," the Proctor said as he gathered up his papers.

Lewrie bowed his way to the street, clapped his hat on his head, and puffed his cheeks as he blew a long *hmmf* of dis-satisfaction, thinking black thoughts about the Proctor's attitude. He looked uphill, imagining that Maddalena might be working at her translations in her lodgings, and that popping in out of the blue would be a grand diversion for her. He set off, with lustful fantasies in mind, that and plans for a supper for two after a passionate *rencontre*.

Rubio, the bearded day clerk at the lobby desk, allowed himself a wee glower of dis-approval, when Lewrie asked him if *Senhora* Covilhã was in. Lewrie shrugged it off, and upon hearing that she was, dashed up the stairs to rap on her door.

"*Quem é?*" came a brusque, irritated cry from within after his knocking.

"Maddalena, it's me," he called back.

"Ah? Alan?" came a second cry, this one much fonder, with a note of surprise. A second later, the bolt was shot, the latch was turned, and she swung the door open. "Oh, get in here, *meu querido!*"

She flung her arms round him, pressed her lips to his, and practically dragged him inside, and Lewrie shut the door with the toe of his boot as he lifted her off her feet and danced her round the lodgings, making her laugh between fervent kisses and breathless endearments.

"Damme, but you feel good!" he told her.

"Oh, so do you!" Maddalena declared, leaning back. "Though, you do smell a bit *too* much of your ship."

He took a whiff of his coat sleeve.

"Sorry 'bout that," he told her, "but sailors do carry more odours than salt and tar. How *are* you, my dear? What've you been up to, the last few weeks? Mountjoy tells me . . ."

"Ah, *sim!*" Maddalena brightened even further. "Come see!" as she led him to her dining table, where stacks of newspapers were littered next to some scissors and a sheaf of writing paper. "These are French. Right now, Mister Mountjoy has me translating and re-writing some of the articles, and the advertisements. See here? I re-write the advertisements, making goods sound very hard to obtain, and make the prices for things *much* higher than they really are, so the French soldiers who read the false papers we print have to wonder how bad it is at home. He, Mister Deacon, and I then create items about hoarders being arrested, people arrested for stealing bread, potatoes, or even turnips, they are so hungry. Who eats turnips, though? Ugh!"

"We English do," Lewrie told her. "The Scots, the Welsh, and the Irish, too. Done right, they're hellish-tasty."

"*Novamente* . . . ugh!" she said, making a face. "Here is one of our latest. Does it not look exactly like a French newspaper? We re-create the banner of the publisher, include the official bulletins, then repeat the local news, with alternations meant to lower the . . . *morale* . . . of the readers. Look it over, see what you think!"

She was more animated than at any time Lewrie could recall, almost giddy with pride in her contributions. Lewrie's understanding of printed French was little better than his ability to speak it, but he took the paper and gave it a good going-over, because it seemed to mean so much to her.

"Damned if I could tell the difference, Maddalena," he said in praise. "It looks completely authentic. As we say in the Navy, 'confusion to the French'. But, how the Devil does Mountjoy get 'em to where the French might find 'em and read 'em?"

"Oh, that is mostly Mister Deacon's doings," she said with a laugh. "He has many contacts among the *Lisboêtas,* who know their way over the border, and Spanish partisans who come over the border for arms, or with information for Mister Mountjoy. They smuggle them, a few copies at a time. Too many would take waggons, and they would never make it over the border. I have heard Mister Deacon say that some of our papers make it all the way to taverns in Madrid, where French soldiers drink!"

"What's Mountjoy done with their defeat at Oporto?" Lewrie asked. "Surely, there's pure gold in accounts of that."

"Oh, Oporto, *meu Deus*!" Maddalena whooped. "You know of it? You were at sea when . . . ?"

"Mountjoy told me, yesterday," Lewrie said. "*Damned* fine, and let Bonaparte stew over that! A whole army destroyin' itself on the retreat? Wellesley's the man!"

"Oh, we have already sent off a special edition," Maddalena crowed, "with a bulletin re-printed from the *Moniteur,* noting even heavier casualties, more suffering, and a hint that Marshal Soult may be tried for such a disastrous failure," she said, a twinkle in her eyes. "Let Emperor Bonaparte . . . stew? Why would he make stew, *meu amor*? Isn't such for celebration?"

"More like, fret in despair, is the meaning," Lewrie explained.

"Aha! Fret!" she said, beaming. "Yes, Oporto! We must have wine to celebrate. I still have some of that *vinho verde* you bought for me. I will go get it!"

Lewrie found a copy of the special edition which purported to be from Bordeaux and looked it over; the so-called official bulletin from the Paris *Moniteur* on the front page was bordered in black, and grim-looking. He thought it too bad that the French, themselves, by now could say that a man "lied liked a bulletin", no longer putting any trust in what their masters told them; the French soldiers in Spain would dismiss it, most likely. Those in power who managed the message, and Emperor Napoleon Bonaparte's vaunted image, would never admit a defeat so baldly, if they mentioned it at all.

"If I knew you would come today, I would have tried to chill it," Maddalena said, returning with the bottle and two glasses. She handed Lewrie the bottle, expecting him to draw the cork.

Damme, more *domestic shite,* he thought, searching for a cork-pull; *ain't that what servants are for? I'll carve the roast, but that's my limit.*

"Ah!" he said, after pouring himself a taste. "It's hellish-fine warm. Let me top you up."

They sat together on the settee with the bottle on a table to one side. "To General Wellesley," Maddalena proposed, to which Lewrie heartily agreed, and repeated.

"Ye know, my dear, now that Oporto's back in Portuguese hands, I've half a mind to transfer my squadron there," he casually tossed out. "It'd save a day or two going to, or coming back, from the Spanish coast. The damned Prize-Court, though, doesn't seem all that eager to go along with me. Too comfortable here in Lisbon, damn 'em. I still could, if I could detatch one ship to escort the prizes here to be adjudged, then return to Oporto a day or two later.

"That's your old hometown. Like t'see it, again?" he asked.

Maddalena had been lounging on the settee's back, but now sat erect, going prim with her wine glass held in both hands in her lap.

"No more than I would care to see my grandparents' hometown up in the mountains, no," Maddelena told him, avoiding eye contact, and staring off into the middle distance. "What about my work here in Lisbon, for Mister Mountjoy and Mister Deacon? It is important work, they tell me, and I enjoy it."

"Well, mean t'say . . . if I'm there, and you're here . . ." Lewrie flummoxed, astounded that she seemed so reluctant.

"No," she said, more firmly.

"Don't want t'see your family, again, your old neighbourhood where you grew up?" Lewrie tried to tease.

"Not . . . really," Maddalena said with a grimace, finally looking at him. "I was never happy in Oporto. My family . . . my father was a brute, and a drunk, and my mother . . . as much as she tried she was never much help to me. Father and my brothers made the wine barrels . . . coopers? We were so poor they didn't even own their own *tools,* and could barely read, or write, or do *sums.* And our neighbourhood? Our house? It was a hovel crammed between two warehouses right by the piers on the South bank of the Douro. *They* thought it suitable," she gravelled, "fitting to who we were, and thankful for it, rented from our employer," she said with an impatient sigh.

"I didn't . . ." Lewrie attempted to empathise.

"Only my brother Emilio was to do better," Maddalena went on, "the youngest, closest in age to me, and he was to be a priest, so he *had* to get a complete education. Hmpf! Emilio was grateful for the education, but he did not dare say that he did *not* want to go into the church. They were proud of *him*. He was an excellent student and won prizes every year. What my father did not know was that Emilio taught what he learned each day to *me*, beyond what little my family thought a girl should know.

"He is a runaway, too, *meu amor*," Maddalena said, inclining her head as if imparting a secret, with a bleak smile. "The grandees in the wine trade sponsored him to attend university at Coimbra, and he went, but he refused to take Holy Orders when he graduated, and it was a great shame to my father, my family. It was as if Emilio had never been born, for no one could speak of him without getting beaten.

"He is a teacher, now, at Coimbra, married and happy, and well thought of," Maddalena said with pride. "They no longer speak of me, either, after I could bear it no longer, and ran off to Gibraltar . . . with the young man who sold wine, remember that I told you? I am a great shame to my father. He does not know of it, but I still speak with my mother. I write our old priest a letter, and mother goes to church every day, so, when my letters arrive, he will read them to her, and writes back what she wishes to say to me. So . . . you see why I have no wish to go back to Oporto ever again . . . not until my father dies."

"Christ," was Lewrie's stunned response.

"I sometimes think of my grandparents, who walked all the way from Covilhã to 'Porto," she sadly mused, taking a sip of wine, "they *must* have had hopes for a better life than being landless peasants in the mountains, but . . . my father, all my aunts and uncles, my brothers and sisters, and their husbands and wives seem *content* to be peasants, almost illiterate, so . . ." She took another sip of wine and looked closely at him. "That is where I come from, Alan, that is *what* I come from, so you must understand why I will never go back, not even for my dear mother's funeral, God preserve her. I will not be cursed and shamed. I will not go back to that lifeless trap, again."

"So, if I do move the squadron . . . ?" Lewrie posed.

"The young man I ran away with to Gibraltar, and you, promised me that someday I would see Lisbon, and be a fine lady," she said with a wistful smile. "And here I am, a *Lisboêta*, and happier than I have ever been. Perhaps I am not yet the fine lady," she japed, rolling her eyes to mock her aspirations, "but we shall see what the future brings. If you do move there . . . I will not follow you. I cannot, do you see why?"

"I do," Lewrie replied, feeling an icy pang under his heart as he envisioned the end of what had been a very pleasurable and affectionate arrangement. Could he dare call their relationship a love affair? Oh, he *liked* her a great deal, found her extremely attractive, and appreciated her wit and her level-headed sense. Maddalena was so easy to converse with, much more so than most women, who knew little or nothing of the wider world. And her passion! She was rare in that sense, too, as eager for lovemaking as he was, not shy or timidly missish when it came to expressing her own desires. Maddalena was not the sort who would submit to a man's desires out of a sense of duty to her mate, would not lay back and endure . . . "lay back and think of Portugal" . . . as most *wives* did.

Did he *love* her? Oh, the endearments of *minha dose, minha amor,* and *minha querida* came as easily to his tongue as "my old chap" to a fellow officer of his acquaintance, but . . . did he really *mean* them? Could he ever consider making their relationship permanent, taking her back to England?

She loves Lisbon, sure as shite she'd hate London, he thought, imagining her melting away in the rain like a clump of sugar dissolved in a cup of her strong, black coffee!

He had been married once, and could frankly admit to himself that he had mostly been a miserable failure at it. In a desperate moment when he sensed that he was losing Viscount Percy Stangbourne's sister, Lydia, and *her* affections, he had blurted out a proposal of marriage, a proposal that had been quickly spurned, for Lydia would not become a lonely sailor's wife; the times apart were too much for her.

Could he propose to Maddalena to avoid losing her, too?

Not a chance in Hell, he told himself; *Might regret that, some day, but . . . no. If it's over, it's over. Dammit.*

"*Meu amor?*" Maddalena asked, after his long silence.

"Hmm? Just wonderin' if Oporto has shipyards big enough for our use if we need repairs," he lied.

"From what I remember, there are companies that build barges to bring the wine casks downriver," Maddalena told him, looking up as if recalling the sights of her riverfront home, "and fishing boats, weed-harvesting boats, but none all that big. The ships that came for wine never seemed in need of repair. If they did, I'd think they would come to Lisbon, instead. A good reason for you to keep your ships here, hmm?" she said with a teasing expression.

"If the Navy ever thought I made the decision 'cause I liked Lisbon wine and food better, they'd have my 'nutmegs' off with a dull knife!" Lewrie hooted. "Stand me up by the taffrails and shoot me like Admiral Byng!"

"Who was he?" Maddalena asked, now in happier takings as she sensed that he would not be removing to Oporto anytime soon.

Even as Lewrie told the tale of the unfortunate fellow who had been court-martialed and executed for not doing his utmost long before said . . . as the cynical French foe said *"pour encourager les autres"*—to encourage the others—he could not help thinking that if he *didn't* move his squadron unless there were some hard, legitimate reasons not to, he *could* face censure, and all for a woman; people in the Royal Navy would say; that "the Ram-Cat" had been too enamoured of his latest "batter pudding" to do his utmost.

The second thought in the back of his mind was about the end of his time with Maddalena. Sweet and pleasurable it had been, but, sooner or later, it would be done. *Sapphire* would come to the end of her active commission in the coming year, he would have to sail her back to England and turn her over to the yards, pay off her people, and walk away, probably never to return to Lisbon, or Spain, or to Gibraltar.

Maddalena's adamant refusal to follow him once more presaged the ending, made them both face it, if even for a brief while, arisen once and quickly suppressed in both their minds, he suspected.

Ride it to the last hurdles, Lewrie thought; *and take as much joy as ye can from it, whilst it lasts. And never think, or speak of it, again!*

CHAPTER THIRTY-FOUR

*T*o his credit (he hoped) Lewrie did enquire about dockyards and chandleries with the Portuguese civil authorities, those left in place when Dom João, the royal house of Braganza, the entire court and all its treasures fled to the Vice-Principality of Brazil. He suspected that local *Lisboêta* pride made them disparage his prospects at Oporto. His conversations with the shipyards along the Tagus waterfront told him much the same; he'd be better off remaining at Lisbon. They even said that there was always an outside chance that the French would come back to re-take the city. The British would protect Lisbon to the last, but Oporto? He even hiked up to the castle where bald-headed old General Beresford reigned, finally got a brief interview, and was informed that the only garrison force available to defend Oporto from a French return would be a skeleton force of Portuguese militia. All troops, British and Portuguese, who had any training were in the field with General Sir Arthur Wellesley, over the border into Spain.

"I gave it a long look and a hard try, gentlemen," Lewrie told his assembled officers, "but no one can assure me that Oporto wouldn't be overrun by the French if they decide to come back. And, no one could guarantee that we'd find a wide spot to careen and fire off our seaweed and barnacles, either. No shipyards worthy of the name, few chandleries, and those picked clean by the French while they were in charge of the city?" He heaved them a large shrug. "It appears that we'll have to continue on as we have, and return to Lisbon when we've run short of hands to man the prize crews, or run short of supplies."

"Little chance of that, sir," Capt. Yearwood said with a deep, rumbling laugh. "The major needs my ship has are firewood and water when we drop the 'hook'. I doubt we've used *half* of our six month's worth of provisions since we struck the Spanish coast."

"And if we, ah . . . take contributions' from the prizes that we torch," Commander Teague heartily agreed, "we wouldn't have to delve into our own stores much at all, hah hah!"

"Except for those sour wines the Frogs supply their soldiers," Commander Blamey said. "Bonaparte sets them a poor table, the miser."

"No word from Admiralty about more ships coming to aid us?" Capt. Chalmers enquired.

"Admiralty sent me a reply to my latest letter," Lewrie said. "Our Lords Commissioners regret our situation, they appreciated my suggestions for troopships, soldiers, and landing craft so we could raid, as well as take prizes, but . . . nothing will be available for some time. Oh, they think it'd be a *wondrous* idea, and they'll consider implementing it, but not for now. The needs of the Service preclude re-enforcement right *now*. They're coming, but not soon."

"Coming!" Yearwood growled, "so is bloody Christmas!"

"Oh, well," Commander Teague quipped, "the fewer of us, the greater the glory shared . . . and the profits."

"Frankly, had we just one more pair, a frigate and a sloop, I wouldn't mind sharing," Chalmers declared. "Not at all!"

"One day Out of Discipline, then, gentlemen," Lewrie decided, "to give our people their ease, if only a brief'un, and we must sail. We've given the French too long a break, and they're most-like makin' the most of it. With our army into Spain, and French armies scurryin' about like poked piglets, they'll be eatin' up supplies like . . . so many hogs, and anything we can deny them'd be more than welcome to Wellesley."

"Allow me to host a shore supper this time, sir," Chalmers offered. "Whilst our sailors are in rut, and full cry? It's always best, I've found, to be well away from all that. I may even take a night's lodging at one of the hotels in the Baixa district, just to get a good night's sleep, away from the din, hah hah!"

So you and your Chaplain won't be tempted t'sin? Lewrie asked himself; *Or catch yourself singin' along to "Sandman Joe"?*

"Same place as before? Would that suit you gentlemen?" Capt. Chalmers asked round the table. "Excellent! I shall make reservations for, oh . . . say seven tomorrow night?"

"What about our First Officers?" Commander Teague asked.

"Well, *someone* has to stay aboard and keep an eye on the revelry, after all," Chalmers said with a little laugh.

Their meeting in the dining-coach was interrupted by a sharp rap of a musket's brass-bound butt on the quarterdeck, and a cry that Midshipman Holbrooke was at the door.

"Damn my eyes," Lewrie grumbled, getting to his feet and going out to the day-cabin. "Enter!"

"Mister Kibworth's duty, sir," young Holbrooke said, his hat under his arm, "but there is a boat making its way to us from the store ship. With a mail sack, he believes, sir."

"Very well, thankee, Mister Holbrooke," Lewrie said. "Once it is aboard, fetch it here."

"Aye aye, sir," Holbrooke said, and bowed his way out.

"Mail d'ye say, Captain Lewrie?" Capt. Yearwood asked, poking his head round the partitions. "Did I hear right?"

"It seems to be, sir," Lewrie said, nodding, "though I thought we'd already gotten our latest. Did anyone see a mail packet enter port, the last day or so?"

As eagerly as letters from home were anticipated, even if they were bills from tradesmen, a London packet flying the "Post Boy" flag would have loudly been announced by the first to espy her, and no one had. All five officers grouped together before Lewrie's desk, awaiting the sack's arrival.

"Hope my wife's sent me some of her ginger snaps," Yearwood said. "I adore them, though one never knows their condition when they do come. Sogginess I can deal with, with a little re-baking, but if they're too long on-passage, I might as well break my teeth on deck planking. She means well."

"I can't remember the last time anyone sent me anything edible," Commander Teague said.

"Sweets and such," Chalmers dismissively commented. "They just draw the ship's rats, who end up eating the letters, too."

There was another rap of the musket, a stamp of boots, and a cry that Midshipman Kibworth was without.

"Mail, sir!" Kibworth said, his eyes alight. "Just in off one of the troop transports newly arrived. The messenger said that there was mail for all ships of the squadron."

"Capital!" Lewrie crowed, clapping his hands together. "Fetch it to my desk and we'll parcel it all out, this instant."

The sack was untied, and at least one hundred letters or small parcels got spread cross Lewrie's desk. For the next few minutes, it was very much like Christmas as five tarry-handed Commission Sea Officers pawed through the pile, separating out "presents" addressed to their own ships. Lewrie sent his clerk, Faulkes, and his steward, Pettus, to find some empty bread bags so the others could carry their, and their crews', mail back to their ships without stuffing them into every pocket or jamming theirs into their waist-bands.

"Oh, Mother, what were you thinking?" Commander Teague asked as he held up a soggy, dripping parcel wrapped in heavy butcher's paper. He sniffed at it, gave it a shake, and they all heard the chinking of what had been a stone crock of . . . "Honey?" Teague bemoaned. He looked about for someplace he could gingerly unwrap it, finally sat it atop one of those empty bread bags.

"That'll be your bag, I daresay," Commander Blamey teased.

"Oh, no!" Teague wailed. "She wrapped it in a new shirt she made me!"

"Not a total loss, Teague," Capt. Chalmers said, sniggering. "You can wring the honey out into a jar, and the shirt will wash out. A little hot water, a little soap, hah hah?"

"Might take two washings," Lewrie said, "before the flies, the wasps, and bees stop swarmin' ye."

"Oh, but once at sea, that'll be no problem," Yearwood japed, "you'll only have your own ship's rats to worry about!"

Sapphire's pile was substantial, and Lewrie, not waiting for Faulkes to sort it out for officers, petty officers, Mids, and hands, pawed through for anything addressed to him in the faint hope that a newer despatch from Admiralty might have come to supercede the bleak reply that he had just briefed his officers about.

He pursed his lips and frowned; there was nothing from Admiralty, not even a promotions list or an update to charts that they'd not use in this commission. "Nothing new from Admiralty," he told the others. "Oh, well. We're still 'on our own bottoms', it seems.

"Faulkes, I'd admire did you sort our mail out for everyone else. Set my own on the desk, and I'll read it later," he ordered.

"Yes, sir," the ever-dutiful clerk replied, scooping up a pile, and finding that Teague's crock of honey had tainted their mail, had tainted everyone else's, with sticky spots here and there. Faulkes sniffed at his fingers, and almost looked as if he would lick them.

"Well, I'm happy that I could give you all an un-looked-for treat," Lewrie told them, "and I'm certain that you wish to return to your ships to distribute your people's mail, and enjoy your own. No ginger snaps, Captain Yearwood? Ah well, the year's still young. Good luck with that shirt, Commander Teague. I will show you to the quarterdeck. Easy Pendant hoisted tomorrow at Eight Bells of the Morning Watch, supper at seven? Capital!"

He stood by the starboard entry-port as they departed in order of seniority, doffing his hat in salute as the side-party and Bosun Terrell rendered departure honours.

"Mail, sir?" Lt. Harcourt asked, rubbing his hands.

"Mail, aye, Mister Harcourt," Lewrie said, in a rush to enter his cabins and tear open his own. "Take joy!" he shouted over his shoulder as he closed the cabin door.

Again, there was no letter from his eldest son, Sewallis, not even a brief plea for spending money, which he'd usually send to his grandfather, Sir Hugo, anyway. There were no bills due to any hatters, tailors, shoemakers, or chandlers, either, for a rare, blessed once, for all his accounts were squared.

There was a new one from his father, Sir Hugo, boasting of his new attire, and how delightful the start of the London Season was.

> . . . *scads of young, eager Not-So-Lovelies in Town with their gimlet-eyed Mamas looking for a Match made in Heaven, or at the Bank of England. Damn my neighbours, for they have let their house next door to mine to a fubsey clan of Midlands cotton Barons, rich as anything, but "Country-Puts" with TWO daughters out at the same time, both doomed, from what I can observe of them, to spend the Season in gilt chairs along the wall of the dance hall. And what a noisy fuss it is, morning to late night with their comings and goings, the parade of dress-makers, milliners, tailors, deliverymen and coaches, and I fear it will go on 'til the Thames begins to reek in August. Your Charlotte is not among them, thank God, for I'm certain that your brother-in-law Governour would try to shame me into putting them all up at my house. And you KNOW how I like my privacy!*

"Damned near shooed me off with a broom, he did," Lewrie said under his breath. "And I wasn't there *that* long."

I fear I put Governour's nose out of join by refusing his request that I use what influence I still possess, as a Knight of the Garter, to have Charlotte presented at Court, which is as ridiculous as my wealthy neighbours letting their house for a little MORE money!

"Gawd, Governour's gotten *high* above himself," Lewrie growled. "We ain't in the peerage. What'd he *expect?*"

Sir Hugo expressed much the same, though he did say that the old *New Peerage* had added the *Baronetage* back in 1800, after Mister Almon turned his bookseller and stationer business over to someone named Debrett. His father had bought a copy, just to see Lewrie's name in it, from the store cross from Burlington House on Piccadilly.

. . . went to White's with an old army Companion, and who did I see but Beau Brummell, in full fig! The Prince of Wales was there, too, and for once he did NOT resemble a corpulent Ottoman Pasha or Moghul Emperor! Prinny the peacock, while still stouter than most breeding bulls, has transformed from a Fashion Disaster as gaudy and colourful as a whole pack of Hindoo women to a Brummell-ite, as sobrely dressed as a parson in "dominee ditto"! Black is the new standard, along with dark blues or forest greens, and what Beau Brummell terms Trousers. Intrigued, I dropped by Meyer & Mortimer in Sackville St. and got shoved into a pair or two, along with the requisite black cutaway coat, white waistcoat, top hat, and white silk neckstock. The trousers fit over the whole leg, with a strap that goes under the arch of one's boots or shoes, and I must say it's a dashing look. Wigs are becoming outmoded, and damn old Pitt and his wig powder tax, for I still must use mine. It seems everyone is wearing Brummell's new dark colours, too, so much so that they begin to look Uniformed! It's all of a piece with this damned new Respectability thing, the Modesty, the Puritanical Earnestness that Wilberforce and Hannah More and their ilk have shoved down our throats. I'm tempted to go out in my old 19th Native Infantry mess dress, just to stand out from what resembles a parade of Arctic Penguins!

His father was considering a long month or so on his estate at Anglesgreen, where he could ride without trampling the summer mobs, for Rotten Row along Hyde Park was becoming impossible with so many brides-to-be and possible suitors crowding it. He had gotten a note from Will Cony, Lewrie's old Cox'n, then Bosun for a short time, saying that the winter's beer was tasty, there was a glut of spring lambs, and, knowing Sir Hugo's penchant for lamb, thought he might drop by the Old Ploughman for a good meal or two. There were strawberries, asparagus, watercress, and his father waxed eloquent on the first of the new potatoes and cucumbers.

All that writing about the freshness of an English garden and its yield almost made Lewrie's mouth water. Ah, but there were plenty of greens to be had ashore in Lisbon.

Surprisingly, Lewrie had letters from Viscount Percy Stangbourne and his other brother-in-law, Burgess Chiswick, the one he liked. It was an odd quirk of Fate, but Percy's self-raised regiment of Light Dragoons, which had been badly winnowed of both troopers and horses on the cruel retreat to Corunna late last year, was now replenished with mounts, weapons, and saddlery, fully re-enlisted and up to top strength. Percy was delighted to announce that he and his regiment would be coming to Lisbon within the next month, and he was as eager as anything to have a proper bash at the French in warmer campaigning weather, this time.

The quirk came when he opened Burgess's letter and discovered that his regiment of Foot had also received orders for Portugal and Spain. Hard as it would be to leave Theodora and the children, three of them now, two strapping boys and a delightful little girl, he had been preparing his officers and his troops for years, he and one or two officers in the mess the only ones who had seen action, his with the East India Company army, and the others who had been part of the invasion of Copenhagen under General Sir Arthur Wellesley a few years back.

"Burgess with three gits?" Lewrie gawped aloud. "Where *does* the time go?" He remembered Theodora, a luscious black-haired, blue-eyed unmarried girl when he'd been introduced at her parents' house, where he had met William Wilberforce, who offered to help him with legal bills when the Beaumans of Jamaica had hauled him into court over the "theft" of a dozen of their slaves to man his disease-ridden ship.

"Wonder if she's turned into a fubsey?" he muttered, for three children usually fattened most women.

One letter left, and it was from Miss Jessica Chenery!

"What more does she have t'write me about?" he muttered as he broke the wax seal and spread it out. He was intrigued, though.

Dear Cptn Lewrie,

I have just received the latest letter from my brother, Charlie, who informs me that you are making a rich young Man of him, with all the Prizes that he says have been taken of late! He also informs me that he has mostly survived the Antics played upon him by his Messmates, some of them involving Crudities best not detailed to a Sister, or my Father, either, for I fear that he would worry about his decision to send Charlie to sea even more.

I do not know and can only imagine how grand is the great City of Lisbon, which beggars my brother's ability to relate, but he does sing its praises of the few times he has been allowed ashore, and how it soars to the Heavens in tier upon tier like an immense Cake, and how brilliantly it glows after dark, when seen from your ship. How fortunate you both are, Sir, to have gone and seen so many exotic Foreign Places, the like of which I can only Envy!

She, along with his father, related how marvellous the Spring and early Summer was in London, and how welcome were the long-gone delights just re-appearing at the greengrocers'; young rhubarb down from Yorkshire, sweet fingerling carrots, the first cucumbers, and the cress, onion, lettuce, and cabbage sprouts, the parsley and new potatoes which could cause riots, so eager were winter-deprived Londoners to snatch them up by the bushel. Her favourites, Jessica happily wrote, were the shrimp dredged from Morecambe Bay, the Cromer crabs from Norfolk; oysters, of course, and Cornish or Scottish lobsters. She even sounded delighted with cockles, mussels, and periwinkles, though she wished that smoked salmon wasn't so dear. The wartime prices were horrendous.

The Illustrations I was commissioned to do for a childrens' Book have been accepted, and, in the course of delivering them the other day, I met a Man well-known to you, Sir, a Mr. Aspinall, the Assistant Publisher of the firm. I saw his previous Titles on Knots, nautical Songs, and Seamanship for beginners, and upon mentioning that my Brother could use them, he enquired which ship he was in, and which Captain, and Mr. Aspinall shewed me the Dedication he had written for his first Book which featured a most Flattering description of you and your Exploits! I must say that his description of your early Career, briefly summarised though it was, sounded most Adventurous and Impressive; which account I told to my Father that evening, who was also amazed. Mr. Aspinall swore he would write you, straightaway, of his doings since leaving your service and bade me to send you his Respects. A very decent man, I daresay, is he.

Jessica went on to tell him that her commissioned portrait for a Bond Street merchant had been received so well that the man had asked her to do a portrait of his daughter, as well, and, upon displaying it at his shop, had drawn the interest of one of his customers from Hatchard's, a bookseller on Piccadilly, who wished to have his portrait done, too! And that fellow was a member of the Royal Horticultural Society, which might result in her, her father's, and Madame Pellantan's invitation to the annual flower show, which was one of the finer events of the London Season.

"Not for me it ain't," Lewrie sniggered aloud. "Flowers and such, hah. Not that it'll catch you a husband, either, poor chit. You ain't dowried deep enough, but . . . who knows?"

. . . we have tried to put our heads together to come up with something to send to Charlie other than one more Letter, something that he really needs, but he gives us no Clue. Might small pots of jam, mustard, or a packet of sweet bisquit go down well, or might he need a new shirt, or some stockings? If it would be no Difficulty, could we beg to prevail upon your Knowledge and advise us as to what would be most Welcome?

"Certainly not honey," he said with a laugh. And yes, he would write her back. Jessica Chenery's letters were becoming a welcome delight.

"Honey, sir?" Pettus asked as he brought Lewrie a tall glass of his sweet, cool tea with a dollop of lemon juice.

"Midshipman Chenery's sister asks me to suggest something the family might send him, something that he needs," Lewrie told him.

"Certainly *not* honey, then, sir," Pettus said, grinning, "or anything else breakable. From what I see of his appearance on watch, new stocks and shirts would suit him better. Miss Chenery is the one who did that sketch of you, sir?"

"Aye, she is," Lewrie agreed.

"A most attractive young lady, if I may say so, sir," Pettus commented. "Quite talented, too. Perhaps she's set her cap for you, sir . . . so she can paint your picture when you're back in England?"

"Set her . . . ?" Lewrie said with a scowl, looking up at Pettus, but he'd donned his "invisible, inscrutable servant" mask and was half-way cross the great-cabins on another errand. "Ridiculous! And damned desperate if she has . . . set her cap for the likes o' me."

He knew just what Pettus intended, though.

Without a husband, it was almost impossible for an English woman with any pretensions to even modest gentility to have a life, and young women without prospects, handsome features, or pleasing frames, and especially those without attractive dowries, usually ended up as some family's governess or nanny, "old maiden aunt" housekeeper for luckier relatives, or even suffered the shame of entering domestic service as some more-fortunate lady's personal maid!

Just like the Mamas his father had described in his latest letter, the better-off gone up to London to ferret out suitable matches. It was a family's prime task to get their daughters married off, assuring them a comfortable and secure life, whether they were happy about it or not. In some cases, it was more a business or political alliance that got arranged, not a love-match.

Despite her seeming ability to support herself with her talent for painting and drawing, was Jessica Chenery any different than any other English lass, raised from their first frock gown to expect to be wed? What else were all the lessons in music, singing, dancing, sewing, and "housewifely" skills for but preparation for the eventual role of wife, mother, hostess, house mistress, and pleasing companion to some man of her social station, or hopefully, a cut or two above?

The young lady was working at several dis-advantages; firstly, was her lack of a Mama, who had passed over some years before, and was not there to guide, poke, prod and steer her into the narrow lane of Acceptability, possibly far away from making a living on her own.

Secondly, there was her father, the Reverend Chenery, who had not struck Lewrie as the Captain of the "Chenery Ship". A slender reed, that'un, too much the book-ish student of natural history and antiquarianism, most-like led by his brother by the nose, if Midshipman Chenery's comments were to be believed. The man had expensive hobbies, with little to spare for the lad's kitting-out, or Jessica's dowry, or paraphernalia.

Trousseaus and hope chests; did she have them? Of course she did, Lewrie was certain. To not amass the necessities was like a girl child who didn't have a single doll! And, she had sisters, *married* sisters, along with girlhood friends who had preceded her to the altar, and an host of young ladies in her father's parish who wed before her eyes.

That Leftenant Beauchamp she'd mentioned in her first letter to him; had she not implied that they were close to becoming affianced? Whether that was true, or really Jessica's hopes, he had no way of knowing.

Damme, did I impress her that *much?* he asked himself, feeling a bit of pride that he might have appeared to be a "catch", even at his age; *And just what* did *Aspinall tell her about me? Did he mention that I'm a widower?*

It was possible that her brother had learned of his situation since he'd joined the ship, and had written her about it.

He had to face the fact that, on the surface anyway, he looked to be a desirable possibility; Post-Captain and temporary Commodore, with a knighthood and a Baronetcy (no matter how ludicrously that had been awarded) shoals of prize-money, a reputation as a fighting Captain with the honourable scars to prove it, rather handsome (if he did say so, himself), and still lean and fit and able to wear the same size breeches as he had when a Midshipman, with lots of his own hair left on his head, and the majority of his teeth remaining, and those mostly in front so he could still smile without frightening children. Add to that the fact that he had been a widower for several years, and all of his children were mostly grown and no longer underfoot, and . . .

His summary of his assets made him feel smug for a moment, but then reality struck. He imagined her shock should she ever learn of his past doings, and what she would make of his kin; Sewallis, prim and prudish, his father's evil leering nature, his daughter's hatred of him or any one he might take up with, and even his brother-in-law, Governour Chiswick's, barely-masked derision.

Run screamin' for the exits, most-like, he glumly thought.

And, there was the problem of, if she indeed had "set her cap for him", did he really wish to be caught? Since his wife, Caroline, had died, he actually had no need of a wife, or time spared from the war to go in search of one. Being a widower, being free to do what he chose when the Navy allowed, felt quite natural, a late bachelorhood.

Now if the long war with France ever ended, and he was cast upon the shore on half-pay, well, maybe. But, did he dare risk becoming a foolish, doting old "colt's tooth", sure to wear a cuckhold's horns as soon as the shine wore off, or he was called to sail out of sight?

Could he actually keep his breeches buttoned, his hands to himself, and cleave to one woman the rest of his natural life?

"Ridiculous," he muttered.

Yet he took out a fresh sheet of paper, opened the ink-well, and dipped his pen into it to begin a letter in reply, if only to advise against anything edible or breakable.

He did not notice that he hummed "Pleasant and Delightful" as he did so.

CHAPTER THIRTY-FIVE

*T*he supper party which Capt. Chalmers had hosted had gone well, as happily boisterous as an Old Boy reunion. The crews of the squadron's ships had had their one-day rut, and, with all provisions replenished right down to spare mustard pots, Lewrie had intended to hoist a signal for them to Weigh the next morning, but the weather had other ideas, for a stiff Westerly had roared down upon the mouth of the Tagus that very morning, a "dead muzzler" that sent waves crashing on the Praia do Guincho, the beaches of Caparica, and sent steep rollers surging into the river's mouth, meeting the regular out-flow in a tangling, churning, white-foamed maelstrom. Along with that wind had come a torrent of rain.

Lewrie had a signal made, the word "Tomorrow" spelled out letter by letter, and then summoned his boat crew. If he was penned in port one more day, he could at least take advantage of it and go have one last bath at that *bagnio,* then hunt up Maddalena for a last day with her. Before he made his way uphill, he popped into Mountjoy's lair, on the off chance that she might be there. Mountjoy was not in, out on some hush-hush work, but Mr. Deacon, when asked, had no news from any quarter, and nothing of the movements of Wellesley's columns.

Much like the old days at Gibraltar, Maddalena was out on her balcony with a fine view of the street as he trudged up to her place from the *bagnio,* and gave him an enthusiastic wave and a blown kiss.

"You look drenched," Maddalena said, finding a place to hang up his sodden boat cloak and cocked hat. "What a horrible morning."

"Oh, fairly dry, really," Lewrie told her, "I got wetter at the *bagnio,* a good, long hot soak. Feel like a new man, I do."

"So, you do not sail today?" she asked, puttering round at her modest cooking facility to put on some fresh coffee.

"Tomorrow, if the weather clears, and the winds shift," he idly said as he sat down on her settee. "Well, hallo, Precious, and how are you, puss? Can't go out on the balcony and watch the birds?"

Maddalena's white-and-tan cat came to sniff at his extended finger, found tarry nautical smells attractive as he always did, discovered the aroma of the *bagnio*'s soap and *eau de cologne,* and a tinge of Chalky on Lewrie's coat and breeches, and leapt into his lap to curl up and accept some stroking and chin rubs.

"I have no milk or cream," Maddalena said, coming to sit with him as the water began to boil. She put an arm on the back of the settee and toyed with his hair. "Black coffee, sorry."

"On a day like this, I'll not send you out to get it, either," Lewrie told her. "Though, we could send old Rubio on an errand."

"Oh, he'd never go," she said with a laugh, tossing her head back for a second, then scooped her cat off Lewrie's lap and held him up for a minute to touch noses and kiss his head before settling him down in her lap. "He would give off clouds of steam where the rain hit him. Rubio is outraged, you see, *meu amor.*" She leaned into him to impart a secret. "Two more young ladies have lately moved in here, both, ah . . . protected by British army officers, and he thinks that the house is becoming scandalous, nothing like it used to be before the French, or the British, came."

Lewrie turned and raised his head to give her a rather chaste peck on her lips. "That's what armies do, *minha dose* . . . piss in the soup. Look at what we've done to the prices, after all?"

"Oh, do not get me started on what things now cost," she said with another toss of her head, this one more impatient.

"D'ye need a little more spending money?" he asked.

"No, *meu amor*, I am doing fine," she fondly assured him.

Well, ain't this . . . domestic? he thought; *We'll be readin' the newspapers and takin' a nap, next!*

"Alan, would you be a dear and grind the beans?" she asked him. "There is not enough already prepared for a full pot, just my one or two cups in the morning."

Damme, what'd I tell ye, he thought.

"Well, if I must," he said with an exaggerated groan as he rose from the settee and went into the cooking area. He found the grinder, he found a sack of roasted beans after some fumbling among her stores, but then was stuck. He'd *seen* it done, but he had no idea how many beans to grind; would one pass be good enough, or might he have to give them a second pass to make them the size of mealed gunpowder?

"How many beans make a pot?" he asked her.

"Hmm, at least two handfuls," she told him from her ease on the settee, still stroking her cat.

"Big handfuls?" he had to ask, shoving his fingers into the sack.

"Yes, *meu amor* . . . big handfuls," she replied, sounding amused. "I will make it up to you."

Rather have some wine, anyway, he thought, scooping out the requisite handfuls into the hopper, closing it, and grinding away. After a peek into the lower receptacle drawer, he poured the results back in the hopper and ground away some more.

"Twice through good enough?" he asked. "Now I pour 'em in the boiling water?"

"Ah! Men! You are so helpless," Maddalena cried, expasperated, and rose from the settee to come to the stove inset with her cat in her arms. With one hand she shoved more kindling under the grill and lifted the lid of the pot to see if the water was boiling properly, opened the receptacle drawer to pinch at the ground beans, nodded in acceptance, and pronounced the task properly done. "And, if you will pare some sugar off the cone in the caddy, we will be almost ready."

Gahh! Lewrie thought.

Once the water was boiling nicely, she took over, setting the cat down, getting down a serving pot, pouring the grounds into a wire filter, and slowly pouring the water over them. "Mister Mountjoy let me have his latest copy of one of his London magazines, the *Tatler?* It is on the dining table. You might like to read it and catch up on what is happening in your country. I will fetch the coffee. Take the sugar and put it in the bowl on the table, would you?"

There was no litter of newspapers, snippets cut out, or false articles on the table, this time; perhaps rainy days brought the work of Secret Branch to a full stop, and left Maddalena with nothing to do. Lewrie sat down and began to read the magazine, flipping pages idly through Royal Household court circulars, the results of the Eton-Harrow cricket match, who had won recognition from the Royal Academy's art exposition, and accounts of the many balls, and who was who and who wasn't, and some hints of gloriously titillating scandals.

"It is very amusing," Maddalena said, coming to the table with her modest coffee service. "London sounds like a grand city, even if you English seem to enjoy your scandals."

"Oh, it is, and we do!" Lewrie agreed, perking up as he spooned sugar into his cup. "Ever wish to see it?"

"Oh, no, *meu amor*," Maddalena said with a little laugh. "From what I read of it, it sounds too cold and wet for someone like me, and from what I hear from the many English I meet in the streets, in the markets, who do not know I understand English, it does not sound too welcoming to people from other countries. I am happy here, being a Lisboêta. What does this mean here, about the cricket? What is a century, and what does it mean to be 'all out'? This is a game or a sport? It makes no sense to me."

They spent a good part of the morning poring over the *Tatler*, with Lewrie explaining the terms and customs which would have been an enigma to anyone not brought up English. Stripped down to his shirt, he drew a diagram of a pitch, the wicket, and how one pitched, and how one batted to protect one's wicket, and how many points could be made from a good swat far out into the un-groomed outfields by running back and forth from one end to the other, acting out parts of it.

Rain continued to lash the city, driving in beneath the canvas awning, the wind setting it fluttering and ballooning, some squalls so thick that the view of the river was blocked out.

"Ah, no more coffee," she said at last, pouring the last few dribbles into their cups. "Whatever shall we do with such a gloomy day?"

"Open a bottle of *espumante*, if there's one left?" Lewrie suggested.

"Yes, let's do," Maddalena agreed, "and then I think that such a day is best spent snug in bed," she said with a coy, promising grin.

"That's my girl!" Lewrie quickly agreed. "Where's your cork-pull?"

⚓

The rain let up late that afternoon, and the winds moderated, allowing them to rise, dress, and go out for supper, yet another very toothsome treat over which they lingered, long after the last plates had been whisked away, a mood which Lewrie searched his memory for the *bon mot*, the French word he'd heard . . . and it came to him.

Tristesse.

She had declared that she would not leave her beloved Lisbon and follow him to Oporto, though shifting his base of operations to there seemed to be right out. She had shrugged off, laughed off, his tongue-in-cheek mention of seeing London, someday, too, perhaps fearful of more than cold and rain and wet, but of being a foreigner in an un-welcoming country.

They had spent the better part of the day in bed, making love passionately, and often, snuggled up close between bouts, cooing and sighing, but with very little meaningful conversation, as if she had a sense that their relationship, pleasing thought it was, was coming to its eventual end. Lewrie damned himself for *ever* mentioning a move to Oporto! They had a touch too much to drink at the eatery, and had a final coffee with brandy, and then it was time to escort Maddalena back to her lodgings.

Too late in the evening for him to go abovestairs with her for one more moment of passion, they had to say their goodbyes in the dim lobby, she with her key already in hand. They held each other in a long embrace, shared a long, lingering kiss, then she leaned back to gaze him in the eyes for another long moment without speaking, as if she was fixing him in her memory, Lewrie could conjure.

"*Ir com Deus*, Alan," she whispered, at last. "Go with God and be safe."

"See you when I get back," he promised, playing up game despite an icy sense of foreboding that he wouldn't.

"I will always love you, *meu querido*," she said, touching his lips with a finger, and then she was gone, up the stairs with her gown and cloak swishing along the flagstoned steps.

And she didn't look back.

Well, damme, he gloomily thought; *I think I've just been sent packing. She thinks we're done, there's no talkin' her out of it. If I know anything about women, I know that for sure.*

He stepped out from the lodging's lobby into the mist and took a moment to look up at her balcony, but the drapes were drawn over all the windows, and not a crack of light showed. He stood there for a long minute or so, then shrugged himself deeper into his boat cloak and turned to walk away downhill. At the corner, he did stop and look back to see a faint streak of amber light between the curtain panels of her main room, the glow of a single candle, but she was not looking out.

Goddamn it, he thought; *This bein' rejected is gettin' old . . . First Lydia Stangbourne, and now Maddalena! Where'd I go wrong, what'd I do t'cause that?*

There was no point in lingering like a heart-sick swain; he'd not play Romeo below Juliet's window. He turned and trudged down to the Baixa's level streets, to the Praça do Comércio to hunt up a boatman that could row him out to *Sapphire.*

People might have said that he took the salute of the yawning side-party a bit more gruffly than usual, that he did not take a final hopping step inboard from the lip of the entry-port. One of his Marine sentries might have noticed that he did not say "Good evening" to him as he raised his musket in salute, but entered his cabins without a word.

There was one overhead lanthorn lit in the day-cabin, and one mobile candlestand going to see him to the bed-space. Jessop had retired, but Pettus was half-awake, slumped over the dining table, and he roused himself when the Bosuns' calls shrilled, and the Marine stamped boots outside the door.

"Ah, good evening, sir," Pettus said, stifling a yawn of his own. "Can I get you anything before you retire?" he asked as he collected Lewrie's hat, boat cloak, and sword belt.

"A large whisky if we have any left," Lewrie told him, tearing his neck-stock loose, shrugging out of his coat and waist-coat. "I will see myself to bed, Pettus. You go turn in."

"Aye, sir," Pettus replied, gathering up the cast-offs first, then heading to the wine cabinet to pour a glass of whisky.

Lewrie sat on a chest to pull off his boots and stockings, got his shirt off, and undid his breeches. Chalky came yawning and making some welcome mews, stretching then leaping atop the hanging bed-cot to wait for his master to join him, tail erect and curling.

Pettus brought the whisky, then bowed himself out of the bed-space, dowsing the overhead lanthorn and wishing Lewrie a good night on his way out to the quarterdeck, and his hammock below on the upper gun deck, leaving Lewrie alone for the night.

Lewrie sat on the chest, again to drink his whisky, welcoming the burn of aged American corn brew, right down to "heel-taps", then blew out the candle and fumbled his way into his bed-cot. The night was just warm enough, yet damp and dank, to slip under the sheet and push the coverlet down. Chalky got tangled in that for a bit, uttered a carping sound of displeasure, then came up to get his head rubbed, butting and pawing for attention before settling down in the crook of Lewrie's left arm.

"That's alright, then," Lewrie whispered in the dark, "at least *you* still love me, don't ye, puss?"

It didn't seem as if anyone else did.

CHAPTER THIRTY-SIX

"Your breakfast is ready, sir," Yeovill announced after he had laid everything from the galley on the sideboard in the dining coach.

"Be right there," Lewrie told him over his shoulder as he wiped the last shaving soap from his cheeks, and splashed fresh water over his whole face.

The last steady shave, Lewrie thought; *The last liberal use of water. A pint a day, from now on.* In a heavy sea, the sort expected off the North coast of Spain most days, even a heavy and solid ship like *Sapphire* could heave, hobby-horse, and roll, making shaving nigh suicidal, an exercise in balance and contortion worthy of a circus acrobat.

"Omelet with onion, peppers, and cheese, sir," Yeovill said as he lifted the lid of the brass food barge, "spicy pepper sausages, potato hash, and tomato slices. Fresh shore toast, butter churned no later than last afternoon, and a Lisbon version of lemon marmalade."

"Excellent, Yeovill!" Lewrie said, impatient for the loaded plate to be set before him. "You indeed do me proud."

"Purser's Clerk and I fetched back three of those *porco preto* cured hams, sir," Yeovill went on as he slid the plate in front of his starving Captain, "though I could only find chickens, no rabbits or quail, for the forecastle manger, and piglets are as rare on the market as unicorns, sorry."

"Oh, I imagine I'll cope," Lewrie told him. "Truth be told, a steady diet of rabbit and quail has lost its lustre. Ah, perfection!" he pronounced his first bite of his omelet.

"I was told, sir," Pettus said, pouring him a cup of coffee, "that the King of France got himself caught when he tried to escape from Paris, before they 'shortened' him on the guillotine. He stopped for supper on the road to Calais, 'tis said, dressed common, and when the waiter asked what he'd like, he said 'omelet; and bread', but then they asked how many eggs in his omelet, and he said . . . never knowing the first thing about cooking . . .'oh, a dozen?' and that's when they sent for the soldiers."

" 'Let 'em eat cake', indeed," Lewrie chuckled, his mouth full. "A very rich and eggy cake, hah!"

He would never admit that, much like yesterday when he did not know how many beans made a pot of coffee, or how to grind them, cookery . . . cooking for himself . . . was a mystery as deep as Egyptian hieroglyphics. The less said of that, the better, and so long as he had Yeovill's skilled services, he would never have to learn.

Yeovill set a bowl of cut-up sausages and potato hash at the far end of the table for a yowling, demanding Chalky, another, larger, bowl near the cabin door for Bisquit, who was only a bit less impatient, and bowed his way out, saying that he would be back for the food barge later.

Lewrie looked round whilst chewing a bite of one of those spicy sausages, and wondered just how much food was in that brass barge. It had always struck him that Pettus, Jessop, his clerk Mr. Faulkes, and Yeovill always looked so sleek and well-fed, better-off than they might had they subsisted on issued rations alone. Once he went out on deck, he imagined a quick, bolting feed off the more than ample "leftovers"! And surely, Yeovill would have to taste whatever he prepared, several tastes, as he cooked, and lay aside a plate for himself before coming aft. He might even share with Mr. Tanner, the Ship's Cook, who could barely manage "boiled to death" everything.

"Lovely morning, sir," Pettus said as he topped up the coffee. "Bright and clear as anything."

"Windy, still, but not a 'dead muzzler', aye," Lewrie agreed. "We'll sail by Eight Bells. Make sure everything's secure."

"Yes, sir," Pettus replied.

"Did those new casks of dry sand come aboard?" Lewrie asked.

"Yes, sir," Pettus told him, "stowed away below in the spare cabin off the wardroom, but for the one in the starboard quarter gallery. Chalky will have fresh litter for at least two more months."

The cat raised his head from his bowl at the mention of his name, licked his chops, sat back to groom with his front paws, then paced down to Lewrie's end of the table, sniffing at other possible things to eat.

"Go on, Chalky, shoo," Lewrie grumbled, "ye haven't eaten a quarter of your food. I know you and your tricks."

So did Bisquit, who took Chalky's abandonment of his breakfast as an opportunity to hop up into the end chair and gobble up what the cat had left in his bowl, licking the last bits of egg and hash from it, sending the bowl crashing to the deck. Chalky flinched, crouched, saw what he had lost, and dashed back to defend his food, but much too late. He hissed and spat, bottled up sideways, to no avail. With a particularly mournful *yowl* he slunk back to Lewrie, sat down on his haunches, and uttered a pitiful wee *mew*.

"Oh, here then," Lewrie said with a put-upon sigh as he handed Chalky the tail-end of a sausage.

"Don't know who's spoiled worse, sir, 'im 'r th' dog," Jessop said, tittering.

"Ah, that was delicious," Lewrie commented after a last bite of toast, heavily buttered and smeared with the marmalade. He dabbed at his mouth, took one last swig of coffee. "I'll be out on deck."

"Good morning, sir," Lt. Westcott said, doffing his hat with one hand, and the other holding his post-breakfast *cigarro*.

"Good morning, Mister Westcott," Lewrie returned, "good morning, all," he added to Lieutenants Harcourt and Elmes, and the Sailing Master Mr. Yelland. "Breakfasted well, have you? And, ready for another go at the French? Good, good. I'd admire that you have all hands piped to Stations five minutes before Eight Bells, and a signal bent on for all ships to Weigh hoisted now." He pulled his pocket watch out and studied its face; it was a quarter-hour shy of eight A.M.

"The ship is ready for sea in all respects, sir," Lt. Westcott assured him, attempting to blow lazy smoke rings before the appointed time, when he would have to toss it overboard. "Damme, I only seem to be good at that indoors," he said, watching his efforts waft alee rather quickly.

"Signal is hoisted, sir," Midshipman Carey reported, "and all ships have hoisted a matching reply."

"Very good, Mister Carey," Lewrie acknowledged. "We'll pay off Southerly, Mister Yelland?" Lewrie asked the Sailing Master.

"Aye, sir," Yelland agreed, taking a moment to study the commissioning pendant aloft, and the feel of the morning breeze on his cheeks. "Bags of room to pay off to larboard and come about, though we'll be hard on the wind to hug the Northern shore and get out of the river mouth on one tack. Once fully under way, nothing to larb'd."

"Ehm . . . time, sir," Westcott prompted, his own watch out.

"Carry on, sir," Lewrie said. "Pipe hands to Stations."

Westcott bellowed that order forward to the Bosun and his Mate, and a moment later, the "Spithead Nightingales", as their silver calls were termed, shrilled, and HMS *Sapphire* thundered as hundreds of shod, or bare, sailors' feet drummed up from below, some hands ascending the masts ready to man the yards, free harbour gaskets, and make sail whilst others stood by the clews, jib or yard halliards and braces to draw the loosed canvas down, hoist the jibs and stays'ls, or raise the tops'l or t'gallant yards up off their rests. Down below on the main capstan, even more sailors stood ready to breast to the bars and walk it round to bring in the messenger which would be nipped to the anchor cable by ships' boys.

Lewrie looked forward, watch still in his hand, to observe the boys at the ship's bell in the forecastle belfry eying the last grains of sand run out from their glasses, and . . .

Ting-ting . . . ting-ting . . . ting-ting . . . ting-ting. Eight A.M. Eight Bells of the Morning Watch was struck, and began the Forenoon.

"Strike the hoist!" Lewrie bellowed aft, and down came that flag signal, which meant Execute, and all five ships of the squadron drummed again, to the rapid clanking of pawls in their capstans as the slack in their cables were brought in-board to be fed down and be draped on the cable tiers right forward, soaking wet and reeking of fish and mud.

The rapid clanking of the pawls slowed as *Sapphire* was hauled up closer to where the best bower had splashed to the river bottom a few days before, the anchor cable's angle becoming almost parallel to the middle or main top-mast stays'l. Men dug in their feet to the oak decks, squared their shoulders, and pushed harder, breasted to the bars.

"Short stays!" came the cry from the forecastle as the angle of the cable steepened. The flukes of the bower had not had time to set deep, to take firm root in the bed of the Tagus, yet the clanking of the pawls got even slower, no longer a drum-roll but an irregular metallic *clunk* more like the beats on a symphony's kettle drum.

"Up and down, sir!" Midshipman Ward shouted aft as the anchor cable went almost vertical.

"Dig in for the heavy heave!" Lt. Westcott roared through his brass speaking-trumpet, and men at the capstan roared and grunted as they made the effort for one more . . . *clank* . . . *clank* . . . *clank,* then a sudden rapid rattle.

"Anchor's free!" Ward yelled, waving his hat in triumph as if he'd done it all by himself, and the head of the anchor stock boiled to the surface in a welter of muddy, discoloured water. "And awash!"

"Make sail, Mister Westcott!" Lewrie snapped, feeling his ship sidle and begin to swing free to starboard. "Jibs, stays'ls, fore and main tops'ls, and spanker!"

"Trice up, lay out, and make sail!" Westcott bellowed as the ship swung wider, her bows which had been facing the river current sweeping the jib-boom and bowsprit towards the South bank as narrow-cut triangular foretopmast stays'l and the inner and outer flying jib rose up far forward, and the stays'ls between the foremast and main, and the main t'gallant stays'l 'twixt the main and mizen blossomed first. The spanker cracked open to the wind over the poop deck with a whoosh, and pulley blocks squealed as the tops'l yards inched up from their rests and the freed squares'ls were drawn down to spread open to cup wind. Falling off the wind and bringing the ship under control would require wearing about, pivotting round to take the wind on her starboard side in as short a distance as could be managed, and the yards braced up taut.

"Respondin' t'helm, sir," the lead Quartermaster, Marlowe, sang out, heaving away on the spokes in a blur as *Sapphire* got a way on at last.

"Hands to the braces, hands to the sheets!" Lt. Westcott bellowed, "harden up full and by!"

Up forward, the bower anchor was being hoisted up right to the out-jutting larboard cat-head beam, a line snatched round one fluke to ring it up so it could be "fished" and secured. The wood-and-leather hawse buckler stood ready to be inserted in the larboard hawse hole as soon as the thigh-thick cable was detached from the anchor stock.

"And what's the rank of the senior officer present?" Lewrie asked to be reminded.

"Rear-Admiral of the Red, sir," Midshipman Fywell crisply replied.

"Pass word to the Master Gunner," Lewrie ordered, "prepare to fire honours for a Rear-Admiral of the Red. Watch your luff, Quartermaster. Nothing to larboard."

"Aye, sir! Nought to larboard!" Marlowe said, cranking down a spoke or two.

"Four knots, sir!" came a cry from the taffrails.

"Very well!" Lewrie shouted back. He heaved a deep breath and let it out slowly. His ship was under full control and under way, and making her way to sea, and nothing had gone smash . . . yet. He went up to the poop deck to watch the progress of the other ships of the squadron. There they were, *Undaunted* a bit over a cable astern, hoisting a bit more canvas to close the distance; *Sterling* close under Captain Chalmers's stern and backing a fore tops'l to avoid running her bow into Chalmers's great-cabin windows, and *Peregrine* and *Blaze* a bit off to *Sapphire*'s starboard quarter, shaking themselves out into a separate pair, in-line-ahead. They would establish the pearls-on-a-string one cable's separation once far enough offshore.

Guns roared in a muted fashion, steady as a metronome, reduced saluting charges barely driving the guns back to the full extent of the breeching ropes, and rotten-egg-reeking clouds of yellow-white powder smoke swirled round *Sapphire* as the honours were rendered.

Ashore, there were stevedores and military waggoners, and men from the Commissary and Quartermaster units that dealt with the vast piles of supplies come from England; there were ragged Portuguese volunteer militias, still armed and garbed any-old-how, and children by the hundreds. All stopped their play, their labours, the volunteers halted their caricatures of proper drill, and idle *Lisboêtas* turned to watch the warships standing out to sea, Union Flags and commissioning pendants streaming, and they cheered. Faint, thin cries of "*Viva l'Inglaterra!*" were more imagined that clearly heard, but arms and hats were waved about, and women closest to the quays blew kisses.

"Think they want us to just go *away*, sir?" Lt. Westcott said with a snigger.

"They'll cheer just as loud when we return, fetchin' in a flotilla of prizes," Lewrie quipped, "and all our randy, thirsty sailors."

"Anchor's rung up and secured, sir," Lt. Harcourt reported as he came to the quarterdeck, "cable stored below, hawse buckler in place, and all halliards, sheets, and braces belayed."

"Very good, Mister Harcourt," Lewrie said with a nod. "Feels damned good, don't it . . . gettin' back t'sea? Once clear of the mouth of the Tagus, and well clear of the North shore, let's ease her a point free and let fall courses. I'd admire did we stand out at least fifty miles to seaward before we alter course to the North."

"Aye aye, sir," Harcourt said with a tap of his fingers on the brim of his hat to Lewrie, and kept his hand in place as he turned to Lt. Westcott. "Sir, I believe I have the Forenoon Watch. I relieve you."

"I stand relieved, Mister Harcourt," Westcott formally replied, returning the salute in the same casual manner.

As the Second Officer took over his duties, roaring for courses to be bared to the wind, Lewrie went to the windward bulwarks to look at Lisbon as it began to fall astern. He had no trouble spotting the green-awninged lodging house a third of the way up the city, even without a telescope. The morning sun turned the glazed double doors along the balcony to sheets of glare, reflecting enigmatically.

Knock, knock, nobody's home, Lewrie told himself; *and won't be again. Go with God yourself, girl. Adeus.*

He looked further astern to his ships, now sorting themselves out into a line-ahead, with the proper one-cable spacing between them.

He strolled aft to the flag lockers and the taffrails, where Midshipman Kibworth was now in charge of casting the chip-log, and he watched as the lad let it fly, let the light line run between his fingers 'til Midshipman Chenery, with the minute glass, called time when the last grains had run out.

"Six and a quarter knots," Kibworth said, unaware that he was being watched by his Captain. "God, this old cow," he said to Chenery, sticking his tongue out as Chenery jerked his head to warn him.

"Six and a quarter knots!" Lewrie took delight in yelling to the quarterdeck for him. "D'ye hear, there?"

Kibworth spun about, his mouth agape.

"You'll catch flies d'ye keep your mouth open like that, Mister Kibworth," Lewrie told him. "Only spiders think them nourishing."

"Ehm, aye, sir."

"Carry on," Lewrie said, directing his "august" gaze to the sea and the ship's wake. Even a paltry six and a quarter knots' speed made a broad bridal train wake, no longer muddy tan from the waters of the Tagus, but a foaming, churned white wake as HMS *Sapphire* met the open sea. Seabirds swirled in their hundreds, gliding and diving into the disturbed water for small fish brought near the surface and confused and vulnerable in the foaming water, or for sloughed-off bits of sea-growth accumulated on the ship's underwater hull. Gulls mewed and cried almost within reach of the taffrails, with beady eyes alert for something edible above water, and Lewrie heard Bisquit scrambling the length of the poop deck, barking at things he could never catch, tail whisking madly, 'til he sat on the flag lockers, whining frustration.

"You're a silly beast, sometimes, d'ye know that, Bisquit?" Lewrie told the dog, ruffling the fur on the back of his head, scratching the spot that made all dogs happy. "Don't you go overboard, now. Hear me? Let's go find one of your nice, slobbery toys. Come on."

There was a rabbit pelt taken from one of the hares kept in the forecastle manger, stuffed with shakings and batt and sewn up, abandoned by the top of the starboard ladderway from the quarterdeck, and though it *was* damp, Lewrie picked it up and flung it aft, and Bisquit went racing after it.

Lewrie looked forward, down the length of his ship. The main course and fore course were fully deployed, by then, blanketing off half the view, and the jibs right forward almost hid the forecastle. The windward bulwark was his by right, though, whether on the quarterdeck or the poop, so Lewrie leaned on the bulwarks, peering out and forward, down to see the bow wave and quarter wave roughly amidships as it creamed by.

Ahead, out to sea, the Atlantic was a glittering, sun-bright bed of tumbling gems right to the ruler-straight horizon under an azure sky, almost painful to look at for very long. For at least one day, they would have splendid weather, and, despite his recent disappointment ashore, Lewrie felt a sense on contentedness. He always got in trouble ashore, but out at sea, ah . . .

Woof! Bisquit was back with his toy, demanding another toss.

"Here ye go, boy! Get it!" Lewrie said as he threw it again. "Whatever makes you and me happy."

CHAPTER THIRTY-SEVEN

*W*hen the squadron got level with Oporto, Lewrie was tempted to send one of the brig-sloops in to make a port call whilst the others idled off-and-on waiting for a report on the availability of chandleries and ship-yard repair facilities, but he decided that they had been too long away from the North coast of Spain, and they sailed on.

It appeared, though, that word of Wellesley's victory had gotten to England, for on their way North they met several British-flagged merchant-men on their way to Oporto, eager to be the first there, and first back to the English markets with ports, sherries, *espumantes* and the very drink-able red or white wines of the ancient Douro region. Admiralty must have had a hole in their wines stores, for they even saw one six-ship convoy es-corted by a Royal Navy frigate!

Lewrie did despatch *Blaze* a little further North as they came up to the latitude of the Spanish port of Vigo, to see if the French had begun to use that port for military traffic, the rest of the ships pacing back and forth under reduced sail for the rest of the day and night, then into mid-morning of the next day. Lewrie was sure that Capt. Chalmers chafed under the delay, but aboard *Sapphire,* Lewrie ordered a full day of Make and Mend, with rich duffs served along with supper that evening, and a free night of music and dancing in the waist.

At last, *Blaze* hove into sight from the East, showing no sign of urgency, and when she was in plain signalling distance, Lewrie had a hoist made for all Captains to come aboard *Sapphire* to discuss the information Commander Teague had gathered.

Teague had brought a chart aboard with him, and Lewrie told him to spread it out on his dining table so they could all gather round it, anchoring the corners from curling back up with wine glasses.

"Took a bit longer than I expected, sir," Lewrie said, making sure that he had a smile on his face so Teague would not take it as a chiding.

"I wished to be thorough, sir," Teague replied, not abashed in the least. "It's not just Vigo that I took a squint at. See here," he went on, bending over the chart with a pencil for a pointer, "there's an host of other little ports. Vigo is the largest, but, on the other side of the peninsula North of Vigo, there's another deep bay, and a harbour called Marin halfway along the North side, then Pontevedra at the back end of the bay. Round the North of *that,* there is yet another wide and deep place to shelter, with several small fishing ports, and a middling harbour halfway along that shore called Vilagarcía. In the end, I could have spent a week or more probing into every bay along the coast, but I broke off after Vilagarcia."

"Any French traffic?" Chalmers said with a grunt, still chafed by the delay.

"None that I could discover, no sir," Teague said. "There are lots of small fishing boats, none larger than fourty feet overall, a few old coasters rotting away at Vigo, Pontevedra, and Vilagarcia, but there's nothing moving," Commander Teague reported. "There *are* enemy garrisons at those ports, with gun batteries erected, and I did see some sizable parties of cavalry or infantry on the coast roads, now and then. I trailed my colours close enough to tempt those batteries and counted their guns, but it doesn't seem as if they have much over twelve-pounders."

"Same calibre as their typical field artillery," Capt. Yearwood rumbled, "those Gribeauval-patterned guns of theirs."

"They thank him, or did he get his head lopped off like all the others in the Revolution?" Chalmers drawled, faintly amused that Capt. Yearwood, a gruff tarpaulin man, would know such a detail.

"So, we can safely leave Vigo astern and not fret about it?" Lewrie asked. "Good. Good work, Commander Teague. We may get back to our hunting grounds, and our necessary delay may even encourage the

French to put a toe in the water, a finger to the wind, and get back to sailing. More joy for us."

"More prizes!" Commander Blamey cheered, relishing the prospects.

"Well, speak for yourself, Blamey," Yearwood countered, scowling and tossing off his glass of *vinho verde* in hopes of a prompt refill. "You and Captain Chalmers get the prime area, closest to the ports of origin, whilst pickings off Corunna and Ferrol are damned thin by the time you've taken them, and frightened the rest to hide in ports East of us 'til we quit the coast, again."

"We are the stronger pair," Chalmers said with a sniff, "more suitable should French warships dare come out as escorts."

"Not by all that much, you ain't, sir," Yearwood groused.

Uh oh, trouble in Paradise, Lewrie thought; *that'll never do.*

"I had a thought that we'd not split up into hunting pairs this time," Lewrie quickly said to head off squabbles, "but cruise as one together, you, Teague, and you, Blamey, out ahead and inshore to do the hunting, and *Sterling, Undaunted,* and *Sapphire* in column a bit to seaward. Let the Frogs see something new . . . something that might force them to sortie warships to challenge us, at last."

He'd had no plan for that in mind, but spun it up on the spot, if only to placate his subordinates' touchy senses of honour and fair sharing. He looked from face to face round his table, and found that the novelty of the scheme, and its chance to offer a real battle, had mollified them considerably, making some of them smile.

"We would still be allowed to separate from the offshore column should the brig-sloops encounter more enemy merchantmen than they could handle, would we not, Captain Lewrie?" Chalmers asked, sounding as if he would be deprived if he had to cling close to the slow flagship.

"In that event, I'll hoist the General Chase and gladly shout 'Yoicks, tally ho'," Lewrie assured him with a laugh, "though I may have to substitute my penny-whistle for a hunter's horn."

"Well, that's alright, then," Chalmers said, much relieved.

"For now, let's sort ourselves out, with our sloops out ahead and landward," Lewrie went on, "and your *Sterling* in the lead, Captain Yearwood, and your *Undaunted* ahead of me, Captain Chalmers. That way, it's easier for the both of you to make more sail and break off should we spot anything. My slow old 'cow' would not be in your way."

"Might work out nicely, then, sir," Commander Teague ventured to say. "The French are used to seeing us by pairs, or your *Sapphire* by herself.

They might have been forced by their losses in bottoms to sortie, *expecting* to see only two of us. Now, if they send out three, or four, thinking that they might overwhelm us . . . ?" he slyly posed.

"And in aid of that, Teague, we'll make it a point to sail all the way up the French coast to Arcachon together," Lewrie promised, "and if that don't sting 'em to some response, then I'm a half-naked snake charmer in a turban!"

"And if they don't," Blamey said, "then we'll know that those snail-eating bastards have no 'nutmegs' at all, hah hah!"

"Well said, sir, well said!" Lewrie exclaimed in praise. "Now, once we're in our new order of sailing, let's continue on Northward on larboard tack, keepin' at least fifty miles offshore. It'll be dusk by the time we strike the latitude of Cape Fisterre, and I'd not wish to be too close to there should we get a blow during the night. At dawn, we'll haul our wind and get within ten miles of Corunna and Ferrol . . . let 'em get a good, long look at us, and see what they do in response. Pettus, refills all round, if you please."

"Coming up, sir," Pettus said as he and Jessop passed among them and their empty glasses.

A toast sprang to Lewrie's mind, one that one of his subordinates had proposed when last he'd been a Commodore in the Bahamas and along the coast of Spanish Florida.

"To us, gentlemen," Lewrie said, raising his glass, "Here's to us, none like us all across the salt seas!"

"To us!" they echoed before draining their glasses and looking for another quick top-up. "Band of Brothers," Captain Yearwood gruffly intoned, evoking the spirit of Trafalgar.

"Indeed," Chalmers agreed with a solemn nod.

Lewrie did not dine them in, allowing them to return to their ships to conduct what drills and exercises they wished for the rest of the daylight. It was gunnery practise for most ships, it turned out, and great clouds of expended gunpowder billowed aloft and wafted to leeward as the squadron did live-firing to ready their crews for any eventuality.

Sapphire's people, once done with gun drill, tried their eyes on musketry and pistol-shooting, using cast-off kegs and barricadoes as targets, then spent a final hour in the afternoon at cutlass practise, and thrusting and blocking with boarding pikes, taking instruction from the Marine officers at how to get in close with a hatchet and kill the foe most efficiently. The ship's crew had not been called upon for any man-on-man fighting for some time, but the practise at such savage skills put them in a prideful mood, sure that they could come to grips and win against any "cack-handed, seasick, lubberly bastard Frenchman."

Lewrie did dine his own officers in, along with Midshipman Chenery, the youngest and newest, to pose the King's Toast from the foot of the table, explaining, as the port bottle made its rounds after supper, how they would cruise, this time, and show the French something new, something that might draw the French out, at last.

"We'll alter course and close the coast just after dawn tomorrow, sirs," Lewrie concluded, "and pray God there's to be good hunting for us all."

"Amen, sir!" Midshipman Chenery, a tad worse for all the wine he had taken aboard in emulation of his seniors; he would not have dared else.

"Think he speaks for all of us," Lt. Westcott said, beaming at the lad.

CHAPTER THIRTY-EIGHT

*F*rankly, Mister Westcott, I don't think this is workin'."

"Sir?" Westcott asked, lowering his telescope from his intense study of the Spanish coast, ten miles alee.

"This cruisin' together," Lewrie groused, "it seems a complete bust. A whole week, Corunna to Arcachon and back, and we've only taken four prizes, and the rest've gone to ground."

"It's the chain of semaphore towers, sir," Westcott commented. "They know where we are, and can warn of our presence, now."

"Damn the French," Lewrie spat. "Only a matter of time before they erected 'em, the bastards. If only we could *burn* a few!"

The sight of the semaphore towers atop headlands, atop church steeples in the small fishing ports, wasn't entirely new. The enemy had begun the chain soon after the squadron's first forays along the Spanish coast, but now they stood in plenty, their arms fitted with large black bladders during the day, and with lanthorns by night, whirling away as soon as shore lookouts espied a strange sail, warning merchantmen to stay in harbour or make for port. None of the prizes they had taken had admitted that the cargo ships' masters could read the semaphore code, and no books of signals had been captured, but the activities of the towers had put a definite crimp in the "trade".

"In a back-handed way, sir, it may be to the good," Westcott opined with a wry grin, "say, one of the isolated towers runs short of bread or wine and sends a signal for re-supply, every merchantman in sight of it dashes into port, sure they've spotted something out to sea. If nothing is moving, then no supplies are reaching harbour from France, and Bonaparte's armies in Spain go without."

"Well, there is that," Lewrie said with a surly expression, not pleased with that result; he preferred accomplishing the same thing by direct action. When Spain had been a French ally, and *Sapphire* had cruised the Andalusian coast of Southern Spain in 1807, they had dealt with semaphore towers, landing raiding parties and burning them to ashes, breaking the signalling chain, and the Spanish, no matter how the ruling French-loving elite wished to emulate the accomplishments of France, and Emperor Napoleon Bonaparte, Spain, did not have the funds to replace them.

Now, if he only had the means he'd had then, Lewrie regretted; troop transports, landing barges, soldiers or Marines to land alongside his own ship's sailors and Marine complement. What fun!

Like boyish sex, he wryly thought; *in, out, repeat if neccesary!*

The ship's bell in the forecastle belfry struck One Bell of the Forenoon Watch; 8:30 A.M. of a passably fine morning of easy seas and non-threatening clouds, with the promise of a clear sight of the sun for Noon Sights, and that mostly a navigational exercise for the ship's Mids, for any fool could make out the now-familiar sea-marks of the coast by now. They were loafing along under reduced sail off Santander once again, tail-end of the column of three, with *Peregrine* and *Blaze* a little further ahead and closer to shore. To their lee, one could almost make out, or imagine, a harbour full of ships, ripe for the picking if they would only come out, and Lewrie sorted through several fruitless schemes on how to double back in the dark and catch them, if only they felt safe.

"Well, dammit," Lewrie said, letting out a long, frustrated sigh. "Send for me if things improve, Geoffrey. I'll be aft."

"Aye aye, sir," the First Officer said in parting.

"Uhm, cool tea, sir?" Pettus asked as Lewrie flung himself onto the starboard-side settee, tossing off his coat and hat.

"Any of that breakfast coffee left, Pettus?" Lewrie asked.

"Aye, sir, and there's some goat's milk in the creamer," Pettus told him.

"I'll have a cup o' that, instead," Lewrie requested, picking up the last of his un-read newspapers gathered during his brief stay at Lisbon off the low, round brass table, hoping that he might find inspiration in the weeks' old London *Times*, if not in the real news articles on the inner pages, then from the pre-printed outer advertisement sheets. All he really got were ink smudges on his fingers.

"Deck, there! Strange sail, four points off the starb'd quarter!" a lookout high aloft in the cross-trees shouted down in an eerie wail.

Lewrie set aside his coffee mug, rose, and went out to the quarterdeck, hatless and coatless, to trade mystified shrugs with the First Officer, and to snatch up a telescope to peer windward and aft.

"Can't see 'em from the deck, yet," Lewrie groused after a long time peering outward. As he collapsed the tubes, he turned to look at Lt. Westcott. "That'd put 'em what, twenty miles to seaward? I can't recall any French convoys sailin' *that* far from shelter."

"Mast-head!" Westcott shouted to the lookouts with his speaking-trumpet. "Can you make anything out, yet?"

There was a pause as lookouts on the fore, main, and mizen cross-trees stood, clinging to the top-masts, and shaded their eyes with their hands. "Tops'ls 'bove th' horizon! Tops'ls an' t'gallants! Two . . . *three* sets o' strange sail!"

"Full-rigged ships!" the mizen lookout added. "Three full-rigged ships, four points orf th' starb'd quarter!"

"It might make sense, in a way, sir," Westcott speculated. "We sail close along the coast, they lose a lot of ships doing the same, so the French might imagine that shaping course almost Due West from Bayonne or Arcachon would avoid notice 'til they steer South to close the coast. And it would only be by dumb luck that they encountered us, or one of the hunting pairs."

"Hmm, perhaps," Lewrie said, frowning over this odd behaviour on the part of the French. He trotted up the ladderway to the poop deck for a slightly better view, but, once steadied against the bulwarks, his telescope still revealed no clues. There *might* be some wee irregularities on the ruler-straight horizon up to the Nor'east, but they could have been clouds below the horizon, or his imagination.

"Deck, there!" the mainmast lookout yelled down, "It's *four* strange sail . . . full-rigged ships, *four* of 'em!"

The commotion had wakened Mr. Yelland from a nap in his sea cabin, and he came bustling out, yawning and swabbing his face with his hands. "What's acting? Sail to *seaward*?"

Lewrie turned to look down at him. "Four strange ships, up to windward, Mister Yelland. Damned small number for a French convoy."

"Maybe troopships, sir?" Yelland opined, "Or horse transports? Marching men and beasts cross the Pyrenees would lame half of them, and exhaust the rest."

Lewrie raised his glass once more, still found nothing tangible, and scowled as he collapsed the brass tubes again, his mind churning.

"I wish a signal hoisted, Mister Westcott," he said, "General Signal . . . Alter Course Two points to Windward in Succession, preceded with two guns t'wake 'em up."

"Aye aye, sir!" Westcott replied, "Master Gunner?"

"Best we recall the brig-sloops, too," Lewrie said, returning to the quarterdeck. "Once the column has come about, make a second hoist with *Blaze* and *Peregrine's* numbers, and order them to investigate strange sails in the Nor'east."

"Aye, sir," Westcott hastily said, overseeing forecastle gun crews assembling to load and fire two saluting charges, and dealing with Midshipman Ward, who would handle the signals.

"No rush, sir," Lewrie said, grinning. "Whoever or whatever they are, they're at least an hour or more off."

"Four troopers, that might be a whole French battalion," the Sailing Master said, rubbing calloused hands together in anticipation, "round an hundred and fifty aboard each, as we do, or two hundred, if the French don't care for their soldiers' comfort. 'Cavalry ships', now, maybe four hundred horses? Five pounds per man, in Head and Gun Money. Four thousand pounds right there, not counting the value of four big full-rigged ships . . . but, I wonder what Head Money is for horses?"

"Guns are ready, sir," Westcott reported.

"Fire 'em, and make the hoist," Lewrie ordered.

"Ah, there it is!" Capt. Chalmers exclaimed with glee when the expected order to alter course finally broke open on *Sapphire's* halliards. He had been pacing, champing at the bitt since his own lookouts had spotted the strange sails on the horizon.

"A small convoy, perhaps, sir, but a valuable one, if they dare sail far off the coast to avoid us," Lt. Crosley, his First Officer, opined.

"Let them be French National Ships," Capt. Chalmers said in heat, slamming a fist upon the windward bulwark's cap-rails. "Give us an honourable, glorious fight, at long last! Mister Crosley, summon brace-tenders and prepare to harden up on the wind. Put the helm down as soon as the signal is struck! Let's be *at* them!"

"Ready to alter course, Mister Cunningham," Commander Teague said to his First Lieutenant aboard HMS *Blaze*. "As to why, though," and he threw in a curious shrug. "Maybe the Commodore is bored with all this fruitless cruising. Damned semaphore towers. Still, there might be some trade further along to the West."

"Signal is down, sir," Lt. Cunningham noted, then issued orders to the helmsmen to steer two points to windward, and to the brace and sheet tenders to adjust the angles of the yards, jibs, and spanker. "Hah!" Cunningham exclaimed a moment later as another signal burst open on the flagship. "Our number, and . . . Investigate . . . Strange Sail . . . to the Nor'east. Odd, sir."

"Odd, my eye, Mister Cunningham," Teague exulted. "They must have spotted a convoy trying to sneak round us! Prepare to wear the ship about. That will slow us down for a bit, let the main column pass ahead, and we can cross their stern and hare off on larboard tack. Acknowledge the signal, and prepare to go about!"

God, I may regret this, Lewrie told himself as he crammed his telescope into his waistband and left the poop deck for the quarterdeck, then went forward to the shrouds of the main mast, clambered up onto the bulwarks, and swung out to scale the stays and ratlines, as high as the cat-harpings below the fighting top. He had been simply terrified, the first time he'd been ordered aloft, nigh-reduced to a quivering, jibbering calf's foot jelly, though determined not to show it, and scrambling skyward hadn't gotten any easier for him. He took hold (a death's grip in point of fact) of the stays, snaked one arm round one, pulled out his telescope, and tried to peer at the ships on the horizon; and trying to appear calm and "tarry" to the sailors already aloft, or peering up from the deck, though his leg muscles shivered in dread, and the damned ocular of his telescope just would *not* stay still.

From that slightly elevated height Lewrie could make out four very wee specks of white canvas, at last, four t'gallants, or the upper halves of t'gallants. Main t'gallants, he reckoned, since they would be higher than fore or mizen t'gallants. And, were there tiny slivers showing before and abaft of those sails that might be those other t'gallants?

Damned white, ain't they? he thought, recalling that most of the merchantmen they'd seen along this coast were dowdy, their sails almost parchment-tan from long use and exposure to the elements, some so old they looked like grimy grey, with patches of newer sailcloth sewn on like a harlequin's costume. *Now who issues clean white sails?* he asked himself, and began a tentative grin.

"How far off d'ye make 'em?" he shouted up to the mainmast lookout.

The lookout shaded his eyes and took his time before making an estimate. "I can see t'gallants *and* tops'ls, now, sir!" he sang out. "Maybe . . . twelve mile off, or a little less! Hard t'say, sir!"

"Very well," Lewrie replied, stuffing his telescope back into his waistband, and very gingerly turning himself about to face the shrouds and ratlines to make his welcome descent. Half-way down the shrouds, though, the lookout shouted again, freezing him in place.

"Deck, there! Th' strange sail are alterin' course! Haulin' their wind, in column . . . in succession!"

Lewrie wished he could race down the stays like a frantic monkey when he heard that, but he forced himself to descend slowly and carefully, chiding himself to appear the stern and cool Captain that the Navy, and a ship's crew, demanded.

Once back on solid oak, he walked aft to the quarterdeck, taking a moment to steady his breath after his exertions before speaking.

"Four ships, in column, alterin' course in succession, Mister Westcott," he told him, "with sails as new and as white as a fresh snow. Warships! They've spotted us, and they're closing us for an engagement. Be up with us in an hour, or less."

"Huzzah, sir!" Westcott cried at that news. "Huzzah!"

"Let's rig chain slings on the yards, and ship anti-boarding nets, now," Lewrie ordered. "Douse the galley fires. It'll be a cold mess for all hands, but there's no helpin' it. General Signal to all ships . . . *Possible* Enemy in Sight, and Prepare for Action."

"Mister Ward, is there a single code flag for 'Possible'?" Lt. Westcott shouted aft.

"Ehm . . . I think so, sir," Midshipman Ward replied, fumbling through his signals book for a moment, "Aye, sir, there is."

"Make to all ships, Possible Enemy in Sight, and Prepare for Action," Westcott ordered.

"Aye aye, sir!" Ward cried back, sounding giddily excited.

"Think I'll have time to shave, Geoffrey?" Lewrie japed with a grin.

"Oh, time enough to don silk shirt and stockings, too, sir," Westcott replied. "And for one last *cigarro* for me."

"Enjoy," Lewrie said, "I'll be aft, making myself pretty for the Frogs. I'm told they appreciate an elegant turn out."

CHAPTER THIRTY-NINE

Lewrie had enough time to don fresh, clean silk stockings, shirt, and underdrawers, even have a quick scrub-up, as his cabins were stripped of anything valuable to be stored on the orlop, and Chalky and Bisquit taken below for safety. There was time to clean and load his two sets of pistols, and for the Ship's Armourer to hone a fine edge on his hanger.

He emerged on the quarterdeck just as the flimsy partitions which formed the forward bulkhead to his cabins, Mr. Yelland's sea-cabin, and the matching chart room on the larboard side were struck down, turning his cabins into a hollow shell.

"Signal, sir, from *Peregrine*!" Midshipman Ward yelled. "It is Enemy in Sight . . . Four . . . Frigates!"

Lewrie mounted to the poop deck to see for himself, raising his telescope for a long look at the approaching warships, thinking them about five or six miles off, and the lead vessel only one point aft of abeam, by then. He turned to look further astern for his pair of brig-sloops which had ventured out far enough to make positive identification, and were now returning to join his main column.

The enemy ships were too far off, still, to count their gun-ports, or to make a guess as to their rates. Strung out as they were in line-ahead formation, they could all be of the same rate and mount the same amount of armament.

"Mister Westcott," Lewrie called over his shoulder, his eyes rivetted on the approaching foe, "I think it's time for us to Beat to Quarters."

"Aye, sir!" his long-time First Officer wolfishly agreed, eager for action. "Bosun Terrell, pipe hands to Quarters!"

The calls shrilled urgently, and the Marine drummer began the Long Roll. *Sapphire*'s hands, long alerted that this moment would eventually come, did not have to dash up from below in a thunder of feet, but almost *strolled* to their duty stations. Gun tools were taken off the overhead racks, tompions were withdrawn from the guns' muzzles, and the ship only grew loud when officers ordered that the gun crews cast off their guns and draw them inboard to be loaded.

"Mister Ward, still on signals, are you?" Lewrie asked.

"Aye, sir," Ward replied.

"A signal hoist to *Peregrine*. I wish her to close and speak with me," Lewrie ordered. "Commander Blamey will have gotten a good look at them, and I want his thoughts."

"Aye, sir. *Peregrine*'s number, and . . . Come Under My Lee?"

"That'd be capital, aye, Mister Ward," Lewrie agreed, then went to the quarterdeck to speak with Lt. Westcott. "Geoffrey, have some Mids pass word to Mister Harcourt and Mister Elmes. They're to tell the crew that I trust their training, their skill at gunnery, and that we will be closing with the biggest bastard, at which point they are to load with roundshot and grape, and aim for the enemy's gun-ports, quarterdeck, and helm."

"Aye, sir, I'll see to it directly," Westcott assured him.

"How many swivels and grenades do we have in the tops?" Lewrie asked. "I want all the swivels up there, and as many grenades as the Marines can handle, when we close to pistol-shot, or closer."

"See to that, too, sir," Westcott replied, summoning Midshipmen Griffin and Fywell to relay Lewrie's message to the crew.

"Sir! *Peregrine* is hauling her wind and falling down on us!" Midshipman Ward shouted from the taffrails.

"Very well, Mister Ward," Lewrie shouted back. Things were speeding up, and he felt a sense of urgency to see that all last-minute preparations that he could think of were done. He drummed fingers on the larboard caprails, impatient for *Peregrine* to come alongside, watching her spread more canvas as she fell astern of *Sapphire,* and began to creep up on the larboard quarter. Lewrie crossed over to the starboard side for a bit to judge how long he had before those enemy ships were up with them, then went back to larboard, snatching up the brass speaking-trumpet on the way.

"Sent for me, sir?" Commander Blamey shouted over to him as his crew reduced sail to keep his ship from dashing on ahead.

"I want to know their pedigree, Blamey!" Lewrie shouted back. "Did you get close enough to count gun-ports? Determine their rates?"

"The lead ship may be a fourty-gunner, sir!" Blamey replied in a odd, sing-song bellow. "The two astern of her look to be thirty-sixes, or thirty-twos. Thirteen ports a side. The trailing ship is maybe a twenty-eight gunner! Twelve ports a side!"

"Go speak with Teague," Lewrie ordered. "I want you to team with *Blaze* and double on the weakest. And all good fortune go with you!"

"Aye aye, sir, and the same to you!" Commander Blamey yelled before turning to his watchstanders to order his ship to haul off and seek his consort.

"Dammit, Mister Westcott," Lewrie growled. "Blamey says their lead ship's a fourty-gunner. We'll have to take her on, ourselves."

He looked aloft at the commissioning pendant, judging the wind direction and strength, taking a moment to note that Union Jacks and battle flags, and his command pendant, were streaming brightly. One more look at the approaching enemy, and he made up his mind. There was just enough time for what he intended.

"Helm down, Mister Westcott, get us hard on the wind and get some *speed* on this barge. Signal *Undaunted* and *Sterling* to reduce sail, back and fill, and that *Sapphire* will take the lead."

"He's going to what?" Capt. Chalmers all but yelped in astonishment when he saw the signal, and saw the flagship turn up to windward. "He won't make it, the enemy's too close, and he'll mask our fire, dam . . . by . . . !" he spluttered, cutting off a curse, and a blasphemy. "The lead ship is *our* pigeon, the point of honour!"

"She's fourteen gun-ports showing, sir," Lt. Crosley told him. "That makes her a fourty-gunner with eighteen-pounders, as I recall from what we know of the French navy. If we are second in line, we will be opposing *their* second in line, which is probably a thirty-six, mounting twelve-pounders. A more equal match, I dare say."

"That man!" Chalmers fumed. "That dissolute, glory-hunting . . . reprobate! Just like he did at Corunna, taking on that French shore battery without orders. My . . . *stars*!" he spat, avoiding another more pleasing epithet.

HMS *Sapphire* was managing to surge abeam of Capt. Yearwood's *Sterling* as both frigates brailed up their fore and main courses to slow down to let the flagship pass and take the lead, whether they wanted to or not.

"We might just make it, sir," Lt. Westcott said, more in hope than certainty. He even winced and sucked his teeth. "The enemy's nowhere in gun range, yet. I think."

"Come on, you old barn," Lewrie urged, pounding the windward caprails like flogging a horse to the finish line at Ascot. "Ye *know* ye want a fight. Come on, *Sapphire*, get a move on, for once!"

The *Sterling* frigate slowly fell astern, *Sapphire*'s taffrails just ahead of *Sterling*'s out-thrust bowsprit. *Undaunted* lay a cable ahead, and she would have to be overtaken and passed, then *Sapphire* would have to gain another cable ahead of her. Lewrie looked over at the enemy ships, noting that their gun-ports were still closed, and he fervently hoped they would *stay* closed for just a bit more.

"Gallop, for once in your bloody life, girl! Go it!" Lewrie whispered. "God, this could all go smash. What was I thinking?"

"Eight and three-quarter knots, sir!" one of Mr. Yelland's Quartermaster's Mates shouted from right astern. He sounded very surprised.

"*That's* the way, darlin'!" Lewrie cheered.

Stern chases, small boat races, they always seem to take forever, hours and hours spent inching up on a fleeing enemy, or the leader in a harbour regatta, then, just of a sudden, one's ship or boat was right astern of the goal, even surging past as if one's own boat had sprouted wings.

There! There was *Undaunted*'s stern, almost even with the bowsprit and jib-boom. And there was Capt. Chalmers, glowering black wrath at *Sapphire*, gripping his windward rails so hard that Lewrie could imagine the sound of wood snapping.

Eat shit and die, you prig! Lewrie thought, feeling a giddy sense of triumph as his ship's forecastle came even with *Undaunted*'s quarterdeck. They *would* make it, they would!

Lewrie looked at the enemy column, and it was a bit less than two miles off, not yet within gun range even at maximum elevation. One good broadside from them could have crippled *Sapphire*'s rigging, slowed her to a crawl, and left his column in shambles, but . . . that broadside didn't come!

His ships were heading West by North, whilst the French were closing almost Due West. They would converge, come to grips, but not quite yet.

He looked astern to see what his brig-sloops were doing, and was pleased to see that *Peregrine* and *Blaze* were lagging back, further astern, so when the French line altered course to lay themselves parallel to Lewrie's, they would even be astern of the trailing enemy ship, that weaker 28-gunner, in prime position to take her on both beams at once, doubling on her.

"By God, we *are* going to make it!" Westcott marvelled.

"Aye, we are, Mister Westcott," Lewrie said, almost crowing with relief. "We finally stung the Frogs to sail out and take us on. So let's give 'em one Hell of a drubbing for their pains."

He let out a great sigh of relief as *Sapphire*'s quarterdeck slid past *Undaunted*'s anchor cat-heads and forecastle. Ships had souls, he'd always believed, gained them after a while under way. *Sapphire* had had a soul when he took command of her two years before, but she'd been accustomed to dull plodding, as if no one had ever asked her for better. As if no one had ever loved her enough, and had consigned her to pulling dray waggons or ploughs, and expecting nothing greater.

"You're a bloody thoroughbred," he said in praise, stroking the cap-rails like he would his favourite saddle horse back home in Anglesgreen. He took a last, satisfied look about as *Sapphire* continued to surge ahead of *Undaunted*, opening the gap to the proper one-cable's spacing. In a minute or two she would be there, and the main course could be brailed up, slowing her down, and reducing the chance of that vast sail catching fire from the discharge of her own guns. She would be ready for battle.

"Mister Westcott, I wish two more signals to be hoisted. The first'd be Number Sixteen, for Engage the Enemy More Closely," Lewrie said. "The second, as I recall, requires only two more flags."

"Which'd be, sir?" Lt. Westcott asked.

"Send, England . . . Expects," Lewrie said, feeling a fey shiver.

"Combine them into one, perhaps?" Westcott suggested.

"Ah, no. One on the main, one on the mizen halliards," Lewrie decided, going back to the windward bulwarks with his telecope to eye the enemy.

Two words.

The first two words of the signal sent to the fleet at the Battle of Trafalgar. Admiral Lord Nelson's signal.

CHAPTER FORTY

*T*he leading French frigate churned onward, slowly closing the range and converging. She and her consorts had yet to brail up their main courses, so they still had frothing mustachios of foam under their bows, making them look fast, and dangerous.

The French naval architects had always designed and built ships that were faster, heavier, and they armed them with more guns than British practise, crammed them bung-full with more sailors to fight and work them, too. Many a British warship was drawn along the lines of French vessels. Oh, there were some who carped that French ships were too fine in their entries, preferring fuller bows that would ride over a heavy sea, that French ships would dip their bows too deep and ship too much water, that they made for unsteady gun platforms when they were engaged in a battle in rough weather.

Still, the British designers and dockyards copied them, for there were so many of them brought in as prizes, re-armed, re-named in most cases, and made part of the Royal Navy.

No, it wasn't French ships that were at fault, it was the men who manned those beautiful creations of the shipbuilders' art. Once, before the French Revolution lopped the heads off most of the "aristo" officer corps, and ran the rest to service in other nations' navies, the ships and the men had been a match for each other. After, though, un-titled officers, jumped-up Bosun's Mates, loud radicals loyal to "The Sovereign People", and the former "Blue Officers" drawn from the merchant service had commanded those ships, dominated by lubberly "No Sailors" placed aboard to keep radical revolutionary enthusiasm high, and suspicious people in line, exceeding their authority over tactical matters because they were the voice of the Directory of Public Safety, the classic consular rulers of the Directory of Five, and even after Napoleon Bonaparte had emerged as the sole Consul, then crowned himself Emperor of the French, that once-grand navy continued to suffer.

Too many defeats, too many over-complicated strategic schemes unraveled, too little time at sea, and a British blockade that was relentlessly enforced kept those fine ships in harbour far too long.

Since 1793, the Royal Navy had, in the main, developed a tradition of victory, and it would be easy for its people, from Admirals to tar-stained Jacks belowdecks, to belittle the French when they did dare head out to sea. A couple of broadsides fired for honour, and they would strike; a half-hour's hammering, and the French sailors and officers would crumble, throw down their weapons and cry for mercy. And when the "butcher's bill" was tallied up, it was British sailors who suffered the least, and the French who paid the highest price in blood, corpses, and piles of amputated limbs.

Victory, gloriously bloody victory, was what people safe and snug at home in England had come to expect, for the newspapers were full of stirring accounts, and even the mildest of men sought out the latest issue of *The Naval Chronicle* for a vicarious patriotic thrill.

Capt. Alan Lewrie had his own tradition of victory, but he could not disparage the French so easily, even though the state of the French navy, and its limitations, were firm in his mind. As the range closed to less than a mile, he felt, despite his seeming bravado, and his "sham posing" as a stoic Sea Officer of the King, that he and his squadron were in for one hell of a fight.

That can't all be lubbers and simpletons, he told himself as he raised his telescope one more time; *they might've been selected specially t'sweep us away and keep the provisions flowin'. They may have sent their very best, sent by Bonaparte himself!*

"I do believe they are opening their gun-ports," Lt. Westcott said from behind his shoulder, his own glass lifted.

"Good luck to 'em," Lewrie said, "it'll be hard to take down our rigging if they wish to fire high. They hold the wind gage, and they can't elevate their guns as far as they need."

The ports were open on all four French frigates, and cannon muzzles, black as Satan's soul, were trundled up to the port sills, emerging in threat. Yet, the French held their fire, and those gun muzzles did not appear to be pointed skyward, with the elevating quoin blocks removed, and the breeches resting on the truck carriages.

"Something new for a change," Lewrie muttered, more to himself than to his First Officer. It had long been a French practise to aim high and fire chain shot, bar shot, and expanding star shot to open an action, hoping to smash top-masts, tear sails to ragpickers' bargains, weaken stays, and bring down masts to cripple a foe which could then be manoeuvred round and boarded with those over-sized crews that they carried.

"Half a mile, I make it, sir," Mr. Yelland, the Sailing Master, commented in a bland voice. Lewrie took a quick glance at him; the Sailing Master was playing "stoic" quite well, Lewrie reckoned.

"Gonna skin th' bastards, gonna send 'em all t'Hell," someone was almost chanting at one of the nearest 24-pounder carronades.

"Silence, now, lad," the gun-captain chid him. "Stop yer gob an' save it fer later, Jessop. We'll cheer when we're done."

Long minutes passed as the range closed to a quarter-mile, and decent gun range even for the inexperienced, yet the French still held their fire. Lewrie began to feel that it was almost uncanny, and the silence, broken only by the sounds of the wind, the creaks and groans of the hull and masts, and the swashing of the sea along *Sapphire*'s sides, was ominous.

"Mister Westcott, you may open the ports and run out," Lewrie snapped, fed up with the waiting.

"Aye, sir!" Westcott replied, then bellowed down to the waist, "Starb'd battery, open ports, run out, aim small, and stand ready!"

The sight of *Sapphire*'s gun-ports hinging up to form a red chequer along her buff gunwales prompted the French, at last, and the lead frigate's larboard side erupted in a sudden cloud of gunpowder smoke, reddish-yellow stabbing flames and a shower of sparks swirling from the cloth powder cartridges.

"Let the smoke clear, Mister Westcott," Lewrie said in rising excitement, "and you may open upon her, by broadside!" Even as he said so, *Sapphire* shuddered, shook, and groaned as French roundshot hammered her starboard side. One ball struck amidships along the sail-tending gangway, blasting a hole in the bulwarks, scattering the taut-rolled hammocks in the metal stanchion racks like so many snakes, and flinging three Marines down into the waist, dead or quilled with wood splinters, and the cry of "Loblolly boys, here, now!" arose.

"By broadside, on the up-roll," officers, Mids, and experienced Quarter-Gunners in charge of several pieces shouted, "Fire!"

Sapphire shook and groaned again as all the long guns in the starboard battery lit off pretty-much as one, then recoiled to the limits of the breeching ropes, making the ring-bolts anchored in the stout timbers of her hull cry out.

"Beautiful!" Lewrie cheered. "Hit the bitch again!"

All that gunnery practise, and the crude notched sights along the barrels, proved their worth, for *Sapphire*'s broadside was concentrated 'twixt wind and water with no splashes of wayward rounds, and almost all round-shot smashed into the French fourty-gunner, staggering her. With her initial broadside's smoke blown clear, Lewrie could see ragged-edged star-shaped holes punched into her along her gunwales and bulwarks.

"Swab your guns . . . serve with powder . . . shot your guns . . . overhaul train tackle and run out!" voices urgently roared belowdecks. "Prime! Stand by . . . on the up-roll . . . fire!"

French guns were barely re-emerging in their ports as *Sapphire* served her another, one which made Lewrie feel like leaping in blood-thirsty joy, smashing into the French frigate, making her hull scream in those peculiar parrot *Rawrks* as 12- and 24-pounder shot blasted clean through stout oak timbers and scantlings.

As *Sapphire* wreathed herself in a dense, impenetrable cloud of gun smoke, the ship was shaken by a massive strike, a shot that ripped through the starboard side of his cabins aft of the quarterdeck, sending clouds of splinters winging about, taking down one of the helmsmen. A moment later there was a second great shaking up forward, and *Sapphire* screamed as her hull was breached.

The smoke pall cleared, revealing the big French frigate, now free of her own smoke for a moment. "Carronades, sir!" Mr. Yelland shouted, pointing at the enemy's quarterdeck. "They've got carronades. One forrud, and one aft!"

"Big'uns, by the looks of them," Westcott excitedly said.

"Two can play that game," Lewrie snapped. "Carronades to load with roundshot and grapeshot, and direct their fire on those French guns!"

Powder monkeys dashed up from below with their wood or leather cases, bearing fresh serge cartridge bags from the magazine, handing the charges over to loaders, then dashing back below. Roundshot was hefted off the piles bound in from rolling about by rope shot garlands, rammed down atop the cartridges, then wooden stands which held plum-sized grape-shot were rammed down. The carronades' slide carriages wheeled about on bulkhead pivots, elevating screws beneath the guns' breeches were adjusted, and the flintlock strikers primed.

"Stand clear!" gun-captains roared, stepping back with trigger lines in their hands, drawn taut, waiting for the moment.

"On the up-roll . . . fire!"

The French frigate had only two large carronades on each side, one near her forecastle, the other on her quarterdeck. *Sapphire* had ten, four on her forecastle and six on the quarterdeck, five on each beam. Hot gases spurted from the stubby carronades' muzzles and the barrels shot backwards on the greased compression slides with loud squeals of wood on wood, and the 24-pound roundshot and a cloud of grapeshot spewed out at the en-emy with a noise almost as loud as a full broadside from both gun decks. And the so-called "Smashers" lived up to their name.

The range had closed to a bit less than three hundred yards, perfect for the short-ranged carronades, the three quarterdeck guns aimed at the en-emy's aft mount, and the stout bulwarks either side of the French gun seemed to dissolve, to shoot skyward in jagged pieces, with a cloud of lesser splinters flying in all directions like a covey of startled quail or grouse. There was a very loud bell-like *bong!* as the enemy carronade's barrel was struck, slewing the entire mount and recoil slide almost fore-and-aft, torn from its anchoring pivot, and un-usable. As for the men who'd manned it, and some of the people on the quarterdeck, the cloud of splinters, and the sleet-storm of grapeshot, swept them all off their feet in a bloody mangle.

"On the up-roll . . . fire!" And *Sapphire*'s great-guns lit off almost to-gether, the discharges becoming more of a stutter all along her sides, the results of their fire seen immediately before the gush of powder smoke blot-ted the enemy from sight once more. More holes punched into the French-man's hull along her gunwale and line of gun-ports, more sections of upper bulwarks smashed clean through.

"Damn the bloody guns!" Mr. Yelland exclaimed, looking up at the sails and commissioning pendant which was no longer standing out, but was limply curling like a weary snake. "We're shooting the wind to nothing. *Always* happens."

Lewrie took a moment to glance aloft, and silently agreed with the Sail-ing Master's opinion; when ships traded fire, the concussions of the guns seemed to still the wind, after a time, blanketing the sea, and the opposing ships, in a fog of gun smoke that would not disperse.

The Frenchman's responding broadside tore his attention back, not quite as organised as the initial ones, but his ship quaked to many hits. At such close range, the French guns could not miss such a big target, even smothered in a reeking fog of powder smoke!

There was a particularly heavy strike up forward, again, and *Sapphire*'s wood screamed in agony as a heavy roundshot penetrated her vitals. The masking smoke did not clear away, it merely thinned, just enough to see that the enemy's forward carronade was still being served.

As the echoes of the broadsides faded, Lewrie noted the sounds of musketry. Marines in the fighting tops were volleying at enemy naval infantry and sailors in their own tops, swivel guns were barking as fast as they could be re-loaded, and Lewrie saw a burly sailor in *Sapphire*'s maintop bracing a Henry Nock volley gun against the main mast as if firing from the hip. All seven barrels went off as one with a sheet of flame spewing from those barrels, and the volley gun, even braced, almost leapt from the sailor's startled hands.

Nice idea, Lewrie thought; *But no one can fire one o' those things without shatterin' his bones.*

Sapphire rumbled as the truck carriages of the great-guns were hauled back up to the port sills, the wooden wheels squealing like a frightened herd of swine. Lewrie peered hard at the French frigate, now nearly one hundred yards off, still closing, and saw only empty gun-ports, a sight which gave him much cheer. All the drills he had ordered, all the live firing once a week, and the almost-daily "dry" exercises, were paying off; *Sapphire*'s gunners were loading, firing, and re-loading much faster than the French, and in this sort of fight, quite unlike his previous battles of manoeuvre, speed was what mattered . . . speed, and proper aim when the time came, when the enemy hull and his were almost touching. And that time would be soon.

His squadron's line stood on bearing West by North whilst the French sailed Due West; his would be un-yielding, forcing the enemy to sidle up to point-blank range, slam hulls together, and duel it out within cursing distance.

Lewrie leaned out to look overboard, noting how feeble was the ship's wake down *Sapphire*'s side, aghast for a moment at the sight of the many shot holes, and a roundshot or two jammed into her timbers like the black bubos on a victim of the Black Death. His guns were jerking, inch by inch, back into battery. At least that was pleasing to see. Despite the risk, he went up the starboard ladderway for a better view aft to see how the other ships of his squadron were doing, but there was almost nothing to see. There were some vague, slate-grey shapes aft, almost lost in a thick, rolling yellowish-grey fog, a hint of *Undaunted* astern of his ship, a hint of her opponent, and some fresh gusts of smoke and fog-dimmed red and amber flames from guns as they fired. *Sterling* and her opponent, and the brig-sloops, were quite invisible. The best that Lewrie could tell, they were still fighting. The cacophonous roar of guns stuttered, crashed, and rattled the sea and air like an host of kettle drums pounded by so many insane musicians.

Something hummed past his left ear, then by his right, and a small chunk of the poop deck's railing flew up in a wee cloud of old paint and wood. Lewrie looked over at the French frigate and saw a party of men in her mizen top, reloading muskets. He doffed his hat to them and returned to the dubious safety of the quarterdeck.

"Mizen top men!" he roared. "Kill those bastards!" and jutted an arm at the enemy top, hoping that his crew's musketry was equal to their skill and rapidity with the great-guns.

Commander Teague had held his brig-sloop close astern of Commander Blamey's *Peregrine* as the trailing French frigate came within gun range, obeying Blamey's last shouted order to make the French imagine that he could deal with the brig-sloops one at a time as they came abeam of his guns. Enemy 12-pounders roared and British 9-pounders answered as they closed, and if Blamey had stood on un-yielding to the original squadron course, *Peregrine* would eventually take the worst of such a duel. Teague impatiently waited, pacing frenetically, fingers flexing and drumming on the hilt of his sword for the right moment. There! *Peregrine* was hauling her wind a point or more, as if shying away from the Frenchman's pummeling.

"Sheet home the main course!" Teague shouted, "Helmsmen, put your helm up and steer Nor'west. Ready, the larboard battery! Got you, you snail-eater, we got you!"

Blaze surged ahead as the French frigate took the bait, too intent on *Peregrine*, perhaps even losing sight of *Blaze* as they all slowly crept into the pall of spent powder smoke from the ships ahead of them. Ports flew up, 9-pounders were run out, and Teague roared cautions to his gunners to aim small and true, the way they'd trained with their new-fangled notched sights.

"As you bear . . . right up her arse . . . fire!" Teague yelled.

The French frigate had been lured far enough off the scant wind to bare her stern to a rake, and Commander Teague rejoiced as his gunners savaged the enemy. Raking fire directed right up the stern of a vulnerable ship would smash through the much thinner transom wood, and there was nothing to prevent the roundshot from bowling the whole length of an enemy ship. With all internal partitions, flimsy to begin with, struck down, roundshot would scour the foe from the helm to the forecastle, contained by the strength of the outer hull, and overturning guns, smashing deck support posts, flinging whole gun crews into bloody gobbets, and creating chaotic mayhem.

"Re-load, and stand ready!" Teague shouted, exultant with the results. "Helmsmen, steer us round to her starboard side. Brail up the main course!"

HMS *Blaze* met the enemy frigate as she writhed about to get back on the wind, to man her bowsed-down starboard guns in the face of a sudden new threat, even as *Peregrine* came back on the wind to match her turn, her starboard guns blasting a fresh broadside.

"Ready, sir!" Teague's First Officer screeched.

"Right into her ports, lads!" Teague shouted. "As they come level with you . . . fire!"

The enemy frigate's starboard gun-ports were jerking upward, the unused guns being hauled to the sills. After the raking she had taken, it was asking too much of a ship's crew to stumble over dead and wounded mates, the chaos of over-turned guns and smashed carriages, trying to ignore the screams of the savagely wounded, and try to fight both batteries at once. No warship carried enough men to do that.

"Oh, lovely!" Commander Teague shouted, pumping a fist at the sky as his re-loaded guns poured roundshot and grape into those ports at less than one hundred yards' range, and he urged his helmsmen to edge his ship down onto the foe even closer. A moment later, and a roar of a controlled broadside from *Peregrine* smashed into the enemy as they doubled on her, sandwiching the Frenchman between them with no chance of escape, nor any room to turn. So close now that even Commander Blamey, dubious of all talk about "aimed fire", could urge his own gunners to point at the enemy's larboard gun-ports. The foe was taking a horrid beating, with barely a shot fired in reply.

"She's striking her colours, she's striking!" Teague could hear Blamey shouting from the *other* side of the French frigate, and he and his crew huzzahed and jeered as the Tricolour which had flown high above her stern came fluttering down to drape over her taffrails and shattered stern windows.

"Cannily done, I must say, sir," *Blaze*'s First Officer said, "and, I don't believe we've anyone killed, nor any hurt!"

"Astounding!" Commander Teague marvelled. "We'll yield honours to *Peregrine*. Blamey's senior to me. We, however, will stand on and see if we can double on another. Go give Captain Sterling our assistance. If we can even find him in all this smoke."

"Good Lord, who can live through that?" Midshipman Hugh Lewrie whispered to himself as he beheld the furious exchange of cannonfire between his father's ship and that big brute of a French frigate. He had a fine view from his post on *Undaunted*'s forecastle, in charge of the carronades and chase guns, the chasers now swung to beam gun-ports.

Great, fire-lit gushes of gun smoke dashed from both battling ships, and the sea between them was flattened by the concussions and rippled by the blasts, as bits and pieces of wood were flung aloft from both. He could *hear* the *Rawrks* and thudding crashes!

Hugh looked over at their own foe, flexing the fingers of his left hand on the dirk at his side, his father's dirk when *he'd* been a Midshipman, given to him just before going aboard his first ship. That, and the pair of pistols in his waistband that his grandfather had sent him, had seen him through Trafalgar, and several actions, since. They would see him through this one.

I am my father's son, he told himself; *and I will bring credit to my family name. For God, King, and England!*

"Ready, lads?" he said to his gun crews. "It's a bit too far for the 'Smashers', yet, but let's try your eyes, anyway. You game?"

"Hell, yes, Mister Lewrie!" they hungrily agreed, unable to stand by idle when the other guns were roaring.

"Maximum elevation on your screws, then," Hugh ordered, and squatted behind them to see to proper traverse. *Undaunted*'s people liked Midshipman Lewrie; he knew what he was about, fought like some tiger, and looked after their welfare, though they could get nothing past him, and he could be a strict disciplinarian at times, a proper sort of "firm but fair" officer that sailors appreciated.

"All guns!" Lt. Crosley was shouting. "By broadside . . . fire!"

"Give 'em Hell!" Hugh cried as the guns went off, smothering them all in smoke. "Swab out and serve 'em another!" he urged. One quick look showed him that the sheet-handlers for the jibs were out of the way, not needed for the moment. "Is that a carronade I see on on their forecastle? Damme, it is! Chase guns and six-pounders, aim small for that carronade and kill their crew. Grapeshot! Load grape atop your roundshot, smartly now!

"By broadside . . . fire!"

His carronades fired again, but the long guns took seconds more to be readied and run out.

"To Hell with it, blaze away, lads!" Hugh ordered.

The long guns fired, spewing roundshot and a cloud of deadly grape-shot at the French ship's forecastle, savaging Frenchmen, gunners, pow-der monkeys, and petty officers, silencing that big carronade.

God, but I love the guns! he thought; *Wonder if it runs in the blood?*

He took a quick moment to look forward at his father's ship, but she and her foe were lost in a rising, dense cloud of gunpowder smoke into which *Undaunted* sailed. Only the stabs of flame showed that they still fought, viciously and rapidly.

"Prime . . . run out!" Hugh cried, seeing that all guns under his charge were re-loaded and ready. "Stand ready, on the up-roll.

"By broadside . . . fire!"

CHAPTER FORTY-ONE

$\mathcal{M}$ ister Westcott, pass word below," Lewrie rasped, his throat raw from shouting commands, and inhaling a constant stream of fouled air reeking of rotten eggs and sulfur. "Load with roundshot and grape and be ready to fire into the enemy ports as they come level with us!"

"Aye, sir!" Westcott replied, coughing a bit as well, as he summoned Midshipmen Holbrooke and Chenery to carry the message.

Up forward, the forecastle 6-pounders and carronades fired at will separate from the great-guns, a fairly concentrated mini-broadside, their shot hammering and peppering, raising screams of terror from the opposing French gunners, and a great shout from his ship's gunners as they finally silenced that French carronade, for which Lewrie was thankful, for that gun had done untold damage to his ship.

Amazingly, neither ship had suffered any damage aloft; none of the spars, top-masts, or sails had been shot away or torn to shreds, so both ships were still fully under reduced sail, creeping now as the winds faded.

There was no time to call for a cast of the log, but Lewrie could almost judge to the knot how slowly his ship was moving, and a look at the French frigate showed him that she was slowly inching up on his, not a pistol-shot off, now, with her surviving guns jerking back into her ports.

"Ready below, sir!" Midshipman Holbrooke shrilled as he came back to the quarterdeck, looking like an imp from Hell with his coat and breeches, his face and hands turned grey from the powder smoke.

"As they come level!" Lewrie shouted. "They are to fire as they bear! And sweep that damned quarterdeck clean, d'ye hear there!" he added, noting that officers and petty officers still occupied the enemy quarterdeck.

The Frenchman was just a bit ahead of *Sapphire*, her first two gun-ports beyond *Sapphire*'s bows, and there was nothing that Lewrie could do about them. He heard Lt. Elmes's voice rise up from the lower gun deck, crying, "As you bear . . . fire!" And then the foremost 24-pounder went off, stabbing smoke and flame, roundshot and a full canister of grape, right into the Frenchman's third gun-port. As each succeeding port came level with the next-aft British gun, pure bloody murder was blown into it. There were loud metal-on-metal *bongs!* when roundshot struck iron gun barrels or muzzles, the rattle of lead grape shot on iron and wood, and screams from enemy gunners clustered round their pieces as they were scythed away.

Quarterdeck 6-pounders and the "Smashers" ravaged the enemy's quarterdeck a moment later, flinging men about like boneless bundles of cloth, taking down all the helmsmen and shattering the drum of the double wheel. Without steering, what wind there still was drifted the enemy ship down on *Sapphire*, and their bows met with a loud thud of wood-on-wood, then, rudderless, the Frenchman rebounded a moment, then came aboard the two-decker, *Sapphire*'s starboard cat-head timber and second bower anchor snagging on the enemy frigate's foremast stays, with the hulls below the gunwales grinding upon each other.

"They're cutting their boarding nets free, sir!" Lt. Westcott shouted. Sure enough, the nets which prevented boarders from gaining easy access were falling like a stage curtain. The French guns fell silent, at last, and everyone on deck could see French sailors come boiling up to her bulwarks with muskets, cutlasses, pikes, and pistols.

"Musketry!" Lewrie shouted. "Get the lower deck gunners up and prepare to repel boarders!"

Game bastards, I'll give 'em that, Lewrie thought as he drew one of his double-barrelled Manton pistols and cocked the right-hand firelock; *Who knew the Frogs'd have this much fight in 'em! Must be desperate.*

Sapphire's anti-boarding nets were still up, hanging in loose, ungainly drapes. Even if French seamen tried, they would sway and struggle to scale the nets, hanging and clawing, arse-over-tit, to get up and over, or cut their way through. And all the while vulnerable to gunfire, cutlass or pike thrusts, as helpless as flies in a spider's web.

"Let 'em come!" Lewrie yelled. "Up, Sapphires! Up, my bully boys! Repel boarders!"

"Now, we'll give them Hell, sir!" Mr. Yelland cried, showing off a pair of four-barrelled duckfoot pistols he'd bought at Portsmouth. One pull of the trigger and all four barrels would go off as one, the barrels angled out from each other to spew death in a fan pattern, murderous in a face-to-face fight.

Sapphire's sailors and Marines came up from below, the men on the 6-pounders and carronades firing their last rounds of grapeshot at the French ship's railings, then taking up small arms. The men on the 12-pounders gave the French a last broadside, then did the same as the French crew surged over their railings, leaping into *Sapphire*'s nets, scrambling down to their chain platforms to cross over to the British chain platforms to make their way up.

"Fire at will, fire at will!" Lt. Keane of the Marines was urging his men. "Fix bayonets and be ready to receive!"

Musket and pistol fire rattled like twigs crackling in a fire, and men in the tops fired down over the edges of the upper platforms while men on *Sapphire*'s weather decks and gangways blazed away.

Lewrie took aim at a man scrambling in the nets, sawing a way through. He fired, and the man fell away to land with a loud *crump!* on his own ship's hard deck. He cocked the left-hand barrel, then turned to say something to the Sailing Master, just in time to see Mr. Yelland's forehead cave in from a musket ball, collapsing him like a sawn tree, as more bumble bees hummed round him, snatching the hat off Lewrie's head and he felt a thump on his left shoulder as a ball lightly clipped his gilt epaulet.

"Kill *me*, ye bastards? I'll *give* ye killed!" he roared, and fired at another Frenchman hung up in the nets, and hit him, making him dangle head-down and lifeless.

Pikes were thrust over the bulwarks, cutlasses thrust or swung at enemy boarders who had gained *Sapphire*'s side with meaty *thunks* as steel cleaved skulls, slashed arms, and necks. The Marines were firing point-blank at one target, then thrusting with their bayonets at one beside. The French attack surged like a wave rushing onto a rocky beach, then ebbed, its courage and fury spent. Sensing the moment, feeling that the heart had gone out of them, Lewrie shoved his spent pistol into his waist-band and drew his hanger.

"Mister Westcott, lower our nets! Cut 'em down! *Boarders*! Away, board-ers!" he howled. "Get at them and *murder* the bastards!"

Sapphire's nets rapidly vanished to drape the starboard side as sailors and Marines clambered over the rails, some leaping from one ship to the other, some going down to the chain platforms to get back up the French shrouds. Loaded weapons on both sides barked and men fell. A Marine was shot and fell between the hulls to be ground to death, screaming his last. Then, as the first Sapphires gained the enemy's rails and decks, their hoarse cheers could not smother the clash of steel on steel.

Not as spry as he once had been, Lewrie swung over the side and low-ered himself to his ship's mizen channel, not daring to leap and leave him-self vulnerable to a defender's blade; not daring to miss his hold and fall into the sea, either, for the very good reason that he, like many British sail-ors, could not swim!

There were no ratlines on the French ship's lower-most stays, but the thick rope shrouds were sticky with tar, making his ascent easier, even as his boot soles scrabbled on the frigate's planking. A handy shot-hole gave him a last foothold, and he was up and over, on the enemy quarterdeck, sailors swarming round him and dashing into combat with loud shouts. A young Frenchman in a neat uniform faced off with him in a fencing pose, but Lewrie had no time for the niceeties. He bulled forward, howling, shouldering inside the fellow's guard, shoving him off balance with his blade wide, then slashed at him back-handed, the keenly honed hanger hacking at his neck.

"Hooalooaloo!" his Cox'n, Liam Desmond, was howling some Irish battle keen, further forward, "Come an' get it, ye Devils! Come on, Pat!" Desmond urged his long-time mate, Patrick Furfy, who was madly swing-ing at two Frenchmen, with a cutlass in one hand and a boarding hatchet in the other like an ancient Viking Berserker.

Lewrie drew his second Manton, cocked both firelocks with his wrist, and stepped forward. He gunned down two French sailors then deflected a pike thrust from a third that caught his coat lapel and brushed it back from his chest. A downward slash with the hanger and he laid the man's shoulder open down to the collar bone. Wrenching his sword free, he looked for another foe, but the French were tossing aside their weapons, raising their hands in surrender, some falling to their knees as if in supplication.

Someone left in authority was calling something like "*amener les coleurs*" and "*reddition*". For a harsh moment, gunfire still popped and swords clashed, raising screams 'til Lewrie heard Westcott roaring "Quarter! Give them quarter, they've struck!"

"Quarter!" Lewrie seconded, after drawing a deep breath with which to do so, amazed at how winded he was. "Dis-arm them and form the prisoners up round the main mast!"

A French officer, his uniform splotched with blood and grime and sporting a deep gash on one cheek, tottered up to Lewrie looking dazed, and it was difficult for him to form words, at first.

"*M'sieur le Capitaine,* I surrender to you," he managed to say with tears running down his grimed cheeks. "Ze *frigat L'Egyptienne* is yours. I present my sword."

Damn *the niceties, damn this honourable thing,* Lewrie thought, his blood-lust still coursing, but he shook himself, sheathed his hanger, and accepted the offered sword, only for a moment.

"After such a hard and gallant fight, *m'sieur,* I can do no less than return it to you," Lewrie replied, even if that was through his gritted teeth. "You offer your parole? Good. *Bon.* You are senior aboard, *m'sieur?*"

"I am, *m'sieur,*" the French Lieutenant responded. "*Notre* Commodore and *notre Capitaine* are . . . *morte.*"

"My sympathies, sir," Lewrie said with a bow of his head, but feeling nothing of the kind. These bastard Frenchmen had harmed his ship, slain or wounded his people.

"A damned hard fight, sir," Lt. Westcott said as he came to report. "Over an hour and a half. What a slaughterhouse!"

"It was?" Lewrie asked, amazed. It had seemed like less than that, much less. "Christ!" he said as he looked over at *Sapphire* from the enemy deck. There wasn't much left of the upper bulwarks above the sail-tending gangways, and the iron stanchions that held tautly wrapped hammocks and bedding, for defence against grapeshot and musket fire, were bent and twisted, their contents spilled. Round the ship's gun-ports, bow to stern, there were un-countable shot holes, some so big he could see clean through to the waist or lower deck. His own cabins were now well-ventilated, open to fresh air in several places. And that precious and dearly obtained lower main mast had taken hits that looked as if beavers had gnawed at it above the line of bulwarks.

"We must have killed or wounded half their crew," Westcott said, pointing down into the French frigate's waist, drawing Lewrie's attention from his ship to the butcher's yard. French dead were piled round the bases of the fore and main masts, several dozen of them, and even more lay scattered about where they fell. A French surgeon and his mates, aided by litter bearers, picked among those whose wounds might be treated, and those for whom nothing could avail.

"We've lost Mister Elmes, sir," Westcott told him, "along with the Sailing Master, Marine Lieutenant Roe . . . Midshipmen Kibworth and Ward, Master's Mate Dorton," he said with a weary sigh, taking off his hat to swipe at his sweaty hair. "I'll have you the full list as soon as I can, but it's sure to be dear. It's a grand victory, but hard-bought."

Lewrie could only nod in response; he was completely spent, as he always was after a battle, badly in need of a sit-down or lie-down, his throat both raw and very dry. Something caught his attention . . . what? It was the silence.

He turned and tottered aft to the French frigate's taffrails, skirting the joyous tars who were hoisting the Union Jack over the French Tricolour, looking astern.

Down to leeward lay *Undaunted*, alongside the frigate that she had taken on, swirled about to show both ship's sterns to him, with British colours flying on both. Off to the Nor'east, he could spot *Sterling* close-aboard her opponent, with one of the brig-sloops on the other beam of their prize, and even further East, there was yet another French frigate, seemingly lashed alongside the other brig-sloop, conquered, captured, and made prize.

It *was* a victory, utter and complete, the sort that men would envy, could spend their whole careers seeking, one worthy of a praiseful resolution in Parliament, but at the moment, all Lewrie could feel was numbness. He turned away and went back to the frigate's waist to seek a dignified way of regaining his own ship's decks, hoping that someone might rig a gangway.

"Oh, arah, sor," his Cox'n said to him, coming up from the carnage below the quarterdeck, with tears on his cheeks. "Th' bastards have done for Pat, sor. Shot him dead, just as they were givin' up, an' none of 'em'll admit to it! Sneakin' damned back-shootin' . . . !"

"Furfy?" Lewrie gasped. "Oh, Christ, no!"

"If I knew which'un done it, I'd murder him, sor," Desmond swore, clumsily swiping his face. "Ye'll let me, sure, sor?"

"No, Desmond, I can't allow that," Lewrie had to tell him as he took him by the shoulders. "Dear as he was to me, too, to all of us . . . they've struck, asked for Quarter. We've already killed more than enough of 'em. We'll have to settle for that."

"Swore to his Mam, time we run off after the Risin'," Desmond barely managed to say, "that I'd look after Patrick an' keep him from harm, and his own foolishness, through thick or thin, an' . . . what'll I tell her, now?"

"That you did your best, Desmond," Lewrie cajoled, "you and me both, we always did."

There was a clatter as several planks were lashed together to make a wide gangplank from one ship to another, and British wounded began to be borne back aboard *Sapphire*. Mr. Snelling the Surgeon and his Mates and loblolly boys had done what they could for those hurt aboard their own ship, and were now assisting the French.

"Ah, here's another of ours, sir," Surgeon's Mate Phelps said, turning over a body. "Poor wee lad. Went game, it looks like. Took a Frenchman with him."

Lewrie left Desmond to his grief and headed for the gangplank, but stopped in shock. It was Jessop! Dead! To Hell with a Captain's required air of aloofness; he knelt and took the fired pistol from the lad's hand, saw that Jessop and a nearby dead Frenchman had shot each other, not three feet apart. He passed a hand over Jessop's face to close his sightless eyes and sat back on his heels.

"Didn't suffer, sir," Phelps told him in a kindly manner, to *his* lights, anyway. "Shot right in the heart, it appears, and didn't have time to take notice before he expired."

"That," Lewrie spat, "is cold comfort to me, *Mister* Phelps!"

He shot to his feet and made his way to the gangplank, bound for his own ravaged decks, his wounded ship, cold and heartsick; so much so that he had no dread of falling between the hulls and drowning as the gangplank jounced under his feet, swayed, and tilted as both ships lazily rolled.

Saws were already screeching, hammers were ringing as people laboured to make what first repairs they could, under the direction of the Second Officer, Mr. Harcourt, the senior Mids, Bosun Terrell and the surviving petty officers.

"Mister Hillhouse," Lewrie bade.

"Aye, sir?" Hillhouse said, coming to him and doffing his hat.

"I am appointing you an Acting-Lieutenant, and Third Officer, in Mister Elmes's stead, Mister Hillhouse," Lewrie told him. "I hope this will be an opportunity for advancement which you have sought."

"Ehm . . . *thank* you, sir!" Hillhouse exclaimed, as if that was a surprise, most-likely thinking that the senior Master's Mate, Mr. Stubbs, would be offered the post, instead.

"Carry on, Mister Hillhouse," Lewrie said in parting, going aft to look over what was left of his cabins. Yeovill was there with Pettus, already trying to set things to rights as sailors re-erected the deal and canvas partitions, and fetched furniture up from the orlop.

"Galley's a mess, sir," Yeovill reported, "and it may be cold commons for a day or two. Someone told me the French carronades did it. *Thirty-six* pounders, they say!"

"Is it true about Jessop, sir?" Pettus asked.

"Aye," Lewrie gruffly said. "Pat Furfy, too, and a *lot* of good men."

"Good God, sir," Pettus could barely mumble. "He wanted to be a real sailor . . . his tattoos and all, poor tyke."

"In the end, he was," Lewrie said, going aft, through the wood door and the jury-rigged twine mesh screen door that kept Chalky safe from going over the side, chasing birds.

The air was clearer and fresher on his little-used stern gallery, with hardly a hint of gunpowder that permeated *Sapphire* and the prize frigate. He took a deep breath of it, heard the flag over his head stirring; the shot-to-nothing wind was returning. With any luck, the squadron, and their prizes, could be back under way in an hour or two . . . back on their hunt along the Spanish coast? Maybe.

Men to promote, he thought; *men to replace, move up. Repairs to be made . . . men, and boys, to bury in the sea.*

The cost of his damned *victory* was more than he could bear.

EPILOGUE

The meeting with his fellow captains had been joyous, full of boyish high-cockalorum, and well liquoured, though the reports which Lewrie had gotten from his officers and petty officers were deeply disturbing and depressing, taking most of the joy from Lewrie's participation in their celebrations.

L'Egyptienne, 40; *Sultane,* 36; *Meduse,* 32; and *Fauvette,* 28. Proud names for grand ships, sure to be bought in and made into Royal Navy ships, perhaps with their original names; soon to enrich every man involved in their taking with prize-money, and glory, far beyond their merchant captures. And, before the wine-cabinet had been opened, Lewrie had made Capt. Chalmers's day; he would take command of the squadron in Lewrie's stead. He would have to, for *Sapphire* would have to sail for the dockyards at Gibraltar, the nearest place that could make all the repairs that she needed. It was there or a yard in England. Either way, he would have to strike his broad pendant, but at least at Gibraltar, Lewrie could keep command of her for even a few months more. He dreaded what Admiralty, and the dockyard Commissioners back home, might do with her.

They had mutually decided that their prize frigates would go to England, though, where their arrival would make more of a sensation with the public, with Admiralty, and, secretly, a hoped-for Nine Day Wonder in the prominent newspapers, for none of the proud, stoic Captains though they might be . . . Chalmers, Yearwood, Blamey, Teague, or Lewrie, in point of fact, were immune to fame, and hard-won acclaim.

Lewrie had seen his Captains off at the entry-port, wishing them all well, sharing some last japes as they had made their way to their boats.

He stared at the weakened main mast once they were gone, and re-entered his cabins, bidding Midshipman Holbrooke to pass word for the First Officer.

"First Off'cer t'see th' Cap'um, SAH!" his Marine sentry called, with a stamp of boots and musket butt.

"Enter," Lewrie replied.

"Sent for me, sir?" Westcott said as he stepped before Lewrie's desk in the day-cabin.

"Aye, Mister Westcott," Lewrie said as he folded his official report on the action, and his decisions, over to make a letter, then began to melt a stick of wax with which to seal it. "No help for it, I suppose?"

"She's shot to pieces, sir, aye," Westcott commiserated, "and I'd not trust the main mast with a bed sheet or tablecloth. It seems we're right back where we were when we got back to Portsmouth."

"Pettus, pour Mister Westcott something, will you?" Lewrie bade as he drizzled a blob of wax and got out his seal. "Whatever he cares for." He pressed his seal, the one with his crest of knighthood, the rarely-used one, onto the wax, blew on it to harden the wax, then got to his feet. "Let's go to the settee, shall we?"

"Welcome, sir," Westcott agreed, taking his ease in one of the chairs while Lewrie sprawled on the settee.

Westcott requested Portuguese *vinho verde*, admitting that it was growing on him, and Lewrie asked for the same.

"We can't remain on station, not in the shape the ship is in," Lewrie began as Pettus got out the wine. Jessop's replacement, a fourteen-year-old lad from the East End in London, Tom Dasher (or so he called himself), who claimed that he had been a waiter and pot-boy, followed Pettus's every movement, still learning his duties.

"Home yard, will it be, sir?" Westcott asked, sounding eager to set foot in England, savour the joys of shore liberty, and hunt up some fresh "mutton".

"I was thinking of Gibraltar," Lewrie said, "it's closer, and there's less chance of something going smash than on a long passage home. The prizes will be going to Portsmouth, though. And, whilst we're in the yards, I've appointed Captain Chalmers to carry on here."

"Oh, *that'll* please him, right down to his toes!" Westcott said, almost hooting in derision. "Mean to ask, sir . . . is your son well?"

"Aye, thank God," Lewrie said, perking up for a moment, "made a brave showing in boarding the *Sultane,* and came off without even a scratch."

"Glad to hear it, sir!" Westcott said, sounding pleased. "He's a fine young man, and a joy to you, I'm bound."

"Aye, he is," Lewrie gladly agreed as the wine arrived. They both took deep sips, then made appreciative noises. "About our prize, Mister West-cott. D'ye think she's in condition enough to make the voyage home?"

"We've made what repairs we could, given our spare stocks of lumber and such," Westcott told him. "Her masts, sails, and rigging are in good order, so she should do fine. The hardest part will be keeping the prisoners in order, what's left of the poor buggers, that is. I never *saw* such an *abbatoir.* Nigh an hundred killed, and almost two-dozen more sure to perish from their wounds? With another fourty wounded or crippled?"

Lewrie nodded, taking no joy from the high "butcher's bill", for *Sapphire* had lost nineteen dead, nine sure to succumb to their wounds in the days to come, and another dozen in the forecastle sick bay, and more hands on light duties from minor injuries. The other ships of the squadron had gotten away far more leniently.

"I want you to take the *Egyptienne* home, Geoffrey," Lewrie said. He held up a warning hand to stave off Westcott's immediate objections. "With my report of the battle, I'll not need all that many hands to get *Sapphire* to Gibraltar, and stand less chance of any *more* French warships crossin' my hawse, so I can spare as many men, and Marines, as you need."

"Good God, sir!" Westcott almost exploded. "Send Harcourt. He'd be pleased as punch. Or Hillhouse. He'd gain his Lieutenancy right off, and we both know that if he has to stand before an Examination Board, he never will make it, else!"

"Or, *you* could be promoted to Commander, and the next time we meet, you could be in command of your own ship, at long last," Lewrie pointed out. "Hell! Do you sail in with four prize frigates, ye might even be *knighted*! I don't know what the rest of the Navy's been up to lately, but after the disastrous mess that 'Dismal Jemmy' Gambler made at Basque

Roads, our success might make as big an impression as news of Trafalgar! Surely, there's a promotion in that for the officer who carries the news."

"But, sir . . . mean to say!" Westcott spluttered. "Why me? And here I thought that we were friends."

"We are, Geoffrey, we *are* friends," Lewrie admitted, "good ones, life-long friends, I hope. And I'm doing this so you can advance, and make your mark in the Navy. You *know* you're more than ready for a ship of your own, and you have me as an example of how *not* to do things."

"Well, you always have been amusing to watch," Westcott japed, flashing one of his quick, harsh grins. "But why now? *Sapphire*'s got time left in this commission."

"Because I'm afraid I'll *lose* her, Geoffrey," Lewrie confessed. "Look here, how many two-decker Fourth Rates are still serving? Four, five? Their days are done. It was a hard fight t'keep her after the lightning strike, and here we are in the same predicament, and where a spare lower mast can be found, or fashioned, is beyond me. I fear a letter from Admiralty saying that we're to turn her over to the Gibraltar yard, pay off the crew, and you and I buy passage home on the mail packet, un-employed and on half-pay. They could turn her into a trooper, like most of the other Fourth Rates have been, a store ship, even a prison hulk. With no quick source of masts to fit her, prison hulk at Gibraltar's the most likely. D'ye want orders t'be Captain o' *that*? To Admiralty, that'd be the most convenient."

"But, what of you, sir?" Westcott asked, looking concerned for his Fate. "You'd be on half-pay, stuck at Gibraltar, sailing home as 'live lumber' aboard a packet, or a returning trooper . . . ?"

"Bein' stuck for a time at Gibraltar's not that bad, we both know that," Lewrie laughed off, even leering significantly. "Besides, I'm a bloody hero, the victor of one Hell of a battle, hey?" He made mock of his accomplishment with a roll of his eyes. "Lettin' someone else sail me home'd be a welcome rest. Just so long as they set a good table. And when I get home, surely there'll be a new commission waitin' for me."

"I don't know, sir. It cuts rough to . . ." Westcott protested, though weakly, as if resigning himself to depart.

"Speakin' of gettin' home, Geoffrey," Lewrie cajoled, "think of the reception you'd get. Dined out on our victory . . . balls and supper parties just drippin' with luscious young lovelies hangin' on your every word, eyes big as saucers, worshippin' your heroism?"

"Well, if I must," Westcott said, sniggering. "Damme, but it's a pity my parents couldn't afford to buy me a set of colours. Once in a regimental mess, you're in for life, and never have to part every three or four years from good friends you most-like will never see in this life, again."

"That's the Navy for you," Lewrie drolly replied. "If ye can't take a joke, ye shouldn't've joined. So. You're amenable?"

"Aye, I'll take her home, sir," Westcott reluctantly agreed.

"Good!" Lewrie exclaimed, "and the next time I see you, there had better be an epaulet on your left shouder, and a ship under your feet. Let's drink to it. Pettus, do we still have some of that Spanish brandy?"

"Yes, sir. I'll fetch it." Pettus said.

"Pettus!" Westcott interrupted. "Given the circumstances, I'd like to sample Captain Lewrie's American corn whisky."

"Of course, sir," Pettus said, smiling.

The First Dog Watch was about to end, and the Second Dog to begin, and the sun was sinking towards the Western horizon, the heat of the day yielding at last to a refreshing breeze. Lewrie mounted to the poop deck for a breath of that cooler air, looking aloft at the sails and commissioning pendant, scanning all about for threatening weather, and hoping that the faint tinges out sunward would turn into a spectacular red and gold splendour.

HMS *Sapphire* loafed along under easy sail, head of the column of warships for a few minutes more, with smoke rising from the galley funnel as the crew's supper was boiled. After the exertions of the day, *Sapphire*'s people were at their ease, some below napping 'til called to their messes, but most were on deck savouring the air and the sights to see. Pipes fumed here and there, and the spit-kids were surrounded by those who chewed. The scuttlebutts did a lively business as hands awaited the second rum issue, taking a dip of water before the real stuff arrived.

And, there were novel things to see. The hard-won prizes were departing, at last, a separate four-ship squadron in their own right, with British ensigns streaming, showing their sterns as they shaped course for England, and some people cheered their departure and the leave-taking of shipmates chosen for the prize crew.

Off shoreward, the few merchantmen taken before encountering the French warships, their civilian crews landed ashore to make their own way to France long before, were burning fiercely. Compared to the prize frigates, their value was paltry, and the demand for more men than usual to sail the prizes home and guard so many prisoners made the men aboard the captured merchantmen needed on their own ships.

Lewrie pulled out his pocket watch to check the time, nodded, and went back down to the quarterdeck for the change of watch. Acting-Lieutenant Hillhouse, very proud of his new status, even if it was temporary, was about to be relieved by Acting–Sailing Master Mr. Stubbs, who would stand watches with the ship so short-handed. Lewrie took a peek into the open door to the re-erected sea cabin which the late Mr. Yelland had occupied. Stubbs had already made it his own, and if God was just, there would be no more noxious reeks emanating from it, or the chart room on the other side of the quarterdeck, either.

"Is my signal ready to be hoisted, Mister Hillhouse?" Lewrie asked.

"Aye, sir, Mister Carey has it bent on," Hillhouse crisply reported. "At the last stroke of Eight Bells."

"Very well," Lewrie said, nodding. He went back to the poop, just to the top of the ladderway, and looked forward to the boy at the forecastle belfry, eyes glued to his sand glass and the whitened rope to the clapper in his hand.

Eight Bells chimed in four double-chimed strokes.

Lewrie looked aft to see Midshipman Carey and the men of the signal party hoisting away, and the hoist breaking open to stream his "Goodbye . . . Godspeed" to his squadron.

His squadron.

The last stroke of Eight Bells was also time for his broad pendant to be struck, and he watched that triangle of red bunting with its white ball in the centre be run down the halliard, un-bent, and folded. Midshipman Chenery brought it to him.

Now it was no longer his squadron, but Capt. Chalmers's.

"Alter course to Due West, Mister Stubbs," Lewrie ordered.

"Due West, aye sir. Bosun Terrell, pipe hands to stations to alter course! Man sheets and braces!" Stubbs roared, in a loud and carrying voice un-expected from such a terrier-like man.

And HMS *Sapphire* peeled away from the head of the column of ships, swinging her bows about to sail into the sunset, one that was pleasingly turning into the sort that Lewrie had hoped for. He went on up to pace the poop deck, his broad pendant held over both hands as if to warm them, wondering if he would ever hoist another, or have a deck under his feet, again.

He snapped about to peer aft at the sound of gunfire! Had the French prisoners risen and re-taken their ships?

No, it was *Undaunted*, firing a departure salute to him; gun after gun, as steady as a metronome down her side, and Lewrie took his hat off and held it aloft long after the last shot fired and died away.

Goodbye, and an end to a too-short adventure.

Godspeed to the next?

He dearly hoped so.